THE THREE GENERALS

BOOK TWO OF THE
SCIPIO AFRICANUS TRILOGY

MARTIN TESSMER

Copyright © 2015

DEDICATION

To George Edward Tessmer, FirstWriter of the
family. And the impetus for all that followed.

"Now Aristotle, he would say that there is not necessarily a conflict between man acting as a good citizen and acting as a good individual, if the state is promoting the common good. But where it does not promote the good of the people, perhaps the man must act contrary to the state's interests, both as a good citizen and as a good man. Is that not so?"

Asclepius the tutor. In *Scipio Rising: Book One of the Scipio Africanus Trilogy.*

Table of Contents

End Notes

Excerpt from Book Three, *Scipio's Dream*

ACKNOWLEDGMENTS

Among 20th and 21st century historians, I am primarily indebted to Professor Richard Gabriel for his informative and readable *Scipio Africanus: Rome's Greatest General*, and *Ancient Arms and Armies of Antiquity*. Similarly, H. Liddell Hart's *Scipio Africanus: Greater Than Napoleon* provided many valuable insights into Scipio the general and Scipio the man.

Among classic historians, I owe a deep debt of gratitude to Titus Livius (Livy) for *Hannibal's War: Books 21-30* (translated by J.C. Yardley) and Polybius for *The Histories* (translated by Robin Waterfield). Cato the Elder's *De Agri Cultura* provided insight into the character of this simple but ruthless and powerful man that so influenced the course of Western History. Appian, Dodge, and Mommsen, thanks to you all for the many tidbits and corrections your works provided.

Ross Lecke has written two fine historical novels about Scipio and Hannibal: they are *Scipio Africanus: The Man Who Defeated Hannibal*, and *Hannibal*. Ross showed me that a writer can spin a good yarn and still stick to the facts, where there are facts to stick to. Finally, I must give a tip of the hat to Wikipedia and the scores of websites and blogs about the people and countries of 200 BCE. The scholarship of our 21st century digital community is amazing.

Sharon, many thanks for your competent proofing of the initial manuscript. And Susan, your copyediting of my humble manuscript was truly excellent. You are a wonder.

A NOTE ON HISTORICAL ACCURACY

This is a work of historical fiction, meaning it combines elements of historical fact (such as it is) and fiction. It is not a history textbook.

The book's major characters, places, events, battles, and timelines are real, meaning they are noted by at least one of our acknowledged historians such as Livy, Polybius, Gabriel, Mommsen, Appian, or Peddle.

The story's Hellenic Party and Latin Party factions are created to capture the mood of the times, when there was real enmity between those favoring a more "decadent" Hellenic lifestyle and those of more agrarian sympathies who disparaged it. Similarly, the creation hobnailed sandals, the cohort formation, cavalry formations, lighter packs, and the falcata sword seem to have occurred during this era, but it is difficult to know who invented them versus who popularized them. In this book Scipio Africanus is given attribution for them to help illustrate the military inventiveness that took place during the Punic wars. A hundred years later, the redoubtable Gaius Marius institutionalized the cohort formation, lighter packs, and reduced baggage trains.

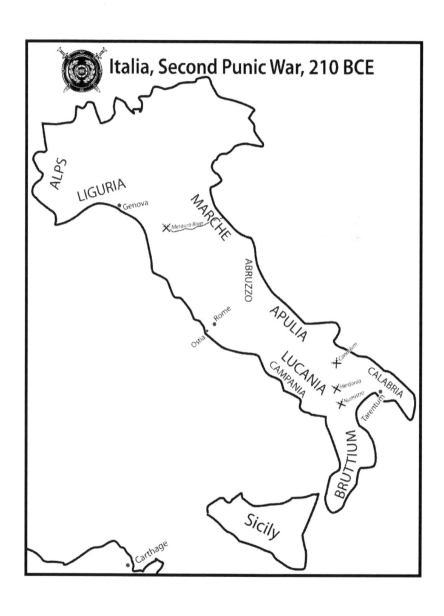

Italia, Second Punic War, 210 BCE

ALPS

LIGURIA

Genova

MARCHE

Metauro River

ABRUZZO

Rome

APULIA

Ostia

Cannium

LUCANIA

CAMPANIA

CALABRIA

Herdonia

Numistro

Tarentum

BRUTTIUM

Sicily

Carthage

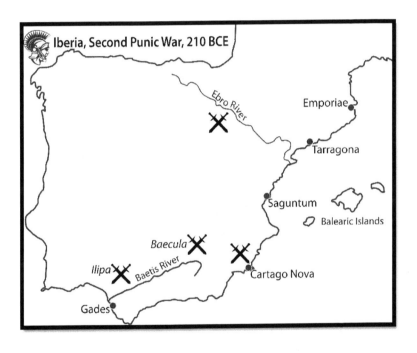

Iberia, Second Punic War, 210 BCE

Ebro River

Emporiae

Tarragona

Saguntum

Balearic Islands

Baecula

Ilipa

Baetis River

Cartago Nova

Gades

I. THE REVOLUTION BEGINS

EMPORIAE, NORTHEASTERN IBERIA, 211 BCE. Thirty quinqueremes ease their 120-foot hulls into the clear bay waters of the port town Emporiae, nudging into its light brown sands. A chorus of horns sounds across the fleet and a hundred oars rise from each ship and slide into its hull, like a centipede withdrawing its legs. The massive warships bob slowly on the shallow winter tidewaters, and for a minute all is quiet.

The lead ship's captain shouts an order, and the ship's buccinator trumpets the command on his C-shaped horn. A loud commotion erupts below decks in each of the vessels, their hulls echoing the sound of boots trampling up to the foredecks. Within minutes, a marine squadron scrambles over each ship's prow and leaps onto the smooth beach. The lightly armored warriors trot forward to set up a guard line in front of their vessels. Knots of sailors follow them onto the beach; they grasp the thick bow ropes and tug the ships' timbered prows deeper into the sands.

A short, heavily muscled warrior vaults off the purple-bordered flagship and lands firmly onto the sands, his sword at the ready. Marcus Junius Silenus, the Tenth Legion Commander, is prepared to kill any who pose a threat to his general. Rome's deadliest warrior glares into the surrounding sea oats as if they were preparing to attack him, looking for any signs of ambush. Dissatisfied with his obstructed view, he pushes through the marines and tramps through the shore-side scrub. He kicks the sand mounds to make sure no assassins are buried there, an old Carthaginian trick. Finally satisfied, Marcus turns around and flashes his gleaming blade at the half-mile line of quinqueremes: all is clear. The sailors on the flagship pivot the ship's weatherbeaten gangplank over the side, and a singular figure descends it.

General Publius Cornelius Scipio, the newly elected proconsul and governor of Iberia, pauses atop the flagship's wide gangplank, savoring the sight of his new command. Scipio, a dignified young man of twenty-four, is of middling height and sturdily muscled, his arms already scarred from his battles in Italia with Hannibal's forces. With no imminent threat present, Scipio has eschewed his armor for a new purple-bordered tunic, wearing a simple bronze cap helmet over his curled raven hair. Scipio studies the terrain with penetrating brown eyes, assessing it for potential campsites—and ambushes. Then he strides quickly down the gangplank, his face alight.

Scipio is enthused at the prospect of leading his first campaign, though it is one that no general would accept after the Three Generals destroyed the armies of Scipio's father and uncle here. He looks up at the low-lying sky: *Father, I promised you I would dedicate my life to preserving Rome, and I am here to do it. Pray I do not disappoint you.*

The young commander turns back to the ship and waves vigorously, and walks onto the shore. Two columns of newly recruited legionnaires hustle down the gangplank and hurry onto the beach, led by an irritated centurion. The veteran officer growls an order at them, and with all the energy and awkwardness of boys, they scramble to form ranks and catch up to Scipio, eager to protect their leader from any marauding Iberians or Carthaginians.

As Scipio walks past the marine guards, it occurs to him that he is taking his first steps to complete his vow to conquer Iberia. *This is it,* he thinks. *With two legions of green recruits, I've got to retake Iberia from the Three Generals.* He looks back on the young men, who are watching him anxiously. *Jupiter help me,* he laughs to himself. *I'm a boy leading boys.*

As the soldiers organize about Scipio, another young commander jumps onto the gangplank and trots lithely down to the shore, wading into the water with a punctilious frown as it splashes onto his gleaming bronze armor. He trots up to stand beside his friend and leader. "Something on your mind, Scippy?" remarks a grinning Laelius. "You look like you are thinking deep thoughts. Or maybe you just have to take a shit, eh?"

Laelius stands at Scipio's right hand, the appropriate position for the leader of the army's equites (cavalry) in Iberia. The lean and graceful youth has been Scipio's best friend since childhood. Now he is Scipio's closest military advisor and confidant, and he embraces those roles with caustic honesty and humor, knowing Scipio will need both if he is to overcome the obstacles he faces as an undermanned novice commander.

Always elegantly dressed, Laelius sports a blood-red cape over the armor that he and Scipio tricked from a wealthy young Roman years ago, back when Laelius was a poor boy with no prospects, trying to wheedle his way into the secure life of patrician society. Now his name is known throughout Rome, where people talk about his combat exploits as much as his unabashed homosexuality.

As Scipio and Laelius step onto the seashore, Marcus Silenus trudges over to meet them. The gruff old infantryman halts in front of Scipio, standing at ramrod attention. Laelius, always amused at Marcus' gravitas in everything he does, steals an amused glance at Scipio. He and Scipio see Marcus as a wise, older father figure, albeit one who could easily kill the both of them with his bare hands.

"The beach is free of any enemy presence," Marcus announces gravely.

Scipio stares across the flat expanse of sea grass, where only a mouse could hide, and suppresses a grin. "Yes, it would seem so. Gratitude for your efforts." Scipio points toward the walled city of Emporiae, looming in the distance. "We will prepare our camp by the south wall, keeping our backs to the river. Start the men to unloading, Marcus. Laelius, get the horses over there as soon as possible. Night comes quickly."

I. The Revolution Begins

As the Roman army debarks from the quinqueremes, Scipio stands at the shore. He watches the proceedings with a stern face, but inside he wonders, *What should I be doing? Giving orders? Moving to the camp? Everybody seems to know what they are doing, but how would I know?* Shaking off his bewilderment, he decides it is time to implement the first of his changes to Roman warfare, the changes he swore to implement after watching Hannibal destroy Roman armies at Trebia, Trasimene, and Cannae. He gestures for the lead tribune of his first legion to come over to him.

"Do you remember those Iberian merchants we brought with us?" Scipio asks him.

"Those six fellows who kept to themselves the whole trip?" the tribune snorts. "Have you seen them, sir? They have more the look of criminals than businessmen, if I may say so. Very furtive."

"Yes, well ...," replies Scipio vaguely. "With these Iberians, looks are deceiving. Just bring them to me." The tribune gives some orders to one of his centurions, who soon returns with six lean, dark-skinned men, all clad in dark green tunics and brown hooded robes—extremely nondescript clothing for merchants. The men keep their heads down, yet their darting eyes register all that occurs about them.

"I would talk with these men in private. You are dismissed." As the tribune and centurion depart, Scipio bids each Iberian to step forward and grasps his forearm in welcome. After each handshake, Scipio leaves a small purse in their palm, which the men quickly pocket. "You two will visit the Lacetani and Ilergetes to the west," says Scipio, pointing at a pair of the men. "You two go to the Celtiberians in the central mountains. You and you travel to the city of Cartago Nova in the south. A larger purse if you return with some valuable information. Get your horses and depart."

The Iberians nod and walk off. Scipio shouts out to one of them. "Tibaste, give me a moment."

The Iberian returns, looking about to see if anyone heard Scipio. "It is best you do not mention my name," the Iberian says in flawless Latin.

Scipio nods. "Agreed. And apologies. I assumed that was a false name you gave me, in keeping with the rest of you. Do you have men up there in Emporiae?"

"Four, and they have recently returned from the tribes allied with Carthage," replies Tibaste.

Scipio holds up another purse where Tibaste can see it. "I need to know everything your men know about Mago, Gisgo, and Hasdrubal. Tonight."

The Iberian bows. "It will be as you request. By the sixth hour." Tibaste hurries off to get his horse. Scipio watches him walk off, takes a deep breath and blows it out. *Fortuna be with me, wait until the men find out I am using spies!* He laughs at his predicament and walks over to help his tribunes finalize plans for the short march to town.

The next day, Scipio and his officers gather inside Emporiae at an abandoned Greek temple, a small colonnaded rectangle littered with fallen statuary of the Twelve Olympians, Greece's most important gods. Laelius and Marcus Silenus stand on the temple's semicircular steps, as do the twelve tribunes who direct Scipio's two legions. The tribunes are looking curiously at a surprise visitor to this tactical battle session: Clastidius Honorius is here with them. The bear-like man is the praefectus castrorum of Scipio's army, making him its third-highest officer, but he rarely attends the tribunes' meetings. Clastidius is a twenty-five-year veteran in charge of infantry combat training, a highly honored position. Two tribunes politely ask the trainer why he is there, but Clastidius merely shrugs. He is as mystified as they are.

Scipio arrives last of all, his heart beating fast. This is his first battle-planning session with his entire staff. Many of the tribunes are young Senatorial hopefuls from powerful patrician families, some of whom are enemies of the Scipios and the Hellenic Party they sponsor. He knows he must take command at the outset because he will say much that will disturb them—many military changes are coming. If he does not gain their respect now, his entire plan may be forfeit. Scipio glances at Laelius and Marcus, takes a deep breath, and commences his fateful meeting.

"Honored Romans, I speak to you with great enthusiasm as we embark on our momentous campaign. Our quest is to recapture Iberia from the Three Generals, the men who used treachery and deceit to destroy our brave legions—and my father and uncle." He pauses to let the reminder of his personal tragedy sink into their minds. "I vowed to my father I would protect Rome, and I stepped forward when no Roman general would take this mission. They were afraid to face the Generals even though they knew they were plotting to join forces with Hannibal in Italia, whence all would be lost." Many of the tribunes nod silently. Some of the oldest veterans merely stare at him, stone-faced.

"Yes, the Carthaginians greatly outnumber us, when they are all together. But their forces are presently divided into three armies, one for each of the Generals. If we divide and conquer in turn, we can retake Iberia. Look here …."

Scipio rummages through a large wicker box that contains the many scrolls he memorized before leaving Rome: terrain maps of Iberia's tribal regions, the histories of the greatest Greek, Macedonian and Persian generals, and—most important of all—his personal diary of Hannibal's battle tactics in Italia. Scipio pulls out a large, papyrus map and spreads it out on the ground, waving for the tribunes to come forward. The officers gather around and study it; they can see it is a map of Iberia, with three freshly-inked red crosses in the northern, central, and southern regions.

A kneeling Scipio points at the crosses. "These are the armies of the Three Generals. They are all below us, south of the Ebro River. Mago's force is far south, on the coast of Gades. Hasdrubal is eight days' march to the north of him near Toletum. Gisgo, he is seven days east from both of them, near the mouth of the Tagus. His army is closest to us."

Several tribunes look at the proximity of Gisgo's army, and frown. Scipio shakes his head. "The Three Generals pose no threat to us until the spring battle season. That means we have several months to recruit Iberian allies, and to organize our campaign." He laughs." And to train our recruits, may Jupiter help us to make them men!"

Scipio walks away from the map to draw his officers' attention to him for what he will say. He stares intently at them, looking into each of their faces. "If we can gather enough soldiers that we match even one of these armies, we will triumph. Because we will engage them one at a time. And they will be no match for us on even terms."

Several of the tribunes mutter among themselves, debating the strategy. A stolid veteran limps over and grimaces at the map. "How do you know where all three of generals are?" he says, his one good eye flashing his irritation. "How could our scouts find all this out? We just landed!"

"No, no scouts revealed this. My spies did," says Scipio, as he steps over to roll up the papyrus and return it to the box. "I am using information from men who were part of the Three Generals' armies. We recruited them three months ago, while we prepared to come here."

"These are Romans?" asks one of the tribunes, scratching his head. "Posing as Carthaginians?"

Scipio chuckles, shaking his head. "No, Castor. Romans would be found out as soon as they opened their mouths—or showed their faces. These are Iberians, tribal allies of Mago. Gisgo, and Hasdrubal."

A paunchy little man vaults to his feet, his jowly face red with anger. He is Nonus, one of Rome's wealthiest patricians, but a man who has never fought a battle in his life. As with many who follow Rome's cursus honorum, the path to political power, Nonus is using his service as a tribune to further his consular ambitions.

"What? This is madness!" Nonus blusters. "You would trust our enemy's word, taking in tales from these half-wit savages? If they lie to

7

you, our lives could be forfeit!" Nonus turns toward his fellow tribunes and spreads his arms to them, appealing for support. "You know the Iberians' reputation for treachery. It is well deserved, is it not?" Seeing several nodding their heads, he whirls to face Scipio. "The Iberians deserted your father for the Carthaginians. It led to his death! Their lies will lure us into another trap."

Scipio glowers at red-faced Nonus, drilling his eyes through Nonus' watery stare. "In the first place, Nonus, 'the Iberians' you speak of are composed of scores of tribal nations, each as different as the nations of Italia. But you are correct—it would be foolish if we trusted but a single source, whoever he would be." He walks away from Nonus and draws closer to the other tribunes. "The truth is, I have several informants at each of the Three Generals' camps, and they are from different tribes. Just now I sent out six to join the ones that are there already, but they do not know each other. We will compare what each man tells me, to spot any lies."

A sallow-faced young tribune named Plinius shakes his head, disappointed with Scipio's words. Scipio is familiar with the boy, knowing him to be a thoughtful lad who is well educated in Greek philosophy and ethics, though Plinius conceals his Hellenic acculturation, now that the Latin Party holds sway in Rome. "My Apologies, General, but I like it not," Plinius mumbles, his voice nervous. "You are depending on men who betrayed their loyalty to the Carthaginians. What worth is the word of such a man? Why would they not betray us?"

A chorus of "ayes" follows Plinius' words, and Scipio can feel his air of command dissolving. If he continues to argue with the tribunes, he will look desperate. But if he acknowledges the merit to gentle Plinius' remark, he will look weak. His mind races to think what to do, when a commanding voice silences them.

"Your brains are shit," declares Marcus Silenus, as calmly as if he were reporting the weather. "Do you know why the Lacetani and Edetani tribes fight for the Three Generals? Because Mago, Hasdrubal, and Gisgo hold their wives and children captive, under threat of death. Because they have crucified the tribal elders of those who would not join them." He looks at Nonus and Plinius and sneers. "Think you they are like the Gauls, fighting just for money? The natives are bound by fear to the Carthaginians' cause. They profess no loyalty to Carthage. They are only loyal to their tribes. Betrayers? Traitors? You are fools."

Though he is not a patrician, Marcus is the veteran of a score of battles, and his word carries much weight. A quiet settles over the group, and Scipio rushes into the void, new confidence in his voice.

"When I was younger, my mother Pomponia taught me that you best win someone's willing obedience through rewards rather than punishment, when rewards are meted with strength and fairness. That wisdom has served me well, and I will use it now. We will gain allies because we will treat the tribes with respect. We will reward rather than punish." Scipio manages a laugh. "They will at least see us as the lesser of the two evils in their country!"

Nonus snorts derisively, not yet willing to give up the fight. "That is not the point, 'General.' It is this whole business of spying instead of fighting. These are tactics of the skulking Carthaginians, cowardly ways for those afraid to stand and fight. Our ancestors would blush at this spying you talk about, much less that you would pay for it!"

Scipio stands quietly for a moment before he replies. "At times, Nonus, I think the Carthaginians have as many spies and informers as they have infantry. And I am tired of them gaining strategic advantages because we are too arrogant to copy their tactics."

Scipio steps closer to the tribunes, looking into each of their faces. "For lack of good intelligence, we did not know that the South Italia tribes joined Hannibal two years ago, doubling his force. We were not aware of it until all those Italians showed up next to him at the Battle of Herdonia. We had not a glimmer that he sneaked thirty war elephants through the Port of Bruttium, until they stampeded across the infantry lines there, destroying our ranks. We are always surprised at what

Hannibal does, yet he is never surprised by us. And you wonder why he defeats us at every turn?" He cocks his head at the group. "I ask you, would you be too proud to have obtained this information about the Italians and elephants by spying—if you could have—and saved thousands of our legionnaires? Would you have 'skulked' about for a strategic advantage then?"

Another tribune starts to rise and speak, but a glare from Laelius halts him. Laelius knows this is the moment Scipio will win over the veterans or lose them forever.

"Nonus, you are a member of the Latin Party, are you not? The political ally of Fabius, Flaccus, and Cato?"

"I certainly am," crows Nonus. "Our party is not trying to emasculate our men with the foppery of Greek education and arts, as the Hellenic Party promotes. We follow the traditions of our Latin ancestors."

"Ah, yes, the Latins. A proud and powerful party," Scipio deadpans. "Of course, one of the ways they came to power was their extensive use of political spies, through planting their ringleaders in the crowds at political rallies." Scipio turns to the other tribunes. "Right or wrong, the Latin Party does such things, is that not so?" When he sees most of them nodding their heads, he turns back to Nonus. "So, Nonus, your party thinks these tactics worthy enough to use against its fellow Romans, but you think they are too ignoble to use against our enemies, it that correct?"

Amid the ensuing laughter, Scipio raises his hands for silence, and his voice softens. "Our spies will gather what I call 'intelligence' about the enemy, intelligent information. In this campaign we will fight with words as much as swords, because we would be at a tactical disadvantage without information about the Carthaginians. Remember the Battle of Baetis? My father Publius had not the slightest knowledge that his Celtiberian 'allies' would defect to Carthage two days before his final battle, when he and my uncle would retake Iberia." Scipio faces his men, his face a mask of anger and sorrow. "That night before the battle, even as my father met with the Celtiberian chieftains, thousands of their men were sneaking over to Mago's camp, and Publius had not the slightest hint of it until they stood opposite him on the day of battle!" He holds his index finger before his men. "One spy, one informant, even one rumor that such a thing would happen, and Iberia might be ours today. ... And my father alive."

Scipio nods his head at Laelius and Marcus. They join the rest of the officers, and Scipio stands alone. He raises his head high, and the next words from his mouth are those of an imperator, not a boy. "Beginning tomorrow, we will construct a new maniple of a hundred and twenty warriors, men we will call 'speculatores.' The speculatores will gather information about the enemy from nearby townspeople, farmers, fishermen, and tribal warriors. They will pose as merchants, slaves, even traitors, to provide us with the 'intelligence' to make intelligent decisions." Scipio sees Nonus start to rise, and his voice rises. "I will brook no further debate. It is done!"

Scipio beckons to Clastidius Honorius, and the bent old warrior limps to the fore of the temple steps, standing next to Scipio. The young general places his hand on the older man's shoulder as he addresses the group.

"Clastidius will lead this new maniple," Scipio declares. "He has served us well as trainer, and now he will train our men in what the Greeks call 'espionage,' that they may mingle effectively amongst the Carthaginians and Iberians." Scipio's eyes narrow. "To those of you who would have this no other way, you may call it 'spying.' But it will be done regardless."

"Each of you will give me ten of your boldest and most clever warriors." Scipio grins. "If they resemble the natives complexion and color, that is excellent. If they are good liars, that is even better!" Several of the tribunes glance sideways at each other, prompting Scipio to add, "If you dare send me your cowards or layabouts, you yourself will replace them, I swear to Mars."

Nonus jumps up and starts to leave. "I cannot stomach this madness," he says. He turns to face the other tribunes, ignoring Scipio's glare. "We have less than a third of the Carthaginian's force, and this … this novice proposes to take even more fighters away from us!"

Scipio walks over and stands in front of Nonus, his back to the rest of the tribunes. He looks steadily into the patrician's florid face. "Get back there, Tribune," Scipio says steadily. Long seconds pass as Nonus stares defiantly at Scipio. Scipio's hand trails down to the handle of his dagger, fingering the knob of its hilt.

"Psh!" says Nonus, and resumes his place among the officers. Several tribunes bow their heads to hide their grins—Nonus is not a favorite among his peers.

There is a long silence before Laelius finally breaks it. "I like the idea of this 'legion of spies,' Consul, but I must ask: can we afford to do this? Where will we get the money to support these activities? The Senate has provided no funds for such pursuits. We have barely enough for supplies and armament. Should I return to Rome and petition the Senate for more support?"

"No, Laelius. The Senate will not support this kind of enterprise while the Latin Party holds sway." Scipio looks away from his men, his eyes hooded. "I will worry about where the money comes from."

The officers look at one another, some quizzically and others suspiciously, but none say anything. Nonus bends and whispers into another tribune's ear, and the solider nods, glancing at Scipio. Scipio stares at Nonus as one would an errant child, and he looks away. *That one bears watching*, Scipio thinks. *He is likely a "skulker" for the Latins.*

"Enough, then. It is done," proclaims Marcus. "What next?"

Scipio runs his finger southward along the map, following the coastline south to Tarraco. "In three days hence we head to Tarraco, our last outpost in Iberia. We will join forces with whatever men are left there, and begin the campaign."

"Who do we fight first?" blurts Plinius, his eyes wide with anxiety. "Mago, Hasdrubal, or Gisgo?"

"We shall discuss it at Tarraco, worthy Plinius," remarks Scipio. "But I will say this," he says, with a knowing grin. "We have a way to defeat them all, without fighting any of them."

Several tribunes rise to ask further questions, but Scipio claps his hands together, twice. "The matter is closed. Now to our final order of business. Clastidius, you will commence a training camp tomorrow for the marines, to train them to fight as well as our legionnaires. From now on the marines will fight on both land and sea. And train the sailors, too. They will more than replace the men who become our speculatores."

"I hear and obey," says Clastidius, extending his arm in a salute. "Apologies, General, but why would you train them all to be ground soldiers?"

"Most of the seamen are war veterans, which we are sorely missing. And we are greatly outnumbered. We need every man we can get." Scipio stares east across the ocean, toward Italia. "Besides, we do not need sailors anymore." He looks at the beached quinqueremes. "We are not going back."

The young general feels his right arm twitch from the tension he feels and clenches his fist to stop its shaking. He lifts his chin and stares at the older men. "One way or another, we will not go back until the war in Iberia is over."

Scipio extends his right arm, dismissing the officers. He stands at attention as his men file out past him, returning to their maniples. Some leave as Nonus does, stalking out without a second glance, their bodies rigid with anger. Others throw a wondering glance over their shoulder at the downy-cheeked general who has just changed the world of Roman warfare. Marcus Silenus nods at Scipio before he stalks away, but Scipio cannot read his field commander's stony expression: does he embrace this intelligence idea, or is he only being a good soldier?

Finally, only Laelius remains, watching the retreating tribunes. When all his men are out of eyesight, Scipio rushes over to a large limestone head of Ares, Greek god of war. He bends over and vomits behind it, his shaking hands clutching the statue's basket-sized ears. Scipio stands up to see Laelius watching him, concerned. Scipio manages a smile. He opens his mouth to speak and suddenly dips to vomit again. Laelius walks over, a reproving grin on his face.

"Is that your opinion of war in general, Scippy?" asks Laelius. "Or Ares in particular?"

"Nerves," Scipio confides, wiping his mouth on a linen scrap. "I thought the tribunes were going to revolt when I told them I was using their legions for my intelligence unit. You'd think I was asking for human sacrifice!"

"You had best tread lightly before you make any more changes, Scippy. Many of those tribunes are veterans of Rome's victories against Greece and Macedonia. For them, the old ways have been most successful, regardless of what Hannibal or the Three Generals have done to us." He winks. "And you had best give them some specifics when we arrive at Tarraco, not these conundrums about defeating all without fighting them, or they might mutiny!"

Scipio manages a laugh. "All in good time, friend. After we arrive at Tarraco, we will send delegates to the mountain tribes that are loyal to Carthage: the Bastetani, Oretani, Edetani—even the cursed Ilergetes, the ones that killed my father."

"Are we that desperate, you would recruit our sworn enemies?" asks Laelius. Scipio shakes his head. "The Iberians are not our sworn enemies. The Three Generals hold them in thrall. We just have to win them over."

Laelius throws up his arms. "Then you'd better do it quickly! The

Carthaginian armies are growing by the day."

Scipio beckons for Laelius to follow, and he starts walking back to his command tent. "We will approach the Edetani nation first. Many of their tribes were loyal to us."

Laelius grimaces with doubt. "Really? Many of them fight with the Carthaginians. We have no money for bribes, and if we go to them with empty hands, they will be wearing our skins before nightfall!" He flexes his arms and poses. "But I would make a very appealing garment, so some barbarian would be very lucky!"

Scipio rolls his eyes and shoves Laelius. "At least you would finally be worth something. We can't give them money, but we can offer them a share of plunder, at least. And something more valuable to those tribes who serve the Three Generals under duress." Scipio puts his arm around Laelius' shoulder. "Remember old Boltar, the family mastiff?"

Laelius makes a face. "How could I forget that dog? That monster used to wash my face with his tongue. Ugh! Your mother would incite him to do it, just to watch the look on my face."

"Hah! You acted like you were being bathed with a spongia from the public lavatories! By Jupiter's beard, for a man who has been covered with his enemy's gore, you are surprisingly delicate about some things! But to my point: I was trying to teach that dog to sit, pushing on his hindquarters, striking him with a rod, and threatening him. And all I got was a cowed dog that bit me. Then Mother showed me how to teach him to sit by giving him some simple rewards and approval, not punishment. That old dog learned in a trice, and he never forgot."

Laelius bugs his eyes at Scipio. "So you're saying you will treat the Iberians like dogs? That could be dangerous!"

"I swear to the gods, why I try to tell you anything is beyond my ken! You know what I mean. The Three Generals are trying to have their way through threats and punishments, when the rewards of respect and freedom would breed the Iberians' obedience and loyalty. Sooner or later their tactics will come back to bite them."

Laelius chuckles. "Perhaps so. I am sure the Generals are beating their Iberian 'dogs' even as we speak. Let us hope that the dog that bites them back is a big one, to save us some trouble!"

* * * * *

NORTHERN IBERIA. The anguished screaming was long in its fading, but the dying man's cries have finally subsided. Now, the residents only hear the despairing moans of a creature who knows his death is upon him. The man's softer laments touch the tribesmen in a way none of his screams could do, making them realize the inevitability of their own mortality—and their vulnerability to the whims and wishes of their hated Carthaginian rulers.

The victim hangs from a cross in the town circle of this Ilergete tribe, suspended from finger-thick spikes driven into his forearms and ankles. Beneath him stands Hasdrubal, Hannibal's brother, a satisfied smile on his predatory face. Unlike Mago and Hannibal, his taller and more regal brothers, Hasdrubal is short and dark, with staring eyes, a fleshy nose, and bulbous lips that give him a fishlike appearance. His physical disadvantages have bred in him a penchant for enjoying the misfortune of more physically blessed men, such as the sculpted warrior who is hanging on the cross. But Hasdrubal is no less brave or resourceful than his famous brothers. He has a long string of triumphs over the Romans, including the killing victories over Publius and Gnaeus Scipio. A harsh and vindictive man, Hasdrubal is feared by friend and foe alike, a sentiment that he greatly savors.

The large tribe's two chieftains, Indibilis and Mandonius, stand next to Hasdrubal, both stoic as stone. The brothers watch as their tribesman writhes in mortal agony on the crossed wood beams, pleading with them for surcease. After several long minutes, Indibilis turns a cold eye onto Hasdrubal.

"This you had to do? Kill one of my people while I watch like a helpless old woman? You think this is important, Carthaginian?"

Though the heavily muscled brothers tower over the slight Hasdrubal, he coolly returns their murderous glare. "It is the way of Carthage, and it has served us well. Our Council of Elders crucified General Harca in the city square, when his stupidity cost us a battle with the Libyans. Do you expect me to do less to one who spied for the Romans? These people must be taught a lesson."

Mandonius takes a step toward the Carthaginian general, his fists clenched. "These people are my people! You are the one that needs a lesson!"

The chieftain takes another step, and Hasdrubal calmly raises his hand, palm out. "No farther, my hairy friend. Is your memory so short you have forgotten that I have your wife and Indibilis' daughters? If you touch a hair of my head, they will be slain—long after wishing they were so."

Indibilis grabs Mandonius' ax belt and pulls him back, glaring at Hasdrubal. "You play a dangerous game with us, foreigner. Someday your plunder will not be payment enough."

"Pssh!" sniffs Hasdrubal, with a flip of his hand, "I pay you enough silver to secure your silence as well as your obedience. Enough for you not to bemoan your wounded pride. Besides, how many men have you two burned or flayed?" He sees Mandonius stiffen and start to come at him again. "Oh for the sake of Baal, if it will stop your crying ...."

Hasdrubal stalks over to his groaning victim. In one motion, he flicks out his dagger and thrusts it up into the stricken man's rib cage. He twists the dagger, and its keen blade slashes across the victim's heart. With a final cry, the man convulses and dies, burbling blood down his torso. The townspeople breathe an anguished sigh of relief. Much as they hate the Carthaginian commander, they are grateful they no longer have to watch Isbitaris suffer for trying to convert them to the Roman cause.

Hasdrubal casually wipes his blade on the dead man's loincloth. He turns about and grins ingratiatingly at the two chieftains. "There now, is that better? Now we can move on to business. That boy Cornelius Scipio has landed north of Tarraco. No doubt he will attack one of our armies in early spring, and I want the honor of defeating him before my brothers do. Meet me at camp by dawn's light tomorrow. We will prepare an assault."

Indibilis and Mandonius look sideways at each other. With the briefest of nods to Hasdrubal, they walk over to confer with their waiting tribesmen, ignoring the Carthaginian general. Hasdrubal shrugs. "Heed me, or your families are forfeit!" he shouts at the two chieftains, who continue to ignore him. Hasdrubal grabs his Numidian pony's reins from a slave and springs agilely into the saddle. As he rides away from the angry villagers, he thinks about his brother Mago. *That prick should have been here to help me,* he thinks. *Telling me he has to block the Romans from attacking us. You'd think he'd killed those Scipios himself.*

Off to the side of the crowd, an aged priest has listened avidly to Hasdrubal and the two chieftains. When the Carthaginian general mounts his horse to leave, the priest backs through the crowd and scuttles to his hut on the edge of town. He pulls a stylus and clay tablet from beneath his sleeping blankets. Nervously watching the hut entry, he etches a note on the small tablet. At the bottom he sketches out the image of a leaping fish, his code symbol.

The old man slides the tablet into a slit in a round loaf of bread, stuffs the loaf into his goatskin pack, and tramps out into the surrounding forest, pausing to sit by a stream that flows next to the merchant road. He kneels next to the gurgling waters and crosses his arms in prayer, oblivious to the drovers and warriors that pass by him. Many bow at the holy man and request a blessing from the gods, but the aged one prays in silence.

As the sun sets, a bent beggar shuffles slowly along the road, huddled beneath a filthy brown cloak. The beggar pauses before the priest and begs for food. The holy man bends into his pack, extracts the loaf of bread, and extends it to him. A deeply tanned arm extends from the beggar's filthy rags, one that is surprisingly muscular for such a frail-looking figure. The beggar whisks the bread inside his cloak and quickly drops a small purse of coins into the priest's open palm. He shuffles off as the priest looks about, quaking with apprehension, praying he will not be the next one on the cross.

II. ROME

ROME, ITALIA, 211 BCE. Emerging from the Senate chambers, Marcus Portius Cato hustles across the spacious Forum Square. He pivots right and plunges into the teeming crowds that fill Merchant Street, Rome's busiest thoroughfare. The stocky young man pushes his way through the innumerable stalls of butchers, pottery makers, money lenders, and bakers—all the shopkeepers and artisans that are not wealthy enough to buy a stand in the Forum Square.

As he distances himself from the Forum, the shops and crowds thin out. Cato ducks behind a pudding-maker's stall and looks back the way he came. Confident that no one is following him, he ducks into a shoulder-wide alleyway between two four-story tenements and speeds his pace, fearing he will be late. He soon emerges onto a wide avenue lined with domus, the elegant townhouses of the patrician class. Cato is on a political mission, one that he feels will save Rome by defeating Hannibal and by undermining the hated Scipios—and one he feels will further his own goal of becoming a consul.

Years ago, Cato was a military orphan, a poor youth tending a small plot of land given to his father for his years of military service, small compensation for a decorated veteran who returned home with fatal wounds. Pulling the rocks from the impoverished soil with his bare hands, the boy-man vowed to make the Porcius family name known to all in Rome, as recompense for the oversights accorded his heroic ancestors.

Now, at twenty-four years of age, red-haired Cato has fought his way from shit-footed farmer to respected city magistrate. He has succeeded by force of his fiery temper, powerful oratory, and unwavering commitment to the simplicity and austerity of an agrarian lifestyle. Cato has also become the adopted favorite of the rich and powerful Latin Party, serving as their link to the plebs, Rome's working class.

This stubby, potato-nosed youth is the avowed enemy of the highborn Scipios. He knows that Pomponia Scipio is a mainstay of the Hellenic Party, the group that would bring education and culture to commoners, at the expense of the rich. But Cato, he would return Romans to their simple agrarian roots, when farmer-kings ruled with a strong hand, and laws were simple and unwavering. Cato is a man without nuance or compromise, liked by few but respected by many, though he cares little for others outside of his mentor, General Fabius.

Pulling a cloak over his sunburned head, Cato quickly crosses the cobbled street and approaches the largest house on the block. He walks up several wide steps to the embossed oak doors of the most powerful man in Rome, the wealthy consul Publius Galba.

Hanging from the front of the massive twin doors is a framed stone tablet bearing these chiseled words:

If a woman steals from me, or a man, or a boy, let the first give me her cunt, the second his head, the third his buttocks.[i]

A three-foot statue of Priapus, the god of fertility, stands to the side of the wide doorstep. The statue portrays a stooped, ugly man with a leering countenance, proudly grasping his two-foot-long erection. Cato sighs. *Typical patrician. Preoccupied with surface pleasures.* Cato carefully steps around the grotesque statue's phallus and pounds the brass knocker on the dark green doors. The doors open, and a portly red-haired Thracian fills the doorway. The middle-aged slave stares insolently at the homely boy, but Cato's gaze bores into him until he looks away. "Tribune Marcus Portius Cato to see Publius Sulpicius Galba," he states. As the slave starts to close the door, he adds acidly, "And that is by appointment, pumpkin," taking pleasure in demeaning the haughty slave.

II. Rome

Cato hands the slave a papyrus sheaf with a bull figure impressed into its yellow-brown wax, the Galba mark. The Thracian takes it with the barest of nods and waves him in. Cato follows the waddling slave to a large open-aired atrium in the center of the house, where the Thracian gestures for him sit and wait by the fish pool. Cato remains standing, ignoring him. With a dismissive snort, the slave patters out.

Consul Galba soon enters, clad in a flowing white toga with a broad purple stripe along its border. He is a lean and sinewy older man with steel grey eyes that match Cato's own. Galba chews languorously on a clutch of ripe grapes, his face wreathed in a smile of self-indulgent pleasure. The consul walks over and claps Cato on the shoulder, a familiarity that makes him wince.

"Young Cato, it is good to see you! How fare my friends Fabius and Flaccus?"

"They send their deepest respect, consul," replies Cato, with a tight smile. "And they send the regards of the Latin Party."

"Ah yes, the Latin Party," exclaims Galba, raising his arms and eyes heavenward. "Ready to set Rome on the path ahead by having it go backwards! I must say, my wife is still angry about that jewelry tax you imposed."

"That was my idea," Cato replies levelly, "and I am humbled and pleased the Party adopted it. Greek frippery has no place in the Roman soul, consul Galba, much less on women who do not know their place. Piety and fidelity are adornment enough, and more beautiful to behold."

Galba sighs, and momentarily closes his eyes. "Ah, yes. Well spoken, young Cato. As always." Galba pops another grape into his mouth and smiles at him. "You are making quite a name for yourself, for certitude, quite a name ...." Galba's smile vanishes. "But you did not come here for compliments, did you? What brings you to my humble domicile?"

Cato looks at the statuary and frescoes that surround him and barely represses a sneer. "Humble, eh? Well, honored consul, you know that Cornelius Scipio has landed at Emporiae. He will be moving south to Tarraco, is that correct?"

Galba reaches inside his toga to scratch his backside, looking away from Cato. "That is common knowledge in the Senate. What of it?"

"Apologies, consul, but Fabius asks for a confirmation: when Scipio comes to Tarraco, will he take command of Marcius' survivors from the defeat at Baetis, as well as Nero's two legions?"

Galba nods. "Most likely. He is the governor of Iberia and commander of the forces in Iberia. Unless commanded otherwise, that is within his power."

Cato stares levelly at him, expressionless. "And if you were to deliver an imperium that Nero return to Rome with those legions …?"

Galba frowns, growing impatient. "That would be different. An imperium cannot be countermanded. But I would not do such a thing. The boy has few enough men as it is." Galba snaps his fingers, and holds out his empty string of grapes. A slave rushes in to whisk it away and returns with a full clutch of them.

He could offer me some, Cato grouses to himself. Then he shrugs noncommittally. "I hear what you say, although many would question giving him any legions in the first place. Especially in light of what Fabius has just learned." Cato takes a step closer to Galba, who studies him warily. "Fabius' scouts report that Macedonian ships have been sighted in southern Italia, approaching the area where Hannibal holds sway. If those ships hold allies for Carthage, we will need every man we can get to combat them, here in Italia."

Galba's brow furrows. He places his grapes on a table and faces Cato. "That is disturbing news indeed. Hannibal already has too many allies—most of whom were once ours. Still, young Scipio does not have enough men to defeat even one of the Three Generals' armies, much less their combined force. It would be a death sentence to deny him Nero's legions."

"But not if Scipio were commanded to sustain a holding action there at Tarraco," replies Cato enthusiastically. "He is too inexperienced to lead a campaign. Warring against the formidable Barca brothers will only waste legions. But a defensive posture, now that is within his ken. All the boy has to do is keep the Carthaginians from crossing the Ebro into Rome, at least until the threat of Hannibal is removed." Cato spreads his hands wide. "Then Scipio could be replaced with a more experienced commander, fortified with veteran legions, and Iberia would fall! Do you see?"

Galba looks heavenward. "You think me a pleb in the street, that can be swayed by rhetoric? I know the boy Scipio. He has the touch of genius. He is not so helpless as you would have me believe, boy."

Cato looks at his feet, hating what he will say next. "Flaccus and Fabius have told me to tell you this," he mumbles. "If Nero's legions return to Rome, the Latin Party will ensure your reelection as consul. Otherwise, they will press for a more suitable commander. Those are their words, not mine."

Galba laughs sarcastically. "You mean a more Latin commander, do you not? Ah, boy, you are too young—and simple—to be making political bribes to a consul!" Galba shakes his head, amused.

Cato's neck reddens, but his voice remains calm. "I offer you nothing. Nothing. I but relay this message from General Fabius himself. He would be here, but being seen with you would not be … propitious."

Galba chuckles again. "For certitude, that is true! If the Hellenics knew what you propose, they would roil the Senate with their protests!" Still laughing, Galba strolls out from the atrium.

Cato's voice rings behind him. "Oh, honored consul, one more thing!" Galba pauses and gives the barest of looks over his shoulder, saying nothing.

"Myself, I think you should do it out of duty and honor, to save the people of Rome. That is what the legendary Dentatus and Cincinnatus would have done. Were they leading the army today, Hannibal's head would already be feeding the crows."

Galba smiles a serpent's smile. "Duty, you say? I have a duty to myself, after all I have given Rome." He walks through the doorway. "I will take the matter under consideration. Tell that to our two friends. Anything that would rid us of Hannibal is worth my consideration." Galba disappears through the main atrium portal, his laughs echoing down the hallway. Cato stands in the atrium, looking at the erotic frescoes that line the marbled walls.

The Thracian slave appears, smiling triumphantly. Cato raises his hand peremptorily. "Do not say it, under pain of injury. I will depart." With those words Cato pads toward the doorway, sandals slapping, eyes burning with frustration.

*   *   *   *   *

APULIA, SOUTHERN ITALIA, 210 BCE. It is very late, but Hannibal still toils on through the humid summer night, plotting his troop's movements for his coastal campaign. Hannibal is a tall, graceful man of thirty-seven, still lithe and muscular in spite of his many wounds and scars. His intelligent face has the high cheekbones and narrow aquiline nose that favors the Barca line, Carthage's mightiest military family. In spite of his impressive physical features, all who meet him first notice his bearing: he carries himself with the posture and attitude of a man born to command nations, a leader at once thoughtful and decisive.

Hannibal stares at his map with the one green eye remaining to him, the other lost after his now-legendary trip from Iberia over the winter Alps to Rome. His tactical genius has allowed him to win battle after battle with a hodgepodge of mercenaries and tribesmen from different nations, all held together in the iron fist of his will. A god to his men and a demon to his enemies, he is an immortal to both. "Bane of

Roma," the legionnaires call him, the title revealing their respect and fear.

For eight years Hannibal has fought the Romans and their allies throughout Italia, determined to fulfill the vow to his father that he would always be an enemy to Rome. Hannibal has never lost a major battle, yet he has never had enough men or resources to take Rome itself. And so the stalemate continues between him and The Republic, each side seeking the one battle that will finally destroy the threat of the other.

After recently decimating Rome's legions in Campania, Hannibal is resting his men in the southern regions of the peninsula below it, secure among Rome's many tribal enemies. But Hannibal is not there to rest; he and Maharbal, his second-in-command, must plot a way to wipe out the last dregs of Roman resistance. Thrice he has assayed peace with Rome, and thrice has Rome rejected his overtures. Hannibal now knows there is only one way to end this war. It is a way that he has sought to avoid, realizing that tens of thousands have already perished in this mercenary conflict, and as many will die if this war continues.

Hannibal bends over his sheepskin map of Italia, studying the placement of Rome's few surviving legions, arguing with Maharbal about where to attack next. A fiercely aggressive combatant, Maharbal is again stumping for a direct attack on Rome via the Appian Way, as he did after they massacred the Romans at Cannae.[ii] Hannibal contends that they must deepen their resource base by adding more food and money to their war stores and by recruiting in the nearby city-states for more allies.

Maharbal argues angrily with his beloved general but Hannibal maintains his composure, in part because his "pets" are outside the tent. Listening to Surus and the other elephants shuffling about, the Carthaginian is comforted; the presence of the enormous beasts is a connection to the home he left so long ago. He feeds and walks the elephants as if they were his dogs, grateful for the calm their stately presence provides him.

"You have a visitor, General," a Sacred Band guard announces, edging his way inside the command tent flaps.

"Who is it?" Hannibal asks irritably, without looking up from his map.

"He will not reveal his name," replies the guard, "only that his business is urgent."

Hannibal lurches up, shaking his head at Maharbal. "The hour grows long," replies Hannibal. "I shall meet him on the morrow, when I hold public court."

A regal voice penetrates the tent walls, one with an undercurrent of impatience. "I will not be here tomorrow, Hannibal. I cannot be seen with you in the light of day. Bid me enter."

Hannibal pauses to think where he has heard that voice before. Then he remembers—when he last heard that voice it was higher in timbre, that of a pubescent boy. Now it has the deep and steady tones of a person used to decision and command. Hannibal turns to his sentry. "Let him in! Now!" He turns to Maharbal. "You have heard my mind on this. We will attack from strength, not desperation. Leave me." With a curse of frustration, Maharbal stalks from the tent.

The tent flaps part and a handsome young man enters the tent, accompanied by four guards in beautifully wrought Greek armor. The youth walks with a dignity and grace beyond his twenty-eight years, as he studies Hannibal's austere domain with his sea-blue eyes. He is clad in thick robes of darkest blue, his head crowned with a nest of curls so high and fine it is almost effeminate. His brow bears the thinnest of gold wreaths, mute testament to his lack of pretension about the power he wields. Though a boyish grin creases his finely defined features, his head is high and his back ramrod straight. He carries the aura of one used to unquestioned obedience. The young man walks to Hannibal and extends his arm, his gesture so decisive it is almost a command. Hannibal hesitates just long enough to show he is a peer, then he firmly grasps the young man's forearm and smiles.

"I am pleased to see you again, Philip. But this is quite the surprise. I did not expect the king of Macedon to travel to enemy country, just to meet me."

The boy spreads his arms theatrically, laughing. "And why not? I set sail to visit our allied territories, and I thought, 'Why not stop over to see my friend Hannibal?' It has been six years since you and I struck our agreement to oppose Rome, and we have much to discuss. Alas, I must leave on the morrow, so do not think me rude."

"Is it a pleasure, Philip, however brief our time. What is on your mind?"

"First, General, I congratulate you on your triumph at the Silarus River. I heard that you destroyed Marcus Centenius' two legions, and those of his allies. Another brilliant victory!"

Hannibal waves Philip to a chair. "A victory it was, but it did not require much brilliance. The Roman Senate gave their legions to a naive praetor (magistrate)," Hannibal replies. "Someone who had lived by the Silarus, a Marcus Centenius Penula. He claimed he knew the region like his wife's thighs; that he could track all my movements and avoid my ambushes." Hannibal chuckles. "By Baal's balls, he was a gift from the gods! I had infiltrators in his army before he left Rome, acting as scouts for him. They gave him all sorts of false leads of my immediate whereabouts." Hannibal sits in a chair near to Philip, shaking his head in amazement. "He took the bait like a hungry dog, starving for glory. It was a simple matter to surround him and 'tighten the circle.' By late afternoon it was over. Of their 16,000, a thousand escaped.[iii] My men were so tired from killing, they sat on the battlefield corpses and watched the remnants flee, aimlessly hurling javelins at them, betting on the swiftest as if they were watching a horserace."

Philip laughs gleefully. "A telling victory, regardless of its ease." He points toward the seashore. "I would provide further help for you to destroy Rome, an objective that is to our mutual benefit, would you not agree?"

Hannibal rises from his chair. He paces about the tent before he withdraws a small ivory figurine. "Destroy Rome, you say? If I must." He shows the figurine to Philip. "I vowed to my father that Rome would forever be my enemy, but I did not promise to destroy it. I seek the restoration of Carthage's land and shipping rights, that we may regain our former glory."

Philip glances curiously as the ivory icon. "That is a figure of your father, Hamilcar?"

Hannibal fingers the image in his palm, his eyes distant with memories. "Yes, the old Thunderbolt himself. It is but a copy of the one my father gave me. I gave his to a dying soldier on the charnel fields of Cannae, a boy named Horace. He saved my life and then lost his, blindly following wherever I led. That has changed what I pursue."

Philip closes his eyes and bows his head in frustration, his voice on the edge of sarcasm. "Peace with Rome? Sooner would I sleep with a nest of adders! Yes, you have changed, Bane of Roma. Six years ago you were determined to wipe out the Romans, and now you would save them by making treaty with them when they are mortally wounded!"

"I have seen much death in my time. And caused even more. I hope for the best, but still I prepare for the worst—a terminal war."

"The worst is what you will get," says Philip. "Rome is not the village of mud huts from centuries past, when our Alexander the Great ruled the world. It seems ever bent on becoming an empire, seeking to take both our kingdoms. They will not rest until they rule the world, heed my words! Thrice you have destroyed their armies, and thrice they have ventured forth with new ones. What makes you think things will change, Carthaginian?"

"Each time Rome's legions grow fewer and weaker, and Rome grows more desperate," Hannibal replies. "Now they recruit slaves and prisoners." Hannibal barks a laugh. "They sent that boy Scipio to Iberia with two legions of unseasoned recruits. He is to somehow defeat my two brothers' armies, and Gisgo's." Hannibal looks at a map of Iberia on his table, pointing to a Roman ship figurine placed near Emporiae. "Scipio has landed here, and moves south. I imagine he will pick up some more men at Tarraco, but it will still not be enough. The Three Generals will crash Tarraco's walls around him." He shakes his head. "When he fought for old Fabius, that boy had imagination. What a waste he is a Roman!"

Philip nods his head, reflecting on Hannibal's words. "That is good news. If Scipio keeps Iberia's veterans with him, they will not come to Graecia and oppose me. Consul Galba's legions are coming there, and I will defeat them. He will not pose a threat to you. How fare your forces here?"

"We are on the cusp of having enough men to attack Rome itself, when the spring fields become ripe for foraging. The southern Italia tribes have come over to my side, except for those near the Roman fortresses. A few more towns, a few thousand more men, and we are ready."

"Ah, that is good, very good. And I can help your cause." Philip rises. "Will you come with me?"

Philip and Hannibal walk out of the tent and are immediately surrounded by scores of their personal guard, who march along with their respective rulers, glancing uneasily at the other ones. Hannibal and Philip walk down to the wide beach near Hannibal's camp, where Philip's triremes lie beached amongst clear turquoise waters. As Hannibal nears the ships, he sees a forest of Macedonian infantry at the shore, standing in full battle array. Hannibal halts and casts a wary eye at the small army arrayed in front of him. His guards nervously finger their sword hilts. Hannibal looks sternly at Philip. "What are all these men doing here?"

Philip waves his arm across the grim lines as if he were showing off a herd of prize cattle. "Them? They are a present for you, General. For keeping the Roman dogs from my home. There are two phalanxes there, a little over 2,000 men. I thought you might welcome some reinforcements."

Hannibal extends his arm, and Philip takes it. "I am very grateful. Your feared warriors will be a welcome addition, as the gods are my witness. And your timing is propitious, for a battle looms."

Philip raises an eyebrow. "So soon after your last victory? For a man who seeks peace, you certainly pursue war."

"War is my only way to peace," says Hannibal. "Gnaeus Fulvius has two legions in the field near Herdonia, bent on besieging the cities that have allied with us. His army is all that stands between me and the Appian Way to Rome. When I take Herdonia, I will use it to muster all my resources. I can move toward Rome before winter sets in. Once my brothers defeat Scipio's little army, they can retrace my march over the Alps and join me. Rome will be indefensible against 150,000 men. Gods damn them, those arrogant pigs will then have to surrender or die."

"Excellent stratagem, Carthaginian. Whence go you to Herdonia?"

"The decisive hour draws nigh," replies Hannibal. "Those who spit upon my peace efforts will be on their knees before me on the Senate floor, begging for mercy."

Phillip grins. "I would pay a king's ransom to see that. But it is more likely that they will lie bleeding on that floor, resistant to the end."

*   *   *   *   *

ROME. Pomponia enters the spacious sunlight atrium of the Scipio family's city house, intent on sending a letter to her son in Iberia. Tall, stately, and full-figured, Scipio's mother is the personification of a Junoesque beauty, her blue eyes and cascading red hair adding to the allure of a woman who carries herself like a queen. Though she is a wealthy patrician of a noble family, her heart lies with the plebs, the freemen of Rome from which her family came. Walking to market in full raiment, Pomponia will pause to talk to the shopkeepers and even the beggars, giving them her full attention.

Many a suitor has come to her door since Scipio's father, General Publius Scipio, perished while fighting the Three Generals. All have been eased on their way, as her purposes have turned to Rome's welfare. Pomponia is now a bastion of the Hellenic Party, and she can take no time for romance. Her passions are given to the political war to save Rome from the Latin Party's depredations. She sees their emphasis on traditionalist values as a façade to preserve the elite's continuing suppression of citizens' education and empowerment, what she sees as the keys to Rome becoming a great city, not simply a powerful one.

The matron stretches out along a low-slung wicker chaise next to the fish pool, pulling her indigo robe about her. She beckons for her slave Marcia to fetch her writing tools, and the bent old woman shuffles off for the wicker basket that holds them.

Marcia remains in the Scipio household even though her worth has long since passed. In keeping with the Scipio tradition, Pomponia retains all family slaves for life, which has inspired a fanatical loyalty from them. She has heard that agrarian traditionalists such as Cato sell their slaves as soon as they become old, treating them like livestock.[iv] But Pomponia learned long ago the power of providing kindness and reward to those accustomed to fear and punishment—provided that generosity is backed by the strength to do otherwise. Pomponia's political power comes from such generosity, as well as her talent at sexual politics, knowing it is a woman's main avenue to political power in Rome.

Marcia hands Pomponia a quill pen and a bottle of octopus ink. "Gratitude," says Pomponia, nodding for Marcia to leave her. Kicking off her sandals, the queenly woman unrolls the small parchment she brought with her and begins her monthly letter to her son.

II. Rome

Beloved Son:

I trust you are doing well there, in the wildlands of Iberia. It must be difficult to be a new general in a strange land, but I know you will succeed once you accustom yourself to being in command. Just remember: your ingenuity is unmatched; it is your key to victory.

As always, Amelia sends her love. The girl you left is gone; she has become a formidable woman. We are organizing a campaign to elect the Hellenic Party secretary, Gabius Veronius, for praetor urbanus. You would like him, he is fascinated by your concept of what you called a "library" to educate the citizens of Rome. If he is elected, perhaps he can make our dream come true.

Your brother Lucius will sail to meet you soon. He is very excited to be joining you and starting his military career. My son, I know you have many tasks to attend to, but please take time to help Lucius succeed. The gods have not favored him as much as you, and he feels the weight of being a Scipio. He needs your help.

I know you have many new ideas about how you will fight this war; you were ever the scholar and thinker. In your last letter you said you have some new weapons and tactics to deploy against the Three Generals, things you learned from Hannibal himself. Like you, I agree with Aesop, your favorite storyteller, that an enemy will often give you the means of his destruction, if you but attend to him. But our legionnaires are proud of Rome's glorious military history. Many will consider your changes an insult to military tradition. Tread lightly and slowly.

You must have much on your mind, but I must tell you that Rome is in dire circumstance. Two months ago, the Latin Party elected Fulvius, Flaccus' errant brother, to lead our remaining legions out to battle Hannibal. You know the temper of Fulvius' metal—more tin than iron. Should his legions be vanquished, we have only old Fabius' tattered soldiery between us and the Carthaginian.

It is so sad. Every day, more of the Italia tribes desert to Carthage. We are desperate for a victory to turn their heads and lift our spirits, yet so terrified of another loss. I pray to the gods that victory will come soon.

May Jupiter be with you,

Pomponia

Six days later, a messenger delivers Pomponia's letter to Scipio as he walks his army's temporary camp far south of Emporiae, preparing his men for the next day's march toward Tarraco. Scipio reads the letter and stuffs it into his pouch, frowning with frustration about Rome's plight. "I will have a return message for you tonight, at the sixth hour. Meet me then."

That night, Scipio takes pen to papyrus and writes a short note.

Dear Mother:

It wounds my heart that Rome is in peril. My spies there echo your distress; Rome's very existence hangs in the balance. Would that I could take my men and sail back to protect you and Amelia.

I do believe I could defeat Hannibal. I know his mind better than any because I am the only one who respects him enough to learn from him. Alas, the Latin Party seeks a political victory over a military one; they will continue with their Latin cronies, Fabius and Flaccus, until our doom is assured.

You know there is only one general who can stop Hannibal, the only one who has defeated him. Rome must recall the Sword of Rome from Sicily. Doubtless you recall the political problem: he favors the Hellenic Party, and the Latin Party will oppose his return because he may succeed where their own men have failed.

You and Amelia must cast the die and take a chance. My beloved has studied how the Persians and Indians use something she calls "propaganda," which she says will bring the people to our side. Use Amelia's genius in this art, and get our message about the Sword of Rome to the Roman people. And give my love to her, Mother, as I give my love to you.

Ever your dutiful son,

Publius Cornelius Scipio

Scipio rolls up the papyrus and seals it with blob of wax, stamping it with the impression of the owl of Minerva, the goddess of wisdom. He wraps the papyrus in sheepskin and hands it to the waiting messenger. "Deliver this to Pomponia Scipio. Do not give it to any of her slaves or attendants. Put it directly into her hands."

Two weeks later, signs spring up throughout Rome, and banners appear overnight on public places. They all echo the same thought:

"Rome is in dire peril. Bring back the Sword of Rome."

*   *   *   *   *

HERDONIA, APULIA, 210 BCE. Proconsul (governor) Gnaeus Fulvius stands in front of a roughshod wooden temple outside his tent. He flaps his chubby arms nervously, awaiting the priest's signal for him to come forward. Still chanting, the priest points his finger toward the massive white bull that is tied to a post next to his acolytes. Fulvius waddles forward and cuts a tuft of hair off the white bull's head. He throws it into the fire, providing his initial offering to Mars, god of war. Then he places an ivy wreath on the bull's head and steps back. The priest's sacrificial assistants, the victimarii, hold the bull by its thick horns, waiting to do their part.

The priest's voice rises as he intones his prayers to the war god, petitioning for victory over the Carthaginians. His prayers completed, the holy man bows his head and glances sidelong at his helpers. One of the victimarii holds the bull's head as the other pulls out a sacrificial

35

knife and slits the bull's throat. They hold the bull's head high as the blood fountains from the beast's neck into a large copper bowl. The bull lows once, piteously, then falls to its side and lies twitching. The blood bowl is handed to Fulvius, who proffers it to the gods before he sips from it, sealing his pact to sacrifice twelve more bulls if the gods give him triumph over Hannibal.

Fulvius is not a devout believer in the power of the gods to influence battles, but he will try anything that will help him avoid defeat—or even worse, physical pain. Although Hannibal has beaten many brash and seasoned Roman generals, Fulvius poses Hannibal's most serious threat because he is a rank coward who will fight only if he thinks he is guaranteed a safe victory, free from mortal peril.

A soft but ambitious man from one of Rome's wealthiest families, Fulvius embraced military leadership as his next step on the cursus honorum to power. After several years of tepid military leadership in the provinces, he has deployed his connections and money to finally attain Rome's highest political honor and become a consul. Now he hopes to engage the Carthaginian army in a light skirmish and return to Rome before Hannibal arrives, declaring himself as a veteran of the Carthaginian wars. He will let the Sword of Rome, the redoubtable Marcus Claudius Marcellus, contest with Hannibal, now that Marcellus has been recalled from Sicily by popular acclaim. *A little dance with the Carthaginian should wipe that grin off Marcellus' face*, Fulvius thinks. *We shall see then who is Rome's favorite.*

Fulvius' minimal-engagement strategy is not without merit because his cautious leadership has served him well in the past. He has two victories from his campaign in far-off Illyria, where his legionnaires overcame the outnumbered barbarians that wildly charged at the Roman front lines, easy victims to the controlled mayhem of the disciplined legions. But Fulvius knows that this Hannibal is a more patient and clever enemy, one who has turned opponents' strengths into weaknesses. He knows that Hannibal has taken Herdonia before and knows its vulnerabilities, making him even more dangerous. So Fulvius plans to avoid the Carthaginian at all costs, especially when he recalls what happened at the first battle of Herdonia.

Two years ago, Hannibal decimated consul Gnaeus Flaccus' army beneath the very walls of Herdonia, killing 15,000 Romans and allies in a single day. The Bane of Roma had used a surprise cavalry attack from the farms behind Flaccus' four legions, collapsing his organized maniples into a milling mob. With his army completely surrounded, Flaccus grasped the inevitable and fled, his retreat a disgrace for the Latin Party he champions back in Rome. As a fellow Latin, Fulvius is determined to bring honor back to the Party before the next elections. He needs only to engage some aspect of the Carthaginian army without suffering a defeat, then his handpicked messengers will return to Rome and trumpet up the achievement to its victory-starved citizens. It is a safe, productive plan with little glory but minimal risk, just the way Fulvius prefers it.

His religious duties completed, the portly general wipes the blood off his hands and strolls back to his command tent for a much anticipated repast. Entering his well-appointed goatskin domain, he immediately grabs a goblet of twenty-year-old Falernian wine and chews on some roasted mice he has brought with him from Rome, quite comfortable with his "battle plans." Tomorrow he will take his army from camp and lay siege to Herdonia several miles away. The city has only a few thousand Carthaginians and local militia inside its walls; he knows they would never come out and fight his numerically superior legions. And Hannibal, dread Hannibal, he is far away in Bruttium, where Marcellus will certainly keep him occupied for months.

Even with little risk to his person, Fulvius does not want to tarry in Herdonia. To that end he has bribed some of the city's most prominent citizens to convince its defenders to surrender peacefully. Fulvius will offer them generous terms, and the townspeople will capitulate without the need of a lengthy campaign. Fulvius pours himself another goblet of wine and grins smugly to himself. *Hannibal is not the only one who can be sneaky*, he thinks. *I will return to Rome before the next new moon. Then I can get out of these fucking camps and into some victory parties held in my honor.* After a final draft of wine, Fulvius plops down among his sleeping cushions. It is barely night, but he wants to rise early. He can't wait for tomorrow, for the safe danger of controlled conflict.

As Fulvius drifts off into a drunken sleep, Hannibal wakes and rises from the ground next to his men. He quickly dons his armor, quietly issuing orders to his officers. Within the hour, the Carthaginian army is treading south toward the plains of Herdonia, barely twenty miles distant, counting on the cover of darkness to facilitate his latest ruse.

Hannibal's spies have tracked this nervous, corpulent little general since he returned from Illyria two years ago. knowing that any victorious general would be sent to defeat him. He also knows that Fulvius will be too cautious to rush headstrong into a trap, as Fulvius' counterparts did at Trebia, Trasimene, and Cannae. No, this patrician would never fight him face-to-face, he would stay safe in his fortified camp, waiting for Hannibal to leave after exhausting his patience or resources. Hannibal has concluded that this wary little mouse must be lured onto the plain of battle, and Fulvius will only come out if he is does not know what awaits him.

The success of Hannibal's battle strategy depends on the force of rumor, one of Hannibal's most effective allies. Months ago, Hannibal enjoined his cavalry commander Maharbal to purchase hundreds of horses from the local merchants. Maharbal told each merchant the same story: he needed the horses because the Carthaginians were heading south to Bruttium to establish a permanent camp. The rumors spread through the city and were soon relayed to Rome.

Before Fulvius departed from Rome, Hannibal marched south toward Bruttium. One night, under cover of darkness, Hannibal reversed direction and headed back into northern Apulia, using a lightly armed force on a forced march.[v] Hannibal's force moves by night and back roads, quickly closing in on Herdonia.

Believing that Hannibal was in Bruttium, Fulvius and his four legions—two Roman and two Italia allies—hastened to lightly defended Herdonia to retake it. And the redoubtable General Marcellus, the Sword of Rome, has taken Rome's few remaining legions far south to engage an absent Hannibal at Bruttium. Such was the strategic power of Hannibal's carefully cultivated deception.

For several predawn hours, the Carthaginians march as silently as an army can go, with scores of black-clad scouts deployed to intercept any Romans ahead of them. As the army nears Herdonia, Hannibal divides his force in two, sending thousands of his swift Numidian cavalry to ride west through the dense Black Forest and circle behind Fulvius' camp. He directs his remaining men to stop and rest. They take food and water and wait for the dawn, horses and weapons at the ready, oiling their bodies against the morning chill. And then they wait, ready to mobilize with the blow of a horn.

The dawn sun is high when the Roman army marches out from its camp to commence its siege of Herdonia. General Fulvius is in the vanguard, surrounded by scores of his elite guard. He leads one of the Roman legions within bowshot of the city gates. They stop there and array themselves in two lines about the front walls, waiting for the Herdonians to battle or surrender. After waiting an hour, Fulvius sends a messenger to the town walls. The messenger shouts that the city is to open its gates or face annihilation. Once the messenger has imparted the dictum, Fulvius delegates his legion to his tribunes and hastens back to camp, past the two allied legions and his other Roman legion, the latter stationed near camp for his protection. He returns to his tent and quickly relieves himself of his armor, to take refreshment and wait for his machinations to take effect.

The Roman army settles in for what they think may be a long siege, with all eyes on the empty city walls about Herdonia. The legions scatter about in small temporary camps and set about making food and sharpening their weapons. They bask in the summer heat, waiting for the sun to go down so that they may return to camp. It is a restful war.

The pacific atmosphere is shattered by the shouts of a scout galloping in from the north: "Hannibal is approaching!" he screams. "He is coming over the hills!" With no time to return to camp, the tribunes and centurions rush their men into their centuries of sixty, and the centuries into their maniples of 120, each maniple arrayed north in three columns of forty men. The legionnaires stand in formation, hearts hammering, as they listen to the sound of distant battle horns.

Soon the first lines of the Carthaginian army flow over the low hills toward Fulvius' men. Hannibal himself is at the front of the attack, lurching along atop his monstrous war elephant Surus. Armored tail to trunk in red chain mail, the pachyderm looks like a demon from the fires of Hades. Many a legionnaire blinks in terror at the sight of the great beast, but they hold fast.

Fulvius is soundly napping when a scout bursts in with news of Hannibal's approach. The general scrambles for his armor, breathless with alarm. *How could this happen?* he asks himself. He gallops out to the legion by Herdonia. Gathering his tribunes, he tells the them to avoid making a deep advancement into the Carthaginian's centerlines if they retreat in front of them, so they will not fall victim to Hannibal's V-shaped encirclement that doomed forty thousand Romans at Cannae. He directs his allies to reinforce the front lines of his first legion, and for his remaining legion to guard the front of the camp. Turning to his Master of Horse, Fulvius orders the cavalry to protect the first legion's flanks and to be wary of a rear attack by the Numidians, as happened at the battles of Trebia and Trasimene. Desperate and scared, Fulvius tries to guard against any trick he can think of, determined he will not fall prey to Hannibal's ruses.

As soon as Fulvius' orders are completed, his commanders dash back to prepare for battle. After the last tribune departs, Fulvius hustles back to his command tent on the pretext of finishing some urgent business. When the Carthaginian battle horns indicate the battle is imminent, he finally orders his horse to be brought to him, intending to direct his men from behind the allied legions, with a Roman legion at his back for maximum protection.

As he waits for his stallion, Fulvius can hear the metallic din of sword on shield and sword on sword. He hears the strident music of the gracefully curved Roman cornu trumpeting the charge, and the shouts and screams of men in conflict. He can even hear the pounding of horses' hooves as clear as day. *That is odd. They sound like they are right on top of us. Is that from our cavalry on the flanks?* Then it occurs to him that the pounding is coming from the rear of the camp, and he steps around to the back of his tent to see which of his squadrons are so late entering the battle.

Fulvius gapes at the sight of a flood of Numidian lancers storming through the rear of his camp. They trample down the soldiers in front of them as their second riders leap off to cut down the camp's guards and sentries. Fulvius can only stand with mouth open as the flood washes past him, out through the open front gates and into the rear lines of his army. He raises his hands in surrender as a tall young Numidian rides directly at him. *Hannibal knew I would be here. How did he know?* is the last thing that occurs to him, before the Numidian's javelin pierces his chest.

As Hannibal's cavalry begin their rampage through the Roman base camp, his infantry storm into the Romans at the front of Herdonia, while its terrified citizens watch from the walls. Hundreds of Gauls lead the charge into the Romans, dashing forward in their tribal gangs, many naked and others wearing only chain mail hauberks. Screaming challenges and insults, they wield their enormous broadswords like axes, cutting through shield and helmet alike. The Gauls are Hannibal's shock troops. They crash into the firmly planted front lines of the maniples, the rows populated by the hastati, which are mainly the youngest soldiers. Each hastati fights at arm's length from his neighbor, maintaining enough space to maneuver around the large barbarians that storm against them.

The berserking Gauls chop down at the Romans' heads and shields, hoping to split either with a single blow. The Romans deflect their blows and stab at unprotected places on the Gauls' bodies, intending to inflict a telling cut rather than a single dismembering blow. The legionnaires thrust with their javelins and short swords, and scores of the large barbarians fall. But many of these unseasoned Romans fall, chopped to pieces by the ferocious Gauls. Still, the Roman lines hold, and many more Gauls fall to the earth.

After a short span of intense fighting, the two sides part to rest, hurling imprecations at one another. The Carthaginian battle horns sound, and the staunch Libyan infantry phalanxes step forward, the African counterparts to the Romans. The Roman tribunes shout line-change orders to the their maniples, and the hastati step back to allow the veteran principes to tramp to the front and face the Libyans. The battle resumes, now becoming a series of controlled attacks between the disciplined ranks of the relentless heavy infantry on both sides.

The Roman army's rear forces are occupied with the Numidians' attack to their camp, and the Carthaginians gradually encircle the outnumbered Romans and allies in the front. The Carthaginians push them closer together, ebbing their fighting effectiveness. Many of the Italia allies fight back bravely, but other groups break ranks and flee as the Libyans and Gauls push into their inner ranks, attacking them from all sides. The Roman lines stiffen, however, as the centurions shove their men back to order and lead a counter march into the teeth of the heavily armored Libyans. Operating again as a coordinated unit, the legionnaires thresh their way through any of the enemy that dares face them, as the African commanders ride back and forth behind their men, screaming for their lines to stiffen.

Hundreds of Roman cavalry break loose from their whirling fight with the elusive Numidians. They gallop in to guard the Roman flanks from a cavalry attack and push the Carthaginian force back up the hill, leaving mounds of enemy dead and dying. The inexperienced hastati soldiers in the front line of the Roman infantry are again relieved by the veteran principes of the second line, and more enemy warriors fall beneath the refreshed lines. Watching the Romans advance, the Italia allies take heart and fight with renewed vigor, battling on each side of the Romans in the center. Hannibal's lines begin to break, and defeat seems imminent.

A trio of Carthaginian trumpet notes echo through the clamor of clashing iron and screaming casualties. The Libyan lines part on each side of the center, and a dozen elephants stampede through from each side, their mahouts riding on their necks. Hannibal leads the charge atop his rampaging Surus, with hundreds of his elite Sacred Band warriors running alongside him. Most of the Romans have never seen anything like these trumpeting monsters, and both horses and men are thrown into panic.

Hannibal lances infantry and cavalry from atop his elephant, using his twelve-foot sarissa with deadly efficiency. He and his Sacred Band cut their way through the center of the principes. Hannibal waves for the Libyans to follow him, and the stone-eyed Africans attack with renewed vigor. Thousands of lightly armored Macedonians follow the them, the deadly gift from Philip. They are fresh and agile troops, eager to revenge the Roman conquests of their land.

The Roman army begins to dissolve into chaos. The Macedonians wedge into the gaps between the disintegrating maniples, and the front line engagement turns into a roundabout melee, with the unbowed Romans fighting opponents from three sides. The first legion and its allies are pushed back down the hill to eventually crowd into the second legion, who are hit from behind by the Numidians who stormed through the camp. The Carthaginian infantry starts to close the circle about the survivors. The battle becomes a rout, and the rout becomes a slaughter. Thousands of Romans and allies run through whatever openings they can find in the deadly chaos, but many of these are hunted down by the wind-swift Numidians.

Maharbal, Hannibal's cavalry commander, rides up next to the general. "I have sent the reserve Libyans to complete the encirclement, General, " he shouts up to Hannibal. "We will kill them all within hours."

"Call them back," Hannibal says. "Let any who flee escape. Kill only those who resist." Maharbal throws him a questioning look and starts to object when he sees Hannibal glaring at him with his one good eye, anticipating his commander's insolence. Maharbal shrugs his broad shoulders and starts to ride off when Hannibal shouts a final directive. "Maharbal! Capture all the tribunes you can find. We have need of them."

From his victory at Cannae, Hannibal has learned that a trapped enemy may fight with more ferocity than one who has an escape; killing every Roman would lead to Carthaginian casualties he cannot afford. He knows that he will not see the escapees in a fight again because he knows what Rome does to legionnaires who leave the scene of battle: it is death or exile for them. But he will need the tribunes; one of them may have the information he needs.

By late morning the next day the Carthaginian army is established inside Herdonia, tending to their wounded and tallying up the spoils collected from the Roman camp. Hannibal has set up a temporary command center in the town square, where he begins questioning the captured tribunes. Maharbal and his allied captains sit at a low table brought from the armory behind them. Two tribunes stand before them, hands tied behind their backs, defiantly staring at their captors. Surus stands a few feet away from the table, pulling stacks of wheat straw into his mouth. A town slave bathes the blood from his tusks and feet.

Hannibal nods to one of the guards, and he drags one of the tribunes forward, a handsome older man who holds his head high, glaring at Hannibal with undimmed hatred. Hannibal smiles in acknowledgement of the man's courage. *Thank Baal these men are commanded by generals who are politicians, else my mission would be impossible.* Out of respect, Hannibal stands to face the man.

"Your name, if you will," says Hannibal.

"Tadius Hostilius Graecus," snarls the tribune.

Hannibal nods in acknowledgement. "I know you have acted as Fulvius' inner counsel, tribune. I have but one question for you, but your life depends on its answer: where is General Marcus Claudius

Marcellus?" Hannibal gestures toward the open door. "Speak and you shall go free, may Baal take my eye if I lie."

"Go fuck a dog," spits the tribune. "Marcellus has defeated you before, and he'll do it again." He grins malevolently. "He's not a puff like Fulvius. He'll have your balls on a cross."

Hannibal pulls out the figurine of his father Hamilcar, a reminder of his promise to forever be an enemy to Rome—and to defend Carthage at all costs. Hannibal takes a deep breath and sighs. "I see you are shy about sharing your knowledge. Perhaps I can warm your heart by entertaining you with my pet Surus here. He knows some interesting tricks. Let me show you." Hannibal points to the other captured tribune, a young and nervous man. "Take him over to that stump."

Two of Hannibal's Sacred Band drag the tribune over to the ground-level stump and lay his head on it. They hold his feet and shoulders, keeping the man's head on the stump. Hannibal waves to his attack elephant, Surus, and the seven-ton beast trots over, docile as a dog, eagerly flapping its ears. Hannibal says but two words, "Surus, step!" and points at the tribune's head. The tribune's eyes start with terror. He thrashes to break free, but the guards hold him in a grip of iron. The elephant promptly places his shield-sized front foot atop the Roman's head and steps down. There is a brief, agonized scream followed by a squooshed cracking sound, as if a pumpkin were dropped from a tall building. The elephant steps back, and there is only a lumpy red blotch on the stump.

Hannibal points at Tadius Hostilius. The guards walk over and grab him, dragging him to the stump as the young tribune's body is dragged away. The guards lay Tadius' face into the gore of his fellow officer.

The tribune remains stoic, staring grimly at the placid elephant towering over him. Hannibal raises his arm, and Surus raises his massive foot over the tribune's head, where it hovers unsteadily. "Down slow!" says Hannibal, and the elephant's foot slowly descends. The Roman's head pitches frantically from side to side, and he screams for Hannibal to stop. "Hold," says Hannibal, and the elephant pauses with his foot inches from tribune's quivering face, completely shadowing it.

The captive's lips move in a soundless babble until he finally spits out a single word. "S-S-Samnium."

Hannibal stares hard into the terrified man's eyes. "Samnium? You did say Samnium?" The tribune can only nod, ashamed to again voice his treachery. Hannibal steps back. "Very well. Remove this man and bring me another tribune. We will see if he confirms your story. If not, my Surus will do his trick for the both of you!"

As the tribune is dragged away, Hannibal turns to Maharbal, his cavalry commander. "Samnium," he says thoughtfully. "Several days' march from here. But not too far, would you say?"

Maharbal snorts. "Why bother? He does not stand between us and the Appian Way to Rome."

Hannibal fingers his figurine again. "True enough. But he would follow us, and I do not want him at our back." His eye takes on a feral gleam. "Besides, we have a score to settle with that smirking bastard."

*   *   *   *   *

BARCILONA, IBERIA, 210 BCE. Rain drizzles steadily on the Roman camp pitched beneath this small Roman outpost. The drizzle turns the cooking fires into hundreds of plumed smoke columns, and the soldiers curse the gods for making them eat a cold breakfast. Scipio sits alone in his tent, listening to the early morning clanks and shouts of his army as they prepare for the march. He inks in the last words of a letter to his mother. With a final flourish to add his signature, Scipio blows on the letter to dry the ink, rolls up the papyrus, and daubs it with wax to seal it. He impresses it with his owl-faced seal. "Send this out from Emporiae. It should be in Rome within the next three days," he orders a leathery little sentry. The legionnaire nods and trots off to find their swiftest messengers.

A few hours later, Scipio leads the legions down the flat coastal road, the coastal hills rolling by on their right. The army stretches out for almost five miles, with cavalry riding on point as the legionnaires march six abreast, followed by a thousand pack mules and a train of a hundred wagons. The march is frustratingly slow for Scipio. With long stretches of sandy trails and soft earth along the coast, his army barely manages a dozen miles a day.

Scipio is accompanied by Marcus, Laelius, and his senior tribunes. They ride along with their red cloaks pulled about them, the raindrops tattooing their iron helmets. At various times, when there is no business to discuss with his officers, Scipio dismounts and joins his men on the march, borrowing a tactic he learned from Hannibal: at all times be a general, but never cease to be a soldier. The men welcome their young general, sharing their rude jests and stories. The troops lug their sarcinas (packs) on poles slung over their shoulders, reaching in to grab an occasional crust of bread or piece of cheese as they march. They offer Scipio a piece of their rude snacks, and he never declines.

The sun emerges as the army wends its way south beneath some low coastal mountains, bringing cheers from the soggy legionnaires. The glistening whitecaps of the Mediterranean stretch along their left side, and the army steps with an added bounce of energy. The sea is so close to this roughshod road that the Romans can see the day's catch being brought in by the native fishermen. Groups of locals bathe and play on the beaches, and many of them are naked women who provide a most enjoyable diversion. The march becomes pleasant, nearly soporific. To Scipio's thousands of untested recruits, the war seems more a concept than a reality.

The legionnaires march on blithely, but Marcus Silenus studies the green highlands to their right, looking for movement in the trees. He knows Scipio sent out a quartet of exploratores yesterday, to check for any enemy presence and to locate defensible camping spots. But none have yet returned from their mission, and the old warrior finds this very curious. He notices that the hills here are blanketed with leafy coastal pines and oaks. *By Jupiter, I could hide a legion in there*, he muses.

Marcus jumps off his mount and trots over to Scipio, who is marching in front of the first row of legionnaires.

"General, we might want to send some scouts into those hills over there," Marcus says. Scipio looks at the hills for a while, and turns back to Marcus, pointing at the light cavalry squadrons riding at the head of the army. "Our men have been roaming along the base of those hills since we left Barcilona town. They have yet to report anything suspicious."

Marcus nods, once. "For certitude, they have not found anything amiss. But they did not go up into the hills, and into the valleys between them. That is my concern."

"And you think the Carthaginians could march unnoticed into our territory?" Scipio smiles. " When I scouted for Fabius' army, I watched Hannibal's men move through a flat open valley, and it took them forever to do it. When the Carthaginians are on the march, their army is even more cumbersome than ours, towing along their oxen, wagons, even women and children!"

Marcus stares back at the hills. "Their army is not what concerns me," he says cryptically.

Scipio stares at him for several long moments. "Very well. Your judgment is to be trusted, that I have learned." Scipio returns to his horse and rides over to one of his cavalry officers. Within minutes, a dozen light cavalry are swarming up into the hills. Hours later the patrols return with nothing to report. Marcus takes the news in silence, still perusing the rocky ridges and hills.

As late afternoon arrives, two of the original exploratores return with news of a wide plain ahead, one blessed with feeder streams and timber, perfect for camp. Scipio approves the spot, and two squadrons of light cavalry race ahead to reconnoiter and to prepare the location. The late afternoon sun is casting long shadows as Scipio leads his infantry columns into the area. They join the cavalry in setting up the camp: foraging for firewood, digging latrines, toting water, marking locations for tents and cattle pens, and building the first levels of the camp palisades. Soldiers swarm busily over the placid plain. The army columns continue to file into the camp area, with the rear columns an hour from arrival.

Scipio and Laelius tour the camp construction, speaking to the supervising tribunes and centurions. Scipio is remonstrating with one of the armorers when he is interrupted by the sound of horns blowing. He looks up into the hills to see a sight that freezes him in mid-sentence. Hundreds of half-naked cavalry are boiling out of the hills around the camp, screaming battle cries as they charge. Riding bareback without reins, each brown-skinned rider carries only a small leather shield, a sword, and a brace of javelins, eschewing armor for the sake of mobility. Scipio would know these feared warriors anywhere: Numidian cavalry, the finest horse warriors in the world—and the bane of legionnaires throughout Italia and Iberia.

The tunic-clad Africans urge their sturdy little ponies across the plain, plunging toward the half-finished camp. An exceptionally tall and lean man leads the charge, a handsome youth with a carefully cropped black beard and a simple crown of oak leaves. Though he wears the same white battened tunic as his men, the man has the unmistakable aura of a leader, erect and commanding, head held high, eyes coldly blazing with determination.

Scipio sees the leader and his mouth drops open. It is the same man who led the Numidian cavalry back at Cannae, who helped to turn the tide of battle into a slaughter of forty thousand Romans and allies, Hannibal's greatest victory. And who directed the killing charge on his father and uncle in Iberia. "Masinissa," he curses to himself. Scipio shoulders through a swarm of men arming themselves and jumps onto his horse, vengeance in his eyes. The Numidians plunge into the camp, spearing Romans as they rush to arm themselves. Scipio ignores the deadly onslaught about him and rides directly at the Numidian prince.

"Scippy, where are you going?" shouts Laelius, as Scipio stampedes heedlessly past him. Laelius runs after Scipio, yelling at him until he is out of earshot. Desperate, Laelius pulls a cavalryman off his horse and jumps onto it, galloping after his friend, joining the clumps of cavalry that rush out to engage the Numidians. Soon the entire plain is the scene of hundreds of individual battles. Scores of dead warriors lie in the streams, the bloody water flowing down to violate the aquamarine sea. The arriving velites dash toward the fight, hurling their pila at the Numidians, piercing the backs of several unwary riders. The arriving Roman infantry hustle into maniples and march into the fight, although the Numidians skirt around them and continue their rampage.

As the raid becomes a battle, Scipio veers to his left, chasing Masinissa toward the edge of the camp. The African stops to issue orders to his chieftains, and Scipio closes in. Masinissa looks up, recognizes his former opponent, and smiles malevolently. Signaling for his men to stay where they are, he pulls a javelin from his saddle scabbard and trots toward Scipio, as relaxed as if he were going to meet a friend.

Scipio draws within a spear's cast of the haughty Numidian. As Masinissa watches, Scipio halts and pulls out his sword, the Iberian falcata he adopted after watching its deadly effect at Cannae. Masinissa pauses his mount, studying Scipio. He slaps his knees against his horse's bare sides, and the pony charges forward, just as Scipio spurs his own mount.

The two commanders close on each other. Masinissa lowers his javelin and thrusts it forward, hoping to spear Scipio's chest. As he taught his cavalry recruits in Rome, Scipio extends his shield and angles it sideways, ready to deflect the thrust. When Masinissa passes him, Scipio swings his falcata at him. The cleaver-like sword hews a large chunk from the Numidian's wooden shield and bites into Masinissa's forearm. Streaming blood, Masinissa rides some distance away and stops to look incredulously at his shield: no Roman sword could have split it like that. Then he sees that Scipio is bearing a falcata, and he grins. With a respectful nod he digs his heels into his horse and gallops back toward Scipio, death in his face.

Scipio turns about and surges forward, his body leaning into his horse's neck to minimize his body, readying for another clash. *Aim for the legs*, he tells himself. *If you cut an artery he will bleed out.* As he closes on Masinissa, he sees the Numidian prince angrily gesturing at someone behind Scipio, as if commanding him to go away.

Scipio does not notice that a blocky young Numidian is closing on him from behind, the rider's approach concealed in the noise and dust of the cavalry mêlée. The squat Numidian lurches forward, jabbing his iron-tipped javelin into Scipio's side as he runs toward Masinissa. Scipio's eyes bulge with surprise; his back arches with agony. He pivots in his saddle and hacks at the Numidian, slashing into his shoulder. The rider howls with pain, but he manages to pivot his horse and ram it into Scipio's mount. The Numidian raises his javelin for a telling thrust, eyes agleam with lust to kill a general. Scipio squirms sideways in his saddle, vainly trying to block the blow.

The African abruptly lurches forward onto his horse's neck, his face a rictus of pain as he clutches at his back. A pilum sticks in the back of his battened tunic, held there by young Plinius, his eyes wide with terror. The pilum has barely penetrated his broad back, but the flesh wound is all the distraction Scipio needs. He swings his cleaver-like falcata into the side of the man's head, splitting into his skull. The Numidian topples from his horse, muttering a death prayer until blood fills his mouth.

Scipio looks behind him and sees Plinius riding up, bareheaded in his haste to join the battle. The sallow young tribune smiles faintly as Scipio raises his right hand, acknowledging Plinius' help. Scipio turns to resume his attack and sees Masinissa standing in the same spot, waiting for Scipio to continue their duel. "Plinius! Get the cavalry over here!" orders Scipio, as much to put Plinius out of danger as to generate a counterattack. The youth nods and dashes back to camp. As soon as he leaves, Scipio faces Masinissa and pulls his heels back to spur his mount into the charge.

"Stop!" roars a voice behind him. Marcus Silenus draws up to Scipio, a squadron of heavy cavalry closing in to join him. Marcus' face is red with anger as he grabs Scipio's reins in his iron grip. "Stop this nonsense," he blurts. "You fall and all is lost!" The cavalry thunders toward Scipio, eager to kill Masinissa. With a sidelong glance at his opponent, Masinissa whirls away, easily outdistancing the pursuing Romans.

Scipio watches the African prince join the main body of his raiders. Waving for them to follow him, Masinissa and his men duel their way through a squadron of Roman light cavalry and disappear into the hills, their passing as abrupt as a desert wind.

Laelius rides up to join the rest of his cavalry around Scipio, and he orders them back to camp. Scipio looks across the plain at the scattered bodies, assessing the damage. He sees that most of the fallen are Romans, killed in the act of preparing for battle. *I have lost a hundred men, all in these few minutes. Gods damn the Numidians!* As he enters the ravaged camp, he sees Plinius sprawled onto the ground, blood seeping from a javelin hole in the side of his head. *In his brave haste, he didn't take time to find his helmet. And I sent him back here to be safe.* Shaking his head to clear it, Scipio rides slowly over to Marcus Silenus, who is directing the rescue of the wounded. Scipio dismounts and questions Marcus, his voice sorrowful and anxious.

"How in Olympus did they find us so soon? My speculatores said the Numidians were way back in Hasdrubal's camp, beneath the Ebro River. This is Roman territory!"

Marcus shrugs. "An army on the march is a large, slow-moving beast. It has taken us five days to cover sixty miles from Emporiae. Plenty of time for an informant to spread the word, and for the Numidians to snake their way through our territory."

"You have it aright," admits Scipio. "We are a big, slow-moving beast, vulnerable to those African jackals. He looks back at Plinius' body, then to the foothills where the Numidians disappeared. "The Numidians have taught me a lesson about mobility. I must figure out how to use it."

*   *   *   *   *

ROME. A downy-cheeked messenger enters the sun-washed atrium of the Scipio domus. Pomponia reclines on a couch there, meeting with the overseers of the Scipio farms. Clad in a simple green gown, she conducts her business with a friendly but firm hand, listening to her men's complaints and questions but brooking no argument on her replies. Marcia stands next to her mistress, inking down Pomponia's decisions onto a papyrus sheet drawn over a wooden plank.

Pomponia has assumed the business manager role that so many other Roman women have adopted since the war started, managing the estates and wealth they inherited with their husband's death. Every year that the war continues, the Roman women become a more powerful economic force, much to the dismay of the agrarian traditionalists of the Latin Party. Women now own much of the farmland about Rome, a fearful prospect to them.

As soon as Pomponia sees the messenger, she knows he has come with news about her sons. Her heart races as she waves her farm managers out of the room. "Away! Out in the hallway," she commands. The freemen grab their clay account tablets and scurry out of the room, pattering down the hall out of earshot.

The boy steps forward and bows his head slightly. "From Proconsul Publius Cornelius Scipio," he warbles nervously, brandishing a roll of papyrus with an owl's head seal,

"Gratitude," Pomponia replies. The messenger walks toward the entrance, stopping to stare appreciatively at Pomponia until she chases him with a frosty stare. *So young. They recruit them younger every year. Soon the children will have swords in their hands.* Pomponia sighs as she plops onto a couch and breaks the message's seal. "Bring me wine," she says to Marcia. Pomponia unfurls the roll and reads the spidery handwriting of her son.

II. Rome

Dear Mother:

My best wishes to you and Amelia. Every hour brings me a fond memory of you both, and with it some pangs to my heart that I cannot be with you. My only solace is knowing that I work to preserve that to which I would someday return, to a quiet life of learning and teaching. But until then, there are many tasks for both of us, are there not? And defeating Hannibal may not be the most important one.

I am loathe to distress you, but I must ask you to employ your political influence for me—and for Rome. I fear I cannot defeat the Three Generals with the undermanned army the Senate has given me. My spies tell me the Carthaginians have thrice my number, or more. And every day they coerce more tribes to join them. Most of the Turdetani and Carpetani are theirs. And the dread Ilergetes.

If I spend my term hiding behind the walls of Tarraco, that would doubtless delight the Latins. If I do, the Three Generals will breach the Alps and join Hannibal. Then it will be too late for Rome to band together: Latin or Hellenic, we will all be gone. I must soon fight Mago, Gisgo, and Hasdrubal, whatever my resources.

This is the task I set to you. One of our consuls—either Publius Galba or Fulvius Centumalus—one must deliver an imperium to Tarraco, ordering Nero's men given over to me. It is the only way I can win against the Carthaginians. Can you intercede, some way or somehow, on my behalf?

Your loving son,

Publius Cornelius Scipio

Pomponia rereads Scipio's letter, taking several deep drafts of wine. When she comes to the part where her son requests the imperium from one of the consuls, her heart pounds. Fulvius is fighting Hannibal near Herdonia, only Publius Galba is in Rome. He is the one she must sway to give the imperium.

She bites her lip at the thought of Galba, thinking how she might influence his decision. Galba is one of the wealthiest men in Rome. He is too rich to bribe, and too open about his sexual deviances to be blackmailed. She reflects on the matter for several more minutes, and then her head droops with realization. There is only one way to sway Galba. All of Rome knows what he, the leader of the Priapus sect, most desires.

Pomponia runs her fingers through her hair, plucking at strands, trying to come up with an alternative. Finally, she rolls up the scroll, tucks it under her arm, and takes a deep breath. "Julia, Marcia!" Pomponia shouts. "Fetch my cloak and bring my litter. We are off to see the meretrices of The House of Calpurnia. I must talk to the harlots."

III. TARRACO

TARRACO, NORTHEAST IBERIA COAST, 210 BCE. The shorebirds skitter away like retreating soldiers as Scipio's vanguard splashes through the shallow seaside river. The army is drawing nigh to Tarraco, Rome's last major fortress in Iberia. Scipio has led his small army south from Emporiae and on through Barcilona, along the rocky trail that rolls between forested hills and the sparkling Mediterranean, fighting through a half-dozen raids and skirmishes. Now they gratefully enter the succoring plain at the feet of the Tarraco fortress, knowing they will have respite from battle.

Scipio's scouts have located a treeless sward near a substantial stream, and Scipio orders camp to be built there. Soon the entire army is bustling about in the afternoon sun, leveling trees from the nearby hills, digging trenches about the walls, etching out street borders inside the camp, and trenching out fire pits. For the hardened veterans, this intense manual labor is an onerous task they would gladly forsake for battle. For the numerous recruits, however, it is an important training activity, one that conditions them to discipline and teamwork.

As thousands of legionnaires swarm to their tasks, Scipio rides up the winding road to Tarraco, a high-walled fortress perched two hundred feet above the sea. Laelius and Marcus Silenus ride with him, along with four of his senior officers. The group is intent on meeting the two men that have held on to Rome's last bastion against the Carthaginian hordes.

Scipio beckons to Clastidius Honorius, his chief of combat training. The old bear trots over to his general. "This road is quite steep, eh?" Scipio asks.

"Very," replies the grizzled soldier, looking at the switchbacked trail to Tarraco. "It is like climbing a small mountain. An enemy would find it difficult to march quickly up that narrow route, and easy to be knocked back down it!"

Scipio nods. "Hmm, that is true. But I see a different purpose for it. After our camp is finished, I want our infantry marching up this road at double our pace. Back, down, and up again. Constantly. Every day." Clastidius looks skeptically at his young general, but he says nothing. Then Scipio adds, "And I want them to carry double their normal pack weight."

Now the veteran trainer cannot restrain himself. "Double the weight of their sarcinas? To what purpose? Are they to carry new weapons?"

Scipio looks at him sideways and grins his mysterious grin, as if he and the gods share a private joke. "Ah, there will be new weapons for them in time, honored Clastidius. But this is a horse of a different color. In fact, the legionnaires are to become horses of a sort. Pack horses."

Scipio says no more on the subject. The aged centurion stares at his general for a few long moments, then he simply nods. "It will be done," he says with a bow of his head, and rides back to join the tribunes.

Laelius, riding next to Scipio, looks quizzically at his friend. "Going to make pack animals of our foot soldiers? They will not embrace that, I daresay."

"I do not plan for them to carry heavy packs," Scipio replies. "Quite the contrary. Their real packs will be lighter than before. But they must be so conditioned that their load is but a feather on their backs, and a forced march will be but a walk around the garden." His eyes narrow. "We will not endure another torpid slog such as we took to get here. It makes us too vulnerable."

Laelius rolls his eyes. "My gods, is it not enough we spend time digging, marching, building, wrestling, and sword fighting? Now the men have to dash up mountain roads? Do you plan to enter them into the Olympic Games?"

Scipio laughs. "Hannibal taught me much about coping with overwhelming force. the Three Generals' armies outnumber us, so we have to use the element of surprise on them, as the Carthaginian did to us. To do that we must move faster than anyone would expect, so we are here and gone before they know it." Scipio's party halts before the gates of Tarraco, waiting for them to open. Scipio looks back down steep road. "Our legions will be faster and more mobile than any before them." He wags his finger at his friend. "And you will soon see its effect!"

"Your efforts would be better invested in securing some fresh mounts for our equites," retorts Laelius. "Some who are fast enough to keep up with the Numidians."

Scipio shakes his head. "What is our tutor's old saying, '*Philosophum non facit barba*'—a beard does not make a philosopher? I'm not too sure we can turn our countrymen into Numidians, just by giving them fast horses. Those Africans were nursed on mare's milk, riding on horses while they were yet suckling on the teat! Better we get the Numidians themselves, would you not say?"

Their argument is interrupted with the clangor of Tarraco's bronze studded gates creaking open. A century of legionnaires emerges and stands in two rows as Praetor Gaius Claudius Nero walks out between them, a tight smile on his cavernous face. Nero is a lean and stringy middle-aged man with prominent brow over this steel-gray eyes. As one of a long line of military leaders from the house of Claudia, he is a veteran of many battles and has literally fought his way up through the ranks. Now, as praetor, he is commander of the provincial army sent from Rome to secure the Ebro River border between Iberia and Italia, Rome's last bastion against the Three Generals' invasion. Although he bears a perpetually doleful expression on his long, drawn, face, he has a Roman officer's unyielding conviction that the mother country will eventually triumph over any foe.

As he meets Scipio, Nero extends his bony hand and clasps the young man's forearm, shaking it vigorously. "Salus, Publius Cornelius Scipio, proconsul of Rome and governor of Iberia! You and your men are a welcome sight indeed!"

"Salve, Praetor Nero. I am overjoyed to see you. This is Legate Gaius Laelius, leader of my legion and its equites."

Nero nods at Laelius and the tribunes behind him, then faces Scipio. "We have made arrangements for you and your men to refresh themselves. Our baths are at your disposal. We will discuss your plans at your leisure, Governor."

Laelius' face lights up. "Baths!" he exclaims, unable to restrain himself. "By Minerva's owl, that is the best news I have heard since we landed here! Pray gods you have fresh linen, too."

Nero blinks in surprise, and his tight smile widens a bit. "I have forgotten how the basic amenities grow in importance when you are deprived of them. Yes, we have all that. And a gymnasium and a wrestling palaestra, should you wish some exercise afterward."

"I do crave some wrestling after I am clean," interjects Laelius, with a sly gleam in his eye, "but not in the palaestra."

Scipio squints reprovingly at Laelius, who only grins. "We gratefully accept your hospitality, Nero," says Scipio. "I congratulate you on the improvements you have made to Tarraco: high walls, baths, a new road. I had heard Tarraco was but a small fort town near the beach."

Nero bows his head slightly. "Gratitude. But your father and uncle started the renovations, before … before they left to fight Hasdrubal and Mago …." He shifts about, suddenly awkward.

Scipio grasps Nero's shoulder. "I know. I respect you acknowledging that." Scipio surveys the inner streets. "They are buried here?"

Nero nods. "Yes, the sepulcher is lately finished. Would you like to go there now?" Scipio shakes his head. "After our work is done tonight. My mind would not be in its proper place, otherwise."

That evening, the Roman officers from both forces gather for a strategic meeting. After providing Scipio with a census of the men at Tarraco and the Ebro, Nero details his estimates of the three Carthaginian armies' emplacements, the size of their forces, and the tribes who are allied to them. Several of Scipio's officers vent their frustration at their lack of manpower, at being forced into a defensive stance while the Three Generals maintain their stranglehold over the Iberian peninsula. But most of all they lament their prospects for victory, as the Carthaginians use terror and torture to conscript more allies. Several Tarraco men query Scipio about his plans to reinforce Tarraco and Marcius' garrison on the Ebro. Scipio gives noncommittal replies; wishing to be opaque about his true plans.

The formal meeting ends, and the convocation turns into a feast. Because it is a special occasion, Nero has ordered a dozen flagons of the region's mysterious Cava wine. It is a delicious drink that sparkles and bubbles from the cave spirits inhabit it, according to the Iberian priests that produce it. Scipio delights in a glass of the spirited white wine but refuses any more; he is determined to maintain a respectfully clear head for his visit to the sepulcher. Ever a man for games, Laelius competes with Tarraco's tribunes in kattabos, a game where they throw their cup's wine dregs at a figure in a pan, the winner knocking it over. Soon, Laelius' purse is bulging, and his face flushed with drink.

After an hour of laughter and stories, Scipio gestures to Nero and the two depart. They walk out into the town square, down the wide main street, and approach a tiny rectangular limestone building situated behind the new armory. Above the narrow oak door is a simple wooden plaque that bears the names of Publius and Gnaeus Scipio. Nero turns his key into the bronze door lock and shoves open the slab door. He takes an outside torch and lights the two inside candles, steps back outside, and beckons for Scipio to enter. Scipio bends over and enters the room.

Two rectangular stone tombs fill the sepulcher, each bearing the ashes of a Scipio general killed by the Three Generals two years ago, when their Gallic and Celtiberian allies betrayed them to the Carthaginians. Scipio stands quietly for several long moments. He bends to the tomb of his father and runs his hand across the top of it. Scipio thinks of Hannibal's army rampaging across Italia, of the Three Generals driving the once-dominant Romans out of Iberia, and of his army being sent here to hold fast to this last major outpost. He recalls the oath he gave as a child to his beloved father, that he would always protect Rome from harm. Slowly his head slumps, then his shoulders, then his body. From behind him, Nero can see his body shudder, as if the boy is cold, or is stifling a sob. Minutes later, Scipio straightens and faces Nero, his face set.

"Nero, I will need your two legions," says Scipio. " I cannot hide within these walls while my father's killers roam about Iberia, while we wait for them to overwhelm us."

"You will certainly have them," says Nero agreeably, much to Scipio's surprise. "And whoever else you want." He hands Scipio a sheepskin document with the seal of Rome affixed to it. "I wanted to give this to you earlier, but I had to wait until we were alone." Scipio unrolls the sheepskin and holds it near the candle, his eyes widening as he reads. "That is a Senatorial decree that was sent directly to me," Nero adds. "It is signed by consul Galba himself."

Scipio pores over the document and looks up at Nero, a question in his eyes. "Yes, it means I am recalled to Rome," says Nero. "I am directed to lead two new legions into South Italia and confront Hannibal and his allies." Nero raises his face heavenward, grinning. "Praise to Jupiter, I can go back and fight, instead of holing up here like some frightened town mayor." He claps Scipio lightly on the shoulder. "And you, you will have command of Tarraco's legionnaires and allies, to do as you wish."

Scipio blinks, discomfited. "I am pleased for the both of us, Praetor. But why would they do this now? The Senate denied my earlier requests for more men."

Nero shrugs. "The gods are less of a mystery than Galba's mind. But now you can go on the offensive, regardless." Nero looks somberly at Scipio. "I do not mean to speak out of turn, General, but I should warn you: if you take both legions with you, Tarraco will be very vulnerable. The city guard might hold out for a month or two, at most. If the Carthaginian armies should attack Marcius' camp at the Ebro, Tarraco could not help him."

Scipio shrugs dismissively. "In another month they will not be interested in Tarraco, or the Ebro, that I can promise you. They will be coming south after me."

Nero looks curiously at Scipio, waiting for further explanation. When none is forthcoming, he nods his head in acknowledgement. "Your reputation for innovative strategy precedes you, my youthful friend. But I must tell you, your life and career hang on what you do next. If the Three Generals take Tarraco, Iberia will be lost to us. Then they can cross the border into Italia." He shrugs. "I but caution you, as a friend."

"I am grateful for the advice, Nero, but my plan stays." He stares curiously at the decree.. "Still, I do wonder about the Galba's change of heart. What made him change his mind?" Then he smiles. "I wager my mother had a part in this."

*   *   *   *   *

Weeks before Scipio arrived at Tarraco, Pomponia paid an afternoon visit to the city manse of consul Publius Galba. As she approached the front door she encounters the same Priapus statue that Cato saw, with the same motto on the tablet beneath it.

If a woman steals from me, or a man, or a boy, let the first give me her cunt, the second his head, the third his buttocks.[vi]

Pomponia winces at the sign. She sighs resignedly and turns to her attendant "You may return home, Marcia. I shall be there by evening."

After her slave disappears from view, Pomponia knocks on the twin doors. The portly old Thracian opens it, clad in a snow-white tunic, and smiles broadly when he see her, ogling Pomponia as if she were a street whore. Pomponia raises her chin. "I am Pomponia Scipio, here to meet with consul Galba," she says icily, her gaze boring into the slave's eyes until he raises them from her breasts to her face. The abashed porter waves for her to follow him.

Pomponia paces her way down the wide marble hallway, admiring the sculptures and frescoes interspersed between its sweeping archways. *He has bought many treasures*, she muses, *as he bought his way into the consulship*. Descended from four generations of successful negotiatores (bankers), Galba is wealthy beyond any need for money, as Pomponia knows all too well. His bribe must be paid in a different coin.

The slave leads Pomponia through an enormous open courtyard filled with roses and palms, and into a large secluded room off to its side. The room is a veritable art museum of erotica, filled with sculptures and murals of sybaritic feasts and couplings. The Thracian grins expectantly at her, waiting for her to be shocked at what she sees. Pomponia sits on one of the reclining couches and stares into her hands, her face expressionless. He wrinkles his nose with disappointment. "The Consul will be here shortly," he says tersely, and departs. Pomponia listens to the fountains burbling in the courtyard pool, calming herself, and finally looks up at the sexual art that surrounds her. *What am I doing here? There must have been another way.*

Publius Galba soon enters, wearing a snow-white toga bordered with purple ermine. A tall, lean man with a crown of thick gray hair, Galba carries his middle-aged frame with regal dignity, his movements spare and sure. His sculpted face with high cheekbones would have an arresting nobility, were it not for his predatory green eyes. Galba smiles when he sees Pomponia. She rises to meet him and slightly bows her head.

"Ah, Pomponia. I am so delighted to see you. By all the gods, you are Aphrodite come to Earth! Such beauty, you are as flawless as a girl!" He takes her hand and strokes it, looking deep into her eyes. She hears his breath quicken and looks away from him. "How might I provide for you today, Carissima?"

Pomponia smiles tightly. "I know your time is golden, consul, so I will be brief. I come on behalf of my son Publius Cornelius Scipio, the general and governor of Iberia. His letters tell me he would benefit greatly from two more legions under his command. It would give him men enough to attack the Generals—and recapture Iberia for Rome. Is that not desirable?"

Instead of answering, the consul motions for Pomponia to follow him out into the courtyard, where they stroll by the fish ponds and palm trees. Galba pauses to deeply sniff a rose. "Ah, the brave young general," he finally replies, "the only man who stepped forward to go to Iberia! I do admire your son's willingness to go on the offensive there, but I fear we have no spare legions."

Pomponia looks sideways at him. "None, consul? We have four here in Rome, don't we?"

Galba frowns at Pomponia, irked by her challenge. "It is true. We are training four legions at the Field of Mars, but those will be assigned to South Italia and to Macedonia. Hannibal and Phillip pose the greatest threats to us." He spreads his arms. "There is naught I can do for you, I do fear."

"What about Nero's men?" asks Pomponia, as if she has just thought of it. "He has six thousand men in Tarraco, does he not? With many allies, too?"

Galba laughs. "So the rumors about you are true. You are a military spy! How else does a patrician woman learn all about all our troops?" He strokes her arm lightly and chuckles. "Do you work for Hannibal, my dear? He has numerous infiltrators who follow my every move, you know."

Pomponia smiles enchantingly. "Oh no, I am only interested in promoting Rome's welfare, and that of my son. Nero's legions would benefit both."

As they finish their walk, Nero stops and looks sternly at her, shaking his head slowly. "The matter is closed. But consider yourself honored, beautiful one. No other woman would even get an audience with me, much less be allowed to venture such an audacious proposal." He stares at her. "Certainly, your plan has merit. But do you know what the Senate would do to me were I to comply with you wishes? Fabius and Flaccus would lead a Senate revolt against me!"

"Ah, the Latin Party," sniffs Pomponia. "So the rumors are true. Cato has been to see you. And he has likely made some threats."

Galba snorts. "I do not fear the Latin Party. But they could make things very inconvenient for me, spreading tales through the Senate, undermining my power." He rolls his eyes heavenward. "I must consider that, of course."

Pomponia grasps Galba's forearm and looks earnestly into his eyes. "I can promise you that you would have the full support of the Hellenic Senators, should you change your mind about Tarraco. Not only in this matter, but in the upcoming elections."

Galba stares at Pomponia's hand on his arm and places his over hers, eyes shining with a feral greed. "Hmm, that is appealing, Domina. Nevertheless, you will be stealing my power, my respect, from the other Senators." He grins slyly. "And you know what the sign says in front of my house." Pomponia looks away from Galba, but he can see her nod. And his smile broadens.

"I do not regard you as a thief, most honored of women. But a debt is a debt, and it must be repaid. In the coin of the realm, the realm of Priapus." He runs his hand up her arm to rest on her shoulder. "Would you be willing to settle your debt for the legions, in such a way?" He waits silently, and the silence between them grows.

Then Pomponia responds. "Yes. Payment in your 'coin of the realm,' consul."

"Excellent," he says. He waves his hand airily. "As the sign says, there are three forms of repayment. It is only fair that you choose which one." His eyes crawl over her body. "In your case, I favor them all."

Pomponia stands silently, sucking on her lower lip. She takes a deep breath and fixes Galba with a stern look. "Dismiss your slaves and guards. I want no one near."

A predatory smile slowly creases Galba's face. "It will be done. But you must tell me: do you do this of your own free will?" he asks mockingly. "The laws must be obeyed, must they not?" Pomponia nods mutely, not trusting her voice. Galba cocks an eye at her. "It must be said," he says.

She raises her head high. "I agree, of my own free will."

Galba rubs his hands together. "Then it is done. I am most pleased. Long have I admired you, despite your bullish determination to embroil yourself in men's affairs." He bows with mock respect. "It will be as you request." With a wave of his hand, Galba sends his attendants scurrying out from the atrium. When they have all disappeared, he closes the door and turns to her, his face expectant. "And now, how is it you propose to pay me?"

She swallows. "The second way."

He nods. "Agreed. But as consul I have the imperium to change laws without a vote, do I not? I think I shall change Priapus' law at my front door. "Payment shall be in the first way, and the second. And you should thank the gods I do not demand the third! It has caused much pain to your predecessors."

Galba walks over to kiss her. As he nears her lips, Pomponia flashes her head sideways, so he only rubs his cheek against hers. He attempts the kiss again and meets with the same reaction. He manages a small grin. "As you will. There are other lips I may penetrate, and I daresay they will not be turned away from me, will they? I would hope not, for the sake of your boy." He kisses her lingeringly on the cheek, as if tasting her, and stands back. "So beautiful," he says wonderingly, and then his face hardens. He gestures with his finger. "All of it."

With a deep sigh of resignation, Pomponia carefully unwraps her palla, the wool rectangle that covers her long, flowing stola. Letting it fall to the floor, she reaches for the owl-shaped clasp on her shoulder and pulls out its prongs from her dress. Pomponia slowly unwinds the thick, rich garment, letting it pool at her feet. She stands in a clinging gossamer tunica that flows to her knees.

Galba draws in his breath. The sheer linen reveals the promise of Pomponia's lush body, of curved hips and swaying breasts. He takes several deep breaths, and gestures for her to continue.

Pomponia stares coolly at him as she grasps the front of her tunica and raises it over her head, turning away from him as she drops it to the floor. She turns and faces him, clad only in a soft linen loincloth. Galba stares at her wide, full breasts with their light tan aureoles, a woman in the fullness of her matronly beauty. He struggles to maintain his commanding air, feeling himself swelling against the thick folds of his imperial toga, hearing himself gasp at the sight of her.

Pomponia notices the effect her nudity has on the consul and finds it pleasing—control is shifting to her. With the smile of a vixen, Pomponia slides her thumbs beneath each side of her wispy undergarment. Galba steps forward before she can remove it, placing his hands gently on her shoulders. "Permit me, dulcis (sweet one)." He bends to one knee and slides the undergarment down her hips, pulling it out from under her feet. He stares at her fiery triangle, entranced at its soft curls and iris fragrance.

The consul leads her to a wide couch and lays her back. He fumbles his way out of his toga and tunic, leaving himself clad only in his subligaculum. "Not every ruler is born with his own scepter," he purrs. "Priapus has blessed me." As he unwraps himself in front of her, Pomponia's confidence turns to dismay. The rumors about Galba prove to be true. There is little doubt why he is chief priest of the god's worshippers. A ten-inch erection juts beneath his stomach, his testicles large as a purse of coins. Her husband Publius had always told Pomponia that she was wondrously tight "down there," and now she fears she could be split in two. Grinning proudly, he steps toward the couch, intent on penetrating her.

Pomponia rolls off the couch and falls to her knees in front of him, cradling his member as she licks and fondles him, halting Galba in his tracks. "My gods, I do crave that rod inside me, imperator!" she murmurs. "But first, I would savor you this way, " she says as she rolls her fingers about his shaft.

Galba says nothing, but he places his hand behind her head, awaiting her ministrations. Pomponia summons all she has learned from her recent visit to Prisca, queen of Rome's fellatrices, and assaults his phallus. She moves her mouth over the top of him, humming her feigned pleasure to vibrate his glans, all the while twisting her hands about him. In a few minutes she feels his penis swell in her hands. Her jaws ache with the effort of keeping her mouth wide enough to encompass him, but she knows his moment is near, and she redoubles her efforts, rapidly milking his foreskin as she nips the underside of his glans. Galba tries to step back from her, but she clings gently to the base of his phallus and twists her tongue down his shaft. "Aaah! Oh my gods! Wait!" he gasps. "Not yet!"

Fearing he will stop and ram himself inside her, she steels herself for her final trick. As he pumps against the back of her throat, she lightly pinches his testicles and stabs a finger into his anus. With a wail of despairing ecstasy, Galba comes violently, flooding Pomponia's mouth as he collapses upon her, sprawling them both to the floor. He lays on top of her for several minutes, convulsing and panting, until Pomponia slides from under him and stands up. She strides over to her fallen clothing and extracts a linen scrap that she uses to wipe her face. She bends and dresses without the slightest trace of self-consciousness, her task accomplished.

The sweaty consul props himself up on an elbow and observes her, avidly watching her body. As she drops her tunica over herself, she turns and favors Galba with a wry smile.

"It appears you have spent all your coin, consul. Unless you are truly Priapus reincarnated."

Galba manages a bewildered smile. "Where in Olympus did a woman such as you learn such tricks!" he says, half in anger and half in admiration. "Even the temple courtesans have not treated me thus."

"Perhaps your whores should study on the matter," she replies, as she clasps her stola together. "My son has a saying: Knowledge is a force. It empowers those who have it, if they but have the courage to use it." She presses her clothing into place and turns to go. "I but used the knowledge at my disposal."

Galba rises and quickly throws on his toga. He walks over and stands next to her, a rueful smile on his face. "I still throb, carissima, so violent was my explosion." He smiles ruefully. "You are well worth the storm of shit I shall receive when I change my orders for Nero."

Galba eyes her speculatively, trying to read her face. "Is there something I can do for Lucius? We can strike another bargain, and you can pay me in another coin." He looks at her speculatively. "Such a bargain may be in your best interest. Who knows what would happen if word would get out about our session? And I cannot assure that it will not!"

Without answering him, Pomponia secures the owl clasp on her robe and smoothes her hair. Only then does she look at Galba, her topaz eyes gleaming. Her lips curl into a tight smile. "Look at me, consul." As he fixes his eyes on hers, she whisks out a leaf-shaped throwing knife, its edge gleaming from a recent sharpening. She holds it in front of his face, her eyes staring at him on either side of the blade. "If anyone should hear of this, I will kill you. If I find out you have willfully reneged on your promise, I will do worse than that. I will make you a castrato and burn your 'gifts' from Priapus at the altar of Athena. And when it is done, it will be slow, and unexpected. That I promise you, on my sons' lives."

A smiling Galba raises his hands in mock protest as he looks into her angry face. "Spare me, Domina, I pray! I am not a man to go back on my word. Your son will receive Nero's legions."

Pomponia nods. "Gratitude," she says sarcastically, and touches her lips to his cheek before she walks into the courtyard. Galba stands in the doorway, watching the sway of her hips as she goes. Quick as a striking snake, Pomponia whirls about. There is a bright flash past Galba's ear, and something thunks into the wall behind him. Galba turns to see the knife buried into the wall, its iron handle quivering. He looks back at Pomponia, wide-eyed with disbelief, and touches his ear.

"That is a demonstration, in case you doubt my words," she says. "That little trick I learned from Marcus Silenus, Rome's deadliest warrior. The man bears much love for our family. Were anything to happen to me, or to one of my sons, he would seek you out, though you hide behind the gates of Hades itself."

Without another word Pomponia continues on, head held high, pausing to spit into the pool. Every iota of her being is devoted to stifling the sobs that well up within her. *Make it to the street*, she tells herself. *He can't see you if you make it to the street. Then you can cry. Then you can die.*

Scipio's mother pushes past the porter who leers at her with a knowing smile. She walks quickly across the street and down an alley between two apartment houses, to then lose herself in the swarms along Rome's main street. She turns left, heading for home, wiping the corners of her eyes. As she passes a pigeon vendor, she feels a tug at her arm. She turns and sees Amelia, Scipio's fiancé, looking sorrowfully at her. Pomponia sobs into her arms as the slaves and citizens flow about them, unheeding.

*   *   *   *   *

TARRACO, IBERIA. Streams of wheat grains cascade through the merchant's sausage-like fingers, hissing as they rain back into their wide earthen jar. The Lacetani grain dealer grins proudly at Scipio. "Have you ever seen such admirable grain, Dominus? Look how large they are! And not a flake of chaff among them! I would be proud to feed this to my family," he expostulates. "Nay, this is too good for my family! It is fit only for a general! Or the gods themselves!"

Scipio runs his hands through the fat grains, digging deep and pulling up handfuls to inspect. He nods appreciatively. "Lovely wheat. I would be happy to make my own porridge with it." He glances sideways at the anxious salesman. "How much of this do you have?"

"Two hundred tons," exclaims the portly man, almost prancing with eagerness. "Enough to feed your legions for at least a month, by my reckoning."

"I see only a dozen jars. Where is the rest of it? I might have need of it all, very soon."

"Why, it is stored in the main granary at the end of the street, very close by. It would be no problem to turn it all over to you immediately," he remarks with a sly grin. "If the price is right for such an excellent commodity!"

Scipio nods. "If the price is right, of course." Scipio walks around, inspecting the other jars as he speaks. "Did you know, Artho, that I served as curule aedile for Rome before I came here?" Scipio asks, referring to his time as public works magistrate.

The puzzled merchant smiles obsequiously. "Oh, yes, it is an honored position. I am sure you did honor to the office, young consul!"

Rolling his eyes heavenward, Scipio continues. "One of my major tasks was to buy foodstuffs for Rome's citizens and legions, an endeavor I took very seriously." He turns to the merchant with a sarcastic grin. "I was the youngest aedile in the history of Rome, and there were many who sought to take advantage of my 'youthful ignorance.' Can you imagine that?"

Artho nods sympathetically. "Ah, it is a tragedy what people will do for an extra coin or two. There are thieves everywhere." He lifts his chin high, eyeing Scipio. "They make business difficult for those of us who merely seek to make an honest living for our families."

"Yes, I could see that some of your clients might be unjustifiably suspicious. I too am a bit cynical about human nature, perhaps from my years as a purchasing agent. So you will excuse me for what I will do next."

Scipio motions to Felix, the army's aged quaestor, and the auditor follows him down the street. They march over to the stone granary, and enter its cavernous storehouse. Scipio sees the merchant's mark on a battalion of enormous earthen grain jars. "These are the ones you would sell us?" demands Scipio. The merchant nods nervously, his mouth tight.

Scipio strides over to a jar in the rear of the room and waits until Felix and Artho catch up. He turns to his quaestor. "Give the man a hundred denarii," Scipio commands. The quaestor dutifully counts out the coins into the confused merchant's palm. Artho stares at the coins in his hand. "What is this for?"

Scipio pulls out his sword. The merchant's eye bug from his face and he cowers, flapping his hands in front of his face. Scipio steps to the jug and pulls back his sword arm. "That is payment for the damage to your jar." The young general backhands the knobbed pommel of his sword into the bottom of the vessel, cracking open a gaping hole. A stream of grain pours from the opening: scraggly, dry grain mixed with chaff. Scipio watches the stream for a minute before he turns back to

Artho, his face a stone.

"As I said, many have tried to take advantage of my youth. For a pampered and ignorant patrician as once I was, it was a wonderful learning experience. I learned much about trade, and the veracity of merchants who think they will never see you again."

Scipio steps back to Artho, his sword dangling from his side. He slowly pulls up the sword in front of the terrified merchant and eases it into his scabbard. He turns to Felix. "We will pay the asking price for the grain." Artho starts to smile when Scipio turns back to him. "You will furnish us with a supply that is the same quality as the first urn you showed me." The merchant starts to protest when Scipio raises his hand imperiously, his boyish face stern. "And half that amount in dried fruit—without additional charge." He stares intently into Artho's face, his right hand resting on his sword pommel. "Agreed?"

The merchant bobs his head like a hen pecking for insects. "Most assuredly, King Scipio, most assuredly! I know not how such poor, undeserving grain was stored here. That was meant for the slaves! I will cane-whip the dolt who mixed up the shipment, I assure you!"

"Ah, caning," muses Scipio, "a timeless punishment. It goes all the way back to the Egyptians, if I remember my scrolls correctly." He pulls out his dagger and plays with it as he talks, poking it into the air. "Quite vengeful, those Egyptians. I remember their punishment for thievery against the state: they impaled the offender by shoving a thick pole up his ass until it came out his mouth. A most effective deterrent, wouldn't you say, Artho?"

Artho gapes at Scipio, blinking with panic. "My gods, yes, yes, I would certainly think so, General!" He claps his hands together and bows again. "But to our matter, I will provide fruit of the highest quality, the best apples and pears in the region, I promise you on my children's lives!"

Felix intervenes. "That is very generous of you, noble Artho," he says sarcastically. "But no need for your assurances. I am certain proconsul Scipio will be desirous of perusing them before payment."

Artho looks blankly at Felix. "I will inspect them, just as I did your grain," affirms Scipio, repressing a smile.

Artho nods energetically. "Of course, of course. It will be an honor for you to do it. Now I will be off, if you will. I must prepare your shipment." He raises his right hand, finger pointing skyward. "I will attend to it personally!"

Scipio simply waves his hand dismissively, and Artho stumbles from the granary. Felix and Scipio soon follow him out, accompanied by two of Scipio's personal guards. As they head for the town gates, Felix looks over at him. "The standard Roman punishment for such fraud is imprisonment. Were you truly going to …?"

Scipio smirks. "I don't know. I don't think so, but I just do not know about myself anymore."

Scipio trudges along with a distracted look on his face, clearly upset. Felix glances at him as they walk, inviting conversation, but Scipio ignores his trusted associate's overtures. As they near the town gates, Scipio halts and takes a deep breath, pondering. He turns to his guards. "Return to camp and attend to my tent. If anyone comes, tell them I will give no more audiences tonight." As the guards march off, Scipio turns to Felix. "Quaestor, we did well today," he says kindly. "We will have grain enough to fill the men's packs for a sustained march, and fruit to supplement their oil and cheese. I figure it at a little over two pounds of food per man, per day, for fourteen days' march south. About thirty pounds total."

Felix nods. "A little under that, I would say, but close." He eyes his general. "Where would we have to go so fast? To the central plateau where Hasdrubal reigns? We would be most fortunate to defeat him there, among his allies."

"*Audaces fortuna iuvat* (Fortune favors the brave)," replies Scipio. "I will reveal all in good time." He gently pushes Felix toward the city gates. "I will meet you back at camp. But now I have some additional business here."

"Business?" says Felix. "Perhaps I should accompany you, and record the transaction. You cannot be too careful with these foreign merchants!"

"We are the foreigners here," observes Scipio, "but I follow your sentiment. No, this business is more personal, quaestor. No money will exchange hands in this transaction—at least none of Rome's money." As he walks off, Scipio casts a final comment over his shoulder. "I need to wash the stink of greed from my person. And the grime of compromise." Felix blinks, shrugs, and patters toward the front gates.

Scipio turns into a street off the main thoroughfare and walks down to the stables. He looks back over his shoulder, ascertaining that Felix is out of sight. With a sigh of relief, he quickly sheds his armor and pays a local stable master to retain it. Wearing only his tunic, Scipio strolls back to the main street and goes straight to Tarraco's famous thermae, an enormous public bathhouse built by his father and uncle. He gives an attendant his purse for safekeeping, hangs his tunic on a hook, and walks into the spacious hall of pools. Stepping down the wide marble stairway to the pools, he eases his nude body into the cold waters of the small first pool, remaining there until his senses are tingling with the chill. Walking up the steps on the far side of the pool, he steps into the warm waters of a second one. Scipio feels his tension and cares wash away as he jokes with several of the local residents. None recognize him, or if they do they have the decency to observe the unspoken code of the bath, and allow him his privacy.

The women's pools stretch alongside the men's baths, separated only by a two-foot wall decorated with life-size statues of nude bathers. Scipio lolls on the edge of the bathing pool; from there he can see dozens of women on the other side of the wall, some with tightly curled raven tresses that testify to their Iberian ancestry. Several young women recline on the stone pedestals along the back walls, chatting happily while a slave girl massages olive oil into the women's' nude bodies. *I wonder what that little prude Cato would say if he saw me now, with all these naked women,* Scipio muses. *He always criticized me for using baths.*[vii]

Savoring the women's lithe nudity, Scipio feels a stirring within him. He recalls the last time he was with his betrothed, listening to her cries of pleasure. The stirring builds into a rising pressure. Red-faced, young Scipio leans face-first against the side of the pool, fearing someone will discover his tumescence.

When a comely maiden bends to sponge her knees, her pubescent rear facing him, he can take no more. He vaults from the tub and hurries to the caldaria, its steaming waters populated with only a few hardy souls. He eases into the pool and feels his urgency dissolve. *Gratitude for building this, Father,* he says to himself, looking down toward Hades. *It is good to be among common people again. No one seeks my favor; no one awaits my decisions.*

Several minutes later he forces himself out of the pool and douses himself in the cold-water bath, whooping with the shock. He pads over to one of the limestone benches along the tepidarium. A slave massages oil into his body and scrapes it off, completing Scipio's cleansing ritual. Refreshed and energized, Scipio dons his tunic and steps out into the cool night air. He walks back to fetch his armor from the stable and prepares to return to camp.

On the way through town, he is spied by several of his legionnaires, who hurry over and snap to attention in front of him. A nervous young centurion addresses him. "Gaius Laelius seeks your presence immediately, General. He has sent out several patrols for you."

Scipio sighs resignedly. "Very well. And where is that gods-damn-him Laelius?"

The centurion points westward. "He awaits by the front gates." Scipio nods mutely and follows the patrol to the city entrance, where he finds

Laelius reclining on the little patio of a popina (wine bar), dipping fresh oysters into fish sauce.

When he sees Scipio, he jumps up and marches over to meet him, his face grave. "Ah, there you are, General. I have urgent business to discuss with you." He glances at the legionnaires. "Well done, soldiers. Return to camp."

As the patrol heads out the main gates, Scipio glowers suspiciously at Laelius. "What is it this time?"

Laelius sweeps his arm toward the popina he just left. "By all accounts, this is the best popina in Tarraco. It is said the gods themselves come down from Olympus to enjoy a flagon here, though they oft pose as local drunkards! Because you are the leader of the army, it is only fitting that you judge this wine bar's worthiness before our men spend their hard-earned coins in it, is that not so?"

Scipio can only laugh. "In truth, I much desire to lift the weight of command, if only for a night." He grabs Laelius' arm and enters the tall limestone building, passing between two enormous Lacetani guards, their bare falcatas tucked into their wide horsehair belts.

Laelius and Scipio immediately park themselves on stools at one of the bar's low-slung stone tables. "Sit down, Governor," says Laelius. "That is an order!" Laelius trots over to the serving-stand and returns with a large bowl of stew and plate of olives. A slave follows him, carrying an amphora of dark red Ribera and another of water. Scipio and Laelius pour equal amounts of wine and water into their bronze goblets, stir them with their fingers, and drink deeply as they spoon stew into their mouths from the bowl. Their conversation wanders from chariot racing to the local olive crops to Senate politics, but never to the war that surrounds them.

Finally, bored of talk, they play several games of latrunculi, trying to trap each other's pebbles on the game board. For the first time since he left his home in Rome, Scipio laughs deeply, carefree. He is a boy again, if only for several hours.

After another pitcher of wine, Scipio mentions his incident with the deceptive merchant and explains how he threatened to kill him for cheating the army. Laelius nods agreeably. "It sounds like you put a scare into him. He will be most hesitant to cheat us again. But why didn't you cut off one of his fingers, or his hand? Then you'd know he wouldn't dare rob us!"

Scipio blinks in surprise, gulps from his goblet, and ponders Laelius' words. "Remember what we learned about Aristotle?" Scipio replies. "A good man does not act out of anger, he acts out of reason—practical wisdom. I would have been acting vengefully were I to cut off his hand." Laelius grins at him and forlornly shakes his head.

"You are a brilliant man, my friend," burps Laelius, as he puts his arm around Scipio's shoulder. "A virtuous man with the best military mind I've ever seen. But old Aristotle did not have to contend with these predatory culi (assholes) that swarm about us. They are as immune to ethics and reasoning as they are to threats." Laelius labors himself up from the table and poses, as if giving an oratory. "Fear—sweet, potent fear—is what they respect, and there is no respect without it. They need to whisper stories of your cold, vengeful wrath, not your sweet, understanding kindness. You want to be merciful to that thieving cunt? Cut off his finger instead of his dick—that is mercy in proper measure!"

Scipio scowls at his friend. "You are as bad as the Carthaginians, using cruelty as your scepter."

Laelius eases himself back down, shaking his head. "You miss my point. A little cruelty goes a long way. You do not have to *be* cruel, hurting people all the time. You have to do enough to have a reputation for cruelty—or severity, however you call it. That will suffice, and it will make your mercies lauded all the more!" Laelius grins. "Marcus Silenus, that old block of stone, he would say the same thing were he here!"

"That has not been my experience," sniffs Scipio. "Remember how my mother Pomponia taught our mastiff to sit? I had beat and threatened him, but he only learned when she gave him rewards and kindness."

"That may work well for a dog, Scippy," Laelius murmurs, "but for these men, kindness is weakness, without cruelty beforehand." He takes a deep draft of wine and slumps his head toward Scipio. "You know I favor humor and beauty over all: it is part of my nature. But I grew up on the docks of Ostia and the backstreets of Rome, and I tell you true: your moral temperance will taint your command and imperil your victory." He lightly thumps his chest and burps wetly. "Must we all die so you can perish as a virtuous man? Pisspots!"

Scipio can only stare at his easygoing friend. "I have never heard you speak such words."

Laelius gives Scipio a crooked grin. "Until now there was no need, but matters are becoming very serious: The Three Generals may attack us here, at any time. You want to make all these changes to the way we march, and fight, and eat? Well, here's a little secret." He wags his finger at Scipio, looking unsteadily at him. "Quit trying to make the men understand why you are making all these strange changes. Reason is beside the point. They will only accept change because they have faith in you, and they will only have faith if they respect you. Which means they must fear you, to some degree."

He picks up his empty cup and stares inside. "Enough syllogizing. I have said too much and drank too much. Odd how those two are so frequently conjoined, eh?" He shoves himself up from the table and slaps Scipio on the back. "Enough wine for tonight, my admirable friend. I must preserve my energy! A young Sicilian waits for me upstairs, the most beautiful young man in Iberia, so I am told." He pats his crotch and grins. "And I will do his beauty justice by saluting it!" Laelius lurches up the popina's stairs. Scipio watches him go, rubbing the back of his neck, where he can feel his tension returning.

He finishes his wine and rises from the table, teetering toward the front door. He pauses at the exit, listening to the laughter behind him, and turns about to follow Laelius' path up the stairs. A wizened old man sits on a couch at the stairs' landing. He is dressed in robes of finest silk and is flanked by two young African slaves, who stroke his bald head as if he were a pet cat. The old man eyes Scipio critically, estimating his purse.

"What pleasure seek you?" says the old man. "Ass, mouth, or cunt? Or all of them?"

Scipio winces at the question—and at himself for coming there. "A young woman," he mumbles.

The old man leers at him. "Of course. And what do you seek, noble sir? I cannot price you without knowing. Everything for a price, a price for everything."

Scipio shrugs, as if undertaking an unwelcome task. "Irrumatio."

The old man snorts. "Irrumatio? Very pedestrian, if I may say. Now, a trio of partners, that would tempt the imagination and the senses! I can arrange that. Say, two women and a boy? You could—"

Scipio waves his hand, cutting him off. "You have heard me."

The old man sighs. "Of course, of course. Whatever noble sir requests. It is but a pittance for such …."

Scipio holds up a small silver coin. "Here is a sestertius. Bring me a gentle woman."

The old man's eyes bulge at the sight of the money. "Gratitude, my king. For such a price, I have a special mouth for you." He quickly pockets the money and leads Scipio into a back room, sparsely furnished with a few wide reclining couches and a featureless brown wool rug. The old man whispers away as Scipio steps about the room, looking at nothing in particular, waiting. The man returns within minutes, leading a comely young woman from the Celtic nation of northern Iberia. Her red hair pours down her finely defined ceramic face like a stream of fire. The woman fixes her emerald eyes on Scipio, reading his mood. She gestures peremptorily at the aged pimp, and he scuttles from the room, pulling the curtains closed behind him.

The woman silently sheds her indigo robe, revealing a supple body that is completely hairless save a triangle of fire beneath. She kneels in front of Scipio and looks up expectantly. Scipio pulls off his tunic, unwraps his subligaculum, and steps over to face her. The Celt deftly caresses his penis, then his testicles, and Scipio begins to breathe deeply. His phallus swells, hardens, and darkens: his moment is already near. He grasps the back of her head and prepares to enter her mouth, but she pushes a hand against his thigh, pausing him. Reaching into the robe at her feet, she pulls out a vial of golden olive oil. She takes a deep drink and swishes it about thoroughly before she swallows. With a sultry smile, she grasps Scipio's buttock and pulls him into her until she kisses the base of his shaft.

Scipio holds her head as he pumps rhythmically into her mouth, his shaft disappearing into the scarlet curtain of her hair. Following the typical practices of irrumatio, the Celt keeps her head completely immobile as he moves within her. Even so, she dances her tongue across his shaft each time he penetrates her mouth, staring up into his eyes, knowing she has him. Scipio shudders, convulses, and erupts into the back of her throat, bracing his hand on her shoulder to keep himself upright. He briefly caresses her hair, turns, and bends over to pick up his tunic and subligaculum and dress himself. When he is finished, he looks up and sees the Celtic woman standing before him, fully dressed. She smiles and asks him a question in her native tongue. Scipio taps his ear, signaling he does not understand. She looks at him, a question in her eyes. He smiles and pats his heart, signifying his pleasure. Then he gives her a silver sestertius as a gift. She smiles and bows.

"Gratitude, General Scipio," she says in broken Latin, and walks out on a surprised Scipio.

Feeling curiously unfulfilled, Scipio heads down the stairs and onto the main floor. He looks about for Laelius, but he is nowhere to be found, as Scipio expected. With a slight shrug he walks out into the cool night air and takes a deep breath. For a few minutes he savors the raucous sounds from the wine bar, knowing it may be his last taste of freedom until war's end, and then he sets out for camp.

The streets are sparsely populated at this late hour, only a few revelers stumble out from the popinas and trattorias. Scipio turns down one of the narrow side streets, heading for the main gates and the road down to his camp. He stops to fumble inside his purse, extracting a short, desiccated rose stem. Fingering the thorny branch, he recalls the time Amelia gave him the rose, before he set out with his father to north Italia, out for his first battle against Hannibal. He remembers how it once pricked his finger as he was shedding his armor after their ignominious defeat at Ticinus, when he was intent on deserting the war madness and living a peaceful life in Greece. He rolls the stem in his hand. *Did you save me from a life of disgrace, little rose, or condemn me to one?*

There is a soft crunch behind him. Scipio looks over his shoulder to see a Roman guard crumpling to the ground, his head slipping from the grasp of the black shrouded figure that has broken his neck. The figure steps boldly toward Scipio. Still clutching his rose stem, the unarmed youth scrabbles for a loose street cobblestone and raises it upright in his other hand, intent on selling his life dearly. The killer reaches for Scipio's neck, and Scipio swings the stone toward his head. In one deft movement, the man catches Scipio's wrist in a viselike grip and effortlessly turns his wrist backward, the stone falling to the street.

"Easy, boy," comes a muffled voice. "You know not who your true friends are."

The killer pulls the black cloth off his head, and Marcus Silenus stands before Scipio, shaking his head disapprovingly. The centurion pulls Scipio over to the fallen guard and pulls off the leather bracelet about the dead man's right hand. Scipio can see a purple dotted tattoo of a skeletal man in a long robe. Marcus waggles the dead man's wrist under Scipio's nose. "That is Mot, death god of the Carthaginians, done in the purple ink of Phoenicia. This man was one of Carthage's Sacred Band, a holy assassin."

Marcus looks reprovingly at Scipio. "I have been following you all night, expecting you might come to some misadventure," he says, as he looks reprovingly at the popina. "Other than the ones you had in there. Did you think I would let you to wander about unguarded in this border town? I am foresworn to your mother: my life before yours." Then he sees the rose stem in Scipio's hand. "Not a worthy weapon," he says drily.

A flustered Scipio pockets the rose stem. "I know. It was foolish of me to venture out on my own. I guess I am not yet used to being a general. I am indebted to you, Marcus. I trust I may repay it someday."

"There is a favor I might ask of you, when this war is finished," says Marcus. "But for now, you can repay me by being more careful!" He inclines his head toward the dead assassin. "The Generals know you are here, and they are coming after you. Whatever stratagems you have in mind, you had best do them quickly. A storm is coming." Without another word the blocky little man stalks toward the main gate as Scipio follows him, thinking about the centurion's words. And thinking about Amelia.

*   *   *   *   *

TEMPLE OF BELLONA, OUTSKIRTS OF ROME, 210 BCE. Cato, Flaccus, and Fabius are sitting on a stone bench in front of the lovely little Temple of Bellona, goddess of war. The domed shrine is nestled among its seven sacred fig trees, making it difficult to see. Flaccus has chosen this secluded spot for a morning meeting of his Latin Party colleagues, knowing that it is outside the sacred boundaries of Rome and that worshippers will not visit it until later in the day. Birds chirp and the wind glissades through the trees' leafy branches. The tranquil setting is disturbed only by the spiteful rage of Flaccus' voice.

"That deviate Galba gave Nero's men to Scipio!" sputters Flaccus. "All for the price of an aristocratic dick-sucking? By Juno, I am glad his consulship has expired and he is out to fight the Macedonians. He was becoming intolerably sympathetic to the Hellenics!"

"He has as much an appetite for glory as he has for sex," snipes Fabius. "He recruited his own legions for the Macedonian campaign so that he could circumvent the Senate. Paying them out of his own funds, if you can imagine!"

"That was a clever move on his part," counters Cato. "These wars overtax our treasury. By doing so he has dissolved much of the animosity our Latin colleagues bore him for giving up Nero's troops." Cato rubs his chin. "I can see why the man is rich. He plays people like a flute."

Flaccus sniffs. "Galba has wounded our cause. That boy Scipio has enough men now to win some major skirmishes, though he is still too outnumbered for major battles. He will not be content to maintain a holding action within the walls of Tarraco."

Cato frowns at Flaccus. "An angry man opens his mouth and shuts his eyes.[viii] Can you not see that his departure is an opportunity for victory? Marcus Laevinus is one of our new consuls. He is a battle savvy general and will not be easily tricked by Hannibal."

"Yes, yes, that is true, very true" mutters Fabius. "A good general, yes, good. But this is the key: he was an associate of the Claudian family, the one that fought the Scipios for control. And he is too old to succumb to whatever inducements that vixen Pomponia used on Galba! Old Laevinus can right the wrong that Galba has perpetrated upon us."

"But he is a man of honor," says Cato, looking pointedly at Flaccus. "As such he will be difficult to manipulate by the likes of you, however sympathetic he is to our cause. And that I respect."

A smug smile breaks across Flaccus' lean face. "Think you, young Cato, I do not have my ways with 'men of honor'? Come with me, dear

colleagues, for a short walk. I have someone I would like you to meet."
Fabius starts to object when Flaccus raises his hand. "Please come
along, General. It will not stress your injured leg. I have arranged a
chariot back to the Forum from there."

Flaccus bows and extends his arm, inviting Cato and Fabius to walk
ahead of him. They stroll down a wide pebbled path through a meadow
to enter a sacred grove of stone pines and fig trees. There, in the middle
of a clearing, squats the mansion-sized Temple of Apollo: a circular
domed edifice belted with marble columns. Sitting on the temple steps
is a small, round man with a cherubic face and smile, adorned in a
gold-embroidered toga. He rises to greet them with open arms.

"Senator Flaccus! General Fabius!" he chirps, "The gods bless me
with your presence!" He studies Cato, who somberly returns his look.
"Ah, this must be young Cato, the notable orator," expostulates the
little man. He grasps Cato's sturdy forearm with his chubby hand and
pumps it enthusiastically, as if welcoming a long-lost brother. "I have
heard much about you, Cato, that you are the very personification of
Latin morality. It is an honor to meet you!"

Cato pulls away from the man's grip and wipes his arm on his
weathered gray tunic. "I am but a farmer and soldier, no more. Whom
do I address?"

Flaccus interrupts. "Cato, this is my friend Apicius, one of Rome's
most successful merchants."

Apicius bows deeply. "The spice and clothing business has been good
to me—and slavery even better since the war. All those widows
wanting help with their farms and houses. I am tempted to make a
thanks giving to Mars to keep up the war!" He grins. "I but jest.
Mercury, our god of trade, has been especially generous. It is to him I
sacrifice, and often."

Fabius nods approvingly. "You must be very successful, if your lavish
banquets are any measure. I have never tasted such foods, drank such

wines, seen such women!"

Apicius bows. "When one has access to the treasures of the East, it is an easy matter to arrange such pleasures." He eases his portly frame back down onto the steps, looking about warily, eyeing his three visitors. "Now, why are you two esteemed Senators requesting my audience out here? I would guess you have called me here for a very special favor, is that not so?"

"A favor to our mutual benefit," says Flaccus, turning to Fabius and Cato. "Apicius can be of great help to our Party."

Apicius bobs his head enthusiastically. "I would be honored to help such noble patricians. For the good of Rome."

"Why would you do such a thing for us?" growls Cato bluntly. "You are a merchant, not a patrician. Tell me you do not seek office among your betters."

There is a brief gleam of enmity in Apicius' brown eyes, but they quickly resume their twinkle. "Oh no, no such pretensions! I seek no magistracy; I know my place. But these Scipios, they harp upon educating the citizens and changing the working conditions for slaves—for slaves! Can you imagine?" Apicius' ready smile fades, and his face reddens. "I heard Publius Scipio, the boy's father, talking about it in the Senate two years ago. He proposed increasing the merchant's portoria (import tax) to three percent! And the slavery tax to four! Can you imagine? I would be bankrupt!"

"It is only too true," nods Flaccus sympathetically. "Raising our taxes again, it is the Hellenic way. And if young Scipio were to be victorious in Iberia, he could be our next consul. The Hellenics would control the Senate, and then where would we be? More taxes for the government to spend on education and free land—for commoners!"

Fabius bobs his head. "Yes, yes, they would steal from we who earn our money." He looks at Apicius. "It is a pleasure to meet a man of true Roman principles, a person I can trust." Fabius blinks as if a thought is just occurring to him, and he snaps his fingers. "You know, Rome is mounting two new legions into the field. They will require weaponry and clothing. That contract could be yours, for a fair price."

Apicius spreads his hands and bows. "I would welcome the opportunity to serve our country, and would provide our men with the best! Now, let us put our minds to similar purpose, crating this Cornelius Scipio so that he does not wander about Iberia. But how? Consul Laevinus will not overturn Galba's imperium about Nero's troops. Young Scipio already has them in his hand."

Fabius looks at Flaccus, who nods affirmatively. Cato looks at them suspiciously, wondering what unspoken agreement has passed between them. "An army is only as strong as its purse, honored merchant," Flaccus says. "If Scipio's war funds were limited to the original amount he was given, with no additions for Nero's men, that would remedy our problem. He would not have enough money to campaign in the field, to purchase supplies from locals or hire tribal allies." Flaccus' fist smacks his hand. "Then he would have to remain in Tarraco. Hah!"

Even as Apicius grins his approval, Cato slowly shakes his head. "I like not that soft-handed Hellenic, but we cannot subvert his military mission for the sake of politics. That is not the Roman way."

"We subvert nothing," interjects Fabius, pointing a gnarled finger at Cato. "We merely assure that he stays faithful to one of Rome's major objectives in Iberia: protecting Italia's northern border from incursion by the Carthaginians. It is paramount that they do not join Hannibal, so we are aiding in Rome's defense!" Cato can only stare at his mentor.

"Besides," purrs Flaccus, "do we really want this untutored general risking our legions against the Three Generals? Best he stay within the walls of Tarraco, helping Marcius defend the border. Time enough to conquer Iberia, when Hannibal is on the cross."

"Your reasons may be appealing, but your motives disgust," grates Cato. He walks down the temple steps and strolls about the edge of the forest, fingering the leaves and earth, ignoring his fellows.

Watching his young protégé, Flaccus sighs with frustration. "Cato is right on at least one point," he says. "The reasons for limiting Scipio's budget can be plausibly argued in the Senate: we simply argue that we need more resources to combat dread Hannibal, and Philip of Macedonia. Fabius and I can secure the votes. But how can we be sure consul Marcus Laevinus will take action upon the Senate's wishes, however he resents the Scipios? If the plebs found out he constrained their hero Scipio, he will be an unpopular man. The consul is well aware of that."

Apicius chortles and spreads his arms. "Now we enter my area of expertise! This is a money problem, so it is best solved by money, would not you agree?" He grins slyly, giving the two Senators a sidelong glance. "Much of my wealth is from my lesser-known business, confidential moneylending to Rome's famous and powerful."

Apicius studies the trees above his head, silent for several moments. "I tell you this in confidence, on your honor as Romans. Marcus Laevinus is an accomplished soldier and politician, but he is not so successful at dice. I have loaned him several sizable sums, which are long overdue—and drawing interest! Our consul would greatly appreciate an absolution of those debts—and would greatly dread any notoriety of his fiscal folly." Apicius winks at Fabius and Flaccus. "When he loses at gambling, it would not surprise me that some of the denarii he leaves on the dice floor came from our treasury. Yes, I see a means of persuading Laevinus."

Flaccus rubs the back of his neck, rolling the thought in his mind. "We must be careful here. You cannot offer a bribe for him to do it. Rather, the absolution of the debt should be part of the celebration of a proposal you favored being passed, similar to debt amnesty during the Saturnalia. You would be making an offering to the gods, you see, on his behalf."

Apicius wrinkles his nose and shrugs. "You make a finer point of this transaction than I would, but it is agreed. I will meet with the consul shortly, to discuss a potential ... celebration."

"Very good," says Flaccus. "The timing of this action is most propitious. We vote on the war budget three days hence. And Fabius here has requested more money for the campaign against Hannibal, so the time is ripe for all this to occur."

Young Cato watches them silently from a distance. *By Jupiter's beard, these men would walk over children if it got them to their doorway.* He walks onto a forest trail, returning to Rome without a backward glance.

Fabius stands and pulls his toga about him, preparing to leave. "That is not how I would have wanted the money to fight Hannibal, friends, but I will do what needs to be done." Apicius and Flaccus merely stare at him. Fabius clears his throat. "Um, very well then. Our decision is made. Let us quickly take action upon it. *Carpe diem!*"

"*Carpe diem!*" the two other conspirators say, smiling triumphantly.

*   *   *   *   *

TOLETUM, SOUTH CENTRAL IBERIA, 210 BCE. Even as Flaccus plots the political ruination of Scipio's career, the Three Generals convene in the Carpetani nation's walled stronghold, plotting Scipio's military destruction. Gisgo is there to oversee the transport of a half-ton of gold to the newly constructed fortress at Cartago Nova. He has called in the two Barca brothers to join him there to plan the spring war campaign and to release some of the captives they hold from the major Carpetani tribes, as is the Generals' custom. With most of Iberia firmly within their grasp, the Generals' thoughts are now occupied with eliminating the last of the Roman threats to their complete dominance: General Scipio and his legions at Tarraco

The Generals convene in the meeting lodge, a large but rude construction of thick pine logs notched together. Gisgo, Mago, and Hasdrubal sit at a wide plank table by the roaring stone fireplace, pushing the table near it to take the chill off the late-winter air.

Masinissa sits next to them, tall and upright, clad in a richly brocaded dark blue tunic. He shifts uncomfortably in his stout wooden chair, tapping his long fingers against the table. Masinissa is eager to be out riding the plains and attacking the Romans, to thus curry the Generals' favor so they will give him troops for his war against King Syphax of Numidia. And, though he is loathe to admit it to himself, to secure the hand of Gisgo's peerless daughter, Sophonisba.

A dozen tribal chieftains sit on benches at each end of the table, arrayed in quilted tunics and plumed helmets. Four elderly men stand calmly in front of this assemblage of roughshod warriors, unperturbed at the challenging looks the barbarians give them. They are bent and gray, their purple-bordered robes hanging loose on their skeletal bodies, but they each are as powerful as any man there. These four are the senior representatives of Carthage's ruling Council of Elders. They have sailed from Carthage to join the meeting, eager to hear the Three Generals' war report. The lead Elder, a man with piercing blue eyes, questions Gisgo.

"How fares your alliance with the tribes? Has the money you requested been spent well?"

Gisgo nods. "We have added another five thousand Lusitani to Mago's force, and almost as many Carpetani to Hasdrubal's army," he says.

One of the Elders eyes Gisgo speculatively. "And our allies, they have cooperated? How many captives do you retain?"

"We have three hundred hostages right now,[ix] " he replies, with some pride.

Another Elder peers in at Hasdrubal. "You are stationed in the north, near the Romans. What is their status?"

Hasdrubal shifts about uncomfortably. "There is great activity within

Tarraco, many troops and merchants roiling about. But to what purpose we do not know yet. The boy Scipio may be planning something."

The oldest Elder stares blandly at Hasdrubal. "Yes, 'planning something,' you say. This is what our spies tell you?"

Hasdrubal flushes. "We do not have to know what he is doing for us to know what we should do." He turns to Gisgo, then Mago. "We agree. It is time to join forces against him, correct?"

"With equal command," interjects Gisgo, eyeing Hasdrubal resentfully. "One of us is not over the others."

The oldest Elder grins slyly. "So, do you propose to act like the Roman consuls do when they are on campaign? Each of you taking turns commanding the army each day? That tact did not serve them well at Trebia or Cannae, did it?" One of the other Elders chuckles briefly, before he covers his yellowed teeth with his hand.

"We do not propose to mimic those fools," says Hasdrubal darkly. "We have yet to work out our command—that is true. But I tell you now, we will march on Tarraco and mow through Marcius' men enroute. Then Iberia will be ours." He looks pointedly at the Elders. "Then we can concentrate on Rome, where Hannibal awaits us."

The Elders stand silently, absorbing Hasdrubal's declaration. "A moment, Generals," murmurs the senior Elder, who motions his fellows to go outside the room.

As soon as they leave, Hasdrubal pivots in his seat and glares at Gisgo. "By Baal's balls, why did you have to mention chain of command?" Hasdrubal demands. "They must see us as a unified front, if we are to gain coin from them."

"I know what you would do," retorts Gisgo. "You would try to secure supreme command for yourself. I will not be your pot-slave in this war. Equal command!"

Mago looks pointedly at his two compatriots and darts his eyes toward the attending chieftains and their interpreters, reminding his colleagues of their allies' presence. "It is not such a problem, is it?" he says pleasantly, his eyes commanding them to agree. "We will each direct our armies, and attack in concert. Three generals, three armies, one big victory."

Hasdrubal nods knowingly. "Ah, your are correct, brother. That is the best stratagem. We make overmuch of the issue, Gisgo." Hasdrubal loudly addresses the chieftains. "One more campaign, with you and your men, and the war will be won," he says to them, as the interpreters translate. "There will be much plunder to share, and your families will be returned to you. We will prosper as one nation, together." Hasdrubal grins ingratiatingly at them, nodding his head.

The chieftains eye Hasdrubal, their faces skeptical. One grizzled chieftain pointedly spits into the dirt and rubs his empty eye socket with his middle finger; an insult. As he does, the Elders return to the room, their faces grim.

"You three command all military operations in Iberia," begins the senior Elder. "So it is your decision when and where to wage war against the Romans." He pauses to cough and clear his throat before he continues, his rheumy blue eyes fixing on each of the Generals in turn. "Be that as it may, the Elders determine how the wars will be funded. We care not how you purge the Roman menace, only that you do it soon and cease this drain on the treasury. Above all, keep the mines functioning and the sea lanes open for trade. Is that understood?"

Hasdrubal begins to sputter with anger. He vaults up in his chair and slams his hands on the table. Gisgo stands up and places a restraining hand on Hasdrubal's shoulder, silencing him before he erupts with invective. "Certainly, we do not want to make this war bad for business," Gisgo says sarcastically. "But did you hear about the Roman orator Cato? Every time he speaks in their Senate, he ends by saying 'Carthage must be destroyed.' I would think that Rome burning our city to the ground would be 'bad for business,' too."

Mago adds, "Keep the purse open, Elders, and we will replenish it with Iberian gold and silver." He crosses his heart with his index finger. "On my life."

The Elders glance at each other and give the barest of head shakes to themselves. "You have heard our position. There is naught else to be said," pronounces the senior Elder. He gives the three commanders a rictus of a smile. "Thank you for your time, Generals. We look forward to news of your impending victory. Soon."

As one man, the Elders turn and shuffle out of the room. When they have closed the door behind them, Mago heaves a sigh. "I swear to the gods, those merchants are more interested in protecting what lies in the ground than what lives above it. We must move on Marcius, and Scipio, before Rome sends any more legions."

"I worry that we may lose more of our allies," says Gisgo. "Two of the Turdetani tribes have rebelled against us. We have crucified their chieftains' sons, but they continue to fight for freedom."

"Send the Ilergetes against them," growls Hasdrubal. He turns toward the semicircle of chieftains. "Indibilis! Mandonius! Your Ilergetes will rid us of these Turdetani rebels. By the next full moon."

Indibilis shakes his shaggy head. "We have no grudge against the Turdetani. We are here to fight the Romans. That was our agreement."

"You are being paid to help us win this war, in whatever form that takes, not to dictate your opponents to us." When Indibilis does not reply, Hasdrubal adds, "Might I remind you, your precious nephew Allucius is one of our hostages at Cartago Nova. We can build a cross for him, too."

Indibilis lurches toward Hasdrubal, but Mandonius grasps the back of his belt and halts him. "We have not forgotten," says Mandonius. "Have you forgotten our bargain?"

"Ah yes, our trial by combat," grins Gisgo. "Our champion against yours, for the release of Allucius and his bride-to-be. You lose, you forfeit next month's wages for your men, correct?"

Indibilis looks at Mandonius, who nods his agreement. "Yes," spits Indibilis.

"Very well. I have prepared an area outside the back door. Our man Rhodo waits there." Gisgo turns to face the rest of the chieftains, smiling unctuously. "We have staged some entertainment for you," he shouts, raising his hands high. "There will be a gladiatorial combat between the Celtiberian champion and our Sacred Band warrior, Rhodo. A duel to the death to settle a 'property' dispute, of a sort. Please attend. You will find it entertaining."

Gisgo heads for the rear door, with Mago and Hasdrubal behind him. The entire convocation files out to gather around the hundred-foot diameter of the fighting circle, outlined with rounded stones. There, in the middle of the circle, stands a lithe athletic man, drawing circles in the dirt with his sandaled foot. Rhodo Gisgon. Known as The NightBringer, is the war champion of the Sacred Band and Carthage's mightiest ground warrior.

Several years ago, at Greece's Panhellenic Games, an unknown youth had won the prestigious Pentathlon, dominating its javelin, running, and discus competitions. The young man claimed to be from one of the outpost Iberian colonies, but the boy was Rhodo, a scion of Carthage's powerful Gisgon family.

Rhodo had moved to a Greek-held colony in Iberia and bribed his way to being declared one of its Greek citizens. This made him eligible to compete in his beloved pentathlon, the competition to be Greece's greatest athlete. Tall and angular, every vein is visible along Rhodo's lean torso; he is warrior god personified. As befits a pentathlon champion, he moves with such a graceful suddenness that more than one priest has declared him a leopard reincarnated from a previous life. Their declaration is lent credence by Rhodo's appearance: his mocha skin is mottled with dark birthmarks, a curse from the gods that has bred in Rhodo a persistent drive to prove himself superior to those who are unblemished, primarily by killing them in combat.

The champion of Carthage is resplendent in a lacquered white linen cuirass with a red-purple phoenix painted on its breastplate, his gleaming bronze helmet crested with the same resurrection symbol. Rhodo hefts a sturdy iron javelin in his right hand, while his left arm carries a round wooden shield with a bronze boss, bordered with a hammered steel edge that gleams like a blade. His silver belt holds a short double-edged sword with a gold pommel, awards given to him as the winner of the Delphi games. By dint of his many kills in the Numidian and Punic wars, Rhodo has earned the right to be The NightBringer, champion of Carthage's most elite infantry. Now he stands quietly, looking bored, waiting for his next death battle.

He does not have to wait long, for Indibilis is already leading his champion into the circle. All heads turn to stare at Gargos, the bare-chested leviathan that tramps into the ring behind the Ilergetes prince. A murdering outcast of the Andosini tribe of the northern Ilergetes, Gargos has earned widespread fear and infamy as a designated champion in death-match disputes between tribes. He has adapted the manners and weaponry of the neighboring Gauls, his six-and-a-half-foot body tattooed from head to toe with blue spirals and knots. Every time Gargos received a battle scar he had it decorated as a blue rope, and his body is covered with them. Broad-bodied and heavy, Gargos' smooth, thick arms mask the coils of iron muscle that lie beneath the surface, a man so strong he wields his four-foot greatsword as if it were a dagger. His light brown hair flows down to his shoulders; his moustache droops below his lantern jaw. His only garb is a pair of bright blue breeches, held up by a wide leather belt circled with the scalps of his victims.

Gargos impatiently steps around Indibilis to stand face-to-face with Rhodo, staring down into his opponent's ice blue eyes. Craning his neck upwards to stare into Gargos' face, Rhodo turns his head toward Mago and Gisgo. He smiles and winks at them. "This is either the largest man I've ever seen, or the smallest giant!"

Mago and Gisgo barely suppress a grin, while Hasdrubal merely shakes his head. They are all aware of Rhodo's macabre sense of humor in the face of death.

Indibilis waves his champion to the outer edge of the ring, and Rhodo steps to the opposite side. Both wait for the signal, Rhodo standing immobile, Gargos smacking his sword against his leathered palm, breathing heavily.

Gisgo steps into the center of the circle as Indibilis leaves it.. Gisgo spreads his arms. "This is a match to the death. Should one of the combatants get outside the circle, whether he is pushed or falls, the wager is won by the man inside the circle—and the other is executed."

Gisgo claps his hands. "Commence!" he shouts, and dashes from the circle. The combatants surge toward each other. Gargos shoves his large rectangular shield into Rhodo's, seeking to knock him off his feet. But Rhodo turns his shield sideways and Gargos' shield screeches off of his as Rhodo slides behind him. As Gargos turns, Rhodo spears him with his javelin, and the head disappears into Gargos' ribs. The Celtiberian roars in pain but he slaps the weapon from him as if it were a child's plaything, and the spear spins away. Rhodo darts over to pick up his weapon. He steps back, his eyes wide with surprise. Then he smiles playfully. "You're a tough little boy, aren't you?" he says to the snarling giant. "Well, come on then, let's play!"

With surprising speed, Gargos jumps forward and whirls his gleaming blade down at Rhodo's head. The agile Carthaginian catches the blow on his shield, but the force of it knocks him to one knee, his wooden shield splintering. Gargos growls angrily, swinging his heavy sword sideways in a decapitating arc. With a deafening clang, Rhodo blocks the murderous swing with his iron javelin, but the force of the blow numbs his arm, and the javelin falls from his grasp. Quick as an adder, Gargos swings back to clang his blade off of Rhodo's helmet, stunning the NightBringer. He falls to both knees, shaking his head, holding his shield in front of his body.

Bellowing his triumph, Gargos grasps the bronze phoenix on Rhodo's helmet to yank him up and expose his throat. Rhodo's fingers fumble desperately to unstrap his helmet as Gargos pulls his head up. The helmet pops from Rhodo's head and Gargos is left holding it, cursing in frustration. Rhodo scrambles on all fours to the edge of the circle, his shield banging against him. He falls on his back, perilously close to going past the edge of the fighting circle.

Gargos pitches Rhodo's helmet aside; then his own shield. He grasps his heavy sword in both hands and lumbers toward Rhodo, roaring with bloodlust. Rhodo grasps his shield and pushes himself upright, shaking his head to clear it. As Gargos closes on him, Rhodo whirls his shield behind his back and twists forward to hurl it like a discus, its spinning metal edge flashing through the air.

The shield's razored edge catches Gargos in the side of his mouth, breaking his jaw and cutting deep into his head. Gargos' eyes start from his head and he gurgles with agony. He drops his sword to clutch at his face, all thought of murder gone. Quick as a leopard, Rhodo dashes in and thrusts his short sword up into the underside of Gargos' jaw, driving until the point emerges from the back of the barbarian's skull. The giant topples, coughing blood, to kick out his final moments. Gasping and glassy-eyed, Rhodo spits on the convulsing Celtiberian and stumbles over to pick up his helmet and polish the dust from it.

Indibilis and Mandonius erupt in frustrated curses, jerking their fists at the Carthaginian champion. Hasdrubal walks into the circle, carefully stepping over its bloody puddles. He steadies Rhodo, and raises the champion's sword arm in triumph, grinning smugly at the two Ilergetes.

The other chieftains watch intently but they are quiet, betraying no excitement at Hasdrubal's win. Hasdrubal glowers at them, irritated. "You all bear witness. Rhodo is the victor. Allucius will remain with us as hostage." He faces Mandonius and Indibilis with a triumphant smirk. "The Ilergetes will forfeit a month's wages, as per the bargain. Praise to Baal!"

The two tribal chiefs can bear no more. "Bring our horses out front. Now!" shouts Mandonius to a stable boy. He and Indibilis storm back through the meeting room and enter the front yard. Gisgo and Mago hurry after them, urging them to wait, but the angry Ilergetes vault upon their horses and wheel their horses around to depart.

"We will honor our agreement," snarls Mandonius, "but bear this in mind: our men will not take kindly to their loss of coin, and they will not blame us for it. Not us. You have won a little but lost a lot." The two abruptly pound off through the fortress gates.

Mago and Gisgo watch them go, seething with anger. They do not notice the wizened Iberian that is grinding corn near the front of the meeting house. The elder's eyes are downcast upon the flour he is making, but he takes in everything.

*   *   *   *   *

The buccinae, the camp horns, are sounding the call for the soldiers to rise and assemble for breakfast, but Scipio is already up and about in his command tent below Tarraco. The groggy young general forces down a traditional hangover breakfast of owl's eggs and roasted canary, washing it down with watered wine he can hardly bear to look at. He ruefully recalls the night's depredations at the wine bar, and of his rescue from an assassin's dagger. At first he remonstrates himself for his foolishness, but then he grins. *That was my last night out until this war is won. But when it is over, let the gods beware, I will make up for it!*

Scipio strolls from the tent with a large goblet of calda, warm water and wine mixed with fragrant spices, the better for his breath. As he woozily inspects the camp, he notes the angle of the sun. *Spring is coming—and with it the spring campaign,* he thinks. He takes a deep breath and exhales, watching his breath fog. *I wonder if I can catch Gisgo's army by itself, over by the Ebro—catch him before one of the other armies would catch me? No, too risky.*

After Scipio visits the trench latrine, he returns to his tent and rinses his body with several linen scraps. Refreshed, he goes to the base of the road up to Tarraco, where he sees his legions marching double-time up the road, carrying their weighted packs. Scipio smiles at the sight, knowing his troops will be the best conditioned in Roman history. *They will have to be*, he thinks ruefully. *We must be quicker than any before us*. He sees Clastidius Honorius, his new intelligence director, standing at the base of the road. The bear-like old man is busy shouting insults and orders to the legionnaires he sends up the road, and he does not notice Scipio's approach.

"How goes the training, Clastidius?" shouts Scipio, making the older man jump.

"Very well, General," replies Clastidius. "They hate that hill more than they will ever hate the Carthaginians, but they have conquered it. I would venture they are good for at least twenty miles a day, with enough left to set up camp."

"What about thirty miles a day?" asks Scipio, "if they were travelling with a lighter pack?"

The old man cuts his eyes sideways, thinking. "Why, yes, that might be possible, were the weather benign. But they must have food and supplies, and the supply wagons are so slow!"

Scipio watches the men. "Food and supplies? I suppose. Wagons? Perhaps not." The praefectus stares bewilderedly at Scipio. "Do not fret about it. Tell me, do we have any new intelligence from our speculatores?"

Clastidius sucks on his lower lip, reluctant to reply. "I wanted to tell you yesterday, but you were out of camp. We have matching reports from Gisgo's and Hasdrubal's camps. The Three Generals are mustering their forces. We think they will join forces to attack Marcius at the Ebro. And then move upon us at Tarraco."

Scipio sits on a boulder and places his face in his hands, rubbing his eyes. "That is sore news, indeed. They have a hundred thousand men now. We have not a quarter of that force. And the Senate denies us money to hire more allies, or even enough food!" He looks guiltily at his veteran commander. "Ignore my complaining—my head aches. So how long do you think we could hold out here, if all three came at us?"

Clastidius shrugs. "It is so early in spring. There is no grain to be harvested, and our stores are low." He turns the sandy dirt with his boot, thinking. "Three months if they lay siege to us. Two weeks if they storm the front walls, which is what I would do ...."

Scipio scratches the top of his unkempt head. "So, if Marcius and his men are destroyed, then we are destroyed, and Tarraco falls. And all those Carthaginians join Hannibal in Italia. And I am supposed to sit in Tarraco and wait for this to happen. Fuck!" He pushes himself up from the boulder. "Apologies, Praefectus. Your intelligence work is gold to me, but I am dismayed at its dark color."

"There is a brighter gleam to it, General," says Clastidius. "The Generals quarrel among each other, especially Hasdrubal and Mago."

Scipio's eyes brighten with interest. "Well now, that is a weapon we may be able to use! See if you can find out about the nature of their dispute, Clastidius."

Clastidius picks at the sword scar that snakes down his right cheek, nervous. "About this 'intelligence work,' General. I should tell you ... our tribunes, they are not welcoming this spying about. They think it cowardly and immoral. That it is too ... Carthaginian." He eyes Scipio meaningfully. "They have become more vocal about it since we caught one of our spies selling secrets to the Carthaginians. The officers fear we will be led into a trap, betrayed by our own spies—I mean, our own men."

"Hmm. I suppose it is up to me to show them that these men will not betray us in the future. We have the betrayer on trial tonight, yes?"

Clastidius nods solemnly. "He was caught by one of our other men in the field, selling Marcius' troop movements to Indibilis' chieftains." Clastidius snorts a laugh. "He did not glean that one of them was in our pay!"

"Hmm. There will be two of us on trial tonight, from what you have said," remarks Scipio, with a rueful grin. He claps Clastidius on the shoulder. "You have done well, old friend. Your honesty is much appreciated. Now I must attend to another matter." Scipio glances at a group of sweaty and exhausted young legionnaires trotting down the road, their faces flush with exhaustion. "Train them severely. They will have need of all that conditioning."

Clastidius salutes and returns to his men. "Up again!" he shouts. "And pick up the pace!"

Scipio sits back on the boulder for a minute and rubs the back of his neck with both hands. He wrenches himself up and stalks back to his tent. "Summon Felix," he growls to an attendant as he enters. He plunks himself onto a stool next to the remains of his meal, playing with a heel of bread. Within minutes, the aged camp accountant enters. Scipio rises to face him as soon as he enters.

"Felix, if I needed to provide food for fourteen days' march, would we have it?"

Felix pulls out the abacus that never leaves his side and begins calculating, talking to Scipio as he goes. "Well, let us see, hmm. Twenty-five thousand men. One and a half pounds of wheat, a half pound of beans, quarter pound of cheese … olive oil, salt … at two and a half pounds of rations per day." Minutes pass as Felix clicks away. He shakes his head vigorously. "No, not even by half. We would have to buy considerably more food from the merchants. But our funds have been cut, as you know. Even if we use our resources allocated for the animals' forage, it is not possible." He stares pleadingly at Scipio. "We have barely enough if we stay at Tarraco and forage the countryside."

Scipio heaves a deep sigh. "Gratitude, you but confirm what I suspected. Good day."

Felix creaks upright and shuffles out the door, pausing as he pulls
back one of the goatskin flaps. "If we had half the men, we could make
it," he adds hopefully.

The young general sits down on the stool again, rubbing his eyes.
"Half the men," he says sarcastically to himself. He grabs the heel of
bread from his plate and flings it at the tent door, where it bounces off
and falls to the floor. He stares glassily at the crumbled heel, lost in
thought. Then he rises quickly and sticks his head out the entry, looking
at one of his guards. "Fetch Felix again," he snaps.

Scipio ducks his head back in the tent and rummages through his
scrolls. He pulls out a yellowed and stiff papyrus roll and hastily
unrolls it, scanning his finger across the words until he fixes at what he
has been seeking. A smile cracks his face. "Buccelatum," he says
aloud. "Why not?"

An apprehensive Felix sidles into the tent. He opens his mouth to
speak, but Scipio interrupts. "You said we might make it with half the
men. What if we had all the men but half the food, and most of that was
wheat?"

Felix's stammers silently, his mouth agape. "Well, yes, that is another
way of looking at it, most certainly. But the men need their food. They
march all day and carry heavy packs. And then there are the animals
and their food, and then—"

"You answer was sufficient, quaestor," replies Scipio, waving off any
further comments. "Now I need you to do something important, and do
it immediately. Return to our merchant 'friend' Artho. Tell him we
want twice the allotment of grain requested, and ten tons of cheese. Our
initial payment will be a down payment for the rest. I know I do not
have to tell you this, Felix, but negotiate a good rate. Delivery in three
days! Go!"

Felix's face is a study in suppressed disagreement, but he scurries out on his mission. Scipio paces about, rubbing his hands excitedly. Laelius and Marcus Silenus enter the tent, weaponless but clad in battle armor. "What did you say to esteemed Felix," asks Laelius with a wry grin. "He did rush past me as if Charon had finally caught up with him to take him to Hades!"

Marcus glances sideways at Laelius and huffs his derision. "The Carthaginians are coming, are they not?" is all he says.

"You have heard then," remarks Scipio as he rolls up his aged scroll.

Marcus gives the briefest of nods. "Clastidius told me," he says. "But it was no surprise. If I were in their place, I would wipe us out now, while we are weakest."

Laelius smirks at the leathered centurion. "Very perceptive! Perhaps you should hire yourself as an advisor to the Three Generals, Marcus. Just think—they would pay you in all the wine and boys you would ever want!" Scipio's face remains serious, but his eyes twinkle with amusement, knowing Laelius is teasing the abstentious Marcus.

Marcus' head turns very slightly toward Laelius, then back to Scipio, his face expressionless. "Hannibal taught me a lesson, boy: understand your enemy, or fall prey to the enemy that understands you," he replies irritably.

"I am in agreement with Marcus," adds Scipio. "It is logical for them to eliminate their last barrier to Italia. We cannot defeat them here, but we can use one of Hannibal's tricks upon them—lure them away from our vulnerabilities." The young general takes a deep breath, anxious at what he will say next. "We will march south and attack Cartago Nova. The Three Generals will have to follow us there."

"That is a month's journey," remarks Marcus. "By then they could be attacking Marcius' men on the Ebro."

Laelius looks at Scipio and shrugs. "It sorely pains me to agree with Marcus, but there is truth in his words. Spring will be in full flower by then. The roads will be dry, and the Iberians will be eager for battle."

"Ten days' march, not a month," says Scipio. "We will be at Cartago Nova in ten days."

Laelius crooks his head sideways, studying his friend. "Not that I question your judgment, General—you always invent a way. But Cartago Nova is almost three hundred miles away, is it not? How can you lead a baggage train there so soon? We could not make it to Saguntum by then!"

"I will not be leading any baggage train, Laelius. You will. Or at least, you'll be sailing one. Let me explain."

Scipio waves the yellowed scroll in front of them, poking it with his finger. "The answer is here, in the early history of the our republic. Two hundred years ago, Marcus Furius Camillus did surprise the Gauls by marching an enormous distance in a short time." He unrolls the scroll and points to a section of it, the edges breaking in his hand. "It says here his men subsisted on 'circles of hard bread' during the entire march. I wager they were eating buccelatum, those hard-baked biscuits we make back in Rome. They contain oil and salt for our men. We just add some cheese to their diet. And maybe some fruit."

Laelius shakes his head. "We still have to haul all our armor and siege supplies. And what of our mules, and the craftsmen? Do we leave all that behind?"

"That is where you come in, 'Admiral Laelius,' " Scipio blurts excitedly. "You are going to sail all our supplies south, down the coast to Cartago Nova. You proceed slowly so that you do not arrive until we do, so as not to alert the enemy. Marcus and I will lead our men on a rapid march. They will only carry their fighting weapons and a sarcina with their food and blankets. No cooking utensils, no extra weaponry. We will post extra guards and sleep without building a camp—that will give us extra time and energy for marching. Thirty miles a day."

Laelius can only stare at him, his mouth open. "More changes,

Scippy? Me, an Admiral? " says Laelius. "You've already turned our sailors into 'marines' and started this strange intelligence work. The men will not be happy. They already grumble about marching up and down that access road. Would you foment mutiny?"

Scipio starts to speak when Marcus interrupts. "It will work," he says with finality. "It will work if we can get the men to believe in it. To believe in your plan."

Scipio eyes Marcus. "You mean, if we can get them to believe in me."

Marcus looks straight ahead, expressionless "I did not say that."

"You make a point that hits home, although it is against my nature," says Scipio. "Those generals who are severe and strict in the observance of law are serviceable to their own men, while those who are easygoing and bountiful are useful only to the enemy. The soldiers of the latter might be joyous but insubordinate, while the others, although downcast, will be obedient and ready for all emergencies."[x]

Laelius extends his arm and Scipio grasps his forearm. "You speak severely for such a scholarly fellow, Scippy. Myself, I would favor reinforcing Marcius at the Ebro, and making a final stand there. But if the both of you think Cartago Nova can be taken, then I am in favor of it." He grins playfully. "Besides, this town has become boring. I fear death by boredom more than death by Carthaginian, for certain."

Moving to the breakfast table, Scipio scatters the remnants of his meal onto the floor, sprawling out his map of the Iberian coast. "It is decided then. We leave in five days. The men will do two more days of intensive training and then rest for the march. We will convene with the rest of the officers tomorrow. No one will be told where we are going. We cannot risk being cut off or pursued."

"How would they not know?" objects Laelius. "The Carthaginians have scouts in the hills and spies in the city! Do you have another 'invention' to prevent them from knowing where we are going? Perhaps a cloak of invisibility, like Jupiter employs to seduce unsuspecting maidens? If so, I volunteer to try it out!"

Scipio smiles. "No inventions, I am out of fresh ideas. But I have two old ones that will help us greatly, more gifts from Hannibal. He used misdirection and camouflage to dire effect upon us, and we will use them upon the Generals when we march."

The three men are quiet for several long moments as Laelius and Marcus wait for Scipio to elaborate. But Scipio merely smiles, enjoying his game.

"I see you prefer to be secretive about what you are doing," Laelius remarks sarcastically. "But perhaps you would enlighten us to our own tasks for the next five days. Other than us telling our tribunes that we don't know where we are going."

Scipio's face reddens briefly. "Apologies, you deserve more. Here is what I can tell you. Before we leave, we will recruit native emissaries for the nations that are loyal to Carthage: the Bastanti, Oretani, Edetani, and the fierce Turdetani. Each will take a purse of gold to the largest tribes of each, as a sign of our respect, and they will be given one for themselves when their mission is completed to our spies' satisfaction."

"For certitude, there are merchants and craftsmen in town from all Iberia," says Marcus. "And the leaders of Tarraco will know who is trustworthy. But to what purpose, General?"

"We need to find a respected elder from each tribe who will tell us about their tribe's affairs with the Three Generals. When the time is ripe, that elder will extend an offer to the tribal council to join us. We need native allies, and for once Rome will have them." Scipio points to the map on the table. "Tomorrow we commence. We send locals to the citadel of Saguntum, halfway between here and Cartago Nova. We will soon have need of some special services there."

"Can we really afford to pay for all of this?" Laelius interjects. "The Senate has given us no funds for such pursuits. Old Felix frets that our coinage is too low to sustain even a few forays below the Ebro! I think

I should return to Rome and petition them for more support."

Scipio shakes his head. "It would be futile. We won't get any more money while the Latin Party holds sway." He fidgets with the handle of his dagger while he looks about the tent, avoiding their eyes. "Let me worry about where the coins will come from. On my honor, I will find a way."

Marcus looks intently at Scipio, studying the thoughts that race across the young man's face. "I trust it is not on your honor, General," he says earnestly. "But these spies, I cannot see the point, wasting good men and coin on bribes and skulking. Why should any tribesmen come to us, when they so fear Mago, Hasdrubal, and Gisgo?"

"That is just the reason. Because they so fear them. We will offer them the greatest 'bribe' of all: the chance to fight for their freedom, as equals among us."

Marcus looks at Laelius, who merely shrugs. They turn to leave when Marcus pauses. "If the men are to finish their training in three days, what will they be doing the other two?"

Scipio stares at them with feigned surprise, and a boyish twinkle momentarily returns to his eyes. "Why, they will be baking biscuits, of course!"

*   *   *   *   *

TOLETUM, CENTRAL IBERIA. The svelte young woman deftly grabs the sword-sized tusk that swings toward her face. "Boodes, stop it!" she chides, frowning into the house-sized pachyderm's face. With a childlike groan of protest, the elephant quits pitching its head about. "I know, I know … it feels good, does it not?" she says soothingly, stroking its face. She retrieves her thick linen cloth and resumes drying Boodes' trunk, careful to wipe the creases between its enormous nose. The elephant utters a low roar of pleasure and wraps its trunk about her slim waist, snaking it down her hips. The slaves scrubbing the elephant's back grin at the sight of Gisgo's daughter washing the dusty beast while wearing a princess' white silk robe and golden circlet. Her father might tell Sophonisba what she has to wear on this high council meeting day, but he cannot not tell her what to do while she is wearing it.

Masinissa strides over to the stream where Sophonisba and her attendants are working, just as she finishes polishing the war elephant's tusks. "Beloved," he says with alarm, "what are you doing?" Wiping her hands on a wool scrap, she makes a face at her betrothed. "Just what I want to do, Prince Masinissa. No more, no less."

He nods his head toward the slaves. "May we have a word. Alone?" She sighs, pitches the scrap to the ground, and walks over to stroke Boodes' head. "I'll be back in a minute, love," she says.

Masinissa shakes his head. "It is beyond me why you engage in such slave work. You could be trampled on a whim."

She laughs at him. "Working with the great animals is the noblest of tasks. There is a dignity and honesty to their souls that I rarely find in men. And a purer love. Besides," she says coquettishly, shaking her hips as she looks over her shoulder, "I am in more danger of being trampled by that horde of suitors that did waddle over to my father, seeking to buy my place in their bed. Fat old men with icy hands," she remarks with a feigned shudder.

Masinissa lays his long fingers lightly on her shoulder, completely covering it. "Those days are past you now, my princess. Gisgo has granted me the treasure of your hand, as long as I serve his ends."

"Is that the only reason you follow my father?" she asks, studying his face.

He smiles sheepishly. "You know it is not. The Generals pledge their troops in my war to take the throne from Syphax the Usurper. When the Romans are driven from here, they will sail with me to Numidia. Then I will reunite the divided kingdoms." A boyish eagerness creeps into his reserved demeanor, an aspect Sophonisba most loves and too rarely sees. "Just think. No more wars against Carthage. No more wars against each other. Two nations in peace!"

Sophonisba reaches up and strokes his cheek, smiling tenderly. "You have such a noble heart. Your dreams are so good, but your means of achieving them are so bad. Do all the Romans have to die? Do you have to be as ruthless as my father?"

His eyes darken, and the grin disappears. "Your father holds my nephew hostage at Cartago Nova. A gesture of 'good faith' on my part, he calls it."

Sophonisba stares curiously at him. "You have not mentioned him before, though your troubles for him have shown on your face. For sake of our love, I beg you, do not hide your heart from me."

Masinissa bows his head slightly, embarrassed. "He is such a bright and trusting child. He cried if he saw even a chicken killed. His parents were slain when Syphax ravaged our village in search of me. I raised him myself. I am all the parents he has. Now his life is forfeit if I do not follow the Generals' wishes!" He sheepishly bows his head. "Forgiveness, beloved. I forget Gisgo is your father."

"No apologies, I know my father. But you must persist in your service," urges Sophonisba. "That oily Syphax sailed to Cartago Nova and met my father there. He still presses suit to wed me."

"It is not a worry as long as my men continue to win our skirmishes with the slow-moving Romans. They are mighty fighters, but very predictable … at least until now." Masinissa walks over to Boodes, running his hand along the beast's massive head, thoughtful. "This new man, this young Scipio, I have seen him in battle, back when Hannibal and I destroyed the legions at Cannae. He is not like the others." Masinissa grabs one of Boodes' tusks in both hands, feeling the beast's gargantuan power as the elephant easily pulls it away from him.

Sophonisba looks puzzled. "This Scipio is stronger than the others? Bolder?"

Masinissa smirks ruefully. "Worse. The boy has imagination."

* * * * *

The setting sun pulls lengthy shadows across Tarraco's wide town square, drawing dusky waves around the Roman officers gathered for the trial. Clad in his battle armor and red cape, Scipio faces a dozen of his tribunes, six from each legion. The tribunal has gathered to judge the guilt and sentence of the prisoner. The tribunes are accompanied by the dux—the leader—of each allied legion, and a handful of tribal chiefs from their Ilergetes and Lacetani allies. The non-Romans are there to bear witness to the judgment rendered by Scipio and the tribunes. Laelius and Marcus Silenus flank Scipio, acting as his counselors. The attendees converse quietly among themselves as they glance at the locked stone storage house behind them, waiting for the guards to bring out the accused.

Marcus bends to Scipio's ear. "However you deal with this man," he says quietly, "everyone will know about it. You cannot let his deeds go unpunished."

Scipio nods ruefully. "That is the good and the bad of it, is it not?"

Marcus looks hard at the youth, shrugs, and says, "If that is what you say, General," then he faces away from Scipio.

"I was unclear. I mean, I can use this gossip as a tool. If we ourselves tell the Iberians that we are trustworthy, will they believe us? But if their own tribesmen talk about some trustworthy act that we performed, that they witnessed, that testimony carries the weight of truth. Do you see?"

Marcus blinks, shrugs again. "Whatever you do to this betrayer redounds through Iberia." He stares levelly at his young general. "And whatever you do not do."

"The philosophers say that mercy is what sets us apart from the savages. It is the mark of a civilized man," says Scipio.

Marcus' mouth twitches in the barest of smiles. "Fear is what keeps the savages at bay," he says, "for 'civilized" and 'weak' bear the same meaning to them."

Scipio stares at Marcus. "I do hear you, Marcus." He turns to look at Laelius. "Difficult choices," Scipio sighs.

Laelius spreads his hands. "But it is your choice to make, at least. You now have the power. You do not have to follow Fabius, or Sempronius, or those other fools." Laelius grins at Scipio. "It is much more preferable than impotently cursing others' decisions that affect you, wouldn't you say?"

Scipio's right hand twitches nervously, then his arm. He bobs his arm to quell its spasms, glancing at the tribunes to see if they noticed. He takes a deep breath. "Bring in the spy," he says flatly. Several guards trot over to an adjoining storage house and unlock the iron door. They drag out the accused, the man who posed as a beggar and took the scroll from the tribal priest. The man is still in his brown wool tunic, but his cloak is gone, revealing a brawny young Iberian with beaked nose and obsidian eyes; eyes that look defiantly into Scipio's face.

The guards drag the unbound Iberian in front of Scipio. The consul unrolls a small scroll and reads from it. "You, Javier Zapater, are charged with treason and murder. While serving as a spy for Rome, you deliberately provided false and misleading intelligence about the placement of Carthaginian soldiers in your town, saying none were there when you knew threescore cavalry were present. You then warned the Carthaginians that our diplomatic party would arrive there to recruit the tribe. This resulted in the capture and flayed crucifixion of six legionnaires and one of our senior tribunes, as well as the priest who was our informant." Scipio rolls up the scroll and smirks at the young Iberian. "Unfortunately for you, you did not know there were other informants in the tribe, ones who witnessed the slaughter. What do you have to say to these accusations?"

The spy proudly raises his head. "I was never a spy for you. I fight for my people. I am Javier Zapater, son of Ander Zapater, chief of the iron-eating Bergestani, a man whom you Romans murdered. I only wish you were with that group, that your skin would be hanging from my tribesmen's hut."

Scipio remains impassive, but he studies the tribunes' faces to gauge their reaction. To a man, they mirror repressed fury at Zapater. "I know not your father, nor do I care about his fate," says Scipio. "You were paid well to serve us, and you rewarded us with betrayal. The priest, your own tribesman, he cursed your name even as they raked the skin from his body." Scipio turns to his tribunes. "You have heard all this from our Iberian allies, is that not the truth?" Several tribunes solemnly nod their agreement.

The Iberian lunges forward to spit on Scipio's legs before the guards pull him back. "Roman pig," he sneers, "you think you could buy my loyalty after your father's men locked us into our own city and burned it to the ground? My family died screaming."

Scipio turns to the tribunal, his arms spread as if giving testimony. "Publius Scipio did what was necessary. The Begistani betrayed us. They joined the Carthaginians and gave them food and weapons—the same Carthaginians who later killed my father and uncle." Scipio turns to the tribunes. "In the matter of this man, what say you?"

One by one, the tribunes extend their right arms and turn their thumbs down. Scipio's mouth tightens. "Guilty as charged." He turns to the betrayer. "You are guilty of treason and murder. As consul of Rome and governor of Iberia, it is my duty to mete punishment. You are sentenced to death."

Javier's voice quavers, but he holds his head high. "I fear not your Roman sword, boy."

Scipio can see the men watching him, and he thinks of Marcus' words. He knows treason is punished by crucifixion, and the legions' designated executioners are waiting. He also knows that many of his men doubt him, this raw young general with a scholar's mien, and that his leadership is in jeopardy. He weighs mercy versus justice, and the impact of each.

Scipio steps back and takes off his armor, carefully laying down each piece as the tribunal members look on, confused. When he has stripped down to his tunic, he bends over and takes his favorite throwing knife from his belt, a leaf-shaped blade which he uses to shave. He walks to the young Iberian. "Hold him," says Scipio. "Hold his legs." Two more guards rush in and lock their arms about the man's trembling legs, holding their grip even as the terrified Iberian's urine runs down his leg and over their fists. Scipio stands face-to-face with the convicted. "If you do not fear my sword, perhaps you should fear my knife."

Scipio lunges forward. He grabs Zapater's hair and yanks his head back. In one swift movement, Scipio digs his knife into the man's upper throat and carves a deep gash across Zapater's neck as his victim frantically twists his head. Blood gushes over Scipio as he steps back, waiting for the outpouring to subside. The dying man slumps in the arms of his captors, his feet kicking spasmodically "Hold his head up," Scipio says.

As one of the guards pulls Javier's head back, Scipio steps in and digs his fingers into the man's throat gash. Reaching up, he grasps the man's tongue and pulls it down through the opening in his neck. The tongue lolls from the Iberian's gurgling throat like a dark crimson tie, flapping on his bloodied neck. The tribunal members gape in amazement, looking at one another.

Expressionless, Scipio hunches over and wipes his knife and hands on the victim's tunic, careful to hide his shaking hands. He turns and faces his stunned officers. "Hang this man from a cross in front of the gates. Hang him at eye level, that all can see him. Let his tongue be a symbol of those who would lie to Rome, that all who deceive us will be paid in kind. This tribunal is over."

Wordlessly, the tribunes and chieftains walk away, many staring at the young general as they leave. Scipio stands with arms crossed, watching them go. Marcus and Laelius walk up behind him.

"Where in the fuck did *that* little trick come from?" bursts Laelius. "That's the most gruesome thing I've ever seen!" He peers into his face. "Who *are* you, Scippy? Who are you becoming?"

"I am not him anymore," says Scipio distractedly. "I can't be, if I would make this army an arm of my will."

Marcus Silenus furrows his brow. "I heard a tale of Cyrus the Persian, enemy of Greece, and what he did to the Spartans he captured, to those who would not talk. Something akin what you have done."

Scipio looks somberly at Marcus. "You are right, Centurion. I read about him when I was a youth. The writing about Cyrus was very ... informative about how he did it. But I did not know if I could do it." He manages a sickly grin. "Uh ... I mean, if I could do it right."

Marcus gives the barest of nods. "The tale will spread like a gale across the nations of the north, I have no doubt." Marcus grasps the top of Scipio's forearm in a stiff grip and shakes it. "You did well, General."

Scipio merely stares at the blood circle in the sand. "I also remember reading a scroll about Aristotle that our tutor Asclepius gave to us," he says dreamily. "Remember him, Laelius?"

Laelius studies his friend's face carefully. "Yes, Scippy," he says softly. "Good old Asclepius."

"It was Plato, was it not?" says Scipio, pacing about as he stares at the twilight sky. "He talked about the philosopher king. What was it? Oh yes, that the philosopher was a person of wisdom and morals, the best person to rule, yes." He stops and looks back at the blood spot, his eyes unfocused. "But such a man would never want to rule because the philosopher knew the corrupting effect of governance, of power. Of being responsible for others' lives."

Laelius manages a confused grin. "It was something like that, as I recall," he says, scratching his head. "Or what I could figure out he said. He said the people had to force the philosopher to govern, or risk getting the leaders they earned by not doing so."

Scipio looks at both of them. "As a child, I never understood those words, but now I think I do. Yes, I certainly do ...."

Marcus Silenus' face tightens with impatience—and concern. "I have only heard about this Plato fellow," he says gruffly, "but I know this: If you were not directing this army, it could have been Fabius. Or that Flaccus character. And disaster would follow."

Scipio sighs. "Yes, that was another thing about inducing the wise man to be king—that the only reason he would do it was fear that a lesser man would rule in his stead. But with that knowledge, you become no less responsible for whatever malice ensues." Scipio rubs the back of his neck. "Ah, I am babbling. I must go to my tent. Tomorrow then, at the third hour."

As Scipio trudges back to his command tent, two tribunes stop at a wine merchant's stand for a goblet of Rioja, the region's famous wine. The younger tribune, a carefully groomed patrician, turns to his fellow officer. "By Jupiter's balls, the boy is not the bookish pussy that Flaccus made him out to be. He has some sand in his ass."

The middle-aged tribune, a gaunt and weathered former Senator nicknamed "Hannibal," scratches beneath his eye patch. "This Scipio has some mysterious new ideas about war," replies the other officer. "But I would no longer call him 'boy,' my soft-handed friend. He took this post when no other would step forward, not even your Flaccus and Fabius." The tribune drains his cup and stalks off, as the other watches.

Scipio pauses in front of his command tent and immediately sheds his blood-soaked tunic and subligaculum, flinging them away from the tent. Naked, he enters. He turns to one of his personal guards. "Is she coming?" Scipio asks as he dips his hands into a large bronze wash bowl. "Is everything as I requested?"

The guard nods. "Yes, General. It took some time in the finding of her, but all is arranged and waiting."

Scipio mops his torso with a scrap of old tunic. "Send her in. Let no one else enter."

The guard disappears and returns shortly with a slim young girl walking next to him, clad in a flowing robe of finest indigo silk. She walks slowly with eyes downcast, stepping as carefully as if she were in a procession. Without a word, the guard gently pushes her forward and exits the tent.

Scipio finishes toweling his muscular body and turns to stand naked before her, as relaxed as if he were wearing robes.

"Welcome to my tent," he says warmly. "What may I call you?"

The young woman averts her eyes from Scipio's nakedness, but she stutters out a reply, nervously twisting the hem of her robe. "My name is Garbi Jasso. I am the oldest daughter of Roderick Jasso, Tarraco's wealthiest silver trader." Garbi reflexively raises her face while talking to Scipio, but her eyes inadvertently wander down to his sizable penis. She turns scarlet and stares down with all her might.

Scipio grins at her modesty and steps over to his clothes chest. He beckons for her to sit on a nearby couch as he shrugs into a short gray tunic. "Salve, Garbi. I am blessed to meet you. I am Publius—for tonight, just 'Publius.' I have had enough of titles for the day."

Scipio sits at the couch adjoining hers, seeing her relax as he keeps his distance from her. He rises and picks up an earthen pitcher and two goblets from a table, bringing them back to her. "Will you take wine with me? I have memories to wash away, and you would help."

Garbi nods mutely, and Scipio fills her glass. He brings over a plate of eggplant, peppers, and roast pork. They dine quietly, Garbi watching his every move, as Scipio stares reflectively at the tent walls. He shakes himself from his reverie, and eyes her appreciatively. "You are, I was told, of fifteen years. Is that correct?" Seeing her nod, Scipio says, "Well, I am twenty-six, almost twenty-seven. How do I appear to you?"

"Why, you are an older man," Garbi responds innocently, "but that I do not mind. What I mean, Gen— ... er ... Publius is you are still young, not hardly wrinkled at all. Just ... older."

Scipio laughs. "Yes, an older man," he says half to himself. "And we older men are all grown up now, with nothing to prove. Gods above, I would it were so." He raises his cup to her and pours a dab of wine onto the ground. "This is a sacrifice to the goddess Venus, for bringing you to me. I am thankful for your presence tonight, beautiful one." For the first time, Garbi looks into his eyes and smiles.

Laying down his goblet, Scipio stands and extends his hand to her. "The hour grows long. Let us to bed." Scipio gently pulls her up from the couch, leading her over to a large feather-stuffed bag. Garbi faces him next to the mattress as he strokes her face until he feels her tensions begin to subside. He reaches his hands behind her, grasping the knot of her dress. A whimper escapes her, which she quickly stifles. Scipio pauses. "Apologies if I make you uncomfortable. You have never lain with a man, is that correct?"

"No, Publius," she says in the barest of whispers, her face crimson. "My father has kept my virginity as a treasure. He said that someday it would be worth much to our family. Is that what you paid for?" She looks up at him, blinks innocently, and looks away. "I have not even known a man's caress, only some boys' awkward fumblings."

"Be at ease, my dove," says Scipio. "This will not be what you think it is. Days ago, when I paid for you to come here," he continues, "I did dream of putting myself into you, of having your mouth consume my seed. But that was long ago, when I was but a lustful boy, not a general doing what I have just done. Now I would ask only one thing."

"I know," Garbi says, moving her hand to cover his limp penis. "I but need your help. You must tell me what to do." She bends over and begins to put her mouth on him. Scipio gently pushes her back. "What I ask of you is to stay with me tonight. Sleep with me, dear girl. I want someone next to me, for just one nigh. "

Garbi nods her. Scipio turns her until she is lying with her back to him. He nestles up against her, cradling his center against her firm little buttocks, his hand draped across her chest.

Scipio pinches the light off the bedside candle and settles back into Garbi, stroking her hair. As he pulls a pillow under his head, he offers a prayer to Febris, the goddess of fever dreams. *Please, not tonight. I have horrors enough for one day.*

IV. THE SWORD OF ROME

ROME, 210 BCE. "You cannot elect this man consul," screams Flaccus. "He brutalized the citizens of Sicily! The man has spent thousands of denarii for which he cannot account!"

Three Sicilian nobles stand on the Senate floor, shifting about nervously. The Latin Party has recruited them to testify about Marcus Claudius Marcellus' wasteful war spending in Sicily—testimony given for a price. One by one, the nobles declare that Marcellus was seen giving silver to his common soldiers, that he bought prize stallions for allied chieftains, and—worst of all—that he purchased Greek statuary to adorn his command quarters.

General Fabius rises from his seat in the front row to echo Flaccus' sentiments. "We have made the mistake of electing Marcellus as consul three other times. Yes, he has won some battles for us, but at what price to the resources we could provide for the other generals and their troops? We must not—not, I say—elect him again!"

Marcus Iulius, a Senator unaffiliated with either party, rises from the third row, his face florid with anger. "What Latin madness takes worthy Flaccus and Fabius? Is this the voice of their heart, or the voice of their Party? Marcellus took Sicily back from the Carthaginians, in spite of the limited resources you gave him. If not for his resourcefulness, we might all be hanging from a Carthaginian crucifix!"

Marcellus stands straight and proud before the Senate, restraining the sardonic grin that never seems to leave his face. He looks at each Senator in turn, his eyes lingering on Flaccus and Fabius. Then he speaks.

"Fulvius is dead, and Hannibal has decimated his army. I know our fate hangs by a thread. I will take the remnants of his legions and restore Rome's honor." He glances back at Flaccus and Fabius, and his grin widens. "Now, for some of you in these chambers, I give you the best news of all: I will defeat Hannibal or I will not return. And if I do return, I will go back to Sicily. One way or another, I will no longer be here for the sport of the Senate. So you had best find yourself another scapegoat."

With a smirk at the Latin Party contingent on the left side rows, he spins on his heel and strides forth from the Senate, his back ramrod straight and his head held high.

* * * * *

SAGUNTUM, EASTERN IBERIA, 210 BCE. "Ah, shit, I'm ready to fall asleep on my horse," grouses Pando, his fingers teasing the curly black beard that envelops his face. The Libyan scratches his broad backside and shifts restlessly in his saddle. "We've been clopping around these puny little hills all night, and all I've seen is a couple fishermen pulling their boats to shore down there by that boulder." He stares at them again. "Huh! Looks like they've got a big swordfish, not a bad night's haul. And look there, one of them has his wineskin out already. There's a man after my own heart!"

"I am thankful we have nothing else to worry about," retorts Leon, his older companion, gesturing with his right hand's two remaining fingers. "I was with Hannibal when we took this city from the Romans. There was killing enough then, boy, enough for my lifetime. Another year here and I return to Africa. I want it quiet."

Pando grimaces. "What kind of life is that, without any death! I haven't killed a Roman since we decimated those Scipio brothers a couple years ago. ... Look, that fisherman is waving us down. He wants to have a drink with us!"

Pando starts to descend when Leon grasps his arm. "Best we stay up here and keep our eyes on the coast," he cautions. "That was our assignment."

Pando shrugs Leon's arm off him. "Fuck the assignment, I need some wine!" He pushes his horse down the shallow slope and trots across the narrow plain to the four fishermen, who by now have tugged their boat up onto the sand. Leon curses Pando, but he follows him down, scrutinizing the landscape as he goes. The two Libyans are soon passing a wineskin around with the lean young Edetani, who are clad only in brief loincloths, obviously weaponless. The Libyans can only speak a pidgin of the local language, so there is little conversation but much drinking. A second wineskin appears, and laughter ensues.

Leon sips sparingly, waiting out his sybaritic companion. He stares out into the moonlit Mediterranean, watching the flickering whitecaps on the sea, and relaxes. Roaming his eyes across the watery landscape, he spies the shadowy outline of a ship in the distance, coming in from his left. He squints harder, and the outline becomes a score of ships, all heading south, each with the unmistakable outline of a Roman trireme. It is Laelius' fleet, heading toward Cartago Nova.

Leon's eyes start from his head, and he spins toward his mildly drunk companion. "Pando!" he shrieks. "Raiders! A Roman fleet! We must get to Saguntum!" Pando drops the wineskin and turns to find his horse. As he does, one of the fisherman yanks a harpoon out of the boat, grasping the thick spear at its bottom and midsection. Running forward, he hurls the harpoon overhand, skewering Pando through his back. The other three pull out their fillet knives and slice Leon's throat in three places; half his blood gushes out before he can fall to the sand.

The fisherman with the harpoon holds a burning torch aloft and waves it back and forth, three times. As soon as he finishes the third wave, four black-caped riders dart out from the trees, scrambling down the hillside and surging north along the narrow coastal plain. The riders wear the short grey tunics and leather skullcaps of the local Edetani. They pull up next to the hulks of several rotted fishing boats, where the lead rider waves his hand thrice over his head and waits silently.

IV. The Sword of Rome

After several minutes, a Roman cavalry scout appears from around a bend in the coast. He trots up to the riders, waving his arm in welcome. There is a quick, hushed conversation, and the riders dash back the way they had come, dissolving into the lowland forest. All is quiet on the beach.

A half hour later, a soft rumbling sound creeps in from the north, growing louder. The first lines of Scipio's marching column soon appear around a bend, the soldiers striding rapidly through the night. Scipio's scout cavalry dash by the fishermen to gallop into the trees and the plains south of the incoming army, reconnoitering for enemies. Scipio leads vanguard of the columns, riding with Marcus Silenus. There is little sound in their passing, other than the cadenced stamping of thousands of sandals. To their distant right looms the Carthaginian fortress town of Saguntum, its thousands of warriors unaware that an enemy army is passing beneath it. Scipio's army snakes by without incident.

Hours later, as the army nears the port town of Valentia, it halts near a quiet cove where several triremes rest at anchor. Laelius and his marines are standing near several large rafts on the shore. Hundreds of sacks of grain and dried fruit are stacked along the beach, arranged as a temporary fort in case of attack. As the army nears the cove, Scipio calls his senior tribunes to him and directs them to pitch camp on the flatlands around the cove. "We will leave at the second hour in the morning, after the men have had some sleep. Organize a detail to distribute the food."

The first lines of legionnaires spread out onto the plain, with guards immediately posted along the perimeter. There is no trench digging or wall building for this mobile army; the men pitch their tents and sleep with arms at the ready, under the shelter of a double guard. Most of them quickly consume the remnants of their buccelatum and dried fruit and immediately stretch out inside their tents and doze. Even as some legionnaires fall asleep, thousands continue to pour into the camp, their centurions leading them to their designated camp spot. The few mules that accompany the army are led to a makeshift corral. They are given their feed for the day and left to rest. Everything is accomplished quickly and silently, part of the attack stratagem that Scipio will employ for the rest of his military life.

The young general dismounts by the feed sacks, where he clasps arms with Laelius. "Thank the gods you arrived on time," says Scipio. "The men were down to the crumbs of their last meal."

"We had to sail out farther than we expected," says Laelius. "Some Carthaginian scout ships were prowling the coast. But everything was fine once we neared Saguntum." He gestures at the food sacks. "Look, we had enough time to unload already. There's some bandages and medicine in those dark blue bags, by the way. And some extra swords and pila on that far raft."

Scipio waves off the offer. "Thank Jupiter, we have had no major engagements yet," he says. "Our Edetani scouts cleared the way for us. They blended right into the fishermen, and the Carthaginians rode right by them." Scipio frowns worriedly. "We just have to make sure they are duly paid. Without money, their loyalty is transient, I fear."

Laelius winces. "Hmm, demon finance rears its ugly face again. How goes our purse?" he asks.

"Not well," replies Scipio. "We will not have enough for legionary salary and supplies, once we pay the natives. We are fortunate we are on the march. We can withhold the men's pay because they have no place to spend it!"

"So that is the answer, to keep marching and fighting so our men won't need money? I do not think that will suffice to fool Felix and the other auditors!" Laelius jingles the purse on his belt. "Thank the gods I have charge of the shipboard treasury. I would have not coin for boys and wine!"

"Ah yes, the necessities," says Scipio sarcastically. "But you are in the same plight as the men, with no opportunity to buy anything!" He looks about to ascertain no one is listening. "Cartago Nova is our break point,

Laelius. If we do not take it, we have not the funds to continue the war."

Laelius shakes his head. "But even if you take it, how will we continue? Our Senate funding will be low, thanks to our Latin Party friends, and all plunder must be sent to Rome."

"Rome," sighs Scipio, "sent to Rome. Sent to the very men who strangle our throats." He turns his head from his friend, looking out into the peaceful cove. "I will but say, let me walk that path when Cartago Nova falls. I have an idea."

"Which is?" prods Laelius.

"Which is something I shall keep to myself," Scipio replies. He looks intently at Laelius. "For your own protection."

Laelius starts to speak, but Scipio raises his hand. "I need some sleep. Let me return to my tent. I shall see you by Cartago Nova, five days hence."

Laelius watches his childhood friend stalk back to camp, slumped with weariness. "Sleep well, Scippy," he calls out to Scipio. "And whatever you plan to do, I know you have our interests at heart."

Scipio heads up the shallow rise to the camp, pausing to exhort the soldiers relaying food. The marines have formed four feeder lines to the camp and pass the sacks of food along to each other, eventually handing them off to legionnaires who distribute it. He goes into his small command tent and flops onto the only bedroll that he has begrudged himself. He lights a candle and stares at the goatskin roof, praying for another dreamless sleep.

* * * * *

LUCANIA PROVINCE, SOUTHERN ITALIA, 210 BCE. Riding high on top of Surus, Hannibal stares down upon the rolling plains of Numistro, watching the dust clouds of the Roman army that is slowly coming into view. *By the gods*, he thinks, *who do they have left to fight us?* He turns back to survey his Libyan and Iberian infantry, stacked in serried ranks so numerous it appears that a forest of spears has grown behind him. He checks the thousands of cavalry on his flanks and affirms that all are there, waiting for the command. *My men are ready. It is up to me.*

"Here they come," says Maharbal, Hannibal's wild-haired cavalry commander. "The Romans approach, or whatever is left of them." He laughs as he cleans his nails with his dagger, studying its point to see what he digs out. "Maybe they are bringing their women to fight. And why not? They could not do worse."

Hannibal squints at the approaching ranks. "I know not. Our intelligence is poor about this army. But those flanking troops might be Umbrians. If so, we should concentrate on breaking them first. They fight like rabble."

Maharbal nods, now picking his teeth with the knife. "They are Umbrians. They have those large crested helmets and thick spears. See, there's a phalanx of them on each side. The center lines are all Romans. Two legions, if I count their standards aright. So there are fifteen, twenty thousand men out there." He tucks his dagger back into his sheath. "I didn't know they had that many left, but no matter. There will be far fewer of them to worry about when the suns sets today.

"Sargon, come here!" Maharbal shouts, and his captain hurries over. "Send the Libyan cavalry to our right flank. Tell the Numidians to join the Balearic slingers on our left. They are to wait for my signal." Maharbal turns back to Hannibal and grins sarcastically. "So, will you take my advice this time and head for Rome after our victory? Or do you intend to become like that old General Fabius, dodging battles with your enemy, waiting for them to die of old age!"

Hannibal laughs and starts to reply when he notices the armor on the commander riding in front of the legions. Even at this distance he can identify its unique configuration: the man wears the ornate bronze breastplates of a Gallic king. There is only one Roman soldier allowed to wear such barbaric armor, the man who killed the fearsome Gallic king Viridomarus in hand-to-hand combat and took his armor. A man who is only the second soldier in Roman history to win the *spolia optima*, the best of spoils, by personally killing the enemy's leader.

He is back, curses Hannibal to himself. *That smirking fool has returned!*

As the armies draw closer, Hannibal can see it is truly him, his worst enemy. The army commander is a tall, gangly, scarecrow of a man, with a dark shock of hair rioting across his helmetless head, his elephantine ears sticking sideways from it. His angular face is creased with the horse-toothed smile that rarely leaves it, even in the midst of battle. General Marcus Claudius Marcellus, the Sword of Rome, has returned to confront him.

Thrice Hannibal and Marcellus have battled, each time for control of the valuable Nola supply depot. The battles endured the entire day, with nightfall the only victor, although Hannibal suffered the more grievous losses. Each time, the Carthaginian lured Marcellus' men into envelopments, surrounding the Romans to break their ranks. Each time, Marcellus' iron determination kept the Romans in formation and discipline. Marcellus would ride across his front lines, ignoring the stones and javelins flying at him, urging his men to maintain shield distance from each other, to defend their brothers, and to always face the enemy. Each time, the Roman lines bent but did not break, as Marcellus would gallop to the weakest spots and muster the forces there. Hannibal knew that breaking those disciplined ranks would cost too many men, so each time he reluctantly withdrew from the field, just when victory was at hand. Now Marcellus is back for another fight, leading two of Rome's few remaining legions.

Marcellus is well aware his old opponent is in front of him. Hannibal is easily visible to him, standing in front of the dread Libyan infantry in the center, riding an elephant garbed in blood red armor. He turns to his Master of Horse and barks out a laugh. "There he is, Atilius. Still alive and feisty, may Jupiter damn him!" He grins and rubs the back of his neck. "I'll wager that one-eyed bastard came to Lucania just to have another go at me. I bet he is quite cocky after his big victory over Fulvius, but we will teach him a lesson!"

Hannibal pulls his sarissa from its saddle pouch and whips Surus' flanks with the fifteen-foot spear. The elephant trundles down the hillside as the Carthaginian battle horns blare the signal to advance. The heavy Libyan infantry march down behind their leader. They tramp toward the center of the Roman lines, which are hurriedly shifting into a more closely packed battle formation.

Well aware of Hannibal's penchant for envelopments, and for capitalizing on his opponents' impatience, Marcellus has rearranged his lines especially for this battle. Instead of a wide front line that is three deep with men from both his legions, he stations the second legion's 4,000 men behind the first legion, so they may quickly refresh their fellows. He has organized his cavalry's two alae in the same manner on each flank. *That bastard will surely have a surprise for me*, Marcellus thinks, *but I will have one for him.*

The Carthaginian army reaches the bottom of the shallow hill and strides toward their enemy as the Roman cornu trumpet the battle warning. Hannibal is flanked by the three hundred members of his Sacred Band, wealthy Carthaginians who fight only for the love of battle; all are superb swordsmen and all have sworn to defend their general to the death.

A phalanx of grim Libyans dominates the center attack lines: 3,600 black-bearded men grouped in squares of thirty-six, each square bristling with spears like a hedgehog of death. Wearing the same stiff linen cuirass that Hannibal wears, the Libyans make not a sound beyond the faint clanking of their domed brass helmets and round wooden shields. Almost all of them wield a short Roman sword that they scavenged from the destroyed legions at Trebia, Trasimene, and Cannae. Of all Hannibal's veteran warriors, the Libyans are the most Roman in their deadly organization and efficiency.

Three thousand Gauls stalk along behind the Libyans, marching with their tribal groups, waiting for a chance to rush the Roman lines. These are tall, broad men, their hairy chests and arms decorated with blue and red clan tattoos. Some wear the chain mail vests the Gauls invented, but many of the most deadly warriors are fighting naked, to show their disdain for their armored enemy. The barbarians heft an ax or broadsword, heavy weapons that can easily cleave a Roman helmet—and the head within it. Singing, shouting, drinking, and cursing, the Gauls tramp forward, lusting to gain honor and glory, or die a glorious warrior's death.

Hannibal's Iberian mercenaries flank each side of the Libyans and Gauls, men with long spears and brightly plumed helmets. The mercenaries are Carpetani and Celtiberian tribesmen recently shipped to him from his brothers Mago and Hasdrubal, to help replace the men he has lost from his recent battles. As untested troops, Hannibal uses them on each flank, to prevent an encirclement by the Roman cavalry or infantry. Though new to Italia, the Iberians lust for the honor of conquering the Romans in their own land, and for the wealth from ransacking their towns. The Iberians march forward, ringing their iron-tipped javelins against their large oblong shields and chanting tribal war songs. They are exuberant.

The Carthaginian army quickly closes upon the Romans, who wait stolidly behind their wall of shields. Scores of Libyan light infantry burst out from between their countrymen's front lines. They rush forward and quickly fling their three javelins at the Romans and allies, raining short iron spears upon them. The infantrymen close their shields in front of them and over their heads, creating a turtle shell to ward off the throws. Even so, some of the javelins find their way through openings, as scores of anguished cries attest. Several legionnaires grab the Carthaginian javelins to hurl them back, only to find that the Iberian javelin heads bend on impact, rendering them useless for a return volley.

Marcellus barks a command, and his velites rush out from under the turtle shell of shields, dashing through the spaces between the maniples. The velites are Rome's light infantry, young men just starting their military careers, most too poor to afford armor or horse. The velites pitch their pila low and hard at the tunic-clad Libyan throwers, ignoring the heavy infantry behind them. Hundreds of the Africans fall, pierced by the pitiless bronze. Many of them try to crawl back to their lines even as they die from pierced lungs and bowels, crying for help, crying for their loved ones. The relentless armored Libyans step over these unfortunates without breaking step, as they prepare to clash with the grim Romans awaiting them.

Hannibal waves his sarissa thrice above his head, and his battle horns sound three times. Five hundred Libyan cavalry ride out from the sides of the infantry lines, looping far around the Iberians on the flanks, heading for the rear of Marcellus' infantry.

The Sword of Rome has prepared for this, however. He leans over and speaks to a tribune, who rushes back to the second legion. Within minutes, the legion has turned to face outward, guarding the first legion's back. Marcellus smiles smugly. *No encirclement this time*, he gloats, *I know your tricks*. The general watches as his Roman cavalry, lead by staunch Atilius, ride out to intercept the outnumbered Libyan riders. A whirling, circling, dust-clouded fight erupts among the cavalries as they thrust and hack at each other. *Strange*, thinks Marcellus, *I thought Hannibal has more cavalry than that*.

The Roman general is distracted from his thoughts by an ear-splitting wave of battle screams from the front lines. The Gauls have charged en masse out through the Libyan lines, hurtling forward in clannish groups, eager to be the first to take an enemy head. Heedless of the armored wall in front of them, the berserking warriors leap onto the legionnaires, chopping them down with shield-splitting force. The centurions yell for their charges to step and thrust, and as one the first line of hastati, the younger soldiers, push back into the Gauls, daggering their swords into unprotected stomachs and chests. Many of the wounded Gauls fall, writhing with mortal wounds, but most battle on, spitting defiantly at those who wounded them, some killing their opponent even as the man's sword dangles from their body. Scores of

Gauls fight their way through the first two lines of the hastati and principes, leaving a wake of Romans on the ground, only to be surrounded and speared to death like a cornered bear.

For a half hour the front-line fight is a swarming tumult of Gauls, Romans, and allies, with neither side giving ground. As if by common consent, the two exhausted lines finally step back from each other, and a lull ensues. The tribunes order their second line of legionnaires forward, the veteran principes. They charge ahead in formation and beat back the ferocious Gauls.

Seeing Rome's best fighters dominating the undisciplined Gauls, Hannibal knows they have used up their shock value, and it is time for a new assault. He shouts a command to one of his Sacred Band officers. The horns sound twice, and the Libyans push through their barbarian allies and clash with the first legion.

Now the infantry battle is a fight between two structured armies, each struggling to maintain their straight lines and rectangular formations, as they swing and stab with their swords. The Libyans duck and dart about in their confined space, aiming their scavenged Roman blades at any unarmored spots, often hacking a man's hamstring to bring him crashing to the earth. The Romans ram their scuta into their opponents' smaller round shields, knocking them off balance and creating openings for a telling thrust. The remaining Gauls attack in the spaces between the Libyan phalanxes, but many of them have wandered back behind the lines, satisfied with their prize of a legionnaire's armor or head.

The Libyans slowly push the tiring principes back. The centurions shout for them to regroup, and the principes back up and pause behind the legion's third line of defense, the triarii. The triarii are the most veteran of all the Roman soldiers, men who have been through the most battles. The triarii kneel down and plant their long spears into the earth, creating a deadly bulwark against any who try to breach it. The older men halt the Libyans in their tracks, buying enough time for the hastati to march out between the spears and plunge back into the weakening Libyans, followed by the principes. Marcellus rages across the infantry lines, exhorting them forward, making fun of the Libyans, even dismounting to fight next to his men. Wherever he goes, his men fight with renewed vigor. And the Romans hold.

Now Hannibal leads the Libyans into a charge on the Romans' front lines, accompanied by his Sacred Band. He rampages Surus into the legionnaires and spears men with his sarissa while Surus tramples many more. The Sacred Band swarm around him, cutting down many of the hastati, heedless of their own heavy losses. The assault breeds chaos and fear among the lightly armored hastati along the front lines. The Gauls and Libyans follow in their leader's destructive wake, breaking into the principes in the second line of defense.

The principes initially retreat under the onslaught, but the tribunes signal for these heavily armored veterans to replace the weakening hastati, and the front line stiffens. Fighting within their six-foot space, the skilled principes exact a heavy toll on the remaining Gauls, and then the Libyans. On the flanks of the legions, Rome's Umbrian allies take heart and push forward with renewed vigor, gaining ground until their phalanx lines are level with their Roman counterparts.

The Carthaginian army slowly retreats back up the hill, dragging their wounded with them. A frustrated Hannibal rampages along his front lines, leading his Sacred Band into his army's weakest spots. The Carthaginian retreat slows, then halts. Both sides pause a scant twenty feet from one another, catching their breath, building courage for another assault on each other.

Hannibal hears the trumpet of the Romans' battle horns behind the first legion. High atop Surus, he can see the Romans' second legion and their allies' back lines tramping toward the front, and he grimaces with disappointment. *Fresh reinforcements*, he thinks, *just when I had the bastards*.

Hannibal summons Maharbal and his two cavalry officers and screams orders at them, pointing toward the Roman flanks. The two officers race away to each side of their infantry lines and head back up the hill behind them. They soon return, each leading a thousand of the agile Numidian cavalry. The Numidians carry only a spear, sword, and small shield, eschewing armor for the sake of speed and mobility. Behind every rider is a Balearic who carries naught but a large lumpy satchel over his back.

The African riders pour down the hill and circle around the battle, heading toward the legion's back lines. Many of the heavy Roman cavalry leave their conflict with the Libyan riders to intercept the Numidians, but the swift Africans elude them, bent on debarking their passengers.

The Numidians pull up on each side of the reinforcing legion, out of javelin range, and their passengers jump off. The Balearic slingers throw down their satchels and stare over at the advancing Romans. They gauge the distance between them and their enemy and undo one of the three strings they have tied around their head. The strings are slings, each one a different length and thickness, each one for a different distance and missile. They reach into their satchel, select the proper stone, and stuff it into their sling. They whirl the sling around their head and release their stones. The egg-sized missiles hurtle into the Marcellus' unwary flanks with lethal force, breaking bones and shattering skulls. The Roman advance halts as the soldiers huddle from the repeated onslaughts, then it slowly creeps forward in their protective turtle shell. Some soldiers march with bleeding noses and mouths, dazed from a missile blow, guided on by their brothers in arms so that they do not break ranks. But still they come on. And the carnage continues.

Dusk arrives with Hannibal's Iberians pressing in on the Roman army's flanks. Hannibal has mounted a sturdy little Numidian horse so he can dash across his lines and allocate his reserves where they are needed. He can see the Iberians winning their battles with the allies and legionnaires on the flanks, beginning an envelopment of the Romans. Elated, he rides back to the rear lines and musters the Gauls for a final charge, promising them first pick of the Roman camp booty. With Hannibal and his Sacred Band leading the vanguard, the Gauls rush back to the front and boil into the tiring Romans and allies, pushing them inward. The Band cuts a swath through the hastati and principes, but the triarii again lock in and refuse to move, forming a spear wall that is backed by the javelins and stones their compatriots hurl from behind them.

The Carthaginian advance slows but it still crawls forward, with the Roman lines on the verge of collapsing upon themselves. The first legion and its allied phalanx has moved to the front again, but they weary under the steady Carthaginian onslaught. The Libyan and Numidian cavalry duel with the unyielding Roman cavalry, who have jumped off their horses to fight the Africans on foot. Atilius falls, the Master of Horse speared from three directions as by encircling Numidians.

Mercifully, the sun begins to set. Maharbal rides up to Hannibal, still raging along the front atop his Numidian horse. "General, I beg you, withdraw!" Maharbal shouts in his ear. "Our men cannot tell friend from foe—we are killing each other!" With a curse at Shalem, the god of sunset, Hannibal gives the command to return to camp. and the horns sound the withdrawal. Hearing their horns, Marcellus immediately calls for his army to return to their base. He eschews any pursuit, knowing that Hannibal might use the darkness for another of his fatal ambushes. The Roman army returns to their fortified camp, exhausted but unbeaten and unbowed.

The battle plain is quiet for two days, neither side willing to institute another conflict. On the dawn of the third day, Marcellus rises slowly, his body still throbbing from his bruises and cuts. He takes a cup of watered wine and trudges toward the camp gates as the buccina sound the first watch of the day. His personal guard joins him as he leaves the tent and follows him up the ladder into the main watchtower. As he did the two previous days, Marcellus looks out upon the field of battle, thinking how he might have changed his alignments or strategy to bring him victory.

One of the tower sentries walks over and points across the plain.

"He is gone," is all the sentry says.

The general looks across the plain to Hannibal's camp, then he looks again: all the tents are gone, and there are no campfires burning. Marcellus blinks, stares, then laughs. *That old fox*, he thinks, *he sneaked out in the night without us knowing. How in Olympus could he do that?* Chuckling to himself, Marcellus takes a deep draft of his wine and leans over the staked wall, listening to the birds welcoming the rising sun. After a while he turns to his guard. "Summon the tribunes to meet me at midday," he says with a grin. "We have a fox to catch."

*   *   *   *   *

CABO DE PALOS, SOUTHERN IBERIA, 209 BCE. The dawn sun shimmers across the aqua sea as the first Roman trireme eases through a gap in an island-sized sandbar and enters a half-mile wide lagoon east of Cartago Nova. A dozen triremes follow the flagship into the tranquil waters, gliding toward the flat sandy shore that borders the peninsula's spine of volcanic mountains. Cartago Nova is only twenty miles east of the Roman fleet, but the ships are as concealed as if it they were back in Tarraco, protected by miles of roughshod land. Scipio's Bastetani scouts have served him well in finding it; the cape is the perfect place to organize his impending assault on the fortress.

Laelius stands in the prow of the incoming lead ship, gazing at the paradisiacal landscape that surrounds him. He grimaces at the towering statue of Baal Hamon, the stern-faced Carthaginian god that looms over a distant point on the cape. "Hmm, we'll have to replace him with someone a bit more friendly when we take over," Laelius comments to an attending marine. "Maybe Bacchus. Or Priapus, he'd make quite the welcome statue, wouldn't he? Imagine, a twelve-foot penis hanging out over the sea!" The marine can only shake his head and smile; he has grown accustomed to his commander's lack of Roman gravitas. Had he not known Laelius has killed a half-dozen enemy with his own hand, he would think him an effeminate buffoon.

The lead ship grounds itself on the beach. Several seamen throw out the landing platform, and the marines march out and establish a guarded perimeter. When all is secured, Laelius eagerly jaunts ashore and surveys the harbor for signs of the enemy. Satisfied no one is about, he sends a scout squadron riding north toward the army, to notify Scipio of the fleet's safe landing.

The sailors and marines soon establish a temporary camp above the sandy shoreline, building a palisade of pine branches. While the camp is being laid out, many sailors rush to net fish in the lagoon, eager for fresh food. The armorers and the soldier-doctors quickly set up their tents and tools. They must ready themselves for the army's arrival because all problems with weapons, armor, and injuries must be quickly remedied as best they can. War is but a day's march from the camp, there is no margin for error.

By early afternoon, the army vanguard descends the northern hills, led by Scipio and Marcus Silenus. Laelius rides out to meet Scipio, and the two trot back to camp, chatting like schoolmates on a picnic. The weary legions trickle in until dusk, setting up their tents and enjoying the treat of a fire to ward off the early spring cold, along with a hot meal of meat and freshly caught fish. After dinner, wine is retrieved from the ships and passed about. The camp has an almost festive air about it as Scipio gives them free rein to savor their final days before they assault the walls of the Cartago Nova fortress.

Scipio enters his command tent and collapses into a long nap. Refreshed, he calls an evening meeting with his commanding officers to strategize for the final assault on Cartago Nova. A leather map of the region is splayed out on the ground, and the officers kneel over it like boys playing Troy, the Roman board game. Scipio has two of his Bastetani scouts review the map for accuracy, and a few areas are redrawn and labeled. The general then places ship, man, and horse icons around the finger of land on which Cartago Nova rests.

"Two days hence we surround Cartago Nova," says Scipio. "Laelius, you will lead the fleet to the east and south walls. I will be camped near the main gates."

"How many men are in the fortress?" asks a tribune.

"I do not know," replies Honorius. "I await the return of our most informative spy, the one who spied for Magon."

At these words, Marcus Silenus frowns. "We are to trust a man who betrayed the Carthaginians to join us? Who is to say he will not betray us in turn, for more gold?"

"Because we do not offer him mere gold," interjects an irritated Scipio. "We offer him freedom, the release of his tribe's captives that Magon holds in Cartago Nova. And one of the prisoners is his brother." Scipio looks into the tribunes' faces and sees doubt in several of them. "You must remember. For the Iberians, the tribe is everything."

"So we attack without knowing their numbers?" asks Laelius.

Scipio shrugs. "Yes. Because it matters not. Our 25,000 will vastly outnumber them. They have a few thousand at best."

A senior tribune sneers. "Thousands of seasoned warriors behind over two miles of thick stone walls some thirty feet high, built on an steep embankment that is surrounded on three sides by water." He turns to his fellows and throws up his hands. "We could lay siege for months and not take it!"

"We will not be here that long because we cannot afford to tarry," snaps Scipio. "By now the Generals will have found out that we are heading toward Cartago Nova, though they know not where we are." Scipio unrolls a map of Iberia and puts his finger on Gades, southwest of Cartago Nova. "Gisgo's army is here, the one nearest to us. He could be here within several weeks, with Mago close behind him. And we would be overwhelmed. Were we to retreat, they might catch us on the march, for all our newfound speed"

"That is why the spy's information is so important," says Scipio. "The fate of our campaign may depend on what he finds out," he smirks. "Or does not find out, gods help us!" Scipio points at the map's sketch of the narrow causeway leading to the fortress. "Either way, there is no turning back. Cartago Nova falls, or we do."

V. CARTAGO NOVA

SOUTHERN COAST OF IBERIA, 209 BCE. Flocks of seagulls dive about the towering walls of Cartago Nova, the prized port city of the Carthaginians, grabbing the breakfast scraps that the sentries pitch over the wall. A scruffy merchant clops along the entry road on his shaggy old mule, towing three with large pottery jugs dangling from their sides. The merchant is part of the steady stream of vendors and street performers that file across the causeway toward the city gates, seeking day entry to the wealthy port city.

A short time later, the merchant stops at the gates. He faces four heavily armed Libyan infantry, who scrutinize him as if he has come to steal their children. One of the sentries walks around mules, eyeing their baggage.

"State your business," says the squad leader in broken Iberian.

"I come to sell and barter," replies the merchant, waving toward the jars on his mules. "I carry amphorae of the finest wines in Baetica. Lusty drink for lusty men!"

"So you say! Would that I buy some of those jugs right now?" jokes the leader, suddenly speaking in Latin. The merchant merely blinks uncomprehendingly at him. "Go ahead, then," says the officer, this time in Iberian. "On pain of death, be out by nightfall."

Once inside the bustling streets, the wine seller moves to the vendor stalls that circle the town square. After several hours of haggling and joking with his fellow merchants, he sells his wine and stables his mules as he wends into the heart of the city. At sunset, the man returns to the stable and pulls his mules out the front gate.

Two days later, the erstwhile wine merchant stands inside Scipio's command tent. The shaggy vendor is now a clean-shaven and elegantly dressed Bastetani warrior, albeit one who acts a bit furtive and anxious. Scipio sits at a table in front of him, with Laelius and Marcus Silenus standing on each side of him. On one side of the table is a black purse of coins. On the other is a dagger, jutting from the tabletop near Scipio's left hand.

"Tell us what you have learned, and I will measure your reward," orders Scipio, glancing at the purse. "If your information proves valuable, the silver may all be yours." He reaches out and fingers the blade of the dagger. "If it proves false, you will be my second lesson to those who would deceive me. The first is hanging outside my tent."

The Bastetani swallows hard. "I saw the withered tongue hanging out there in the front, and heard the tale of why it is there. I have no wish to suffer the same fate, by my children's eyes." The man reaches into his satchel and pulls out a rude drawing of Cartago Nova's streets and surroundings. "The land is fairly flat all about the front, and the back walls are shielded by the bay that surrounds them."

Scipio frowns. "We know that. You can see it from miles away. Do you think we do not have eyes?"

The merchant smiles smugly. "I am certain you do. But, did you know that the lagoon recedes on the first full fishing moon, as the waters become so shallow that a man could wade up to the walls?"

Scipio glances at Marcus and Laelius, who shrug their ignorance about the matter. "How do you know this?" asks Scipio.

"I was talking to one of the local fishermen at the market, a salty old man who looks like he was born on the sea a century ago. I asked him where he obtained the fine crabs he had for sale. He told me that the bay tide retreats when the full moon is high, leaving the lagoon so shallow the fishermen can sludge through it and pluck out their crabs and clams. It is a local secret. He doubts the city-bred Carthaginians even know about it. They never ask him how he got his crabs."

Scipio takes the purse and empties half of it onto the table. He flips the purse to the spy, who snatches it in midair and tucks it into his robe. "Laxos, I am not sure how valuable your information is," says Scipio, "but come back after the next full moon. If your story is true, you will receive the rest. Tell no one, on pain of death. Now go." The man hustles out and Scipio watches him depart.

When he is sure the spy is gone, Scipio looks at his two commanders with a broad smile, his eyes alight. "This could be it. The rear wall could be the Achilles' heel of that impregnable rock. The Carthaginians may be lax about guarding that back wall, thinking it unassailable. When the waters recede, we could attack it!"

"So we try a sneak attack from the bay?" asks Laelius. "Then we should send out a night party to essay a mock assault, and see if it is truly negotiable. Otherwise, our men could be mired in mud and picked off from the parapets."

"No. First, we talk to several more of the local fisher folk, to confirm his story," says Marcus severely.

Scipio shakes his head, and his right hand begins to twitch uncontrollably. "Perhaps I am being too hasty in seizing on this bayside attack idea. We have yet to test the mettle of Cartago Nova's defenders. And there may be another way. We could negotiate with Magon for a surrender, or see if our infiltrators could open the gates at night somehow. There are other options."

Marcus looks at Scipio. "Perhaps you think overmuch, General." He walks to the map of the area and moves all the map's infantry pieces on top of Cartago Nova. "As you say, let us test their mettle. Attack the front gates at dawn. There are only a few thousand of them. They have the walls, but we have the army. And we are Romans, they are not."

Scipio looks at Laelius, and he shrugs boyishly. "Why not? We might be able to storm the fortress without any tricks." Scipio exhales, and laughs ruefully. "Perhaps I do overthink sometimes. We will try it the old Roman way and hit them in the mouth."

*   *   *   *   *

ROME. "You know, Fabius, the boy's moralizing is beginning to irritate me," says Flaccus as he gnaws on a slice of onion pizza. "We have to do something about him."

Flaccus and Fabius are perched in a stone booth inside a large thermopolium, a hot food shop in the Forum Holitorium, Rome's largest vegetable market. The two are plainly dressed in order to be inconspicuous, choosing this modest diner because no patricians would ever frequent it.

Fabius and Flaccus are here to meet one more time before Fabius returns to his troops in South Italia. They are discussing their two favorite goals: winning the war against Hannibal and the war against the Hellenic Party. But now Cato has become a topic for discussion.

Flaccus' face mirrors his mood—dark and angry. "At the Party meeting last night, Cato criticized our plans to start a rumor campaign against Marcellus, and then he openly refused to be a part of it. We should send him back to his farm!" A dark look crosses his face. "Or, we could ...."

"We have need of a fellow like Cato," interrupts Fabius hastily. The old general gestures for an attendant to refill his clay wine cup as he looks at the beer-drinking commoners about him. "Cato's presence mollifies these plebs. He gives them hope that they might become a patrician, too. That hope mitigates their dissatisfaction about their wages."

Flaccus arches his eyebrows. "Well, we certainly don't want another work stoppage by the citizens. You couldn't get fresh bread or meat, or even a wine delivery!"

141

"So we keep the boy!" declares Fabius. He grins. "Besides, I am quite fond of him. He has an uncompromising attitude that is refreshing."

"Unless you are on the receiving end of his unwillingness to compromise!" snaps Flaccus. "He has a growing following as an orator. I am worried that he will speak out against one of us." Fabius nods. "Then we will keep an eye on him." He looks meaningfully at Flaccus. "We don't need to do anything drastic right now."

Fabius and Flaccus are silent for a bit, chewing on pizza and dipping their cucumber slices into honey. Dozens of farmers and craftsmen stream past them, each throwing a coin to the baker as they grab a wedge of pizza and step back into the thoroughfare. Fabius snaps his fingers. "We need to keep Cato in the party, but he does not need to be in Rome. When he returns from campaign with me, we can push for him to take the next step on the cursus honorum."

Flaccus grins. "Get him an appointment as quaestor?" Fabius nods enthusiastically. "Yes, but as an army quaestor. We might be able to make him the army auditor for Scipio."

At those words, Flaccus' grin widens. "Those two together? I may join Scipio's army myself, just to watch!"

*   *   *   *   *

CARTAGO NOVA. Magon Rhodanus, governor-general of Cartago Nova, is shaken from slumber by one of his personal guard. "Forgiveness, Commander," the soldier says, his voice agitated. "The Romans are here."

"Wh-what?" sputters Magon, pushing himself up from his sleeping pillows. "Romans?"

"Please, sir," urges the guard. "come to the east wall."

Magon sighs. "May Melqart take me to the Underworld, what would Romans be doing here? Very well, I'll take a look." Cursing the hour,

Magon rinses his mouth with diluted wine vinegar and pulls a purple-red tunic over his head, then donning his sword belt and helmet. He grabs a wall torch and rushes into the field-sized courtyard that fronts the main gates, stepping up the limestone stairs to the wide plank walkway that encircles the city's thick walls. Two gate sentries gesture furiously for him to come and look over the parapets. Magon joins them and looks over the east wall, staring onto the gray shadows of the dimly lit plain below him.

Clanking and rumbling sounds echo across the plain, punctuated with the occasional faint voices of officers dictating commands. Magon can see hundreds of vague shapes moving about in the morning shadows below, shapes spreading out in a wide semicircle about the city. As Magon and his men watch anxiously, the rising sunlight creeps across the sea and lightens the shadows. Now Magon can see them, and he watches in horror as the Roman army fills the plain a mile away, dragging in pack animals and battering rams behind the incoming infantry maniples.

"That must be the army of Cornelius Scipio," mutters Magon's captain of the guard. "I thought he was up at Tarraco."

"Impossible!" sputters Magon. "Our spies saw him there but a fortnight ago! This must be an invasion from somewhere else. Perhaps Sicily."

A sentry runs up to Magon, his eyes wide with alarm. "General," he shouts, gesturing behind him. "The south wall! The ships!" Cursing loudly, Magon strides along the wall until he comes to the side facing the Mediterranean Sea, and he halts in dismay. Laelius' fleet is bobbing out in the bay, a dozen warships blockading any ingress or egress to Cartago Nova. Magon studies the ships for several minutes, composing himself, developing his plans. The battle-hardened commander then trots down the stairway to his headquarters, calling for his officers to meet him there immediately. As soon as they are gathered, Magon wastes little time in discussing possibilities.

V. Cartago Nova

"Prepare for an attack by tomorrow. Every soldier is to be at the gates or on top of the walls. How many infantry do we have ready?"

A short, muscular Carthaginian officer steps forward. "By yesterday's count, we have 985 men ready for battle. And 89 wounded," he reports.

Magon grimaces. "Not nearly enough. We have over two miles of wall to cover with those few. And we need to concentrate men on the front gates—that's where they'll attack." He looks at his officer. "Put the wounded up on the wall. They can at least stand watch."

"What about fetching Mago's men at Gades?" asks a senior Libyan captain, his face masked with a thick gray beard. "We can send messengers for help and hold the Romans until he arrives."

A Carthaginian officer shakes his head. "We should do that, but he is at least twelve days' march from here."

"Send out four messengers tonight," commands Magon. "At least one should make it through to him. In the meantime, we will arm the citizens. Give every man a sword, spear and a shield. Organize them into phalanxes and muster them near the front gates tomorrow. We will show these Romans that Cartago Nova is not easily taken. Report here in four hours!"

The Libyan and Carthaginian officers scramble out to execute their various duties, still a bit stunned that in the blink of an eye a quiet tour of duty has turned into a frenzied hive of battle activity.

Magon takes Balon, the sturdy older Libyan who is his second-in-command, up to the walkway over the entrance. They watch the army massing a half mile away, at the top of the narrow causeway that leads in to Cartago Nova. Magon squints out at the legionary standards being carried into the camp and barks a tense laugh. "Gods defend me, that is truly the Scipio boy. He somehow flew down here from Tarraco!" Then he shrugs dismissively. "Ah, all the better. When we crush him, we end the last Roman threat here. Then on to Rome."

Balon watches the battering rams being led to the front of the tents, and he grimaces. "You think we can defeat them, with our few men?"

"We do not have to defeat them. We have to detain them," Magon replies. "These walls can repel an army for months, but we only need hold them for a fortnight. By then Mago's men will be at their backs, with Gisgo's army following, and we could charge out from the front. With Scipio gone, we march to Tarraco. And over to Italia!"

By late morning of the next day, the walls of Cartago Nova are lined with Carthaginian soldiers, and the courtyard is filled with Cartago Nova citizens and expatriated Carthaginians, sturdy men armed with swords, spears, and farm implements. An hour later the buccinae sound from the Roman camp, and a thousand infantry march across the quarter-mile-wide causeway toward the main gates. On each side of them trots a score of escaladers, each lightly armored pair carrying a long wooden ladder for scaling the walls.

All is quiet along the top of the wall until the infantry draws within a spear's cast of the entrance. The escaladers dash out to spread beneath the walls. They lean their ladders on each side of the front gates as the infantry marches toward the front gate, pulling along a stout battering ram. The Carthaginians rise up from the walls and rain stones upon the Romans, crushing the skulls and shoulders of any escaladers who are tardy in raising their shields.

The gates open abruptly, and a horde of two thousand inhabitants rush out and assault the oncoming infantry, led by the Carthaginian officers. The Romans are taken by surprise and are pushed back by the ferocity of their opponents, slowly withdrawing from the causeway, leaving their fallen ladders scattered at the base of the wall.

Scipio watches the retreat of his legion, and his enthusiasm for victory turns to dismay, then anger. "The locals are driving them back," he snarls. Scipio turns to his two senior tribunes. "This is unacceptable! Prepare the second wave. I will lead them myself."

V. Cartago Nova

The buccinae soon sound a second time, relaying the command that the assault force is to withdraw to camp. The first assault force moves to the south side of the causeway, near the protecting sea, and are passed by five maniples of fresh troops striding into the militia, led by a grim Scipio. The hastati of the front lines cut their way through the disorganized ranks of the determined citizenry, beating them back toward the gates. As more of the defenders fall, their slow retreat turns into a rout, and the locals run for the shelter of the front gates. Seeing that the city gates are open, Scipio's eyes light with excitement.

"Onward," he screams, "into Cartago Nova!" Scipio urges his horse forward, but one of the senior tribunes grabs his arm.

"General, please," the veteran urges. "You will outstrip your men and be unprotected."

Scipio pushes his hand away. "I lead my men," he exults. "We will take this city before nightfall! Call forth the escaladers!"

Scipio turns to face his infantry. "Remember Cannae!" he screams and pushes his stallion into the pack of spears and shields ahead of him, his guard and tribunes following. Swinging his falcata like an ax, he splits several shields and helmets, the bloodlust upon him. His entourage follows him desperately, casting fearful eyes about them as they press ahead of their legionary lines. The maniples essay to follow their general and yet maintain ranks, and begin a fast trot. Seeing fresh legions approaching, the militia run for the gates, and Scipio rides ahead in pursuit, chopping at any within reach. He can see the gates slowly close, and he pushes toward them, shouting for the Romans to penetrate before they close.

As the Romans enter the shadow of the walls, the defenders again rise from the parapets, raining rocks and javelins upon the unwary Romans. A small boulder rings off the top of Scipio's helmet, and he follows it to the ground, stunned with the impact. The fleeing militia roar enthusiastically at the sight of the fallen general. Two dozen of them turn about and rush back, eager to take Scipio's head. A mêlée ensues around Scipio as his tribunes raise him to his feet and the front line infantry battle off the determined militia. More of the fleeing locals reverse their flight and rush toward the Romans, and scores of enemy surround Scipio and his defenders.

Marcus Silenus steps in from the back ranks, a look of nightfall on his face. The older man steps in front of Scipio's few protectors and becomes a whirling dervish of thrusts and counterthrusts, his blade seemingly in three places at once. A half-dozen attackers fall at his feet, several of them headless, as he cuts his way through Scipio's would-be killers.

The citizen soldiers lose their taste for facing this murderous machine and withdraw into the fortress, the gates closing behind them. The tribunes drag Scipio back to the front ranks of the legion. As soon as the deadly hail of stones begins anew, the officers raise their shields above their heads and to the sides, forming a protecting shell as the legionnaires slowly pull back from the causeway, to the exulting cries and jeers of the Carthaginians on the wall.

Scipio is assisted to his command tent, where his officers stretch him out upon a sleeping mat. A helmeted Marcus Silenus stands off to one side, his breastplate spattered with gore, his bloody sword still bare in his hand. He glares angrily at the dazed Scipio, as a father might to an errant son.

A Greek medicus rushes into the tent. His fingers probe the top of Scipio's skull and pull back his eyelids to examine his pupils. The medicus stands up and nods at the anxious tribunes. "Be at ease. He is stunned, but not injured," he says in halting Latin.

Scipio rises to a sitting position and blinks at his officers. "Cartago still stands?" he asks blearily.

Several tribunes merely stare at each other, barely repressing a smirk. "We failed to take it," finally replies the oldest of them, his voice tinged with sarcasm.

Scipio glares at the senior tribune, then smiles at the rest as he rubs the top of his head. "Ah, but that failure was a success. I have seen where they concentrate their forces during a frontal attack. Now we know how to defeat them!"

*　*　*　*　*

ROME, 209 BCE. "Ah, gods, there is nothing like a good mouse!" exclaims the tipsy Senator. He bites into a large mushroom-stuffed dormice he has pulled from a dinner platter being passed around and flops back onto his pillows. "Quite the party," he slurs. "Pomponia should receive a triumph for giving such a marvelous feast!"

The Scipio domus is alive with talk and laughter this late summer night. Pomponia is entertaining a number of Senators and magistrates. Ostensibly, she is giving a party in honor of the upcoming Ludi Romani games, but true to her nature, she has a deeper purpose.

The aristocratic guests are sprawled around the low-slung couches that line the atrium walls, sampling the many platters that the house slaves bring to them. The meal has been lavish even by Roman standards, with oysters and peacocks as the appetizers, followed by main courses of eel, pork, and dormice. All of it is washed down with flagons of prized Falernian wine, perfectly blended with fresh spring water. Even the Latin Party Senators manage to have a good time, although they know the Hellenics will profit from the goodwill generated at this event. After the dessert, biscuits are passed about with cups of honeyed wine, and the guests rise to chat with each other, as the lyres and flutes waft soothing harmonies.

Pomponia and Amelia move among their guests, making sure everyone is in good spirits. Pomponia wears a lush burgundy robe adorned with an emerald necklace that reflects her blue-green eyes, the robe clasped together with a gold likeness of Minerva's owl. Her red hair cascades down her shoulders, adding a touch of wildness to her elegance. She has arrayed herself in powerful colors and textures because she has given this party to lobby for her party's immediate political objective, keeping the Sword of Rome.

The Scipio matron chats her way through a knot of former consuls who are exchanging war stories, waiting to corner the portly Appius Claudius, one of Rome's senior Senators. She needs to talk with him about the upcoming Senate vote to remove Marcus Claudius Marcellus, the Sword of Rome, from military office.

Because Marcellus has lost so many of his men to his battles with Hannibal, the Latin Party moved to remove the Hellenic sympathizer from military command. Senator Appius is not affiliated with either party, but the senior Senator's vote will influence many of the younger Senators. If Pomponia can persuade him to vote for Marcellus, she will have recouped all her time and expense for this fest.

The Senators' conversation lags, and she eases in to take Appius' arm, leading him over to the fish pond. "You are enjoying yourself, Senator?" purrs Pomponia as she smiles into his rheumy eyes.

"Oh yes," replies Appius. pulling a fig from a slave's serving platter. "The pheasant was a wonder. And the honeyed wine would seduce the gods themselves!" He pats his ample stomach and burps to show his approval. "As you can see, I am as stuffed as one of your mice!"

"I am happy that you are pleased," she replies with the slightest of bows. "My husband and I often hosted parties when he was alive, and I carry the tradition in his honor." She sighs mournfully. "So many of our best generals gone, so many fallen to the Carthaginians!" She wrinkles her nose, eyeing Appius. "Especially that terrible Hannibal!"

Appius nods sympathetically. "Yes, yes, so many men, too. Rome looks like a city of women and children. And now we are training convicts to be legionnaires. Can you imagine that?" He shakes his head. "What will follow, women in the army?"

" It is true, Senator," she somberly replies. "All the more reason to keep the few good generals that we have. And that is what puzzles me about this upcoming Senate reprisal vote. Why would anyone want to remove Marcellus from command, the only man to best Hannibal?"

"Well, I don't know if 'besting him' is the term I would use, Pomponia," Appius says cautiously. "Hannibal is still alive, and still threatens to sack Rome."

"What else would could you call it?" she counters. "The Sword of Rome has thrice battled Hannibal, without defeat. He drove the Carthaginian from the field at Numistro, with Hannibal leaving a trail of dead men behind him!" Pomponia motions for a platter-carrying slave to come over, and she pulls off two smoked sardines, offering one to Appius. "Marcellus has fought Hannibal better than anyone," she says in between bites. "He has killed thousands of his men, and forced Hannibal to retreat. He is quite formidable, wouldn't you say?"

"Well, Marcellus did win that fight," huffs Appius. "But he lost a lot of men. And then he slinked off to Numistro to rest."

"Slinked off?" retorts Pomponia, her eyes glinting angrily. "Most of his men were wounded, he stayed to ensure they were being treated well, and then went after Hannibal. What more would you expect?" A light dawns in her eyes, and she looks intently at Appius. "Apologies if I be rude, but have you been talking with Flaccus about this?"

Appius avoids her eyes. "Well, yes. He is an old colleague of mine. And I talk to all the Senators."

"Do they all tell lies?" she retorts, her composure fading. "Flaccus is naught but a purveyor of poisonous rumors about any who oppose his Party's interests. And Marcellus seeks to provide land and education for the citizenry, with a tax increase to accomplish it. That is all you need to know about Flaccus' motivation for what he says about him!"

"You have given me much to think about," placates Appius, edging away. "And I will truly consider it. But I cannot promise that I will vote for Marcellus."

Pomponia takes a deep breath and calms herself. "As you say,

Senator. I am but a woman, I cannot tell a Senator what to do." Appius smiles conciliatorily and starts to walk away when Pomponia adds, "But I will tell you this: two weeks from today, when the Senate does vote on Marcellus' fate, there will be some plebs in the public gallery. They will record each and every Senator's vote, whether he says yea or nay."

Appius halts, staring at her in dismay. She nods congenially at a few of her guests and takes a deep draft of her wine, letting her words take effect. Then she looks into Appius' eyes. "The plebs will know who voted against their hero, as will the Tribunes of the Plebs." She smiles wickedly. "This upcoming year, I predict there will be a large number of veto ("I forbid") declarations by the Tribunes of the Plebs. They will be directed at certain Senators' proposals in the Senate. Do I have to tell you who those 'certain Senators' will be?"

Appius can only nod at her, as he searches for his composure. Pomponia abruptly switches moods, smiles gaily, and puts her hand on Appius' shoulder. "It is merely an observation," Pomponia lilts. "I have no say in the matter, of course." She lifts the goblet to her face and stares mockingly at Appius as she drinks. "No say at all." Appius huffs and stares into his goblet, as if auguring the wine lees for an answer.

"Well, I must be off," says Pomponia as she bends to kiss Appius lingeringly on his powdered cheek. "A hostess' duties are interminable! I must introduce myself to some of the new Senators." Hips swaying seductively, Pomponia strolls away from the flustered Appius, pausing to talk to three younger men in purple bordered togas.

Appius watches her, takes a deep breath, and blows it out. "My Gods!" is all he says.

While Pomponia entrances the new Senators, Amelia moves about to ensure everyone is enjoying themselves, turning heads as she moves through the domus. She is simply attired in a flowing moss-colored robe, her shining auburn hair tied back into a bun. Devoid of jewelry or decoration, her ravishing face and form is all the adornment she requires to attract the men's attention. At the urging of her future mother-in-law, Pomponia, she is mixing with the crowd to tell them about Scipio's plight in Iberia, in hopes that the Senate may soon provide more funding and troops for him.

Amelia spies a simply dressed young man in a corner of the atrium, standing alone and looking quite displeased with the proceedings. She studies his expression, puzzled. She has seen his face before, but she cannot remember where. Amelia steps over to introduce herself.

"Salve, honored guest. I am Amelia Tertia. I saw you sitting with Flaccus at the dinner table. Welcome you to Scipio House!"

The potato-nosed youth attempts a smile, but his furrowed brows betray him. "Ah yes, Amelia, the betrothed of Publius Cornelius Scipio."

"I am that, among other things," she acknowledges with a faint smile. "Are you enjoying the dinner party?"

Cato stares into his goblet of watered wine, as if searching for an appropriate answer. "Not as much as your other guests, I venture. I am but a farmer at heart. To me, these luxuries are but a waste of good money. It is a sign of the times that we have such frequent nonsense now."

Amelia is taken aback for a minute, and then her eyes light with recognition. "Oh! You are Cato, are you not? Your reputation for … clarity precedes you."

"Tribune Marcus Porcius Cato," he replies solemnly. "A man of the people and for the people."

She nods at him, her face blank. "I have heard you speak in the public square," Amelia says evenly. "I think you are a very persuasive orator, though I do not embrace the austerity you espouse. Myself, I would provide art and culture for everyone! To make Rome the greatest city in the world."

"Such beauty comes at a price," says Cato. "A price to be paid by taxing those who have earned their money and are loathe to give it to those who did not."

Amelia fingers her wine cup. "Well, I do favor people being able to keep what they have earned, to a certain degree. But there should be room for the most fortunate to give back to the state that has enabled those riches. It is a complex issue, I confess."

"I do not see it as complex," retorts Cato. "It is as simple as those who earn keeping what they earn, not losing it to those who do not deserve it. Your 'complexity' implies compromise, and compromise is weakness—the kind of thing a Greek would espouse."

Amelia raises an eyebrow. "Complexity and compromise are weak? As opposed to the cowardice of simplicity, of being afraid to admit there are nuances to every 'truth,' that politics and economics will never allow certainty, only educated guesses? I see no courage in such an avoidance of reality. Give me the man who acts in spite of his doubts, and I will show you a man of true moral bravery."

Young Cato glowers at her, frustrated that his conversation with lovely Amelia has taken a factious turn. "You sound like one of the Hellenics, always wanting to steal private money and give it the public. I tell you as truth, the real war for Rome is right here in the city, and it is not with the Carthaginians." He shakes a callused finger under Amelia's nose, his face reddening in spite of himself. "Greek decadence versus Roman austerity, that is the battle! Whose side are you on, young Domina?"

"The side that will make Rome a great nation," Amelia huffs, "not just a powerful one." Without another word, Amelia gathers her skirt in her hand and paces away, her sandals clopping across the marble floor.

Cato watches her slim ankles and feels the sting of the resentment he has harbored for beautiful women, feeling they ignore him because of his humble agrarian roots, thinking that they are better than he. He barely notices Flaccus sidling up to him.

Cato's lanky patrician mentor puts his arm around his shoulders. "So you have been coddling up to the Scipio boy's woman," leers Flaccus. "I must say I admire your taste. She has breasts like cantaloupes, and her hips sway with lust. She is long overdue for a dick in her!"

"I am not interested in some powdered patrician's puss," snaps Cato, still seething at her departure. "I am angered by this lavish foolishness, all this money spent on superficialities. It tells me these Scipios do not know the value of a denarii—perhaps because they have never had to earn one." He looks at Flaccus. "That Cornelius Scipio may be wasting Roman money over there in Iberia, too. If he is anything like his mother or betrothed, he bears watching."

Flaccus rubs his chin, eyes agleam with speculation. "Hmm. The idea has merit. Especially if we can catch him wasting Rome's money. It would show just how the Hellenics would waste any tax money they would gather with those proposed increases." A sly grin crosses his face. "Just think what might happen if you were his army's quaestor, auditing his accounts, monitoring his spending. How delicious that would be!"

There is a silence. Cato looks steadily at the older man and then speaks, his voice tinged with outrage. "I would only demand an honest accounting of funds, Flaccus. I will not besmirch my own honor in a quest to impugn another's."

Flaccus laughs, unperturbed. "Knowing these Hellenics, you would only have to faithfully record Scipio's expenditures. He will knot his own noose!" Flaccus nods his head eagerly. "Cato the quaestor. I shall look into that for your sake, for certitude I will!"

"Look where you will," growls Cato. "I have more concern with these Scipio women. They reach beyond their female station, another sign of our degradation of good Roman values." He throws his wine into a palm plant. "All mankind rules its women, and we rule all mankind, but our women rule us." [xi]

Two days after the party, Amelia calls a night meeting at an abandoned insula, an apartment house, in the center of Rome. Her attendees are an odd collection of artists, tradesmen, and patricians. But they all share one goal: to improve the welfare of Rome's freedmen. Amelia has arrayed scores of small paint jars and twig brushes on a table. Wearing only the dark tattered tunic of an indigent, she is dressed to blend into the streets, which she must do to accomplish her mission tonight. She hands out three vials of paint to each person and stands before them.

"You know what you need to write, and where to write it. You each have your own section of the city. You can also use any public buildings near the Forum, but no private residences, except those who we know are Latin Party members. And no temples, understood?" All nod silently. "Then into the night, and back before dawn. A righteous man's fate depends upon you!"

The twelve attendees scurry out of the building and into the starlight night. The next day, Romans awake to find their city awash in slogans supporting Marcellus, sayings such as *"Support General Gaius Marcellus. He makes good bread," "Marcellus will keep Hannibal from Rome's gates," "The virgins of the Temple of Vestas support Gaius Claudius Marcellus,"* and finally *"The late drinkers admire Marcellus, the Bane of Hannibal!"*

The next week Marcellus is reelected as consul for the coming year, much to the dismay of the Latin Party. The office is given to him with one proviso: that he again face Hannibal in battle, as soon as possible. An overjoyed Marcellus hastens to Rome from his outpost at Canusium to stand before the Senate and accept the arrangement, a grin tugging at the corner of his mouth, his eyes twinkling with his amusement at politicians.

*   *   *   *   *

V. Cartago Nova

"Ptuh!" Shuffling around outside his command tent, Scipio brushes his teeth with a frayed twig, then rinses his mouth with vinegar and water. His toilet complete, the proconsul of Iberia walks through the camp gates and stops to gaze at the Cartago Nova, its walls looming before him a quarter mile away. Off to the right he can see Laelius' fleet strung along the bay, with men moving about the decks—a quiescent but ready threat to any Carthaginian excursion. Scipio scratches the back of his sleep-tousled head and grimaces at the fortress. *Can't fail again*, he chides himself. *You'll lose your men.*

Footsteps crunch on the graveled earth behind him, and Scipio turns to see Marcus Silenus marching forward, stern-faced as always. Scipio's lieutenant commander raises his arm in a formal salute, though no one else is near. "Salus, General Scipio," says Marcus.

"Ave, Marcus," Scipio replies.

Marcus stops next to Scipio and looks out upon their target. "That city is more fort than a town," Marcus comments. "It will be a difficult nut to crack. The walls are thick and high, and we have no catapults or towers." He pauses before he continues, as if weighing what he will say next. "I can hear the men talking. They wonder if we can ever conquer it."

Scipio says nothing. He flings a flat rock at the city, and then another, watching them skip across the ground. He turns to Marcus, challenge in his eyes. "And after that attack two days ago, they wonder if their young general is in over his head, is that not true?" He studies Marcus' face. "No, you do not have to answer. I hear what people say. I walk among my men at night, wearing just an infantryman's cloak. The men talk quite freely when they think no officers are about." Scipio pitches another rock, watching it skip across a pool to his left. And he grins. "Five skips! I know there are those who do not trust such a young general with their lives, Marcus. But they do not know that I have potent forces on my side."

Marcus' mouth twitches in the faintest of smiles, expecting something outlandish. "And what would that be, General?"

Scipio looks at him innocently. "Why, the gods, of course. Neptune is on our side. ... He will join us tomorrow!" He grins mischievously. "I would address the men before tomorrow's battle. They should know that the gods favor me. And them."

For the briefest of time, Marcus rolls his eyes heavenward. Then he bows his head. "I will ensure they are all before you by the seventh hour."

As Marcus turns to leave, Scipio casts a final comment. "Make sure no one but our legionnaires are about, not even the doctors or craftsmen. And no one is to leave camp. No one else must know what I tell them."

Five hours later, with his legions mustered before him on the field, Scipio steps up to a seven-foot-high rostrum, elevated so that all his men may see and hear him. The legionnaires can see he is wearing full battle armor, his bronze plate gleaming like a summer sun. He removes his plumed helmet and places his hands on each side of the speaking platform, eyes staring intensely into the hushed silence of thousands, his body rigid with purpose.

"Romans, allies, brothers-in-arms!" he shouts. "Last night I was visited by Neptune, the god of the sea. There I was, fast asleep, and suddenly fearful Neptune appeared above my head! His beard was green seaweed, his robe a net of living fish." Scipio pauses and looks at his men's faces. His men watch him raptly—they have heard the stories of their commander's prescient night visions when he fought in Italia. "The god bore a mighty trident in one hand and a Roman sword in the other, ready for battle." Scipio raises his arms heavenward. "And he promised to lead us to victory!"

The troops roar their approval as Scipio stands with arms upraised, allowing the cheers to crescendo. "Hear me, hear me now, soldiers! I know we planned to attack at night, but Neptune would have it otherwise. Tomorrow, at dawn's first light, when he sees we are mustered for battle, Neptune will pull the seas back from the land, that we may storm the walls there. You will see our own men walking across the water—this I swear! And when you see this wonder happening, you are to attack the gates with every iota of will and strength within you, before he again closes the seas. If we do this, victory will be ours! Cartago Nova will fall!" A great shout rises as Scipio raises his sword high, holding himself like a statue. He slowly turns his entire body, boring into the eyes of his men as he repeatedly screams, *"Victoriae, gloriam, aut mortem* (victory, glory, or death)!"

With the troops thundering their cheers, Scipio steps down and marches away without looking back, as if heading into battle. He strides back to the command tent and disappears inside. Once inside, he quickly sheds his armor and plops into a large wooden chair, his feet splayed out before him. He takes a deep breath and exhales it with a whoosh, then turns to his tent slave. "Wine," he says, and the slave hurriedly fills half the cup from a wineskin, mixing it with stream water. Scipio takes the cup with a trembling hand and drains it. He is on his second cup when Marcus and Laelius enter, followed by a quartet of the senior legionary tribunes.

"What a story! Neptune comes to you to lead us to victory!" chortles Laelius. "Why did he not just strike down the walls for us and save us some trouble? What a lazy god!"

"You know I often have dreams, when Febris is upon me," replies Scipio noncommittally. "And the gods are often in them." With a reprimanding look at Laelius, he turns to his tribunes. "I meant every word I said. Break your fast at dawn. We will attack the front gates at the third hour. We will sound retirement early tonight, that all may be rested for the morrow. Go and attend."

The tribunes file out, but Laelius lags behind. When they are gone, he frowns at his old friend with reproving humor. "You are learning the politics of generalship, that much is obvious. I cannot believe you turned those fishermen's tales about the lagoon into an intervention from the gods!"

"Confidence is as important a weapon as any," says Scipio. "And doubt a loss of armor. The men must believe they can take those monstrous walls. If it takes the belief that the gods are on our side, then so be it." Scipio waggles his finger at Laelius. "Your time would be better spent preparing your ships than mocking my speech, Admiral! When the infantry charges, I expect you to unleash Hades upon the seaside parapets! Use every catapult we have. Use every missile, every firepot. Spare nothing, for there will be no tomorrow if we fail."

He gently pushes Laelius out the door. "Now go to your rest, old friend." Scipio slaps Laelius on the back as he exits. After Laelius leaves, Scipio quaffs the last of his watered wine and leans over the map, staring at it for minutes, immobile. He spends several more hours calling in various infantry and cavalry commanders, including the centurion of the escaladers. When they have all gone, he has a private audience with Marcus Silenus about the lagoon assault. Finally, young Scipio sheds his clothing and crawls onto his sleeping couch, his heart still racing with anticipation, his brow burning with the onset of fever.

He lapses into a fitful sleep, and then the dreams come upon him, dreams that have plagued him since he was a child. Twenty years ago, when Scipio was but a boy of seven, a plague of mosquitoes enveloped Rome after the summer monsoons. From that time forward, the boy has been visited by Febris, the goddess of fever, who occasionally "blesses" him with fever dreams. Scipio has learned to heed these messages: many have come true, while others have given him visions of glorious futures for Rome and his family. But other dreams paint nightmarish situations that portend of the future, dire warnings that he knows he must heed, if he can but interpret them correctly. At times, desperate for a portent of the future, Scipio has taken a measure of opium with his wine, hoping the hallucinations would furnish him guidance. Such were always incoherent, however; only those bought with his fever have ever given him revelations—sometimes.

As Scipio thrashes in his troubled midnight sleep, muzzy images play inside his head, darting shadows with elusive shape and substance. Finally, they coalesce into a scene.

Scipio is standing inside the ancient Forum Boarium, the site of Rome's first gladiatorial contest. There, in the middle of its large circular floor, is a mansion-sized weight scale, with townspeople sitting in one plate and Roman soldiers resting in the other. The people's plate rests near the floor, pulling the soldiers' plate into the air. One of the soldiers grasps a legionary standard with both hands, and Scipio can see it is his own; these are his men.

An eight-foot-tall man stands in front of the scale, a sinewy elder with curled silver hair and beard, piercing blue eyes, and a thin beaked nose. The man beckons Scipio forward, his regal attitude brooking no disobedience. As Scipio nears him, the man turns to face the scale, as if inspecting its contents. But when the man turns to look at the scale, Scipio sees the man's face staring at him again, from the back of the man's head. Then Scipio realizes: he if facing Janus, the two-faced god who looks to the past and the future. The god of changes, and passages. And endings.

When Scipio draws near to him, Janus puts his enormous arm around Scipio's shoulders, as a father might with his child. They stand together, looking at the scale, when Janus finally speaks. "Do you not see it, boy?" he booms. "An imbalance. Those people there, they tip the scales against your men!"

Scipio stares at the scale, sees all the civilians sitting along the round scale plate, their legs dangling casually off the side as if they sat near a pond, the scale almost touching the ground. The legionnaires are all standing anxiously on their scale plate, holding tightly onto the plate's chains, afraid they might fall off.

"Those are my men!" Scipio expostulates. "You should bring them down lower so that they can get off!"

Janus shakes his head. "That is for you to do. You must put something on the their side to increase the weight. That will tip the scales."

Scipio looks about, but the area is empty. "I have nothing to put on there," complains Scipio.

At that remark, Janus merely grins. "Oh, I think you do, if you will but give it. Give of yourself, something of great weight, and it will restore the balance." The god gestures toward the side where the civilians are sitting. "Or maybe you should throw some of those others off. Or perhaps do both. Both would certainly solve it, General. But the balance must be restored."

The camp bugle rouses Scipio from his sweat-soaked bed, and he props himself up on trembling arms, waiting for the fog to clear from his mind. Blinking himself back to consciousness, he snatches at the memory of his fading dream, ruminating over its images. The dream foretells that a sacrifice must be made and loss will follow, no matter what. But what sacrifice, what will be saved, and what will be lost? He smiles regretfully to himself. *I will know when the situation has come upon me*, he thinks, shaking his head regretfully. *But gods help me, I know not what to do about it.*

* * * * *

Magon stands on the parapet over the main gates, looking out into the dawn bustle of the Roman army in front of him. Last night he stormed about his headquarters, alternately praising the citizen militia for defending the gates and cursing his officers for allowing half of them to be killed. Today, though, Magon is calm: every defensive preparation has been made, and his two thousand defenders are ready for any attack on the stout front gates. Rocks are piled along the front wall, ready to be hurled. Firepots are ready to be lit and thrown. Spears are stacked like firewood along the wall, ready for thrusting or hurling. Every item that might damage a Roman has been co-opted and put to use, somewhere.

Magon himself will direct the defense. He never shied from hand-to-hand combat when he was a soldier, and he will not stop now. He has stationed some of his Sacred Band warriors behind the militia, to ensure that no one runs or turns from his post. Magon knows it will be a bitter fight, but he is unperturbed. He has the calmness that comes from doing everything you can to prepare for what lies ahead. *From here on, it is in the hands of Baal Hamon, may he strike them all dead.*

*   *   *   *   *

The next day dawns bright and sunny, and buccinae sound the call to breakfast at the camp cook tents. Today is a battle day, and the cooks serve that rarest of treats: meat. As the men eat and arm themselves, the tribunes do a last-minute review of assault tactics with their centurions. The horns sound to muster into formation, and Scipio leads the two Roman legions out for Cartago Nova, with the allies following. When the buccinae sound the march, the legionnaires can see several of their ships begin to hurl stones at the south wall, and they know this will be an all-out assault on the fortress, with no retreat.

Laelius stands on the deck of his lead trireme. He watches his ships catapult their rocks at the walls, crashing through the parapets and crushing the defenders behind them. He notices there are few Carthaginians defending this portion of the wall, so he implements the second part of his attack plan.

Laelius draws his command ship and two others closer to the walls, as the rest continue their pummeling. He calls his 120 marines to the deck and steps up onto a peg hammered into the bottom of the mast, so all can see him. Laelius grabs the mast with one hand and leans out over his men, grinning with excitement. "Marines!" he shouts. "Soon our legions will overwhelm those Carthaginian dogs inside there, and history will be ours, with all the glory that comes to the victors. Now I tell you, it is time for us to win the legions' respect, to show them that marines are every bit as good as the army!" Laelius' eyes gleam mischievously. "Our General Scipio, he has promised a gold corona muralis to the first man to breach those walls.[xii] " Laelius' eyes widen, as if telling an exciting story to children. "Have you seen the corona? It is a circle of little towers. It looks like you are wearing a golden fortress!" As his men murmur their excitement, Laelius' tone becomes catty. "I am certain General Scipio thinks that it will go to one of his legionnaires on the causeway. But we will surprise him!"

Laelius pivots around the mast, waving his arm to take in the men gathered below him. "You and I know those land-lovers think we marines are not their equal. They think all we do is float about on our boats while they win the battles. But I ask you: what if it was one of us who first breached those walls? What would the army say then? Their faces would be as red as their unwashed assholes!"

Laelius grins at the hoots and curses that erupt. He reaches out to one of his sailors, and the man gives him a knotted rope with a grappling hook attached to it. The young commander holds the hook up where all can see, as if showing them a great prize. "The walls here are ten feet lower because the Carthaginians think they are safe from attack here. Well, men, we are going to launch these climbing ropes onto the walls while the Carthaginians cower from the rocks of our catapults. And the first man to the top of the wall will win the crown! Imagine the looks on those legionnaires' faces!" As the men cheer, Laelius holds up a bulging leather purse. "And I will give the first man a purse of silver. Consider what you can do with this purse—it will be whores and wine for a month! Who needs a crown of gold?"

As the men roar their boasts and jests, Laelius motions for his marines to follow him down a rope ladder and onto one of the four small boats bobbing alongside the ship. They paddle the short distance over to the steep rocky shore beneath the wall and unload their piles of mounting ropes. Laelius grasps one rope a few feet below the hook end and whirls it about to build momentum. He hurls the hook over the parapet and yanks it to set the hook. As he does, a Carthaginian pops up and hurls several rocks at him, and another pitches a javelin. But Laelius stands calmly, waiting while his men cast return volleys to suppress the enemy missiles, a feral smile upon his handsome young face. A bold Libyan leans over the wall to cut Laelius' rope, and he is pierced through his neck with a Roman javelin, to the cheers of the men in the boat.

Laelius yanks the rope taut, showing it to his men. "Who will be the first up there? The purse will be yours, unless I get there ahead of you!" Laelius sheds his breastplate and greaves, throws a small shield over his back, and begins to clamber up rope knots to the wall. "Follow me!" he shouts over his shoulder.

A dozen men grab their ropes and pitch them over the walls as their compatriots rain javelins and rocks at any Carthaginian who raises his head. The surrounding ships hurl boulders on each side of the attackers, adding to the suppressing fire. The unarmored marines scramble up the rope. Several are killed by the determined defenders, plummeting past their fellows, but the others continue, aching to be the first to scale the wall. Moments later, a bloodied young marine named Sextus Digitus clambers onto the top, stabbing down a guard as other marines clamber up after him. There is a short but furious clash of swords as the walkway erupts in individual duels. The outnumbered Carthaginian defenders are killed, one by one, and pitched over the wall to the rocks below, some still alive, their screams drowned in the crashing surf. Laelius waves his hand, and the marines pad along toward the main gates.

*   *   *   *   *

While Laelius' ships were closing in on the seaside wall, Scipio has launched his attack on the front gates, leading his legions and cavalry across the causeway. His infantry rumbles in a new battering ram toward the gates, a massive log with an iron goat's head, suspended on chains beneath a protective roof. As the ram nears the gates, the Carthaginians rain stones and spears upon it, but the soldiers under the roof are protected, and the flanking legionnaires raise their scutum above their heads, the curved rectangular shields forming a tight protective barrier. And the ram grinds on to the gates.

Magon screams commands for more wall defenders, and his captains race along the walkway to transfer men from the walls by the lagoon and sea, dragging in all the soldiers and remaining militia. The ram reaches the main gates, and the men inside the roof slowly push the tree trunk back on its chains and run forward with it. The iron head booms into the thick iron doors, but they barely budge. Again the ram crashes into the gates, and again. The iron-barred wood begins to splinter, and the defenders become frantic. They hurl firepots onto the roof of the ram, then flaming javelins. Soon the area is a conflagration of small fires and burning wood, with burning legionnaires rolling about the ground to douse the flames, screaming horribly. Scores of Romans fall, but the ram still booms the gates.

Scipio rides about on one side of the front lines, overseeing the frontal assault. Instead of watching the battle on the causeway, however, his gaze is fixed on the distant promontory of land that fingers out into the wide lagoon. He notices the tide lines on the shore, signs the water is receding, but still he is not satisfied it is low enough. Then the morning winds come, blowing out to sea, pushing the lagoon waters farther back. Scipio sees a glint of metal on the promontory, three quick flashes, and he quickly rides over to the senior army engineer, who is supervising the attack with the ram. "Bring the ballistae to the front," Scipio shouts. "Aim for the parapets!" The engineer sends his men to the rear of the assault legion, and they soon wheel up the four enormous crossbows they have built. The soldiers ratchet back the thick rope bowstring and yank the release, rocketing smooth river boulders into the walls, crushing its limestone blocks and any unfortunates behind them.

Scipio commands the ballistae attendants to use every missile at their disposal immediately: his purpose is not to win the battle with them but to induce Magon to use every available man to defend the front walls. Scipio knows he cannot conquer these doughty walls; this battle will be won on sea, not on land.

As the north wind blows the deep water from the lagoon, Marcus Silenus leads five hundred infantry out from the trees along its border. When he sees the ballistae sending their missiles at the gates, he knows that is the signal to attack. Carrying tall wooden ladders over their heads, the trained escaladers follow Marcus across the submerged finger of land the fishermen described to Scipio, the only low-tide path to the seawalls.

The armored Romans sink into sand and water up to their chest, and many look anxiously at the quarter mile of lagoon they must cross to the wall. Marcus Silenus plows heedlessly forward; the water rises to the short man's neck, but he never pauses or looks back, forcing his men to follow him. Marcus fixes his eyes on a large rock outcropping on the opposite shore, a dung-speckled pinnacle filled with raucous cawing seabirds. He remembers the words of the fishermen they talked with last night in Scipio's tent. *Walk out from the point and straight toward the seabirds. Do not stray to deep water on the side.* Marcus recalls these words well; he cannot swim.

Halfway across the wavy lagoon, legionnaires step onto a submerged sandbank. The water descends to their stomachs, and the men take heart and pick up their pace. Marcus studies the walls above them, but no helmeted head appears to sound the alarm. He looks to his right toward the causeway, and he can see the plumes of smoke and hear the booms and thuds of the projectile assault. *The boy has pulled them all to the front*, he thinks. *We may have a chance.*

The men finally step onto the rocky shelf beneath the wall and pause, gasping with relief. Marcus gestures for them to spread apart, and trios of legionnaires spread out along the base of the wall, their ladders at the ready. When all have placed their ladders, Marcus steps to the ladder in front of him, puts his foot upon the rung, and nods to his waiting men. They begin to climb up the ladders, their swords and shields hanging from their backs. Marcus is the first to the top; he scrambles through a space between the thick blocks and lands on his feet, sword at the ready. But there is no one there.

Looking toward the distant front gates, he can see hundreds of Carthaginians clustered about the walkway there, busily hurling projectiles and firepots. He nods to his men. They trot lightly down the walkway until they come to a turn in the wall. Marcus halts and waves for two of his centurions to come forward. The three spin around the corner and dash forward. There is a quick, clashing commotion, followed by the scraping sound of bodies being dragged. Marcus reappears around the corner and motions his men forward with his dripping sword.

The walls on each side of the city converge near the front gates, and Marcus looks across to the opposite wall, to see if any Carthaginians have spied the Romans. He gapes when he sees a thin line of marines pacing toward the front gates, led by Laelius. One of the marines notices the legionnaires, and he trots up to tell Laelius. When he hears, Laelius looks over and waves cheerily, as if he were greeting a friend at a festival. Marcus slowly waves back, half-amused at the sight, and jabs his finger downward, telling them to get down from the wall and out of sight. Laelius nods and leads his men forward, looking for a descent.

As Marcus' men round the last curve toward the gates, they run into a half-dozen militia, who freeze in surprise at the sight of the Romans. Marcus and his men storm into them, and Marcus rams through the Carthaginians to turn and block their escape, that none will run to the front. After a brief, fierce fight, seven bodies are pitched over the walls, one of them a young legionnaire.

Marcus sees an unattended stairway that leads down to a nest of apartment houses, and he leads his men down it. Darting through the side streets, the men head to the main gates, pausing only to dispatch anyone who might warn their enemies. Most of the townsfolk dart inside the nearest buildings as soon as they see the Romans, and Marcus ignores them.

The raiders can see the large open courtyard ahead of them, and Marcus gestures for his men to halt. He sidles forward against the apartment walls and cranes his neck around the corner. Marcus notices there is a large group of townsmen and militia bracing the gates with wood pilings, supervised by a small group of soldiers. The walls above the defenders are dense with Carthaginian infantry and militia as far as his eyes can see. He notes the position of the stairways nearest the gates and waves for his centurions to come to him. Marcus points to the stairway that each is to defend.

As they prepare to charge, a pair of older women shuffle across the courtyard, crossing between the gates and the Romans. They head toward the right stairway, carrying armfuls of javelins for the defenders. One crone looks over her shoulder, sees Marcus and his men standing in the shadows of the narrow street, and drops her weapons with a crash.

"Romans, Romans!" she cackles, pointing a bony finger at them. Several Carthaginians at the gates turn around and shout a warning.

"Now, now!" bellows Marcus, turning to his officers. He whirls to one of the centurions. "Your century follows me, now!" Marcus dashes across the courtyard for the gates, followed by a century of eighty men, as the other centuries fan out toward the stairways. The gate defenders drop their pilings and rush for their weapons, and scores of legionnaires hurry to block the stairways leading to the courtyard. Marcus and his men are upon their enemies within a minute, while they are still stumbling to form ranks. "Get the soldiers first!" Marcus shouts, gesturing at the heavily armored Libyans. As the Romans swarm into them, the defenders back up to the gates, desperation lending fury to their defense.

Marcus stalks toward the leader of the Libyan infantry at the gates, a short, squat man with tree-trunk arms. The Libyan bellows a challenge and rushes for Marcus, raising his war axe over his head. A brash young legionnaire attacks the Libyan from the side, thrusting his sword toward the African's chest. With one swing of his axe, the Libyan knocks the sword from the Roman's hand and delves through the side of the man's helmet and into his brain pan, crashing him to the ground. Marcus notes the awful power of the man's blow and closes on him, moving to the Libyan's shield side. The man chops a fearful blow at the Marcus's head, but he blocks it with his shield, the axe sinking so deep into the shield that it gashes Marcus' arm. The Libyan jerks his weapon backwards to yank it out of the shield. As he does, Marcus releases his shield and the Libyan crashes it back into his own face. Marcus dips down and thrusts his sword up under the Libyan's chin guard and deep into his head. As his opponent gouts out his life from his mouth and nose, Marcus grabs the dead legionnaire's shield and hurries to the gates. He knows there is little time remaining before the walls' defenders break through the Romans who are blocking the stairway.

Fighting like a man possessed, Marcus Silenus jabs and slashes his way to the wood beam crossbars that seal the gates. Scipio's ram still booms from the other side, so deafening that Marcus can only gesture to his men: come here, now.

The Romans are disposing of the last of the gate defenders when a large group of Sacred Band infantry plunges into them from behind. A tall and leanly muscled man leads the Carthaginians. Even in his stiff linen armor, he moves with the fluid grace of a dancer. His white cuirass bears the emblem of a phoenix, the symbol that he is the Champion of Carthage. It is Rhodo, The NightBringer, felling any Roman who dares face him, determined to preserve the gates.

Marcus sees his men giving way and gnashes his teeth with frustration. He rushes into the fray and yanks four burly legionnaires back with him toward the gates. "You are not to fight, though you see us all being killed," he screams at them. "You are to get those gates open! Now!" He shoves them toward the massive crossbars that bow inward with each blow of the ram. They scramble up the low stone steps on the side of the gates and push at the top crossbar, shoving it into its niche in the wall. A spear throw takes one in the back, but as he tumbles off the platform another legionnaire rushes into his place. Shoving and cursing, the Romans push the second beam off the gates. The lowest beam, however, is too bent from ramming to slide through its iron clamps, and the gates hold fast.

The Romans at the stairway slowly draw back into the courtyard, overwhelmed by the number of defenders who descend to attack them. Then Laelius and his marines storm into the courtyard and run to the east stairway, clashing with Balon and his Sacred Band just as they cut down the last of the Roman defenders there.

Balon recognizes Laelius as an officer and hurtles toward him with upraised sword. Fighting without armor, Laelius deftly ducks past Balon's charge and plunges the tip of his falcata into the back of his head. The Carthaginian falls spasming to the earth as Balon's men cry out in dismay. The legionnaires and marines regroup and take control of the stairs, preventing any descent. Several of the Scared Band push in a wagonload of straw, and the wall defenders leap into it and scramble down to fight Laelius' men. They soon overwhelm Laelius' forces and push them away from the steps.

Slowly, the Romans in the courtyard are pushed together about the closed front gates, led by Rhodo and his Sacred Band. Cursing and muttering, Marcus shoves his way through the crush in front of him, stalking toward the haughty Carthaginian that leads the assault.

Rhodo sees the plumed helmet of an officer heading toward him, and a grim smile crosses his face. *There's the leader of this mess. Now we can end this.* He darts behind the young Roman fighting him and slashes his hamstring, dodging the boy as he topples sideways to the ground. Rhodo slips around two dueling soldiers and faces Marcus Silenus, who crouches before him with raised shield and sword, his eyes green lamps of fury. Rhodo stops and laughs at the shorter man.

He gestures haughtily for him to attack. "*Veni, ignavus* (come at me, coward)," he says in his pidgin Latin and waits for the Roman to rush him. Instead, the soldier stalks slowly toward Rhodo, moving around him in a circle, studying his opponent's stance and armor. Rhodo smiles in grudging respect as he revolves to follow Marcus: the Roman is doing what he would do with a dangerous opponent.

Seeing an opportunity, Marcus leaps forward and shoves his shield at the Carthaginian. Rhodo is surprised at the blocky little man's speed, but he manages to deflect the force of the blow sideways with his shield. Even so, he is knocked to one knee by the strength of the blow.

Marcus lunges forward to put his sword through Rhodo's face, but
Rhodo is quick as a serpent, and he dodges the thrust and gashes
Marcus' sword arm. The legate does not even change expression as he
counters with a swipe at Rhodo's head, making him leap backwards to
avoid decapitation. Nonetheless, Marcus' lightning strike has left a
deep slice on Rhodo's cheek. He wipes his hand across his face, stares
at the blood, and smiles broadly: *a worthy opponent, indeed.* The two
men back up for another charge at each other, each streaming blood,
when there is an earth-shattering crash behind them.

*　　*　　*　　*　　*

Scipio stands under the roof of the battering ram, urging his tiring
men to essay yet another plunge into the gates. In front of him, he can
see scores of escaladers throwing up wooden ladders to scale the high
walls as the scurrying defenders fling most of them down. Scipio eyes
the thicket of Carthaginians at the top of the gates. *They are all up here
by the gates, so Marcus has a chance.* He turns around and orders his
second legion to replace the one in the front. He can see the tired
resignation on many of his men's faces as they march to the fore,
fearful that they will be beaten back again. And for the first time since
the battle started, doubt creeps into Scipio's mind.

Suddenly, a chorus of dismayed shouts breaks out among the
defenders above the gates, and he sees many of them darting away from
the wall, out of sight. Then, as the ram thuds into the portals, he can see
a narrow space of daylight opening above the middle of the two gates.
Scipio realizes that Marcus and his men must be on the other side,
fighting to open the passage into Cartago Nova.

Scipio vaults on top of his horse and rides along the front lines of his
men, screaming wildly in triumph as he goes. "Neptune has fulfilled his
promise! He has led our men into Cartago Nova! They are on the other
side of the gates! Victory is ours! Break the gates, damn you, break
them!"

Scipio gallops back to the ram and jumps off his horse. He grabs the thick post and pushes for all he is worth, his face red with effort. The incoming legionnaires see him and rush to his aid, pushing aside the exhausted rammers. Every inch of the ram is covered by a Roman hand, and the soldiers shove with all their strength. The ram speeds into the gates with a splintering crash, and the gates bow farther inward. The legionnaires can see that a cracked beam is all that holds the barrier together, and they scream with excitement and yank the ram back. With a last surge of demonic strength, the Romans rocket the ram into the gates, and the portal splits open.

Scipio rushes onto his horse. "Ah my gods, through the gates!" The legionnaires surge from each side of the ram and shove the gates wide open. The tribunes scream for them to maintain ranks as they march in. Thousands of Romans delve into the opening, eager to wipe out the enemy that has tormented them.

Magon is standing on top of the wall over the gates, directing his few thousand men for maximum defensive effect. When Marcus' men break into the courtyard, he screams for his elite Libyans to get below and attack them, and for Rhodo and the Sacred Band to join them. When he sees Rhodo cutting his way through the Romans below, Magon nods with satisfaction: those fools will soon be disposed of. Then he hears the crunch of his gates giving way and looks over the wall to see the battering ram halfway through the gates. In an instant he realizes the city is lost, knowing he has too few men to win a pitched battle.

He gestures for his field captain to come over. "To the citadel. Get every man to the citadel."

Magon's Sacred Band guards lead him down the stairway and into the courtyard mêlée, where Scipio's Romans are methodically threshing through the Libyans and Carthaginians. He sees Rhodo angrily hacking back at a sturdy little Roman who is fiercely attacking him.

As Magon's guardians fall about him, he shouts over to his champion. "Rhodo! To the citadel, now!"

Rhodo steps back from Marcus Silenus, gives him a mocking bow. "Another time homunculus (little man)," he says and dashes to join his leader. Marcus stands with sword in hand, momentarily taken aback. Then he turns and resumes killing Carthaginians, frustration lending fury to his hand.

Magon's remaining defenders close ranks about him and retreat down the wide main street, backing into a tall, thick tower built into the rear of the town, its sheer sides even higher than the fortress. The iron tower gates close behind the last of Magon's retinue, and the Romans are left standing in the plaza that surrounds his impregnable refuge, stabbing down the unfortunates that did not get into the citadel.

Scipio rides into the plaza and dismounts. He walks up to the citadel's front doors, holding his shield over his head. He can see Magon leaning over a battlement some fifty feet above him, watching the Roman army surround the tower. Marcus Silenus and Laelius stand near Scipio with the rest of the officers, awaiting orders. The city is quiet as the citizens cower within their homes. Only the scattered screams of the last defenders interrupt.

"Magon, surrender! The city is mine," Scipio yells.

"Boy, do you think I will give in to the likes of you, who have not yet learned to shave?" Magon sneers. "The Generals will be upon you by the next moon! I can wait until then."

Marcus eases next to Scipio, speaking so only Scipio can hear him. "He is right, General. It will take months to starve them out of there."

Scipio frowns. "Those doors are solid iron. If we assault that bulwark, we will lose many men. Yet we can't wait, either."

"You must show Magon that you will do anything to take this city," Marcus mutters intently. "The Roman way, as your father would do." Scipio's right hand twitches nervously as he looks at the old centurion with moist, frightened eyes.

Marcus understands his young commander's dilemma, and his voice softens. "If Magon does not surrender, we must assault or retreat. If we retreat, the Generals will be upon us in Tarraco, and many men will be lost. If we assault it, centuries of men will perish. To make him surrender, you will have to demonstrate you will do anything for victory. No matter what you do, people will die."

Scipio swallows and looks back up at Magon. "Magon! Surrender or I will kill you all! If you surrender now, you and your officers will be spared for ransom in Rome—I swear on my father's grave. But once the ram touches the gates, all will die!"

Magon mutters something to a guard, and he hurls a javelin at Scipio. It thunks into the ground in front of Scipio as he stares up at Magon, unmoving. Scipio looks at his nine remaining tribunes and the legionnaires behind them. His eyes glaze with tears, but his voice is firm as he issues his orders. "Tribunes, purge the town. Starting here," he says as he points at the homes about the perimeter.

The tribunes pivot about and step over to issue orders to their waiting centurions. Soon squads of legionnaires are kicking in the doors of each surrounding mansion and apartment house, barging in with swords bared. Screams erupt throughout the city, cries of dying men, women, animals—and children. Their victims' heads, limbs, and torsos are thrown into the street, a grim testament to the Roman's mission to destroy Cartago Nova. Several women burst into the square, running desperately from their houses, but the waiting legionnaires catch them and chop off their heads, bouncing them off the citadel's gates. Through all the slaughter Scipio stares steadfastly at Magon. From that distance, Magon and his men cannot see the trembles that wrack Scipio's body with each scream.

Magon watches the carnage, knowing that many Carthaginian nobles and dignitaries are below him. He sees four of Carthage's ruling Council of Elders being led out by the soldiers, rich and powerful men who were visiting dignitaries. The Elders are quaking with fear as they are dragged to the tower base. The Elders look entreatingly at Magon, who cannot tear his eyes from them. Scipio mutters a few words to Marcus Silenus, and Marcus strides over to the middle-aged men. He turns to the nearest one, a portly, elegant man in robes of the finest purple linen who is pissing himself with terror. "Hold him," Marcus says as he withdraws a leaf-shaped throwing knife from his belt. In one swift act, Marcus pulls up the man's fine robe, slivers his knife into the man's abdomen, slashes him open, and pulls out his entrails. The man wails in anguish as he falls to his knees and rolls over, screaming out the last seconds of his life.

A stone-faced Marcus throws the intestines toward the citadel as he turns to the other man, who is writhing on the ground, begging for mercy, as his fellows yell for Magon to give up. "Magon, I beg you, surrender!" he screams. "The Elders will pay your ransom—I swear it!" Marcus grabs one of the man's frantically kicking legs as a soldier grabs the other, and raises the man's shit-stained robe.

"Enough, enough! Stop!" wails Magon, his face in his hands. "I surrender! No more!"

As soon as the words leave Magon's mouth, Scipio spins about to face his troops. "Cease now!" he screams. "No more killing! On pain of death, cease now!" The officers rush to halt their men as the battle horns sound a call to order. When all is quiet save for scattered cries and sobs, the citadel doors clank open. Magon walks out, head held high, carrying his sheathed sword to a waiting Scipio. Magon bows his head, glaring as he does it, and proffers his weapon. Scipio takes it and addresses Magon. "Your men are mine," he says, then points toward Marcus Silenus. "No weapons. No armor. Follow him," Magon disappears back inside to organize his retreat.

"Put them in the armory," says Scipio, "under heavy guard. Do it as soon as possible, that our men may sleep long tonight. The townspeople are to be unharmed."

In a short while Magon, Rhodo, and his remaining soldiers file out of the citadel, unarmed and unarmored. They walk through a double line of legionnaires, led by Marcus Silenus and two centuries of men. The officers will be captive until they are ransomed; the soldiers face a life of slavery.

Scipio watches them go, barely able to keep his eyes open for his weariness. When all the Carthaginians are inside the armory, Scipio summons his horse and rides out of the city toward the Roman camp. After a quick meeting with his Master of Horse and the infantry tribunes, Scipio sends everyone out, including his guards, with orders not to be disturbed. Scipio picks up a wine goblet to pour himself a draft, but immediately puts it down on the table as he pours: his hand is shaking too much to hold it. He sloshes some wine into the goblet on the table and bends to drink from it, and then drinks another. And another. Nervous and tired, he stumbles over to the miniature family altar he has brought with him, and kneels in front of it.

I pray I have done you proud, Father. I keep my promise to preserve Rome. But I fear I am lost forever.

*   *   *   *   *

APULIA REGION, SOUTHERN ITALIA, 209 BCE. Returning to camp from Rome, Cato wastes no time in unpacking his scant belongings. He walks from his tent to Fabius' pavilion and pokes his head through the entry flaps. "Do we know where Hannibal is, General?" asks Cato. "We've idled two weeks at Rome while he moved about freely. He could be hiding near us in one of his ambushes."

Motioning for his protégé to follow him, the senior commander rises from a heavily padded chair and hobbles to the table map of south Italia. He sticks his finger on a small town south of them. "According to our scouts, he is here in southern Bruttium. Yet a ways off. Ease your worries."

"I am still not an ease," says Cato. "If Hannibal comes here and defeats us, he has a clear path to Rome. Marcellus is way over at Venusia, and his force is too undermanned for an open battle."

176

"That Marcellus may be a Hellenic," says Fabius, "but he is no fool. He will attack Hannibal's rear guard while it is on the march and cut off his supply lines. That will slow his progress. So, if we can take the supply depot at Tarentum before Hannibal gets there, he will not have the resources to advance to Rome!"

"You plan to attack Tarentum?" says Cato skeptically. "It is a redoubtable fortress."

Fabius scratches the back of his neck, looking away from Cato. "No, not against those walls, we would lose too many men. But I have been considering another way," he says, with some embarrassment. "I have been using a cadre of native speculatores, as Scipio does at Iberia. And they have found a way."

Cato can only gape at his mentor, the man he idolized. "You copy that soft-handed patrician, with his sneaking and spying? Are we as bad as the Carthaginians?"

Fabius shakes his head vigorously. "No, and we are not as effective, either. That is what Scipio has taught me." Seeing a red-faced Cato start to object, he raises his hand imperiously. "Suppress your enmity and attend to me, Tribune Cato."

Fabius beckons his abashed pupil to his side, and he speaks softly. "Philomenus is the garrison commander inside Tarentum. He fought against Hannibal when Tarentum was one of our allies. My spies tell me he would help us get into the city."

Cato nods decisively. "That sounds excellent. If we can storm that portion of the walls, we could open the gates."

"Yes, well, there is the matter of pay," Fabius says, smiling ruefully. "He wants a sizable portion of gold to do it. Romans do not pay foreigners for betrayals."

Cato stalks about, thinking the matter over. "I would see it this way.

Promise Philomenus that he can have his share from the Carthaginian spoils inside the city. If we win Tarentum, Rome pays nothing; the payment comes from our enemy. If we lose, there will be no one alive to claim the payment or issue it." [xiii]

Fabius returns to his chair and sits quietly, holding his chin in his hand as he reflects on Cato's words. After a while, he nods his head. "Your logic has the taint of sophistry, but I believe it is the only way," he says. "Do not think ill of me if I commit this wrong. I do it for Rome."

"I would not think ill of you, General," says Cato. "I can forgive anyone's wrongs—except my own." [xiv]

Fabius waves for Cato to go, and the sturdy young tribune stalks toward the tent exit before he glances back at Fabius. "This Scipio is an enemy more nefarious than Hannibal, for he would change how we fight and live. And I will stop him."

*　*　*　*　*

CARTAGO NOVA. On the night before the Cartago Nova assault, the Roman camp had been quiet as a tomb. Those who could sleep had gathered their rest for the impending conflict, and those who could not silently pondered their fate. Two nights later, after the men have recovered from the conquest, the summer evening is filled with the boisterous revelry of victory, of men who drink and fight as if there will be no tomorrow, because now they know there will be a tomorrow for them.

Amid all the furor, Scipio collapses onto his sleeping mats, burying his head beneath some large pillows in an attempt to blot out the world. His brow is hot, and his body begins to ache. He knows the fevers will again be upon him, so he rises and smears oil of lavender about his face and shoulders, hoping its sleep-inducing aromas will take him to a dreamless sleep. Another cup of wine, and he drowses, then sleeps.

In spite of his prayers, the dreams are soon upon him. At first, murky shadows dance behind his mind, sliding gray ghosts that repeat the screams he heard in the square today. Roman Senators' faces flash past him: Flaccus from the Latin Party, General Fabius, his mother Pomponia, the young contrarian Cato, and his dead father Publius. And finally, Amelia, his love. He then lapses into a deep and dreamless sleep until cock's crow, when his dream takes him back to Rome.

Scipio walks through one of Rome's narrow side streets off the main entrance to the Forum, lined with merchant stalls. He pushes his way through the shoppers and vendors; he can see the street opening up into the Forum Square ahead of him. A purple-robed street vendor shouts at him as Scipio passes by, offering him fame and riches if he will drink the potion he sells, a murky-looking viscous liquid that is entirely unappealing.

Further on, a sinewy old man stands on one of Rome's public speaker podiums. The man wears a simple gray tunic and leans on his weathered staff, but his commanding voice bespeaks him as a person of power. As Scipio nears, he is startled to see it is his beloved childhood tutor Asclepius, deceased for years. The old Greek warrior expounds on one of the favorite lessons he gave to Scipio and his friends: ethics and service to the state. Scipio halts in front of his old mentor, who seems not to notice him among the small crowd at his feet.

Asclepius spreads out his arms and shouts entreatingly, "Heed me, citizens. Heed the words of the immortal Aristotle, greatest of the philosophers. He has a question for you." Asclepius looks into the crowd and locks eyes on Scipio. "You all know that a good citizen works to preserve his country, but a good man works to do the right thing, to be a good person. And these two oft come into conflict." Asclepius smiles slyly as he often did when posing a conundrum to Scipio, Laelius, and Amelia. "Aristotle would ask you: is it nobler to act in the interests of the state over the individual, or should the individual sacrifice his honor for the interests of the state. Which would you choose?"

"What honor is there in allowing the state to decay that you may preserve your personal merit?" counters Scipio. "Is the greater good to be sacrificed for the individual's ethos?"

"If citizens act honorably, the state's interests are always served," shouts a woman. "What has a state become if its citizens are not moral?"

Scipio shrugs. "Perhaps the citizen and the individual are all the same. Serving the interests of the state is the most honorable act an individual and a citizen may do because they are one and the same."

Asclepius cocks his head wonderingly at Scipio. "Even if the individual must commit dishonorable acts? Such as murder, or lying?" He looks pointedly at Scipio. "Or theft?" Scipio bites his lip, thinking.

"If it meant the preservation of the state, I would steal," Scipio declares firmly. "Though it impugn me or imprison me."

Asclepius nods, rolls his eyes appreciatively, and then looks back at Scipio, another sly smile on his face. "Would you steal from the state in order to preserve it, if you believed its best interests were served by taking its wealth or power?"

A stout young man in the front brays a laugh. "What nonsense is this? You think you could steal from me and tell me it's for my own good, and have me thank you for serving my interest?"

The crowd laughs, and Asclepius stands silently, his face as reproving as if children were taunting him. "Have you ever withheld drink from a drunken man, my friends, knowing he would hurt himself if he drank it? Or hidden a knife from a person bereaved at a sudden misfortune, though they beg for it? You do it because they are sick, sick in body or sick mind, and so you deny them until the time they will be well." The crowd stands silent, as Asclepius looks across them.

"Sometimes the greatest honor an honorable man can do is to dishonor himself for others."

The camp horns wake him, and Scipio rises, a befuddled smile on his face, thinking about his dream. At last, he reconciles himself with what he has known he must do to win this war, though he feared to admit it to himself. *I now cast the dice for victory*, he thinks as he pulls on his tunic. *Let us see where they fall.*

VI. AFTERMATH

CARTAGO NOVA, 209 BCE. Scipio sits in a large, high-backed wooden chair that rests on a dais in the city's main meeting hall. It is four days after his army's conquest of the fortress, and the exuberance of conquest has given way to the tedium of administering a conquered city. There is plunder to be collected, wounds to tend, mass burials to be quickly completed, and disputes to be resolved. Scipio is now attending the last of these matters as he holds court on the fate of prisoners and townspeople. Laelius and Marcus Silenus stand on each side of him, acting as his advisors.

Laelius studies Scipio's bleary-eyed face and frowns. "You look depressed, my friend. Are you having regrets about the … the surrender?"

Scipio stares straight ahead. "I have no regrets. Only nightmares," he says tonelessly, his face a mask.

Laelius reaches out and gently squeezes Scipio's shoulder. "It needed to be done. If you think of all the legionnaires who are still living because you forced surrender, you will know it needed to be done."

Scipio shrugs off the consolation. "At night I still hear the innocents' entreaties. Their screams."

Overhearing their muted conversation, Marcus Silenus leans in from Scipio's other side. "Heed Laelius. You tilted the scales of life in our favor. Had you not shown your iron to the Carthaginians, we would still be fighting them. Had you not shown it to our men, you would have lost their respect." Marcus snorts derisively. "I also hear screams at night. The screams of men who tried to kill me, before I put a blade through their chest." His mouth twitches with a smile. "It helps me sleep."

The young general shakes off his mood and lurches himself upright. "What is the next issue, Servilius?" he shouts to his attending tribune.

The older man consults a scroll. "General, we have hundreds of Iberian captives. Men, women, and children of high placement. Magon held them prisoner to maintain tribal loyalty. Should we kill them or ransom them?"

Scipio reaches for his goblet of honeyed wine and sips it, pondering. He looks at Laelius and Marcus. "Set them free," he says.

Marcus leans in. "Free them?" he asks incredulously. "Their kin did kill many of our soldiers, perhaps your own father or uncle!"

Scipio returns a coldly reproving look that takes Marcus aback. "Set them free," he says in a tone that brooks no dissent. "We need live allies more than dead enemies. We will show leniency to these tribes, that they may join us in battle, or refuse to fight against us." Scipio blinks. "After killing those townspeople, we must prove we can be lenient."

He waves his hand at Servilius. "Give each tribal group an escort to their homeland. Have it done by the evening horns!" Servilius bows and mutters some commands to two of his centurions, who rush out of the meeting room. "Next," says Scipio.

Servilius motions toward the open front doors. A squat, barrel-chested centurion drags in a tall and willowy Iberian maiden and throws her before Scipio's feet. The centurion gives Scipio a gap-toothed grin. "We found this tasty morsel hiding in Magon's kitchen, Maximus." He leers at Scipio. "I thought you might like to sample her first, given your taste for the ladies and all."

Scipio frowns at the impudent officer. "Gratitude," he says coldly. "Now be gone, you pumpkin."

Abashed, the centurion withdraws amid jeers from the attending soldiers as the young woman picks herself off the floor and looks coolly at Scipio, her head held high. Looking into her face, Scipio has to restrain a gasp of awe: she is one of the most beautiful women he has ever seen.[xv] "They found you in the kitchen?" he says with a wry grin. "I would venture you are neither cook nor serving wench."

"I am Carmina," she replies haughtily. "Daughter of Dario, chieftain of the Bastuli. I was held prisoner here to guarantee my father's loyalty." She looks deep into Scipio's eyes. "His reluctant loyalty."

"I understand, Carmina." Scipio steps off the dais and goes to her, taking her by the hand. "You are lovely beyond words," he says softly. "A fitting present for a king. Or a general." In spite of herself, Carmina's eyes moisten with apprehension. Seeing her alarm, he smiles sadly. "And you remind me of the one at home who holds my heart in thrall." He sighs and then grins regretfully. "You are safe from my depredations, Carmina."

"I too am betrothed," she says enthusiastically. "To Allucius, prince of the horse-loving Oretani. He is—he was—a prisoner of Magon. That bastard Carthaginian threw him into the prison cells below. Now he is in your power." She suddenly falls to her knees, making Scipio jump. "Please do not harm him!" she begs as she clutches his knees. She tries to look at him beguilingly, though tears roll down her cheeks. "I will be yours in whatever way you desire. Just set him free."

Feeling her arms about him, Scipio can feel himself rise in spite of his fevered weariness. He shifts his belt about, hoping no one can see the bump of his erection against his tunic. She is his for the taking, part of the spoils of war, as all would acknowledge. And she will do anything he wants. He can see himself entering her from behind, hearing her cries of despair and pleasure. *If I fuck her, I make two tribes my enemies.* He looks at the swell of her fulsome breasts. *But they already toil against us—nothing will have changed.* Scipio gulps and releases her hand. He looks at the supervising tribune. "Fetch this Allucius from the prison chambers. Now!" The tribune sends three guards dashing out the door. Scipio points for Carmina to sit on a chair to the side as he returns to the dais to conduct other business.

The guards soon return with a slim young man who wears only a filthy loincloth over his light brown limbs, but who walks with an upright dignity in spite of his rags. The boy cries out when he sees Carmina, and rushes to embrace her. The guards grab his arms and roughly pull him back, but he shakes off the guards' restraining grip and turns to face Scipio, looking warily at him.

"You are Allucius, prince of the Oretani?" inquires Scipio.

"I am," replies the handsome youth with obvious pride.

Scipio nods. "I am—"

"All here know who you are," Allucius says, interrupting. "King Scipio, chief of the Romans."

Scipio winces at the kingly appellation. "I am but a soldier, no more," he says impatiently, "here to do my duty." He points at Carmina. "This maiden is your betrothed?"

Allucius nods enthusiastically. "Carmina is my life," he says as he smiles at her. She smiles back nervously, wringing her hands, her expression evidencing her fear for him. Allucius turns back to Scipio. "Please do not harm her," he pleads. "I give you my life in exchange for hers. Or I will bring gold from my father's mines. Much gold, if you but return her home."

Carmina surges against the guard holding her. "No! Allucius, he will not kill me. Let him have his way." She looks earnestly at Scipio. "I will do whatever you want if you will but free him, General."

Scipio looks calculatingly at Allucius, as if conducting a business transaction. "So you offer your life for hers?" he asks.

Allucius nods, then finds his voice. "Y–yes …."

Scipio looks at the two guards restraining Allucius. "Kill him."

One guard nods to the other, and he pins Allucius' arms back as the other yanks out his shortsword. Allucius strains his neck out for the cut, eyes clenched shut, surrendering to his fate. The guard raises his arm to strike, but when he does, Allucius writhes free and strikes the other guard in the face, wrestling his sword from him. The boy leaps up and dashes forward to face an unarmed Scipio as Laelius and Marcus whip out their swords, knowing they will be too late to stop him. When he is within a few feet of Scipio, Allucius abruptly turns the sword upon himself, grasping the pommel with both hands and pointing the blade under his chin.

"Swear you will spare her," he says through clenched teeth, as blood trickles down the blade point where it has pierced his throat. "Swear and I will do it myself!"

Carmina screams with alarm. She pulls a dagger from her bodice and stabs her captor on his hand. The guard yelps with pain as Carmina rushes to Allucius and clutches him. "Take me first," she urges Allucius. "I would rather die than live without you!"

The guards close on the despairing couple, blades poised to kill them, when Scipio raises his hand. "Halt! Withdraw from them!" Scipio walks down and gently takes the sword from Allucius' hands. He raises the sobbing Carmina from the floor, pushes her into Allucius, and steps back.

"Forgive me. I had to be assured that your word is your bond." He smirks. "I have lately been in our Senate, where words have the value of a grain of wheat, and are more numerous." Scipio looks about the room. "Carmina and Allucius are free!" he proclaims loudly. Scipio turns back to the guard that held Carmina. "On pain of your life, escort this woman, and all of her tribe, back to their homeland."

The guard starts to lead Carmina out when she dashes back and throws herself at Scipio's feet. "The gods bless you, King Scipio."

Allucius watches her being led from the building, then faces Scipio, his tear-stained face radiant with relief. He kneels and kisses Scipio's hand. "The earth gods bear me witness," Allucius declaims for all to hear. "I will repay this man a thousand times."

Scipio draws him up and grasps his forearm, as Allucius does his. "It pleasures me to see two so in love become reunited. Would I could do the same with my Amelia, but duty chains me here." He turns the boy about and gently pushes him. "Go, Allucius. Tell the Oretani that they need fear no Roman, as long as they do not serve Carthage."

Allucius nods and starts to walk out when a thought occurs to Scipio, setting his eyes alight. "Allucius, one favor before you depart. How many of your tribesmen are captives here?"

Allucius reflects. "There are about twenty still alive, as I recall. The sons of chieftains and warlords."

Scipio rubs his chin, musing. "So, they are strong men, then." He points to the west. "You and your tribesmen will meet me by the city storehouse tomorrow at dusk. I have a task for you to complete before you go. It will take but a few hours, but it will serve us well. All of us."

Allucius bends to kneel and bows his head. "I hear and obey," he says.

Scipio turns to one of his tribunes. "Go with this man to the prison cells. Release those he selects; they are free to depart whenever they desire." The tribune salutes and heads toward the door, gesturing for Allucius to follow. Scipio watches them leave as Laelius draws up behind him.

"What in Hera's cunt are you going to do, Scippy, that you require those savages instead of our own men? Are you having another of your fever dreams?"

Scipio merely smiles into his friend's eyes, a slight grin on his face. "Balancing the ledgers, Laelius. I need the assistance of those who have no connection to Rome—especially no connection to Felix, our quaestor."

Scipio walks back to his chair and slumps into it. "Who is next?" he says moodily. "Bring them up quickly. I have much to do today." He turns to his master of supplies, a wizened former soldier. "Bring four wagons near the storehouse. We have some grain transports that must be done for the locals."

The supply master blinks his rheumy eyes, confusion evident on his face, followed by the blank resignation of a lifelong civil servant. "It will be done," is all he says.

Late that afternoon Scipio stands in the town square with his tribunes and centurions, watching the Carthaginian citizens march out toward the docks. After taking a blood oath to Baal that they will not leave Africa, they are allowed to take an old transport ship back across the strait to resume their life in Carthage, leaving all their belongings behind. Magon and his officers will board another ship, a trireme bound for Rome, where they will be delivered to the Senate along with the first load of Cartago Nova plunder: the gold and jewels of Magon's elaborate palace. The hundreds of surviving Libyan and Carthaginian soldiers are assigned to the galleys as slave rowers, freeing up the Roman oarsmen to become part of Laelius' burgeoning marine force.

Scipio and his men stand on the wide speaking platform above the square, watching hundreds of captives march out. Rhodo walks in the van of the prisoners destined for the galleys, his arms manacled in recognition of his deadly skills. The elegant Carthaginian looks disdainfully into Scipio's crowd of officers on the platform, searching faces until he finds Marcus Silenus. Rhodo looks at Marcus' face until Marcus notices him. Marcus nods his head, and Rhodo does the same. There is an unspoken agreement between them, about their unfinished business.

As the prisoners fade out of sight, Scipio points for Laelius to stand in front of the Roman assemblage that is facing Scipio. Laelius jostles his way to the front and stands with arms crossed, a puzzled look on his face. The young navy officer is wearing an embroidered tunic that he pillaged from an enemy commander's manse, knowing that the commander will have little use of it in Rome's prisons.

Scipio extends his arm out and turns in a semicircle, commanding his men's attention. "Hear me, men of Rome! Through Gaius Laelius' blockade of the harbor, we have captured eighteen Carthaginian ships[xvi] that will now become part of our fleet. And without shedding a drop of Roman blood, he has also procured dozens of trade ships filled with all manner of grains, foods, and treasure. Through his exploits we now have resources to wage war across the country, to take the offensive against the Generals' armies! Gaius Laelius, step forward!" Scipio's friend solemnly steps next to Scipio, who puts his hand on his shoulder as the two face the crowd. "I hereby appoint you Admiral of the Iberian Fleet. May the gods bless your every venture." Most of the tribunes and centurions applaud loudly. Laelius has become a favorite among those who look beyond his unabashed homosexuality to the warrior beneath.

Scipio places a ropy green wreath onto Laelius' head and grins at the crowd. "It's seaweed," he exclaims. Amid the laughter he raises both his arms, and his face turns serious. "Quintus Trebellius and Sextus Digitus, step forward!" The centurion and the marine stride out proudly from the crowd to stand before Scipio. "You two were the first to breach the walls, coming from different places." Scipio smiles. "And I have heard about the fights between army and marines about who was first!" Scipio gestures for Spurius, who brings up two gold leaf crowns bearing the shapes of walls and towers. "For the first time in our history, I award two corona muralis, for two men of exceptional bravery."[xvii] As the crowd cheers and bangs their armament, Scipio places a crown on each.

When he steps back from them, Laelius bends and whispers in his ear. "Thank Jupiter you did that. We were going to have a mutiny on our hands!"

Scipio spreads his arms wide before the crowd, signaling he will speak. "The day after tomorrow, we begin a new training regimen. Our men will learn how to fight on Iberian terrain, as Iberians. How to fight in both mountain and plain. How to wield a new sword that is more deadly than any before. How to change formations immediately. When we conquer Iberia, we will become the army that all future legions will emulate!" There is a scattering of cheers, but most of the officers are quiet, waiting to see what their inventive general has dreamed up now.

The grin returns to Scipio's face, with a trace of boyish mischief. "But tonight, we relax. Let the wine flow free as we celebrate our capture of the richest city in Iberia!" Now the cheers erupt from everyone, and Scipio nods their acknowledgement.

Scipio turns to address his officers. "Laelius, your marines will guard the city in shifts, and my infantry will take shifts watching the camp, that all may partake. I will personally see to the celebration." He spies a look of concern on several tribunes' faces. "No, the task will be a pleasure to me. I did such as curule aedile for Rome. Now go, notify your men, and release them to their pleasures. I will order wine and food for this fest. The best we can buy."

Pushing into the back of his officers, Scipio finds his nervous old quaestor standing off to the side of them. "Felix, I will procure these myself, that I know we have a fair price. But I will not scrimp. I will purchase much of the best, whatever the cost." The army's accountant gasps in fiscal horror, his mouth burbling like a fish's, and he raises his hands to object. Scipio waves him off as he steps down the side of the platform and walks with his guard to Merchants' Row, where the local vendors are already preparing their wares for their new clientele.

Moments later, Scipio paces up to a large stone building with rows of sealed urns in front of it. The sign's Iberian words are foreign to him but the grapevines on it speak a universal language: this is the business of a wine merchant. The manager stands out front directing the unloading of large urns from a wagon; he is a richly attired and portly Greek. He begins speaking Latin when he sees Scipio approaching. "General Scipio, our liberator. It is my life's honor to see you at my humble establishment!"

Scipio nods at his effusiveness and points to the urns. "The citizens tell me that you have the largest stores of wine in this city, is that correct?"

The merchant rubs his hands together. "Oh yes, with wines from all over the world—including the very best of Iberia! What may I get for you? Perhaps a flagon of Baetican, the pride of the south?"

"This wine is for my men. And I have little time for negotiation." Scipio hands him a scrap of papyrus, hastily scribbled. "Here, I desire this quantity of wine, of a good drinkable quantity, but not lavish. Delivered as soon as possible. What is the cost?" The merchant glances at the list and writes a figure on the tablet. "Have a care," Scipio interjects as he writes. "My good will would be priceless to you." The merchant glances sideways at Scipio. He pauses, then erases one figure and writes in another. He hands back the papyrus to the general.

Scipio glances at it and nods agreeably. "You will be paid that figure in coin within three days. Now, I want you to write me a bill for this amount of wine, at this cost." Scipio scribbles another figure and gives it to the merchant.

The Greek looks at it and stares wide-eyed at Scipio. "This is a king's ransom in fine wine! What is this bill for?"

Scipio takes a step closer to the nervous little man. "It is a receipt for an accountant that does not know wine from beer, but who has a head for figures. You will give the receipt to me without delivering anything that is on there, only the other wine." Scipio takes a step closer to the merchant, his hand on his sword hilt. "You are not to mention this to anyone, on pain of imprisonment for slander. Do you understand?"

The merchant bobs his head furiously, speechless with fright. Scipio turns him about and pushes him toward his office doors. "Make the bill out now." The salesman rushes in and hastily writes it up. He starts to give it to Scipio when Scipio raises his hand. "Seal it," the general says. The merchant gulps and makes his wax seal on the receipt and gives it to Scipio. "You will be delivered the higher amount of money, and not the first amount. I will have someone come by to pick up the difference." Scipio turns and walks back the way he came, his guard following.

The young general stops at several food stalls, where the he makes similar arrangements. After several hours he is back at his headquarters, ready to hold the last of the day's meetings. He enters to find Marcus Silenus waiting for him. "Where have you been?" Marcus asks.

"Learning how to fight a war on two fronts," replies Scipio, as he eases into his magisterial chair. "Now, who is next?"

*   *   *   *   *

ROME, 209 BCE. The street vendors are closing their stalls as Amelia and Pomponia skip by them with the rest of the celebrants, returning from the midsummer festival of Zeus. The two women are chatting and laughing as they enter the side streets off the Forum. There is a spring in their steps this evening; both are giddy with wine and success. Amelia's propaganda campaign and Pomponia's coercive dinner parties have helped to get Gaius Marcellus elected as Rome's proconsul, much to the dismay of Flaccus and the rest of the Latin Party.

Seeking to represent the interests of ordinary people, Marcellus wasted no time expending his newfound political capital. After his election, the Sword of Rome collaborated with the Tribune of the Plebs to ensure the veto of several tax-reduction measures for the wealthy. The sponsoring Latins gnashed their teeth in frustration but kept their silence.

Then Marcellus marched his new legionnaires and allies from Rome to join his old army, heading down the Appian Way to engage Hannibal. He exits the city portal amid the wild cheers of thousands of plebs, hard-working commoners who hail him as their potential savior. Marcellus has thrice battled Hannibal to a draw, even as he wins the war of attrition against the Carthaginian and his dwindling supply of mercenaries and Italia allies. Hope has returned to Rome's populace— hope that the Bane of Roma may yet be defeated, that Marcellus will end nine years of fear and sorrow.

Amelia and Pomponia are happiest, however, at the events in distant Iberia. The news of Scipio's victory has arrived like a thunderbolt in Rome. One week the populace hears that the young general is dug in behind Tarraco's thick walls, guarding the frontier in a defensive action. The next they find out he is far south at Cartago Nova, storming over the seemingly impregnable Carthaginian fortress, bringing hope to Rome's victory-starved citizenry.

From the lowest pleb to the highest patrician, Romans now feel the war tide turning, with Scipio and Marcellus on everyone's tongue. For the first time since her husband Publius was killed in Iberia, Pomponia is truly happy. And Amelia—calm and resolute through all the public jokes and comedic performances about her betrothed's tender age—she can finally laugh at them all.

"It is almost beyond belief, that Cornelius won such a battle," exults Amelia. "Was it just a few years ago that the two of us wrestled on the tiles in your atrium?" She chuckles. "That seems so long ago." Pomponia playfully shoves her future daughter-in-law, grinning slyly. "Ah, you were wrestling, but by that time it was not the wrestling of children," she says. "As I recall, the wrestling holds were in quite unconventional places, and pinning you became a very extended exercise!"

Amelia reddens, but she manages a shy laugh. "We did grow from innocence to passion in our play, though I do not recall exactly when that happened."

"It is not something you watch happen, but it is something you notice when it has happened," smiles Pomponia. "I did think my husband Publius an arrogant boor. And then one day, all I could think of was having his body against mine, just like that!" She snaps her fingers. "I am glad you are so strong, dear. I fear my son will need your strength in the years to come. With every victory the resentment against him rises."

"Perhaps the Senate will begrudge Scipio some more money," Amelia says hopefully. "Last month he had written me that he barely had enough coin to feed his men, much less wage a campaign. And he must deliver all the spoils of Cartago Nova to Rome." She sighs. "All that money spent on the military. Where is our flowering of civilization, like Greece had?"

Pomponia snorts. "Get money from that Senate? The Latin Party may dislike Marcellus for his Hellenic sympathies, but they hate my son even more. They will do what they have always done: use Hannibal's presence in Italia as an excuse to restrict Scipio's resources." She shrugs. "And why not? If the Latins can limit my son's success until the next election, they will replace him with a party lackey, and let him have the glory of conquering Iberia." Her mouth tightens into a line. "This is becoming a party war for Rome's future."

"Well, they cannot restrict his genius," replies Amelia. "He will figure out a way to win. He has always learned more from his opponents than his friends, from the evil more than the good. And he turns it against them."

Pomponia nods. "My little boy is learning to play the politics of war," she says. "I hear the stories from Iberia that he called Neptune to his side, that he communes with the gods." She laughs. "I remember how much he liked Aesop's fable about the Wolf in Sheep's Clothing, that people could be so easily fooled by appearances—and stories!"

Amelia pouts. "He would never lie," she says. "But he knows the power of myth!"

The two friends are so busy chatting they do not notice the dark, hooded figures who are following them through the twilight streets. Pomponia and Amelia turn away from the crowd and into a narrow side street between two tall apartment buildings, a shortcut to the Scipio domus. As they reach the middle of the street, they hear a clattering behind them. They turn to discover their two male slaves lying in the alley with their throats cut.

Two cloaked men fall upon the women, pulling sacks over their heads and hustling them into an abandoned apartment. The men push them into different corners of the large windowless room and slam the door shut. Amelia and Pomponia scrabble off their head coverings and back into corners of the room, eyes wide with fright. A scarred and rangy older man blocks the front door, with a short and stocky youngster standing next to him. The older man stands with hands on hips, a gloating sneer on his whiskery face.

"You two have been messin' where you should not be," he snarls. "And we're here to teach you a lesson about your messin'!" He laughs and snaps his fingers at the younger man. "We'll beat 'em about, and give 'em a good fuckin.' Then we get out of here."

The young man looks at him apprehensively. "That wasn't part of the arrangement," he says. "Just slap them about."

"Fuck the arrangement, and fuck them. I'm going to get meself a piece o' patrician ass! And you do the same, or I'll slice yer throat!" He leers at Amelia. "You're a pretty one, aren't ya? Maybe I'll give you a go when I'm done with the redhead," he crows as he stalks toward Pomponia.

Pomponia pushes herself into a corner and musters her voice. "I have coin. You can have it all—just let us go."

The youngster glances hopefully at the lead man, who only snorts. "I've plenty enough coin for the doin' of this. And I'll have yours too, before it's over."

The leader grabs Pomponia and throws her down, ripping down the top of her tunica to expose her breasts. "Ahh, fine set you have, Domina. Bet they're goin' ta jiggle when I'm a-pumpin' ya!" He pulls out a dagger and shows it to Pomponia, who glares mutely at him. "You scream and I'll slit yer throat fer sure, bitch." He turns back to his companion. "See to the young one. Give her a good fuckin' boy. Them's orders."

Hesitantly, the youngster grabs a cringing Amelia and forces her down along the wall to the floor. "Off me, you little pig," Amelia spits. She kicks and elbows him furiously, but the muscular youth eventually pushes her flat.

"Settle back and take it without a fuss," he mutters. "It will be easier that way." He climbs on top of Amelia and pushes up her robe, yanking off her silk loincloth. As he leans forward to enter her, Amelia lunges up and bites his ear, tearing off a piece of the lobe. She writhes from under him and starts to rise when she is knocked down with a blow to the back of her head. "Curse you! I tried to be nice to you! You want it hard, that's what you'll get!" He throws her down upon her stomach and pins her arms back. He yanks up her tunica and pries her legs apart, ignoring her screams.

Thunk! Thunk! The young man's eyes start from his head, and his mouth gapes wide. He collapses on top of Amelia, who squirms from beneath his writhing body. When she stands up, she sees two leaf-shaped throwing knives wedged into his back. One razored blade is buried to the hilt in his shoulder, but the other knife dangles loosely from the base of his neck, stuck in his spine. Her attacker convulses on the cobbled floor, his legs twitching helplessly as he loses all motor control, unable to do any more than claw feebly at the earth.

As if from a great distance, she hears Pomponia's voice. "Amelia, Amelia! Are you all right?" She sees a blood-soaked Pomponia standing by the corpse of her rapist, pulling her gown back down her legs. The man lies on his back, blood still pouring from a deep gash that splits his throat. "I am sorry it took me so long to help you," Pomponia says, her voice shaking. "I had to wait until the bastard's dick was inside me, so he was distracted. Then I gave him a second mouth." She spits on the body. "A Thracian, by his tattoos. Someone's house slave. I will make enquiries and find out, on my life."

"Who would do such a thing?" Amelia sobs. "Who hates us that much?"

"The Party. They hate women interfering with their politics, hampering their efforts to make gold at others' expense. Pricks!" Pomponia smoothes her hair with a trembling hand, her green eyes shining with anger. "I have no doubt that someone in the Latin Party is involved in this. Someone with enough money to pay this scum. I will settle accounts with him, whoever he is."

Pomponia takes another look at her bloodied outer sheath and throws it into a corner. "Our revenge will not be in killing. We will redouble our efforts for the Hellenics to take control. When Marcellus conquers Hannibal, we will go to the plebs and get them to elect Marcellus dictator, so he may reign supreme without obstruction from the conservatives. That will be death to those Latin bastards."

"Then they will come at us again, Pomponia," says Amelia. She sobs for a moment, then straightens her shoulders. "I will be ready next time. Can you show me that trick with the knives, how to throw them?"

Amelia is interrupted by a gabbling sound at her feet. She looks down to see her young attacker clutching at her shoes, eyes bulging with the desperate terror of a dying man. "Puh-please, help me!" he drools. "Helppugh mae!"

Amelia puts her hand to her mouth, horrified. She looks at Pomponia with a question in her eyes. "Leave him," says Pomponia coldly as she walks for the door. "I have already given him too much help by putting that knife in his back. The bastard will die sooner than he deserves." Pomponia gives Amelia one of the throwing knives and opens the door. After a quick look outside, she leads Amelia out the front door and into the night, where they straggle for home.

*   *   *   *   *

VI. Aftermath

CARTAGO NOVA, 209 BCE. It is a break day for the legionnaires, a time to rest from the mock war games and weapons training. Ever since their lavish party to celebrate the fall of Cartago Nova several days ago, the centurions have drilled their soldiers mercilessly. Now it is a day to recuperate and prepare for the morrow's rigors. But that tomorrow is far away this late summer afternoon, and there is relaxation to be had before retiring early for the next day's grind.

"Fortuna, bless me one more time! Give me a Venus and I'll sacrifice a cock to you. But not my own, of course!" Amid the laughter, Crassus, a veteran decurion of the Tenth Legion, raises the dice high, shaking them vigorously in his three-fingered hand. He has just won his third consecutive cast with the dice, and his pile of shiny *sestertii* has grown from a handful to a mound. He prays again to Fortuna for luck, prompting other prayers from those who have bet against him.

"Just throw the dice, fool!" grouses one of the losers.

"Off with you, this it too big to rush!" Crassus casts the four numbered knucklebones along the packed earth. They show a total of nine, neither a win nor a loss. He picks up the dice again and starts shaking them. "Come to me, fourteen, come on Venus!"

If he casts a Venus, Crassus will have enough to buy two skins of the region's prized Rioja wine. "If I win this cast, I'll buy the grape tonight," he declares. "Nothing like a good drunk to break the monotony of all this odd new training."

"Aye," says one of the players. "Drilling to follow those cursed whistle commands in that formation the general calls a 'cohort.'"[xviii]

Another adds, "It is nothing more than a big maniple, if you ask me. And worst of all, we are double-time marching with all those supplies on our backs, as if we were mules. Just like at Tarraco."

Crassus shakes the bones in his hands. "The General has a plan, though only the gods know what it is. But enough whining. One more Venus, we will all be worshipping Bacchus tonight!"

Crassus is so intent on his throw that he does not notice that the crowd around him has grown oddly silent. He rears back to make his cast when a commanding voice halts his throw, a voice with the unmistakable tone of command.

"You have prayed to Fortuna for luck, I trust?"

Crassus looks over his shoulder to see General Scipio standing behind him, a wry smile on his face. The centurion's fellow legionnaires are all standing at attention, wide-eyed with apprehension, but Scipio grins and signals them to be at ease. "I just came by to inquire about your welfare. Is camp life decent enough for you?"

A triarii stares boldly into his commander's eyes. "Life here is good enough for now, General. But it grows a bit tedious. We do naught but drill about like a gaggle of raw recruits. Just yesterday, we had us triarii breaking in one direction, the principes in another, and the hastati in a third! Turning this way and that as if we were prancing in a summer dance, mock fighting with those strange Iberian swords. Ach! When do we fight the Generals and settle this war? The harvest will be coming at home, and I would return!"

Scipio nods, a small grin on his face. "I want to settle this issue as soon as we can. But the Three Generals outnumber us. We must learn how to fight in Iberia, if we are to have a chance against them." He squats down next to the players. "Hannibal taught me a lesson at Cannae, that our maniple formations cannot take the shock of cavalry attacks. They break apart like cracker bread. We have to be more fluid, especially when we fight those swarming Numidians, or when we fight on uneven terrain."

Scipio stands and spins about, striking a battle pose and then swirling to strike another from a different direction. "We must be quicker than any legions before us, to change direction in the blink of an eye. To break into small groups when needed, and quickly join again." He sees the men quietly staring at him and he grins. "Enough of that for tonight!" He turns to Crassus and throws several sestertii on the ground. "Make your cast, centurion. My money says Fortuna is with you."

"As you say, General," replies Crassus as he picks up the dice. Two older legionnaires bet against Scipio, a hint of resentment in their eyes. Crassus matches their bet and looks at Scipio. "If I may be so bold, would you call upon the gods to help my cast? We know that Neptune favors you, pulling away this place's waters so we could conquer it." Crassus looks meekly at Scipio. "Perhaps a prayer to Fortuna?"

Scipio laughs. "I will not attest that Neptune was by my side! But even if he was, Crassus, I cannot ask the gods' favor in all small matters. Soon they would not listen to me. Do you recall Aesop's fable of the boy who cried wolf too often?" When Crassus nods, Scipio slaps him on the back. "Just so. But I will offer a wish that Fortuna blesses you. That much I can do! Now, *carpe diem*, and make your throw!"

Crassus nervously shakes the dice again and throws them onto the ground. The dice show a Venus. A winning cast. Crassus rakes in his winnings among the curses and cheers of his compatriots, and Scipio does the same, dribbling his winnings into his purse. "I keep my promise," Crassus crows. "The best of this magnificent city's wines are on me tonight! Thank you, General," Crassus says as he turns to Scipio, only to find him gone. "Did you see what he did?" Crassus blurts. "He brought Fortuna to visit me! He does truly communicate with the gods!"

"What gods?" grumbles one of the losing bettors. "The dice took their own course. Now you must take yours and buy us some wine! And women, too!"

As the others laugh, Crassus shakes his head. "No, the General is truly touched by the gods. His attendants tell me they visit him when he dreams. They can hear him threshing about and muttering in his sleep. They say he awakes exhausted, as if he had been to Olympus itself that night!"

VI. Aftermath

"Perhaps, perhaps he just runs a fever," says a middle-aged army tent maker. "Myself, I hope he can call down the gods when the Three Generals band together and come after us. We will need them then."

Crassus rises, brushing the dust off his bare knees. "Then they had best come soon, gods or not. Winter will be coming. And we cannot all stay here." He starts to walk away, then looks over his shoulder. "There is a wine merchant who has a tent on the edge of camp. I would go and sample his wares. Who will join me?" As one, the soldiers scramble up and run to catch up.

Scipio walks through the camp, talking to the men who are cooking their daily porridge, conferring with the tribunes and centurions he meets, visiting the wounded in the medical tent. He stops in the armory lane, where more than a hundred blacksmiths are forging and repairing all types of armor and weaponry. Most are busy melting down the Carthaginians' weapons, forging Roman spears and armor. Scipio calls the lead smiths together. They are a group of stocky, black-faced older men, most with arms as thick as legs.

"There is a task I will set to you soon, to make a new sword for our army, the deadliest sword a Roman has ever wielded. It will resemble this one." Scipio withdraws his falcata, the cleaver-like weapon of an Iberian he killed years ago. "I have killed four men with this sword, and I tell you true: it can chop through shield or helmet. But look at this!" Scipio holds the blade over his head and bends it into a wide U-shape. He releases the tip and it snaps back into place. "The blade is impossible to shatter, yet it will break a Roman sword in the blink of an eye." He grins. "I know—I broke a Roman's sword in a mock fight with a tribune named Cato, some time back."

Scipio hands over his sword to a nearby smith, who examines it. "To do this, you will have to take some lessons from our captive armorers, the Iberians who have been making these swords for years. There are hundreds of them to help you make the iron that they call 'steel.' I don't know how they do it. All I know is that they bury the metal in the ground for years before they forge sheaths of it into a weapon." He

VI. Aftermath

holds it before their eyes. "This is the sword of Rome's future."

He looks each of the craftsmen carefully in the eye. "Embrace the Iberians' lessons without wounded pride. If you learn to make this 'steel,' Rome will have the finest swords in the world. Do you hear me?" The smiths nods mutely, awed that their general would even deign to visit them. "Good," says Scipio. "Ten thousand of these swords by the late fall moon." As the smiths stare at each other, dumbfounded at the magnitude of their task, Scipio strolls away.

* * * * *

Two dozen legionnaires circle Cartago Nova's town square, watching for thieves as the riches pile up before their eyes. The treasure wagons unload their booty onto a hill-shaped pile that grows larger by the hour. The Romans are busy gathering every scrap of Carthaginian treasure and coin from their mansions—and from the corpses of their soldiers. Moving through the city with typical Roman orderliness and efficiency, the soldiers and slaves gather plunder for resource-starved Rome.

The plunder pile contains much of the treasures of the town: jewelry, coins, ceremonial weapons, expensive robes, spices, and art. Felix, the army's chief accountant and paymaster, tallies the value of these items. Aided by his assistants, Felix dutifully records each type of booty, placing checkmarks next to an icon of each type of treasure. Felix is a former Senator and is a decorated legionary tribune. He is a jovial man with a reputation for exactitude, honesty, and incorruptibility, the perfect man to monitor military spending far from home.

The quaestor regularly tallies up all the army's war revenues and expenditures and ships a report back to Rome. As the financial watchdog of the Senate, his position is an honored and important one. As a former city magistrate, Scipio respects Felix and his office. But he knows that Felix is one of his greatest opponents in his war against the Three Generals, his fiduciary responsibility no less an obstacle to triumph than a Carthaginian army.

VI. Aftermath

Nearby the first pile, another rambling pile is mounded with enemy weapons: swords, shields, helmets, breastplates, greaves, javelins, and daggers. Each time a wagon unloads its weapons, slaves wash off the blood and body parts before arranging them into their respective mounds. Prize weapons and armor are rewarded to officers and their heroic subordinates. Among the tribunes, the patricians prize these as souvenirs of their military experience and heroism, to be exhibited at parties and when they run for *praetor* (magistrate), the next step on the cursus honorum. The centurions distribute workable swords and daggers to their men, whoever requires a new blade, and others are given to the allied troops, who may sort through the piles.

All leftover metals go to the blacksmiths for melting and forging. Having metals for forging is particularly important now, for Scipio has asked them to forge an army's worth of swords modeled after the Iberian falcata, the revolutionary weapon that will be called the *Gladius Hispaniensis*, an elongated, leaf-shaped sword that the Romans can use for slashing, thrusting, or chopping.

After the piles are tallied, the quaestor spends the next several days in the fields outside the city. There he spends his days accounting for all the captured livestock and foodstuffs, a messy and arduous task for him and his assistants. The food tally is especially important to army strategy now, as fall nears. Scipio will march to Tarraco, and he must know how much food he has on hand and how much his army must forage en route. Even though his army moves faster than any before it, Scipio must carefully plan for the transportation and gathering of food, for his men and for the pack animals.

When the field accounting is finished, the quaestor gathers his men and turns his attention to the most exciting task of all for a quaestor: accounting the wealth of the city treasury. Felix and his cohorts return to the treasury for the first time in weeks, when they did a cursory assessment of the city's wealth. Scipio accompanies them, ostensibly to oversee the transfer of the now-organized plunder from the city square into the rooms of the storehouse. As they enter the miniature citadel that is the treasury, Felix immediately goes to the coin room, where

Cartago Nova's monies are stored. He pushes open the door and freezes, staring inside it. Scipio looks at him questioningly. "What is wrong, Felix?" asks Scipio.

Felix blinks his eyes several times. "The money. I would swear there was a lot more gold and coin than the first time I visited here, right after the fall!"

Scipio looks at him, unperturbed. "Exactly how much money was in here?"

Felix throws up his hands. "I don't know. We didn't do an accounting of it, General, I just looked around. But there were piles and sacks of it in the corners over there, and more in the back room, I am sure."

Scipio places his hands on his hips, surveying the stacks of gold and silver coins, the man-high pyramids of precious metal ingots. "It looks like there is a lot here for Rome. That's all I know." He turns to Felix, staring intently at him. "Would you say there is a lot here for Rome?"

Felix waves his hands in frustration. "Well, yes, certainly, there are a dozen fortunes here. But I would swear that—"

"The treasury has been under guard since we took Cartago Nova, under my personal supervision," Scipio says, interrupting him. "Make an exact accounting of what is here, and trouble yourself no more about it."

"B–but," stammers Felix, looking bewilderedly at his assistants. "Someone must have …."

Scipio transfixes him with a stern look. "If I am not worried about it, you should not be. Make your accounting, quaestor. Or Rome will know of your dereliction." Scipio spins on his heel and strides out, followed by his guards, leaving Felix to stand there, open-mouthed.

*　　*　　*　　*　　*

GADES, IBERIA. "Suck my cock," curses Hasdrubal. "That little prick sneaked down there and took Cartago Nova! How in the Seven Shadows did he get there so fast?" The dark little man flings his wine goblet, and it shatters against the room's thick stone walls.

Gisgo and Mago dodge the flying shards, and Mago stomps over to confront his brother. "Your infant outbursts do naught for us! The truth is, we don't know! A spy tells us he was setting out from Tarraco, and suddenly he's at Cartago Nova!" Mago throws up his hands. "No Roman army moves that quickly; Romans are plodders!" Mago rubs his black-bearded chin. "The boy must have marched them day and night. Or they all rode mules and horses. Maybe he gathered a fleet of ships and sailed them in. But from where?"

"Who cares? Now that pussy patrician has our money, and most of our weaponry," grouses Hasdrubal. "One of us has to get down there and take it back before winter sets in."

Gisgo shakes his head in denial. "You want to attack that fortress, when it is held by an entire army? Hannibal himself couldn't get in there without a long siege! What are you thinking?"

Mago grins wryly at them. "A long siege? That 'pussy patrician' took the city from us in two days! Perhaps it is time we quit underestimating him, Hasdrubal. He does not think like a Roman. He thinks like Hannibal, always coming up with some ruse or trap."

Hasdrubal sneers at his brother and rubs the corner of his eye with his index finger. *Go fuck yourself,* he signs. Mago rolls his eyes heavenward.

"Maybe taking Cartago Nova isn't the answer. We do not have to conquer Scipio to win this war," interjects Gisgo. "We just have to hold him at bay. If Hannibal can win one more battle against the Romans in Italia, Rome will not have the men or money to help out the boy," observes Gisgo.

"That is easier to say than to do," muses Hasdrubal. "My brother

Hannibal now has two consuls coming after him, each with a different army."

Gisgo shrugs. "Of what matter is that? He has destroyed all who dare face him, much less some soft-handed patricians leading a spate of boys and convicts."

Mago snorts. "One of them is the Sword of Rome. And Fabius is not to be ignored. You all may do as you wish," continues Mago, "but I am not wasting my time trying to take that fortress. I am going out to recruit more allies. We'll need them if we are to wipe out Scipio next spring."

"For once, you are making sense," comments Hasdrubal. "We do need more men. I will be visiting some chiefs of the Celtiberians and the Ilercavones." He glares at his brother. "And when I get them to join us, I will take Tarraco while it is undermanned. That will open the gateway to Italia, and reinforcements for Hannibal. Scipio can rot down there in his fortress." He glares at Gisgo. "We'll go help Hannibal but he will prevail, regardless. Sword of Rome, my ass!"

*   *   *   *   *

CANUSIUM, APULIA REGION, 209 BCE. The late summer sun arcs low across the morning sky as Marcus Claudius Marcellus leads his army into a third day of battle against Hannibal. He is desperate for a decisive victory today; casualties have reduced his consular army to half its force, with food becoming scarce in this ravaged countryside.

A week ago, Marcellus led his army out to skirmish with Hannibal's force, to forestall the Carthaginian from attacking Fabius at Tarentum. After several indecisive skirmishes with Hannibal's Numidians and Libyans, Marcellus wearied of using Fabius' harassment tactics. "I will not follow him around like a barking dog," Marcellus was heard to say. "Let us drive the Africans into the sea and be done with it."

The seasoned general essayed a full-scale attack that chased Hannibal south to Canusium. After several skirmishes, Marcellus met Hannibal again in a full-scale battle, intent on destroying the Carthaginian's entire army. But the fight did not fare well for the Sword of Rome. Hannibal's battle-hardened Iberians and Libyan infantry broke Marcellus' front lines and threw them into the soldiers behind them. The Carthaginian cavalry hit the Roman flanks at the same time, delivering maximum shock. Thousands of Marcellus' men died before night halted the destruction. Five Roman standards were captured from the fleeing maniples, adding to the ignominy.

The normally jovial Marcellus has become grim and stern. All the maniples that lost their standards are given barley to eat instead of the preferred wheat ration, and the entire army is subjected to a tongue-lashing about their will to win. Though Hannibal challenges him to battle the next day, Marcellus reluctantly refuses, using the time to restore his army's courage.

Marcellus convenes his allies and legionnaires and heatedly berates them. "I can at least praise and thank the immortal gods for one thing," he snarls. "Our victorious foe did not actually attack the camp itself when you were making your panic-stricken dash for the rampart and the gates. I am sure you would have deserted the camp with as much terror as you quit the fight!" xix

One by one, Marcellus chides the centurions and tribunes who failed to control their men, not even sparing his two hardened legates, Lucius Lentulus and Gaius Nero, the latter recently returned from Iberia. As one, his men cry out for a chance at vindication, swearing death before dishonor. Marcellus agrees to give it to them; he calls for battle on the morrow. The Sword of Rome knows that he must quickly gain a victory before news of his previous defeat reaches Rome and the Latin Party again works to recall him from the field. He needs a political victory as much as a military one.

After breakfast, the Romans march out for their third day of battle. Marcellus has put all the repentant Romans and Italians on the front lines. They are surrounded by their compatriots, and have no place to retreat. The Umbrian allies hold the left side and his legionnaires maintain the right, with himself and his main legion in the center. Marcellus has made the disgraced soldiers give up their belts and scabbards; they march with blades unsheathed, a symbolic promise that they will not quit fighting until death or victory comes to them. Marcellus knows that many of his men are too wounded to fight beyond today. This is their day of decision.

Hannibal is as determined as Marcellus, for both have Rome at stake. If Hannibal can rid himself of his worst adversary, he is certain he can outwit the unimaginative Fabius and open his way to Rome. But Marcellus has been too wary to fall into Hannibal's ambushes, so he has resorted to holding some of his ablest force in reserve, to play a morale-breaking trick upon Marcellus' men. This morning, as he sees Marcellus marching his troops out in battle formation, Hannibal puts his plan into action.

The Roman army halts a half mile away from the Carthaginian camp. They stand for an hour in battle formation, blowing their battle trumpets, challenging their enemy to fight. Then the horns echo out from the Carthaginian camp, the gates swing wide, and the army tramps out in machine-like unison. Hannibal rides atop his war elephant Surus. His staunch Iberian warriors again fill the center lines, with Libyan and Gallic infantry on their sides. Hannibal's Libyan heavy cavalry ride on the right flank and his nimble Numidians on the left. The phalanxes and columns flow slowly across the undulating plain. They halt less than a spear's cast from the legions. And they wait.

The stoic Romans stand immobile with shields up and swords bared; only their eyes betray their determination for vindication. Minutes flow slowly by, as thirty thousand men stand silent. Hannibal holds his men, taking the measure of his weakened foe, looking for vulnerabilities. Then he nods to Maharbal, his second-in-command, and the war horns blow. The Balearic slingers rush out and rain their stones upon the Roman army, but Marcellus' men form shield shells, and the missiles wreak few casualties. Marcellus' velites sprint out to hurl their javelins into the retreating Balearics and the front-line Iberians. Scores of anguished cries tell them that many of their throws have hit home, and the young soldiers cheer. Three javelins fly toward Hannibal, but he calmly deflects two of them with his bronze-embossed shield, and the third bounces off Surus' mail-covered head.

Hannibal waves this sarissa thrice, and the battle horns sound again. With shouts and curses, the Iberians stamp forward, crashing into the Romans' center lines. The relentless Iberians chop through shield and limb with their falcatas, stepping over the wounded and dying. The Roman lines begin to bend inward under the Iberians' charge. Then the disgraced allies and legionnaires fight back fanatically, determined not to bear another humiliating loss, and they push the Iberians back.

Marcellus rages across his army center, cajoling, praising, and threatening, his face flushed with excitement. Off to his left, the Roman cavalry hold the Libyan riders at bay in a roundabout sword duel, while the Latin and Umbrian horsemen chase the outnumbered Numidians far out onto the plain, negating their threat. The two infantries fight at a stalemate for several hours; thousands lay dying or wounded. The heedless sun begins its journey toward the horizon, and long shadows stretch across the carnage. The Roman cornu sound a position change, and Marcellus' rear legion tramps to the fore as the remnants of the front legion begin an orderly withdrawal, the fresh maniples moving between the retreating ones. The Carthaginian lines take the opportunity to refresh their front-line troops, and the battle begins anew.

Hannibal watches the legions switch, and it occurs to him that the fresh legionnaires' have dimmed his chance for a victory before the sun sets. He nods to Maharbal: it is time to play their final gambit. Maharbal sends a Sacred Band officer to the rear lines with one simple order: release the elephants. Within minutes, two dozen elephants rumble to the front. They stampede in on each side of the Carthaginian army's center, guided through the gaps by the Carthaginian mahouts riding on their backs. Four phalanxes of Libyan heavy infantry follow behind them, ready to capitalize on the disorder the beasts will create.

The wildly trumpeting elephants rampage through the Roman front

lines, creating havoc wherever they go. The front-line hastati scatter
back into the second-line principes and their backup triarii, disordering
the maniples. Their formations broken, the backup lines mill about,
trying to dodge their own men as well as the random assaults of the
trampling elephants. The Libyan infantry are soon upon the vulnerable
Romans and Umbrians, fighting with a deadly efficiency the Romans
have lost.

The Carthaginian army senses victory and pushes into the Romans
with renewed vigor. In spite of his maniacal calls for order, Marcellus'
front maniples dissolve, and they begin the same disordered retreat they
made two days ago. Hundreds of Romans and allies are killed with
their backs to the enemy, easy prey for a javelin throw or stone cast.

As his rear maniple marches toward the front line, tribune Gaius
Decimus Flavus watches the elephants appear and wreak havoc on his
comrades. Flavus is a quiet and mannerly older veteran, a self-made
man who is lean and sun-browned from his many years of working on
his farm. Until now he has been an inconspicuous member of the
consular armies, content to do his job and follow orders. But his place
in history is about to be secured.

Furious that a Roman would cower before mere animals, Flavus grabs
the horse-head standard from its fur-capped bearer. He rushes forward
with it, screaming for his men to follow the standard. Using the
standard as he used a goad on his farm animals, the wiry little tribune
rushes to the elephant in front of him and jabs it repeatedly with the
spike end of the standard, putting the pachyderm to flight.[xx] The beast
crashes into several other elephants, and they turn and stampede back
into the Carthaginian infantries.

Flavus shouts with triumph. He yells for the maniple following him to
throw their javelins at the remaining half-dozen elephants nearby, and
the soldiers fling their weapons into the elephants' sides. The elephants
trumpet with pain and stampede back they way they came, their
mahouts vainly switching at their ears to stop them. The exuberant
legionnaires chase them, flinging their javelins to goad them farther

into the enemy.

A Libyan captain sees Flavus running with the standard and grasps his deadly purpose. The captain jumps off his horse and calls his men over to him, pointing at Flavus. The Libyans thresh through the Roman lines in front of Flavus, determined to stop him.

As they move toward Flavus, the tribune runs at one of the remaining elephants, raising the standard over his head to stick it in the beast's side. Flavus is so intent on his task he does not notice the Libyan captain stalking in from behind. The African captain shoves his sword deep into Flavus' lower back, grievously wounding him. Flavus' eyes start from his head and he screams in agony, but he holds onto the legion standard. As he drops to his knees, he jabs its spike deep into the Libyan's stomach, piercing his intestines. The captain falls to his hands and knees, crawling back to his men while moaning in agony. The angry Libyans run over to finish off Flavus and capture the prized standard. Flavus' maniple rushes in and swarms all over the Libyans, slashing frenziedly until naught remains but a pile of mutilated corpses. The legionnaires drag the bleeding Flavus back behind their lines, then carry their standard back into battle.

Marcellus observes the little tribune's heroic actions with amazement, then pride, then horrored dismay. When Flavus falls, the general grabs a javelin from a nearby velite and rides toward the elephants. His surprised guards hasten after him. Ignoring the furor about him, Marcellus races to the fourteen remaining pachyderms and jabs his javelin repeatedly into the foremost beast's side, and it tramples away from the Romans. When his men catch up to him, Marcellus directs them to mimic his actions on the surrounding elephants. The soldiers hurl their javelins into the elephants from all sides. Maddened with pain, the elephants reverse course and crash into the oncoming Libyan reserves, throwing them into chaos. The surviving mahouts eventually scramble to the top of their elephant's head and drive a spike into its brain, but the damage is done: the Carthaginian advance is ruined.

With their victory over the elephants, the Roman army regains its courage and regroups. The rear maniples relieve the exhausted front-line men, and the Umbrian allies bring their remaining troops to the fore. Undaunted, Hannibal calls for the remaining Libyan phalanxes to step forward and replace the fading Iberians and Gauls. A renewed battle erupts as the afternoon sun edges down the horizon. An hour later, nightfall becomes the victor as it sends both armies back to their camps.

Hannibal returns to his command tent and storms about it, furious at the turn of events. He has lost almost eight thousand men in this three-day battle, meaning he must forestall his march to Rome so he can recruit new troops. Even worse, the cursed Sword of Rome is still alive, although Hannibal is consoled by the thought that he has left thousands of Marcellus' men dead on the battlefield, again decimating his army. *He has won this time*, Hannibal thinks. *Rome will treat this as a victory because I did not destroy him. Their politicians will play this up as his triumph.* He picks up a recently prepared treaty he was going to deliver to Rome after his victory, and burns it. *They will not listen to my peace terms while the Sword is still alive. I must draw him out, one more time. He will be carried from the field as a corpse, or I will.*

For two days, Hannibal gathers information for a new battle strategy. He roams among this troops, conversing with the soldiers about their experiences in the battle. He rides out to reconnoiter the terrain, looking for spots to hide cavalry and spearmen. Satisfied, Hannibal and Maharbal meet with the cavalry and infantry officers, drawing out a battle plan that employs Hannibal's favorite strategy: ambush.

The elephants are to be sheathed in heavy mail and sent to battle with their own contingent of guards, to prevent them from being prodded into their troops. The Numidians will move into the far hills that night, sequestering themselves near the Romans. After a prayer to Baal for victory, Hannibal's officers disperse to prepare their troops for Marcellus. Hannibal looks across the plain to the barely visible Roman camp, listening to the buccinae sound the change of the watch. He takes a bowl of fruit to the stables and feeds Surus by hand. "Tomorrow we settle this, old friend," he says, stroking the great beast's trunk. "When that grinning bastard dies, Rome must accept peace."

At dawn's first light the Carthaginian army marches out into the plain, presenting themselves for battle as the Numidians lurk among the trees. Hours pass but the Romans do not emerge from camp, though they repeatedly sound the call to muster their forces. Reluctant to move his men beyond the ambush he has set up, Hannibal boldly rides out with a contingent of his Sacred Band, thence to challenge Marcellus to a duel. As they approach the camp, Hannibal sees that there are only a few campfires burning, and the palisades are devoid of activity. With a curse he stampedes his contingent headlong toward the Roman gates. His men crash into an abandoned camp, empty save for a quartet of Roman buccinators, left behind to sound the camp watch as if the army was there. The brave hornsmen are quickly killed, and Hannibal rides back to recall his army. *He used the same trick I used at Trasimene. Perhaps Romans are not too stupid to learn from their enemies.*

Days later, Hannibal's spies report that Marcellus has withdrawn his army to a fortified camp near Venusia, with more than half his army nursing wounds. *He will pose no threat this summer*, Hannibal decides, *but yet he is still alive.*

Hannibal scratches the empty eye socket beneath his patch. He stares at the tent walls about him, already deep into his next plan. Soon a feral gleam comes to his eye. He motions for a slave to bring him wine, takes a deep draught from his goblet, smacks his lips, and burps with satisfaction. *While he is still alive.* Hannibal sticks his head outside his command tent. "Fetch Maharbal. We have a trip to plan. We are going to draw out the Sword of Rome."

*   *   *   *   *

CARTAGO NOVA HARBOR. 209 BCE. Laelius stands on the shore of Rome's new Iberian fortress. He basks in the low autumn sun and smiles as he listens to the seabirds screeching at each other in their war for the harbor scraps the fishermen are pitching out. As the new Fleet Commander, Laelius is there to oversee the loading of the three quinqueremes he will sail to Rome: 140-foot warships filled with the captured riches of Cartago Nova, a vast treasure to be delivered to the Senate. Scipio walks over to join Laelius, unattended by any guards.

"How fare you, Admiral Laelius?" asks Scipio jovially.

Laelius gapes at his friend. "I cannot believe I have an entire fleet now! Amazing! It is good to see you happy for once, Scippy, though your eyes look tired. But what are you doing down here by yourself? Did your attendants get sick of following you?"

Scipio jerks his thumb over his back. "The guards are right over there, talking with several women from town." He smirks. "It was not difficult to convince them to remain with those lovelies."

"I need to talk to you about your trip to Rome. Alone," says Scipio.

"Of course," Laelius replies good-naturedly. A movement behind him catches his eye. "Why are those four wagons pulling up to the side dock?"

A guilty look flashes across Scipio's face, but it is quickly replaced with the stern visage of command. He places his hand on Laelius' shoulder. "Those wagons will be loaded onto a cargo ship that will accompany you. That ship will not dock at Ostia."

Laelius looks at Scipio suspiciously. "You are up to something, aren't you?"

Scipio locks eyes with his friend. "You will moor that ship at the fishermen's port just south of Ostia. Notify my mother that the ship is there. She will know what to do with it."

Laelius huffs impatiently. "Scippy, what is this all about? What is in that ship? As fleet admiral, I have a right to know."

Scipio's face is a stone. "Rome's future is there, no more and no less." His voice grows officious. "I command you, Admiral, under my authority as general and proconsul of Iberia: you are not to ask any further questions about it, nor look in its contents. You will transport that ship under my orders, understood?" Scipio sighs, and a sad smile breaks his face as he looks at his lifelong friend. "Forgive me, but this way the responsibility will be mine."

Laelius looks reproachfully at his friend. "This is not like you. Not like you at all ...."

Scipio glares at Laelius. "Like who?" he says sarcastically. "Like the boy who was a quiet scholar before he was pushed into service against his wishes? Like the idealistic young man who was betrayed by the Latins when he volunteered for Iberia? Or like the man who murdered the Cartago Nova townspeople? Who am I like now?"

Laelius looks wonderingly at him. "You are like all of those. I fear they are all inside you, fighting for control." He takes a deep breath, and his posture suddenly stiffens. "General—my beloved friend—I will follow your orders."

Scipio slumps, the tension leaving his shoulders. "Good. There is a war to win Rome, within its own borders. And our warriors need resources to do it. That is all I will say."

Laelius nods dubiously. "You play a dangerous game, against dangerous men."

Scipio looks at the ships, avoiding Laelius' eyes. "Let us talk of other things. The Senate will not provide our army sufficient coin while the Latin Party holds sway, would you agree?" Scipio laughs, briefly and bitterly. "In truth, they would likely see it as abetting the enemy."

Laelius, indecisive, shuffles his feet. "Well yes, possibly. But I will speak to the Senate about more money. We have just won a great victory, after all."

"Do what you will," Scipio replies tightly.

Laelius looks awkwardly at Scipio. "Very well. I had best get on board. We have to prepare for the launch." Laelius gives his friend a final, sorrowful look. He turns and begins to step toward the gangplank when he feels Scipio's hand on his shoulder, turning him about. Scipio leans in and kisses Laelius, deep and lingeringly. He leans back and smiles, his eyes moist.

"Forgive my furtive ways. I would bare my heart to you—I need to bare my heart to you—but protecting you is one of the only honorable things I can do right now." He squeezes Laelius' hand. "Go now, and may Neptune be your friend until you get to Ostia."

Scipio's friend manages a wisp of a smile and stalks off onto the weathered gangplank of the ship, his red cape flowing from his shoulders. Scipio watches him, fingering the dagger his father gave him when he and Laelius were children, an eternity ago.

*   *   *   *   *

SABINA HILLS, ROME, 209 BCE. Flaccus walks among the heavy-headed wheat fields around his lavish country villa, admiring the bounty that will be his in this exceptional growing season. The gangly Senator is lost in the beauty of the waving fields, a place he often visits to find solace from the depredations of political fighting in the Senate. He has brought his field manager with him, to help estimate the yield.

"The fall harvest is upon us, Thrax. I think we should give the field slaves some extra food next week. They will have to work from dawn to dusk. Thrax, do you hear me?" He looks about for his Thracian slave, but the rows behind him are empty and quiet. "Thrax! Where the fuck are you? Get over here!" The fields whisper in the wind as Flaccus strains his ears for footsteps, suddenly feeling very alone.

Flaccus hears the wheat stalks rustling and glares toward its source. "If you're in there taking a piss, be done with it!" As he cranes in to see, a thick sack slips over his head and strong hands yank a drawstring tight around his neck, muffling his cries. Another set of hands grabs his shoulders and throws him to the earth. Flaccus thrashes, cursing and pleading. His silent attackers pull his hands behind his back and rope them together, then his feet. They yank up his linen tunic and rip off his subligaculum underneath it. The wealthy patrician feels a blinding pain in his anus, as if he is being split apart. Another thrust and the pain grows deeper, lancing into his bowels as his muted screams fill the heavy bag.

The hands release him, leaving him to thrash about on the ground like a maddened snake, rolling into the wheat fields in his effort to free himself from the agony in his nether regions. Later, two of his field slaves find him and cut him loose. Sobbing with pain, Flaccus scrabbles his fingers between his buttocks. He extracts a bloodied Greek oblisbo, an eight-inch marble penis crafted in the Hellenic style. Flaccus stares at it in angry wonderment, then he flings the instrument into the field.

The Latin Party leader grasps the import of the sex toy's style: this rape is his recompense from the Hellenics. Or, more likely, a certain member of the Hellenic Party. He raises himself from the torn earth and waddles slowly back toward his villa, supported by his slaves. Grimacing with each step, he repeats "fucking cunt," as if it were a religious chant. "I'll get that bitch," he screams at his alarmed slaves. They merely nod, mystified as always by the impotent rages of a man who has wealth and power beyond their dreams.

VII. BAECULA

PILLARS OF HERCULES, CADIZ PROVINCE, IBERIA, 208 BCE. Pulling his purple cape about him, Mago stares into the windy drizzle blowing out from the narrow strait separating the Mediterranean from the Atlantic. He can barely see the coast of North Africa in this showery gray seascape, but he knows the rain is a blessing: the reduced visibility will conceal the Carthaginian quinquereme and transport that are coming to him. *This time*, he thinks, *they may get through.*

Durro, a senior member of Carthage's Council of Elders, stands next to Mago on a high rocky promontory, looking decidedly irritated. The aged dignitary is there to observe the safe delivery of money and supplies for Mago, Gisgo, and Hasdrubal. The Three Generals had claimed that a prior shipment was intercepted by Scipio's navy, the Barcas' political enemies ensured that one of their own would come here to audit the delivery and distribution of government resources. Durro's presence only adds to the natural enmity between Carthaginian politicians and the military, but Mago must tolerate him.

After an hour of staring, Mago wipes the rain off his face and looks at Durro, who is now sitting in a canopied chair. "Will you take wine with me?" he asks reluctantly, hoping the old man will actually return to Gades. Durro gives the briefest of nods, and the two repair to Mago's tent. They dry themselves and plunk down among Mago's thick reclining cushions, sipping the hot spiced wine the slaves bring them.

"This will be the last shipment for a while," states Durro. "Business has been bad at Carthage. The Romans are hampering our sea trade with Greece and Macedonia. The treasury's war funds are low." Durro sips his wine, then adds, "Besides, you lost our last convoy to their patrols."

Mago grows agitated. "We must expect some losses there. We no longer own the seas! That Scipio has made a navy out of our captured ships. Now his boyfriend Laelius patrols all of south Iberia, places where they couldn't reach us before."

"There are alternatives. A treaty would be good for business," muses Durro, gesturing for a refill. "We could negotiate trade permissions with Rome, I am sure of it." He takes a long gulp. "And get some of our mines back."

"You mean a treaty would be good for the aristocrats in the Council of Elders, don't you?" hisses Mago. "They don't care who wins or loses, as long as they can make money. Pfah!"

"It makes no sense to keep sending ships to you. We lose them to Rome, and they profit. We are twice damned!"

"No sense?" says Mago incredulously. "Have you heard about this Roman orator Cato? He concludes every speech by saying Carthage must be destroyed.[xxi] These people do not want peace, unless it is to plot our destruction. You are as bad as Hannibal has become, talking peace!"

A Sacred Band guard steps into the tent. "A ship has been sighted," he reports, and withdraws. Durro and Mago rush out to the promontory. There, heading in from the Mediterranean side, they can see the outline of the sleek quinquereme gliding into the strait, the ninety oars on each side working in unison to push it along. A bulky supply ship follows it, destined for the harbor on the Atlantic side of the promontory.

Two Roman biremes enter the strait from the Atlantic side, plunging toward the larger quinquereme. Their fifty oars stroking at full speed, the patrol ships slice through the choppy seas and close in quickly on the towering warship, heedless of the giant spears that shoot from the deck crossbows. The scene plays out directly below Mago and Durro's overlook—they can see the Carthaginian soldiers assembling on top of the deck, preparing for a boarding fight.

The biremes suddenly split apart, turn wide, and head straight back at the quinquereme's sides. Rowing at a full eight knots, the Romans crash into the enemy ship's sides, ramming holes beneath its waterline with their submerged rams. The quinquereme starts to sink, and the Carthaginian warriors jump into the sea. After hurling javelins at their foundering enemy, the biremes stroke backwards and head for the supply ship, which has turned about and opened all its sails in an attempt to escape with the wind. The Romans do the same, and the agile little vessels close rapidly to draw alongside the transport's sides.

Cursing futilely, Mago watches the Romans throw out their hooked mounting gangplanks and collar the slow-moving transport. Scores of armored marines dash up the gangplanks and vault over the ship's sides. There is a furious battle on the decks as javelins fly and fighters plummet over the sides. Soon the activity lessens, and Mago can see the marines rounding up captives and returning to their ships. A Roman captain now stands in the prow of the Carthaginian ship, directing its capture. The transport and the biremes turn about and head back to the Atlantic side, drifting out of sight.

Durro has watched the disaster unfold without saying a word. Now he turns to Mago. "Another capture! That ties the knot. There will be no more money sent to you, but we will send men later. General Hanno has suppressed King Syphax' rebellion in Numidia. He will come when Hasdrubal's army moves to join Hannibal in Italia. But not until then."

Mago explodes. "We need more money now! We have to pay the mercenaries and recruit more Iberians! How do you expect to win a war if you won't support it? You think the citizens of Carthage will join the army? Hah!"

Durro gazes out across to Africa, at the scenic silhouettes of the low coastal hills. "Very well. You will have half of whatever you can cull from the remaining silver mines near Baecula, as determined by *our* auditors."

Mago splutters a curse at Durro, and the Elder turns back, his face flushed with suppressed anger. "You think me unfair? I must tell you, this war has become very unpopular in Carthage, even with the common people who once thought a Barca could do no wrong. You have lost all those mines, and Cartago Nova itself!" He holds up two fingers. "Two years. If Rome is not ours by then, Carthage will press for peace, as we did in the first war." Durro wipes his palms on his robe, as if they were smeared with something unpleasant. "When Hannibal was heading to Rome's gates and you three ruled Iberia, it looked like Carthage would extend its empire—and wealth—beyond all measure. Now Hannibal talks of peace, and Scipio sends our gold to Rome. This conflict has become far too … unprofitable."

"You cannot afford peace, my wealthy friend," rejoins Mago, suddenly calm. He stalks back to his tent, waving for his staff to follow him. "Peace means our destruction. What good is money when your body smolders beneath our fallen walls? And Rome, it will have no less."

*   *   *   *   *

"Shit!" Scipio exclaims, as he again pricks his thumb with the thick iron sewing needle. This autumn morning Scipio is altering a pair of *calceus*, the ankle-length boots favored by Rome's legionary officers, but it is not without its casualties. He moodily sucks his finger and gulps some watered wine, then bends back to finish his latest invention: hobnail sandals. The man who is consul and governor of all Iberia is sewing a toe strap onto the sandals he has cut out from old army boots, sandals that will be a model for his captive Iberian cobblers to produce during these final autumn weeks. Scipio plans to outfit his legionnaires with these shoes for the spring campaign, giving them footwear that better suits Iberian conditions. Scipio runs his finger over the studs in one of the soles, pushing against them to test their resilience. Satisfied, he begins adding them to the other one.

Years ago, Scipio was elected as Rome's youngest public works magistrate, charged with inspecting and maintaining the city's food supplies and services. The patrician boy eagerly embraced a position that for many was no more than a political stepping-stone, believing it would help him learn more about the plebs' lives and needs. As he probed into the city's daily operations, he devoted the same zeal of learning that he had committed to his philosophical studies and war training. The dreamy young scholar became a focused analyst, assiduously inspecting water lines, grain purchases, even the public toilets—all to ensure their quality and efficiency.

From his experience as an aedile, he acquired his now-legendary attention to military detail; no aspect of army preparation eludes his careful investigation, from horse feed to armor to breakfast food. After conquering Cartago Nova, Scipio has set up a production plant, populated with hundreds of artisans devoted to the development of military resources,[xxii] including his new *Gladius Hispanicus*, the falcata-like sword the legions' infantry will employ. Scipio intends to leave Cartago Nova with a new army, one more deadly and mobile than any before it.

Immersed in his task, Scipio does not notice Marcus Silenus pushing his way through the tent flaps until it is too late to hide his work. Marcus stops short at the sight of a patrician general sewing shoes. He stifles a grin and strolls over to Scipio's scrap pile, where he casually fingers the remnants. "So, General Scipio, let me venture a guess." Marcus picks up several of the leather cuttings and looks at them as intensely as if they were the intestines of an augury. "If you survive this campaign, you will renounce your oath to become a scholar and take up life as a cobbler. I have hit the mark, have I not?"

Scipio pauses to stare incredulously at Marcus. "Did I hear you right? Did you truly make a joke?" Scipio shakes his head. "I but prepare our men for our march back to Tarraco. And for war." Scipio cuts out a final strip of leather and holds up the shoe, which is now an open sandal webbed with leather strips. He turns the sole over and taps in the final three hobnails in the thick leather sole. Satisfied, he picks up the sandal's finished mate and proffers them to Marcus. "Here, try them on."

"What are these things?" asks Marcus with no small amount of trepidation.

Scipio blinks. "I don't know. I didn't have a name for them. Uh, let's call them *caligae*—that's like calceus. Go on—try them. They won't bite—too much." Marcus gingerly retrieves them from Scipio's hand, cautiously sniffs the leather, and puts them on. "Walk about," says Scipio, "out of the tent and back." Marcus takes a few tentative steps, nods approvingly, and strides out of the tent, marching as if he were heading to battle. Long minutes pass, then Marcus stomps back in to stand in front of Scipio, hands on hips.

"Well, what do you think?" asks a nervous Scipio.

Marcus bends over and fiddles with the straps, pulling them higher up his ankle. "They need a darker, more uniform leather, perhaps some metal bands across the forefoot to protect against cuts. And a good olive oil rub to …."

Scipio rolls his eyes. "Yes, yes. How did they feel, Legate?"

"They felt … good. Light on my feet. And … cool, that's what I would say: my feet were very cool." He frowns critically at Scipio. "Of course, you made me a laughingstock just now, prancing around in these raggedy boots." Marcus frowns toward the exit. "I had to shut a few mouths before I returned."

For the first time, Scipio grins as he rubs out the tension in the back of his neck. "Exactly! These … these sandal-boots will lend wings to our feet for the summer campaign. Now give them back, commander." Marcus takes off the shoes and hands them to Scipio. The general picks them up and smiles. "Hundreds of our men contracted foot rot from hiking in the damp heat. We marched so fast and long, their feet sweated." Scipio holds up a sandal by its straps. "I noticed that some of the Iberian tribes wear this type of shoe, so I thought we would try them in place of our boots." Scipio runs his fingers lovingly across the soles. "The studs on the bottom will let us scramble over the rocky terrain in the north, like the Celtiberians do." Stretching and yawning, he rises and walks about. "I'm going to give them to the shoemakers and have them design a cartful. We'll test them on the march north to Tarraco."

"But fall is here. Why do you need them now? Just to keep their feet from stinking?" deadpans Marcus. "Not that I favor stinking feet."

Scipio laughs. "Well, that alone would be sufficient reason! We have to try them out, and make adjustments. Then we finish them over the winter." He shakes his head. "It's so they can march faster, with little discomfort. Our army will cover ground faster than anyone thinks possible. That will be our little trick for the Three Generals." Scipio makes walking motions with two of his fingers, moving them quicker until they are a blur. "No mules, no wagons, no strolling along—just marching, marching fast and light."

"All that from nubby sandals," observes Marcus. "I think you have overmuch faith in them."

Scipio shrugs. "We marched down here faster than the Carthaginians expected. That worked well, did it not?"

"So why play with the shoes? We are travelling light, moving faster than ever. Besides, the men grumble about all the changes you've already made. Do you want a mutiny on your hands?"

"We need more speed—more agility. The amassed force of the Generals greatly outnumbers us. If the three of them catch us, we are lost. And Rome is lost." Scipio takes the sandals in hand and heads for the tent exit. "I'm taking these to Craftsman's Row. We'll make enough for two cohorts. Certainly, we have captured enough artisans to accomplish that in a trice!" Scipio hurries out the door. Once he is gone, Marcus shakes his head in wonderment. *That boy and his ideas*, he thinks. *But he's been right so far.*

As twilight settles over the Roman camp, Scipio picks his way among the mule droppings beneath his feet, leading his officers over to the pack animals and supply wagons. He pauses there, his back to the corrals.

"I am selling most of our mules, save for a few to haul some wagons to follow us later. Pack animals will not be part of our army on the march back to Tarraco. Nor after it." As several tribunes voice their protests, Scipio raises his hand, glaring peremptorily at them. "This is not a matter for discussion. We will have to cover ground faster than ever. That means we cannot take pack animals with us."

The tribunes look at one another as if to confirm that they have heard correctly. One grizzled veteran cocks a sarcastic eye at the young general. "You did say we would take no pack animals? No mules to carry our food and supplies?"

"That is correct, Fontius. We did it on the way down here, and we'll do it on the way back up."

The old tribune cannot help but laugh. "So, you think the cavalry can carry all we need on the backs of their horses? And just drop it all when it's time to attack?"

Scipio takes a deep breath and looks into his officers' skeptical faces. "No, the horses will not carry the men's food and supplies. Our men will carry it. Just as they did on our march down here."

The general picks up a sarcina and hefts it. "Every man will carry a satchel for their food and belongings, as well as a shovel, a bowl, a kettle, a cup, and a cooking pot. Every man will carry five days' rations of grain, beans, olive oil, fruit, and cheese. And nothing else. All told, their sarcina should weigh about sixteen libra (twelve pounds). There will be no meat. Meat can spoil, and we cannot drag along animals for slaughter."

"I beg you reconsider, General. Many of our men are used to riding the mules for at least part of the trip," pleads Fontius. "The older men of the triarii often ride the mules to restore their energy."

Scipio merely looks away from the tribune. "Older or not, no one will ride on mules," he says impatiently. "We march as one." When the tribune starts to speak again, Scipio raises his hand imperiously. "For what can you expect in a war from a man who is not able to walk?"[xxiii]

The officers do not reply; they have learned it will do them no good. Since capturing Cartago Nova, the young general has a confidence in his decisions that borders on arrogance, and a determination to follow them that borders on fanaticism. His self-doubt has fled, and along with it his naiveté—some would say his idealism—about waging war. Scipio waits a minute longer for comments. Hearing none, he resumes. "The evenings grow ever longer, leaving us less for marching. We must leave in two weeks."

Marcus Silenus reads the confused looks on several of the tribunes' faces. "Why so early?" he asks, a tinge of challenge in his voice. "We can make Tarraco in a fortnight, and the weather will be good for a month. If we stay here, we can drill more on the cohort formations." He grimaces. "And learn how to use that new sword."

Amidst grunts of approval for Marcus' words, Scipio raises his voice. "It will take much longer than a fortnight. On the way down here we were an invading army. On the way back up we will be a protecting one, protecting the land we have won. We have many stops on the way."

He gestures to two attendants, and they unfurl a map of the southeast Iberian coast, with red crosses marked between Cartago Nova and Tarraco. Scipio points to each of the four crosses. "We will garrison each of these towns with our legionnaires and allies, and part of our intelligence force." He points to several blue dots on the map. "The towns are near Akra Leuke, Sucro, Saguntum, and Valentia. If the Carthaginians try to move through there to regain Cartago Nova, our infiltrators there will know, and we can mount a ready defense." He gestures for the attendants to roll up the map and faces his officers. "It will take several days to garrison each town. Our trip up will be longer, so we must leave earlier. And we have much preparation to do when we get to Tarraco."

A thin young man rises, facing his general with frightened eyes. Octavius is a new centurion. The only reason he is present at this meeting is to attend to his century's tribune, a friend of the family. When he hears Scipio's words, he cannot restrain himself. "If you leave men at every town, how many men will we leave behind?"

Octavius' tribune glares at him, but Scipio raises his hand. "Well said. It is a question that must be on all your minds. Six thousand, roughly, including allies."

Marcus looks at him. "Then we lose a quarter of our force. How do you expect to defeat one army, much less three of them?"

"Recruit or die," replies Scipio. "Rome will give us nothing. We must turn to the Iberians. And their cousins to the north, the Celtiberians."

One tribune glances over at his fellows. "The Iberians," he says sarcastically. "The very people we have come to fight. People who killed your father and uncle."

"Many of those tribes were held in captive loyalty by the Generals," retorts Scipio. "We have liberated those tribes, who once were chained by threats and bondage. We can only hope that the mercy we showed them will bring them to our side." Scipio shrugs fatalistically. "Besides, we have no choice. It's them or no one."

The air of anxiety and disagreement is palpable, but no one voices disagreement. Finally, Marcus Silenus speaks. "If that is what we must do, we will." The officers look at him, and then back at Scipio, their faces resigned.

Scipio smiles wearily as he looks at his men. "I know some of you doubt the wisdom of these actions, but experience will bear me out. It is done."

Two weeks later the Roman army disassembles its camp and heads for

Tarraco. A score of supply ships follow them north from the city, transporting animals, artisans, and weapons to the Roman stronghold. For Scipio's army, the excitement and glory of their victory has faded over months of training and preparation. Now they grimly anticipate a spring season of battles for control of Iberia, battles against an undefeated trio of generals with a superior force.

The legionnaires march rapidly up the coast, passing field harvests that make the common soldiers long to be back home, attending to their own fields. The streams and rivers are low this time of year, so little time lost in fording them. The army heads for Akra Leuke, the first town it will garrison with troops.

The extraordinarii lead the vanguard this time, a newly designated branch of the allied infantry, composed of men who distinguished themselves in the battle for Cartago Nova. Scipio rides behind the vanguard, sometimes jumping off his horse to march several miles with his men, other times riding back to join the rear cavalry. Each time he marches, he makes sure he shoulders one of the new sarcinas, eating the same food his men carry. His message is clear to the skeptical veterans inured to traditional Roman tradition: if a patrician boy can do it, you can do it. And say no more about it.

The army is a scant ten miles from Akra Leuke when two scouts return from the north with alarming news: a large force of Iberian cavalry is coming over the ridge toward the middle of Scipio's infantry columns. Even as the buccinators sound the alarm, hundreds of Iberians stream down the distant ridge to catch the Romans on the march. The infantry hastily forms three defensive lines toward the riders, preparing to hurl their pila.

Scipio starts to order a cavalry attack when he notices the Iberians are led by a young man wearing only a purple tunic and a black crested helmet, his sword sheathed at his side. "Hold!" commands Scipio. "Hold your weapons!" Scipio studies the oncoming wave as his officers glance anxiously at him. He abruptly rides out alone toward the oncoming barbarians.

"General, wait for us!" yells one of his surprised tribunes and chases after him.

"I know this man!" Scipio yells back as he rides out from the front lines of his waiting infantry.

The young general rides out from the front lines and raises his arms in welcome. The young Iberian rider enters the plain in front of Scipio and returns the salute. He pauses a stone's throw from the anxious Romans, as hundreds of armored Iberians line up behind him, silent as stones, long spears at the ready. The Iberian trots his horse forward. As he approaches, Scipio smiles broadly.

"Hail, Allucius," Scipio shouts.

"Hail, King Scipio," returns Allucius.

Scipio again grimaces at the term, but ignores it. "Whence come you, and why?" commands Scipio.

"I bring fourteen hundred men from my tribe and our neighbors, hand-picked by myself."[xxiv] The young man draws nigh, ignoring the bared swords of Scipio's accompanying officers. He grasps Scipio's forearm and shakes it firmly. "I did promise I would repay you a thousand times over for my beloved Carmina. Here I am to repay that debt, and submit to your command." He smiles into Scipio's eyes. "It was not a difficult thing. I told them about this young soldier who communes with the gods. A man who was victorious everywhere, as much to his kindness and generosity as to his military prowess."[xxv] Allucius laughs. "And when I told them this man was fighting the Carthaginians, that was all they needed to hear!"

"You are indeed welcome," says Scipio, his eyes moist. "Join me as an equal, Prince Allucius. Together we will release Iberia from its bondage." Scipio trots to the rear, and Allucius and his men follow as the Romans watch in wonderment.

Scipio's expanded army continues on its way toward Tarraco,

stopping every several days to station troops at one of the towns that favor the Roman cause. In each town Scipio abandons his camp tent and sleeps in the quarters of the city magistrates, demonstrating his trust in their commitment to Rome. But he also sleeps there in quest of a sound and dreamless sleep, a sleep devoid of the screams of the innocents at Cartago Nova. A sleep without the shadowed play of unfocused visions that dance through the back of his mind until cock's crow announces blessed daylight has come.

*   *   *   *   *

PORT OF OSTIA, ROME. Laelius bounces onto the wide oaken dock of Ostia as the oarsmen tie up his quinquereme. He grins triumphantly as he looks around. The young admiral has docked his fleet at same port he patrolled as a wharf rat in Ostia.

Before he met Scipios, the boy Laelius survived by cutting bait fish, scraping hulls, and stealing food scraps. Happiness was any time when there were no pain and fear. Then he and Scipio met at the wrestling fields for boys, and became fast friends. Now he commands the Iberian fleet; thousands of sailors and marines follow his commands. He cannot help but laugh out loud at life's caprices, a behavior to which his men have grown grudgingly accustomed.

It is his twenty-eighth birthday, and Laelius is resplendent in a snow-white tunic with gold embroidery, covered over with thrice-polished armor that blazes like the sun. Looking every inch a fleet commander, Laelius marches quickly toward the port streets, flanked by a personal guard of marines equipped in decorative armor that would do credit to a legate—Laelius' personal touch. Laelius watches the roughshod dockworkers that toil along the wharf. *There, on the Avenue of the Fisheries*, he recalls, *that's where I sold myself for food—and for drink for my father*. He looks down at his armor and bends over, hands on his knees, stifling the sob that overcomes him.

"Admiral, are you well?" asks his new tribune, the young marine who first scaled Cartago Nova's walls.

Laelius coughs and pushes himself upright, a forced grin across his face. "Ah, it is nothing, Carbo. Just a slight pain in my groin. Perhaps it's these new caligae our general dreamed up. Haven't quite broke them in." Laelius puts his hand on Carbo's shoulder, the familiarity surprising him. "Did I tell you this dock was where I first met Scipio? He had come to the public fields here, to wrestle with the other boys. I threw him three out of five falls, and we became fast friends after that. Then he copied my moves, and beat me!"

"He has the mark of greatness on him," comments Carbo. "The men have learned to trust him in spite of his youth. And to love him." Carbo smirks. "Well, most of the men, anyway."

Laelius stares into the distance. "Yes, we all love General Scipio," he says, as if to himself. "Each in our own way, as much as we may …." Laelius steps onto the bustling thoroughfare and walks over to the horses waiting for him and his retinue. He grabs the saddle and prepares to mount when he hears a scream behind him.

"Laelius! Blessed Jupiter, wait for us!" He turns and sees Amelia and Pomponia scurrying toward him, pulling their elegant robes above their ankles. The two women dash through his marines and swarm upon him, covering his face with kisses.

"Oh my gods," says Laelius through his tears. "I feared I might never see you again!" Carbo gestures to his men, and they take themselves and the horses a discreet distance from the reunion.

"I am so happy to see you," sobs Pomponia as she caresses his face. "I missed you so, my boy. You are so like a son to me."

Amelia holds his hand tightly in both of hers as she stands back to study her childhood friend. "Look at you! You look like the commander of the world, in your shiny armor. Admiral Laelius!" She kisses his hand. "I am so happy for you, boy of the streets. You have come so far!"

Laelius laughs. "Remember when you and I and Cornelius would argue with each other during our tutoring sessions with Asclepius?" He sighs. "Seems like that was a god's life ago, back when your front was as flat as your backside!"

She swats him playfully. "As if you cared what my front looked like!" She grows suddenly somber and clenches his hands tighter. "I am so glad you are with him, Laelius. There were so many people who doubted him. He needed you to remind him who he truly is."

"In truth, he has done the gods' work there, accomplishing wonders!" A shadow of concern passes over his handsome face as he manages a bittersweet smile. "But he has to make so many fateful decisions." Laelius looks away from them. "Such terrible, terrible decisions to make." Seeing their concern, he summons a grin. "Ignore me, he is truly doing fine. His father would be very proud."

At the mention of her dead husband, Pomponia bows her head. "Publius was wise. He knew Rome would need our son's genius to defeat Carthage. He made him promise to become a general and defend Rome, when my boy would have been happier with his books and scrolls." She smiles wanly. "Though it broke my own heart to see him denied his heart's desire, Publius was right to do it. Who else could have conquered Cartago Nova?"

Amelia looks out at the fleet floating in the harbor. "You have quite a few ships out there, Laelius. What are they all for?"

Laelius looks over at his quinqueremes and quadriremes. "They hold the plunder of Cartago Nova, the coins and gold from its treasury. And jewels and art. It's incredible what they had! I'm here, to give it to the Senate." Laelius holds up a thick scroll. "Old Felix, our quaestor, he has given me a detailed list of what we are bringing. They should be pleased."

"Mmhmph," Pomponia sniffs. "Some of those Latins would be more pleased if you reported that Scipio had lost. But you bring good news and money, both are grievously needed. Our legionnaires and allies here are fighting without pay. That can weaken any fighting man's arm, after a while."

Laelius jumps onto his horse. "I will see you tonight, after I meet with the Senate." He looks over his shoulder to see if anyone is near and leans down to whisper to them. "There is another ship on the far side of the harbor, with unmarked sail. The sailors await your orders for disposal of its contents." He looks innocently at Pomponia. "Whatever those contents are."

Pomponia nods slowly. "I know. I did receive my son's letter about it. Rest assured, the matter will be settled within two nights." She steps nearer to Laelius, placing her hand on his thigh. "It is a good thing you are doing. Good for the future of Rome. Let us say no more about it."

Laelius shrugs noncommittally and turns his horse about. "Carbo!" he shouts. "We are off for Rome." His attendants hastily mount their horses and chase after a galloping Laelius as Amelia and Pomponia somberly watch him disappear.

That afternoon, Laelius reports to the Senate about the actions taken to topple Cartago Nova. When he is done, the Senators loudly applaud him, and the image-wise Latins take part in the accolade. Scipio has brought new hope to Rome: a great citadel was taken with relatively little bloodshed, an act unparalleled in the Carthaginian wars. Laelius enumerates the money and treasure he has brought for the Senate coffers, which brings another round of accolades. He concludes his report with Scipio's request that another legion be sent to Tarraco for the upcoming spring campaign, with money and food to support them for a year. The request is coolly received, with a guarantee from the Senate leader that the Senate will take it under advisement in their upcoming sessions.

Laelius snuffs derisively when he hears these remarks, knowing he has brought them fifty times the amount requested. His face expressionless, he presents Felix for his auditor's report. Laelius steps down from the podium, standing near his quaestor with arms crossed, his posture shouting his outrage about his tabled request.

Felix steps to the podium and details the army expenditures, from animal feed to medical supplies. When he summarizes the costs for Scipio's legendary victory party, a dozen Senators shout their dismay, led by Flaccus' chants of "Thief! Thief!"

Flaccus rises from the front row of the Senate seats and glances over at Cato, where the younger man sits in the side rows reserved for the citizenry. Cato's intense stare conveys his message: *Get after him.* "Why did Scipio waste so much money on a drunken fest for common infantry?" blazes Flaccus to his peers. "Couldn't these battle-hardened soldiers find their own wine and food in the city?" Flaccus turns and spreads his arms in sarcastic wonderment. "Surely Cartago Nova has a few people who drink wine and store it for themselves. Rumor has it they do the same for food!"

There is scattered laughter as Laelius shoulders Felix out of the way in front of the podium. "The Carthaginians had been under siege. There were few stores of either resource in their homes, Senator," says Laelius. "Many of our men had just finished their first battle. There was a need for them to celebrate, to release the horror of battle."

"Puf! I daresay your defense of these indefensible expenditures is prompted by your … what should I call it … *friendship* with young Scipio?" purrs Flaccus.

Laelius stares coolly at Flaccus, evidencing the same haughtiness he has oft used on the mockers of his sexual persuasion. "General Scipio commanded that the city was not to be plundered, to preserve the citizens and their belongings, and thus win their loyalty. I must say it was a wise move. Half the city has worked to resupply our army, which was necessary because you have not given us the coin to do it ourselves!" He arches an eyebrow as Flaccus, smiling sarcastically. "As to the celebration, Flaccus, I have seen you indulge yourself and your officers after observing a minor skirmish from a distance. Would you do less for the men that risked death on the bloody front lines?"

Amid several laughs and jeers, Laelius steps back from the podium as a red-faced Flaccus shouts at him. "They are naught but foot soldiers, boy," he snarls. "They did not need it."

Laelius sniffs. "You mean, they are not of noble family," he says archly. "As if that were the true measure of a man!" Cato looks at Laelius thoughtfully, a new appreciation dawning in his eyes.

Laelius' voice takes on the tinge of rage and envy he has always felt for the undeserving rich, for those who mocked his poverty. "The celebration was for our countrymen and our Italian allies. The gods be my witness, I would have given them my own money for their day's surcease, if I had any to give!" Laelius spins on his heel and strides away from the arguing voices behind him, trembling with frustrated anger. *You were right, Scippy*, he thinks. *We will have to get our resources ourselves.* He trods from the Senate chambers and down the wide steps of the Forum, merging into the everyday bustle of the city, seeking solace in the streets from which he arose.

The Senate concludes its business, and Cato rushes over to join Flaccus. "Can you believe those expenditures?" blurts Cato. "This Scipio and his effeminate 'friend' have been throwing lavish parties at the state's expense! They waste monies on expensive wines and foods."

Flaccus pats his protégé on the shoulder. "These Hellenics, they worship the decadent Greeks. If they had their way, they'd spend all our money on scrolls and art!"

"Still, Laelius had the truth of things about the worth of deeds over ancestry," says Cato. "Our founders were farmers, as well as our greatest generals."

Flaccus sniffs. "This Scipio might have won a battle for Rome, but his heart is with Greece. He lacks Latinitas, my friend, the three essences of being a true Latin: purity, simplicity, and devotion to duty!" He turns to Cato. "The more I see, the more I think you should be the next quaestor for them, to restrain their spending."

Cato is thinking that Flaccus seems to be lacking in all three of these elements, but he holds his tongue. "I would certainly like to observe firsthand his use of our finances," he says. "I suspect there is more waste than Felix has noticed. Far more ...."

That night, Laelius reclines on a couch in the Scipio family's domus. Pomponia and Amelia are with him, eager for any news about Scipio. They studiously avoid talking about the ship delivered to Pomponia, with so many slaves and attendants present. After dinner, the discussion eventually turns to the Latin Party's efforts to rescind the Sword of Rome's command before the upcoming consular elections.

"Your arrival was propitious, Laelius. Now I have the ... resources to combat this injustice. Amelia and I can work with the other Hellenics to publicize how valuable Marcellus has been to the war effort."

"I do like the man, but he is not a true Hellenic," observes Laelius. "He has no interest I know of in public museums or libraries. He's more of a land-rights and food-for-the-masses type, wouldn't you say?"

"Marcellus may not be a Hellenic, but he is a man of the people," says Pomponia. "He will prevent the patricians from taking more of our public lands under their so-called agricultural reforms."

"I only remind you, he is a military man, Mother," says Laelius. "He may not support public works for culture. Now, if you want a road or an aqueduct built, he is your man!" Laelius grins and takes a deep draft of his wine. He smacks his lips. "Mmm. Falernian. It's delicious, but I have grown accustomed to the hearty wines of the Iberians, they have reds that would please the gods!"

"Yes, well, Marcellus would be a worthy ruler, and I will help elect him," Amelia says. "Once Marcellus defeats Hannibal, he will be given a triumph and become the idol of Rome. At that point we begin his campaign to be elected dictator, so he can rule with the imperium of absolute power." She pours herself another glass of wine. "That should put him beyond any depredations of the Latin Party. And then, when my fiancé returns victorious from Iberia, he can become the next consul—with my help, of course."

"You make it sound so easy," chuckles Laelius. "The Senate might assassinate Marcellus. It has happened before, and it will happen again."

Pomponia sips her wine, smiling to herself. "Perhaps, but I think Flaccus knows there would be, let us say, 'repercussions' from me, were he to do so." She looks stonily at Laelius. "Do not ask me why I say that, dear, but Flaccus knows it is in his best interests not to be a pain in the backside ...."

Amelia giggles, looking away from Laelius. "Hmm ... private joke," says Laelius. "Very well for you two."

Amelia looks back at Laelius. "More of a joke about privates, dear friend," she says, with a wink at Pomponia.

Pomponia chortles as she pours more wine. "I think Rome will be led by whoever is victorious in the next battle: Marcellus, Scipio, Fabius, Flaccus, the gods know who else. So who will rule Rome, what direction will we take? The last piece of that puzzle lies on the battlefield." Pomponia sighs. "For all its stink and horror, the it is cleaner than the Senate."

*   *   *   *   *

TARRACO, IBERIA, 208 BCE. The winter rain shows no sign of abating, and that pleases Scipio mightily. Time grows short before the army leaves for its campaign against the Generals, and his men will likely encounter early spring rains on their march. He knows that rain fighting cannot be explained. It must be experienced—legionnaires learn how to maintain footing in the midst of conflict, when a slip can mean death.

Scipio watches Lucius Marcius drill the marines and infantry in the new cohort formations, pleased with his selection of him as his new infantry trainer. Marcius is a survivor of Publius Scipio's army, and a legend among the legionnaires that made it to Tarraco after the defeat. Three years ago, when the senior Scipio's force was massacred in the Baetis River valley, the wily old tribune marched the disheartened survivors through miles of enemy territory to arrive at the Ebro River. There he assembled the army remnants into a single oversized maniple, designed to maintain formation in the face of the concerted infantry and cavalry attacks that it subsequently repelled. Scipio became enamored with the idea of a large and mobile maniple and recruited Marcius to help train the men in the infantry formation that Scipio has adopted for the entire army, referring to it as a "cohort." After months of drilling, the legionnaires can divide into maniples, move lines in different directions, and merge back into cohorts. More important, the veterans have grown to accept the wisdom of the formation changes, and army morale has improved.

In unison, the cohorts break into maniples and execute a rapid flanking maneuver, all to the signals of the trumpeters that Scipio added to each cohort. Having been in four major battles, he has learned that a centurion's shouted commands can be lost in the din of battle, and whistles may not be heard. For the cohort to be an effective weapon, his men must respond instantly, as one man, so a soldier with a trumpet is near the centurion. Scipio drills his men relentlessly in these formation changes: the memories of Romans milling into each other at Cannae and Trasimene are too vivid for him to ignore.

Scipio sees Laelius standing off to the side of the troops, dressed in full battle regalia, studying the cohort movements of his legion of marines. Desperate for men, Scipio has beached all but the dozen ships that patrol the sea lanes and converted the seamen and marines into a highly trained infantry legion. Laelius the admiral has become Laelius the legate, a lieutenant who commands his marine land forces with an oddly effective mix of discipline and humor. He joins Marcus Silenus and Lucius Marcius as Scipio's primary officers and advisors.

Satisfied that the infantry training has gone well, Scipio rides over to the plains to watch the cavalry alae practicing their new maneuvers, dismounting and remounting on the fly. *They are certainly not Numidians*, he chuckles to himself, *but they will have a few surprises for the Carthaginians.*

Scipio returns to the Tarraco town hall, resigned to sit through his usual spate of afternoon meetings and adjudications. This day he receives visitors from neighboring tribes, ones who have heard of his merciful treatment of the captives at Cartago Nova. Scipio has barely plunked himself into his large throne-like chair when his Quintus announces his first visitor: Edeco, warrior prince of the Edetani. A hirsute, barrel-chested man stomps into the capacious room, a bright blue robe flowing about his iron armor, an antlered helmet on his head.

Edeco nervously strokes his curly black beard and fumbles with a few Latin words before Scipio signals for his interpreter, a gaunt old Edetani priest, to speak for him. The prince speaks a few sentences to the interpreter and looks at Scipio expectantly as the interpreter translates. "He says you have his wife and his two daughters, brought here from Cartago Nova." The interpreter looks at the prince, who growls a single sentence. "He says that he may be crazy, but he would like them back." Scipio suppresses a grin and bows his head slightly in acknowledgement of the man's blunt request. Edeco speaks again. "In return he offers you—"

"Tell him he does not have to offer me anything," Scipio interrupts. "I am pleased to give them their freedom and apologize for the delay—it was a time of much confusion. Tell him that they may all leave, with the gods' blessing."

When the interpreter relays this message, the burly prince's eyes light up, though his expression remains stoic. *The man has as much gravitas as that tedious Cato,* Scipio thinks.

The tribesman suddenly releases a long, passionate sentence as he looks steadily at Scipio. "He says you are now a friend of the Edetani," says the interpreter, "and that they are an enemy to all of Carthage. His tribe will not fight for the Three Generals, and his scouts will inform you of their movements about the Ebro." The interpreter smiles mischievously. "He thanks King Scipio for his mercy." Scipio winces at "King," but he nods his head and dismisses the prince.

Scipio turns to one of his attendants, a longtime Tarraco citizen. "Is mercy such a rare commodity here? Is that why it becomes so impressive to Iberians?"

The older man rubs his stubbled chin. "More that its opposite is so prevalent!" he retorts. Scipio grunts a laugh and waves for the next appointment.

"Our next visitor is a very well-known tribal chieftain," proclaims the chief attendant. "But he requests a private audience with you, General."

Scipio looks curiously at his Roman attendants. "Why did he ask for this?" An attendant walks over and speaks softly into Scipio's ear. Scipio's eyes widen, and he turns to his attendants and tribunes. "Wait outside, all of you." He points to his guards and interpreter. "You remain."

After everyone has left, a solitary hooded figure enters through a side door, scrutinizing the entire room, as if assassins were waiting. "There is no one else here," says Scipio. "Come forward." The figure stops ten feet from Scipio, where Scipio's guards pull back his hood and quickly inspect him for arms. Though he wears but a simple gray slave's tunic, the heavily bearded man looks at Scipio as if he were his peer, holding his head high and calmly staring into Scipio's eyes.

Scipio's mouth is a tight line when he speaks. "You are Indibilis, chief of the Ilergetes." The man hears the translation and nods. Scipio leans forward and looks stonily at him. "You helped kill my father and uncle at Baetis." The translator looks questioningly at Scipio, who glares his command.

The translator conveys the message to an impassive Indibilis, who nods and speaks. "I did not have the honor of killing him myself, but I know he died a noble death, fighting to the end. He was a great warrior."

Scipio gulps and blinks back his tearful anger. He breathes deeply several times. "What do you want, enemy of Rome?"

Indibilis receives Scipio's reply without expression. "We have a saying, 'It is best to be the dog of a man who does not treat you like a dog.' The Ilergetes know about your release of the captives at Cartago Nova. You come as conquerors to our country, but you at least show respect. The Carthaginians have treated us shamefully." He shifts about uneasily. "My family was held captive by the Generals at Cartago Nova, and now they are free. We are no longer bound to them. My brother Mandonius and I would join you, and bring our men to your side."

Scipio frowns at the chieftain. "How do I know you will not abandon me when the Carthaginians come to you with gold?"

Indibilis looks insulted. "The only gold they have is chains that appear as coins. We will not wear them again." He gestures toward the door. "I can give you my firstborn and wife as hostages. They are here."

Scipio waves off the offer. "I do not want hostages. I want your word."

The Ilergete chieftain takes out a carved wood statuette of a demon-faced man with four long clawed arms, each grasping a falcata. He holds it in front of him. "I swear to Semnocosus, god of war, that I will fight alongside King Scipio until the Carthaginians are driven from our land. May he take my family if I prove untrue."

Scipio stands and walks down to embrace Indibilis. "It is done. You are my ally. Return home. You will soon be called to join us." Scipio leans in and speaks softly. "There will be gold for you, as well."

Indibilis bows slightly and pulls the hood over his head, walking quickly to the side entrance. When he is gone, the interpreter turns to Scipio, who has slumped in his chair, looking like a child who has been forced to eat something he does not like.

"Apologies, General, but I am curious," says the interpreter. "That man led the attack on your father and uncle. You could have cut his throat and been done with it."

"Which he knew I would not do because it would destroy my connection with the tribes," says Scipio with a sigh. "Revenge is a luxury I cannot afford right now, especially if it costs me thousands of Iberian warriors." Scipio steeples his fingers together and bends them in and out, watching their movement. "Besides, I have a special purpose for Indibilis and Mandonius. A loyalty test, if you will."

That night, Scipio meets with Marcus Silenus and Laelius in a feasting room in the town hall. Scipio spreads out a five-foot map of southern Iberia, drawn by the captured mapmakers of Cartago Nova. The map is a work of art, exquisitely detailed with the region's mountains, rivers, valleys, and towns. Three phoenix figurines are placed on top of the map, one for each of The Three General's camps. One marker is at Gades on the southwestern coast, another hundreds of miles north of Gades near the mountains. Scipio points to a third phoenix two hundred miles northwest of Cartago Nova, near the center of Iberia.

"This is where Hasdrubal's army is wintering, above the plains of Baecula, by their last silver mine. Our exploradores tell me he is planning to move his army across the Ebro and into Italia, to join his brother Hannibal. We don't have the men to guard the entire border, so he will likely make it over."

Laelius stares wonderingly at Scipio. "That would give Hannibal another thirty thousand men, more than two Roman armies!"

Scipio nods. "It would double Hannibal's force. And they would be battle-hardened warriors, worth twice their amount in Roman recruits." Scipio moves his finger farther north. "But look here. Gisgo is only two or three weeks' march from Hasdrubal, leaving most of Iberia unoccupied. We must conclude that the three armies are planning to come together very soon, perhaps to take over Hasdrubal's territory when he marches for Italia. If we are locked in an extended battle with Hasdrubal, they could come to his aid before we could escape."

"And destroy us," interjects Marcus.

"Yes, they could," Scipio says, as he moves Hasdrubal's figurine over the Alps to Italia. "Now, we could allow Hasdrubal to move on to Italia. Then we take on Gisgo and Mago. That reduces the odds from three to one to two to one." Scipio turns to Marcus Silenus. "What say you, Marcus?"

Marcus shakes his head, once. "No. We came here to take Iberia and thus starve the beast that Hannibal has become. If Hasdrubal goes to Italia, we might conquer Iberia, but Rome would fall, and eventually we would, too."

Laelius chuckles. "I hate to agree with Marcus, but for once those history lessons from Asclepius are worth something to me. I remember that the great Pyrrhus of Epirus won all his battles with Rome but lost the war, when he ran out of resources. I fear we'd be the same here. Besides, I'm sick of being called a soft-handed Hellenic by those Latins. Let's beat all three generals! That would send a message to Rome."

Scipio can feel his right hand twitching from his anxiety, and he reaches to grab the table edge to quiet it. "I share your sympathies, but either way we have to win, or Rome will fall—it is that simple." He rubs his neck, looks up at the tent roof for several long minutes. Then he looks back at Marcus and Laelius. "We have to get to Hasdrubal before Mago and Gisgo can join him. We'll have to surprise him."

"Maybe those tricks of yours will pay off after all, making pack mules of the men and having them wear those odd sandals," jibes Laelius.

Marcus merely looks at his general. "If we make it there first, Mago and Gisgo will not be far behind, that is certain."

"Well then," says Scipio, "we had best prepare to leave soon, while the edge of winter is still upon us and no one would expect us. We'll have to meet with some of the Iberian tribes as we go, so Baecula will require at least a fortnight march."

"Their scouts will be about. They will discover we are coming," says Marcus.

Scipio nods. "I will send out the speculatores. They will spread rumors in the wine bars and taverns that we are departing for the Ebro border. Their spies will relay that information back to the Generals, I am sure. When we leave, we will march northwest as if we were heading for the Ebro, then turn south."

Laelius grins. "Perhaps the Latins were right about the Scipios: they are full of intrigue and deception."

Marcus stares hard at Laelius. "Would we had used such stratagems at Cannae," he says flatly. "We might not have lost forty thousand of our men to Hannibal."

Scipio claps his hands, excited and fearful. "It is done, then. We must detail our plans at tomorrow's military meeting. Be prepared: our older tribunes will certainly have some ideas about how to proceed! But we will not change our battle strategy for this conflict: win quickly and decisively. We cannot endure a drawn-out series of battles with Hasdrubal."

Marcus shakes his head. "That will be difficult to accomplish. He is very crafty, and he has a large army of seasoned fighters, more than we do."

"Ah, but we have one advantage," smiles Scipio. "He thinks he is fighting a bunch of stupid Romans, and we know we are fighting a bunch of clever Carthaginians!"

*　*　*　*　*

UPPER BAETIS VALLEY, IBERIA, 208 BCE. "Fuckin' hot enough already, itdn't it?" asks the infantryman.

The Carthaginian corporal glares at him. "Put more fire under the belly, you sow's afterbirth! I want that belly red!" He cuffs the soldier on the ear, and the forlorn little man shovels another pile of wood under the bronze bull. The corporal takes a thick stick and pries off the lid of the statue, throwing a leaf into it and watching it curl into ash. He nods and walks back to Hasdrubal's palatial command tent. Hasdrubal is inside, sitting on a pile of cushions while he converses with the visiting Gisgo and Mago. At the rear of the tent stands Agon, his cavalry commander, and the fearsome Rhodo, who has recently escaped from a Roman prison.

Two Sacred Band guards hold a captured speculatore between them. The rotund young Roman watches the party nervously, trying to comprehend the Carthaginian they are speaking, hoping for some hint of his fate.

"Spring is coming, my brothers," says Hasdrubal. "The rains are gone and the ground is firm. It is time to move against Tarraco and Ebro and rid us of the Roman menace. Then I can reinforce Hannibal." He grimaces. "The Council of Elders has sent me a reminder that I am to cross the Alps before winter, and they will send me nothing until I do!"

"Cornelius Scipio should be our first target," urges Mago. "The Iberian tribes are defecting to him. We are losing thousands of potential allies. If you take your army to Italia, Hasdrubal, we have to replace it with Iberians. So we get rid of Scipio first, and claim his allies."

Gisgo scowls. "That little bastard is a threat to our stability. I am going to send my forces north to the Ebro and eliminate him. Our Tarraco spies say the boy is headed there, to block your entry to Italia."

"Hmm ... I can be there about the same time as you," muses Mago. "We could join forces for a massed attack."

Hasdrubal raises his hand to silence them. "Be not so quick to your strategy. Let us see what our little pigeon has to say about Scipio's movements. We need to be careful. This Scipio seems to be a bit more devious than the usual Roman. He is more … Carthaginian."

Mago shrugs. "Why not? Put the question to him."

Hasdrubal throws up his hands. "Ah, but I have already asked him nicely, with just a few blows of encouragement! He confirms that Scipio is heading to their garrison on the Ebro."

Gisgo cocks his head in puzzlement. "That is good, eh? Now we know what we suspected. We can attack there."

Hasdrubal's muddy brown eyes darken with a vicious gleam. "Ah, but he said it so readily, without sufficient duress! Perhaps he would sing a different tune, with the proper encouragement."

"And you have prepared the proper encouragement, haven't you, my brother?" Mago says while he looks knowingly at Mago. "That is your specialty."

Hasdrubal bobs his head, smiling. "Why yes, I have prepared my latest toy for him: The Sicilian Bull."

Gisgo looks disgusted. "The Bull? I thought that was only a disgusting Greek myth."

Hasdrubal grins excitedly. "Oh, no, it is real, very real, as our friend here will find out!" The Roman captive hears the pleasure in Hasdrubal's voice and looks expectantly at him, hoping it somehow, some way, signifies mercy for him.

Hasdrubal heads out of the tent. "Come on out and take a look at this. I had my little treasure imported from Sicily." The four Carthaginians follow Hasdrubal to the rear of the tent. They see a seven-foot-long brass bull standing over a bonfire, its belly reddened with heat. Hasdrubal walks about it, chattering as proudly as if he had a new chariot. "What do you think? It is a handsome beast, isn't it? It's like the one that Phalaris used on poor Perillos in Greece, those centuries ago. A masterful instrument!"

Mago looks at Gisgo, shaking his head disapprovingly. "Is this truly necessary?"

"Necessary?" Hasdrubal splutters, " Oh yes! We have to know about little Scipio's whereabouts. What do you want me to do? Ask this prick politely, and thank him for his answer? No, we give this Roman cur the shit test, see if his words ring true." Hasdrubal gestures for the Roman to be brought near him and the bull. The speculatore's eyes start from his head, and he writhes to escape as he is dragged forward and stood up in front of Hasdrubal.

"Where goes Scipio?" says Hasdrubal in his pidgin Latin. "Where he goes?"

The shaking young man swallows. "Ebro," he says. "River Ebro garrison."

Hasdrubal gestures for him to be pulled closer to the searing heat of the bull. "Where goes he?" asks Hasdrubal, carefully studying the Roman's face.

"Ebro, Ebro, Ebro!" screams the spy. "I swear, the Ebro garrison!"

Hasdrubal frowns. "Mmm, I doubt your sincerity." He takes the thick stick lying on the ground and props open the door in the back of the bull, revealing a man-sized hollow within it. He motions for the sweating guards to throw the spy into it. The young Roman struggles like a maddened snake, screaming in horror as they prepare to lift him into it. In his terror he abruptly voids his bowels, urine and feces running down his legs.

Hasdrubal grabs the front of his tunic. "Tell truth or in you go!" he yells.

"Baecula! Baecula! He goes to Baecula!" the Roman screams to the heavens, over and over, as if calling down the gods. Hasdrubal slaps his dazed victim and gestures for the guards to pull the still-screaming spy back from the sizzling bronze statue.

The dark little general grins smugly at his fellow commanders. "You see? I give him the shit test. When they shit themselves, you can believe what they say." He stabs his finger into his chest. "This pussy boy Scipio, he is coming at me, coming to take my last silver mine, the last of our money sources. Very smart! And very stupid!"

Gisgo turn to Mago, who nods. "By Mot's underworld, this Scipio is closing in on you," Mago says. "We will join you as soon as possible. I'll leave tonight."

Gisgo looks at the slumped spy, crying as he writhes on the ground. "I believe what he said. I will muster my men as soon as I return. If the Romans come at you, hold them at bay until we get here."

"Not to worry, Scipio must be weeks away." Hasdrubal laughs. "But maybe I kill him myself, if I am bored. Maybe I put him in the bull!"

Hasdrubal starts to walk back to the tent with the rest of the officers. One of the guards holding the Roman shouts over to Hasdrubal. "What about this one?"

Hasdrubal turns about. "Fuck him. Throw him in the bull."

The guards wrestle the demonically terrified Roman inside the burning bull and close the trap door. Within seconds his screams erupt from the mouth of the bull, coming through a series of fluted pipes that make his agonies sound like the bellowing of a bull. The bull's bellows build, and crescendo. And then fall silent.

*   *   *   *   *

BAECULA PROVINCE, IBERIA. The vast Roman army sprawls over the fertile tree-ringed river valley, their camp palisades looming over lands green with budding crops of wheat and grapes. "Where is he?" Scipio presses his scouts. "Where is Hasdrubal's army? How many men?"

The two riders look at one another, embarrassed. "Hasdrubal is in the Guadalquivir Valley, General, but we could not find out where. There are two cavalry outposts at the valley mouth, and the road out of it has another outpost. We could not get in."

The other scout pushes in front of his fellow. "But we did see an enormous hill in the center, tall and wide as a mountain, with nothing but watered plains below it. That would be a likely location for his camp."

Scipio looks at them for several long seconds. "Dismissed," he says abruptly.

After they are gone, Scipio hisses with frustration. "You know what their Numidian scouts would have done?" he declaims to his attending tribunes. "They would have figured out a way to steal into that valley. Then, and only then, they would have ridden back to report." He frowns at his officers. "And you think we have the best cavalry in the world? Roman vanity is our worst enemy, not the Carthaginians!" He stalks about the command tent as the tribunes stoically wait for him to continue.

Laelius moves over to Scipio's side. "The scouts' words have value, nonetheless. We know he is next to Baecula, on the high plains. And that is only two days' march from here."

Two men jostle their way through the tribunes to face Scipio, rough men wearing wolf's head caps over their unkempt halos of hair. "We send our men there, they will find out," says Indibilis through Scipio's interpreter.

"Our men will count the teeth on every soldier, and be back by tomorrow!" says brother Mandonius. The two chieftains have kept true to their word: they entered Scipio's camp last night with four thousand Ilergete warriors, defecting from the Carthaginians. With the three thousand Iberians that have joined Scipio since his army left Tarraco, he stands with a force of thirty thousand men, an even match for Hasdrubal's formidable force.

Scipio bows slightly. "My gratitude. I do appreciate the offer of the fierce Ilergetes, you who are first to fight and last to quit." He motions to the back of his command tent. "But we have another ally who knows well this area."

Allucius, prince of the Oretani, steps to the front. The young man wears a snow-white tunic with vivid purple stripes, his only ornament a thin band of gold about his brow. He bows deeply before Scipio. "We live here. We know the ways of forest and plain," he says in his newly acquired pidgin Latin. "I send our men now. Back by cock's crow, King Scipio."

Ignoring the muted chuckles from the tribunes, Scipio places his hand on the young man's shoulder. "Gratitude. Send them immediately." Allucius walks out from the tent as the Ilergete brothers eye him with no small amount of jealousy. "Who knows?" says Scipio to his officers. "They just might make it happen."

Marcus Silenus gives a derisive snort. "Might? They are Oretani, masters of stealth, and they are in their homeland. We should have told him to bring us Hasdrubal's head." At that, even Scipio has to laugh, which he finds more difficult to do every day.

"What about Mago and Gisgo? Where are they?"

A senior tribune looks at his fellows, embarrassed. "We have no certain knowledge. We know they left their camps many days ago. They must be near."

Scipio blows out his cheeks. "Well, all the more reason to act quickly. Hasdrubal must know our general location. He will think we are two days' march from him and will be preparing accordingly. But we can still surprise him." He turns to Laelius. "Send the rest of the Oretani into the region. They will find any Carthaginian scouts that may be in front of us. Tell them to make sure that the road is clear to the valley. They are to stay out there and intercept any scouts that venture our way. We must have the element of surprise."

"So, we prepare for a two-day march, starting tomorrow," says Marcus.

Scipio shakes his head. "We turn two days' march into one day, and that is today." Scipio faces his officers. "Strip the men's packs down to a half-day's cold rations and their weapons. The mules can bring the rest later. Tonight we march. We march as if our life depended on it because if Mago and Gisgo catch us, it will be forfeit."

*　　*　　*　　*　　*

The African horses neigh impatiently, pushing their noses against the unshorn timbers of their rude stockade. Their morning feeding time approaches, and the nimble little ponies stir restlessly. Two Libyan cavalrymen soon enter the pen, leading a knot of slaves carrying extra rations of horse feed. Today will be a long day of patrols; the scouts must ride out until they find the Roman army's location. The cavalry outpost has been warned that that the Romans will arrive in two or three days, and its two hundred men have been readying their horses and sharpening their spears.

The slaves shovel in grain and forage, pushing it about so that all are fed. "Get some over there to my horse," says one scout.

"You want him fed proper, you'd better feed him yourself," says the other cavalryman. The first man starts to reply, but he pauses and cocks his head, listening. There is a barely perceptible drumming sound in the air, familiar but not yet recognizable.

"What did our scouts report yesterday, have you heard?" The other rider merely shrugs. "They haven't been back yet."

The Libyan looks curiously at his fellow. "They have not reported? Hmm … look, I want to check something. You finish here."

The African quickly secures a leather saddle and bridle onto his horse. He trots through the outpost gates and gallops south toward the low-lying hills that border the wide plain, heading toward the drumming noise. The dawn sun lightens the river-bottom fog, and the scout perceives four shadowy figures coming toward him. Jabbing his heels into his mount, he rushes forward. *There they are, dragging in late again.* The officer prepares to berate them when he notices that the four shadows have other shadows emerging behind them, bobbing dots in a light gray sea. Then he sees the unmistakable outline of a Roman legionary standard, and his mouth gapes. The Libyan wheels about and hurtles back toward the outpost, shouting "Romans! Romans are coming!"

As the Libyan darts back to his men, the four Roman scouts turn about and gallop back to their legions. Scipio is leading the vanguard, his eyes fixed on the murky plains ahead. The lead rider pulls up in front of Scipio, stammering his news. "We sighted an enemy scout. He rode away before we could catch him."

"Gods be cursed," Scipio mutters. "We have lost surprise after marching all night to preserve it. Tell the Master of Horse to send our cavalry!" Within minutes, thousands of Roman and Iberian cavalry plunge across the plain toward the Carthaginian outposts at the entrance to the Baecula River Valley. The courageous Libyans ride out to engage their enemy, but they are quickly encircled and overcome. Several escape, however, and rush to Hasdrubal's camp at the base of the hill.

"How in the fuck did they get here already?" storms Hasdrubal. "Where are our scouts?" A Libyan informs him the scouts have not yet returned. "Not yet returned?" sneers Hasdrubal. "They haven't returned because they're dead!" He turns to his commanders. "Get our men together as best you can. Go now!" The officers scramble from the tent, shouting for their subordinates. Thousands of Libyans and Iberians rush into formation, many of the men unarmored, as they hastily prepare for a Roman assault.

Scipio's victorious cavalry quickly return to the marching army, and cheers erupt when they break the news of the fate of the Libyans. The Roman army steps up their pace and they soon tramp through the Guadalquivir Valley entrance. The fog has lifted, and Scipio can see Hasdrubal's vast camp sprawled near the base of the tall, wide hill that dominates the valley.

The legions spread out across plains, each divided into ten cohorts of 480 men, steadily advancing toward Hasdrubal's camp. When Scipio can discern the Carthaginian formations, he signals for a halt. The young general hurriedly calls a standing meeting of his war council; he and his officers dismount and stand in a circle on the plains as the tumult of their arriving army boils about them, and halts. The centurions direct their men to take food and water, not knowing when the next opportunity will present itself.

"What say you?" asks Scipio. "Should we attack now? Hasdrubal's camp is there before us."

Laelius looks at the reticence on the faces of his fellows and raises his voice. "Our men have marched all night at double paces, with little sleep or food. Is it really wise to send them out against a rested foe?" A half-dozen tribunes murmur their agreement.

Scipio's face turns red momentarily, and then he chuckles. "For once I will agree that I may be moving too quickly. Let us make camp for tonight, but we cannot tarry beyond tomorrow, is that agreed?" The officers salute and immediately set off to organize the camp streets and tents.

Night falls on two winking constellations of campfires. The large camps are quiet, the expectation of mortal battle dimming even the most raucous spirit.

The next day, Scipio's Iberian scouts give him a rude awakening: Hasdrubal has moved his army up the hill during the night and is hastily constructing a permanent camp on the plateau.

Scipio confers with his officers, and Laelius is again the first to speak. "That little bastard must be feeling quite smug, camped on top of that rocky mount. It's unassailable—we can't maintain formation up those inclines." Laelius stumbles about, teetering and waving his arms. "You see what would happen?"

"We have drilled in many formation changes," replies Scipio evenly. "Now it is time to put them to practice. Break the cohorts into maniples. That will make it easier to keep men together when we negotiate the hill."

"It is very steep and rocky," says Marcus Silenus. "It will still be difficult to stay together while going up it. There's too much scrub and too many boulders."

"Perhaps not," replies Scipio. "I checked my scrolls of ancient battles in this land. There was a Carthaginian general named Hanno, who fought the Greeks and Iberians here some two hundred years ago. The scrolls say that the Iberians would seek mountainous terrain to mount their defense, making it difficult for Hanno to attack in a direct assault. He learned to seek the path of least resistance, oft taking his men sideways up the mount to maintain order. We will do that today."

"Today?" blurts an angry older tribune. "We need another day or two to prepare for this." He looks at Scipio defiantly. "Or we should just return to Tarraco."

Scipio stiffens, and the voice that comes from his mouth is that of an imperator, not a young man. "There will be no retreat, and there will be no delay. We have to get up that hill before the other two armies join Hasdrubal. That is our only chance."

A young tribune interrupts. "But, what happens if Mago and Gisgo come here afterwards? They will have more than twice our force!"

Scipio nods. "Yes, but we can hold them off if we have that plateau." He looks at the tribune, a sarcastic smile on his determined face. "And if we can't, our lives will cost them so dearly they will not be sending anyone to Hannibal for years, that is certain. In two hours we start up that hill. For once, we will not use our heavy infantry for a frontal attack. They will come around the sides of the hill." Scipio grins. "This time we will be the ones playing a trick on the Carthaginians!"

"Then who bears the brunt of the middle?" asks Marcus Silenus. "Let me lead our young velites up there. They will not retreat, I assure you!"

Scipio slaps Marcus on the shoulder. "Mars himself would fear to disappoint you, Marcus. It will be a short, steep dash up that center. Just keep them moving steady."

Scipio looks around. "Indibilis! Mandonius!" he calls out. The two Iberians step forward. "You said you wanted to avenge the wrongs the Carthaginians have given to your tribe. Now is that time, I tell you. Will you lead some of your light infantry up that hill, while the rest follow me up the side?"

Mandonius glances at Indibilis, who gives the barest of nods. "Middle is fine. Side is fine. We kill them anywhere," he says in Latin.

Scipio looks at his tribunes. "Then the die is cast. Get back to your cohorts. The battle horns will be sounding soon."

*   *   *   *   *

Hasdrubal stands on the wide hilltop plateau, watching the Roman army fall into battle formation beneath him. Squinting to discern the enemy armor and standards, Hasdrubal can see that the Romans are massing thousands of velites and Iberian light infantry for an attack, with none of their dread principes or hastati. "They are looking to have a skirmish," concludes Hasdrubal, "but they will fetch themselves a slaughter!"

Hasdrubal pulls his infantry commander over to the lip of the plateau, pointing to the men lining up below. "Yaroah, I want our light infantry to occupy that shelf halfway down the hill. Use the Balearics and Libyans. They are our best."

"Very well," answers Yaroah, a muscular older man with the scars and nicks of a hundred battles. "I will station our Iberian heavy infantry at the top of the hill, in case the Romans send in the legionnaires behind the velites."

Hasdrubal nods, then turns to his Master of Horse. "Agon, place your Numidians down there on the flanks. If they send up their cavalry, Masinissa's men can ride circles around them."

"As you command," replies Agon. "But I should tell you, the Numidians are not as agile on that steep and rocky terrain."

Hasdrubal waves away his remarks. "Those little ponies of theirs are like goats. They'll still be better than the Romans." Hasdrubal steps back from the lip, turning toward camp. "Agon, I need you to take command of this skirmish. I have to get our camp built—we don't even have walls up yet." He shakes his head wonderingly. "Baal's balls, they weren't supposed to be here for days!"

Scipio has moved to the front of the velites and Iberians, accompanied by Marcus Silenus and Mandonius. They look over the steep hill, studying the fissures, rocks, and scrub trees that blanket its uneven landscape. The savage Balearic infantry stand above them, stamping about on each side of the unmoving Libyans, with the lithe Numidian riders waiting on the Roman's left flank. Four thousand warriors look down at the Romans from the wide, gently inclined shelf that forms a semicircle about the hill.

"They've got their Libyans in the middle," comments Marcus.

"They will be the toughest opponents," says Scipio. "But they are all light infantry and cavalry, so they expect us to skirmish today and attack later, as Romans often do." Scipio turns to his officers, his eyes gleaming with excitement. "This time, we have a very un-Roman surprise for them," he crows. "Laelius, I want you to take your marines and the cavalry. You will loop around the left and come up on their right hand. I will lead the infantry around to the right and attack their left flank. [xxvi] We depart as soon as our center force engages their attention."

Scipio points to the ridgeline above them, jutting from the steeply inclined slope. "It is not a long way to get there, but the going will be slow. Look how rocky and fissured that land is! Keep the velites together. Marcus, I will depend on you for that." Scipio points to the side of the hill. "As I said, Laelius and I will skirt around the sides of the slope. They won't expect Romans to sneak up on them. Then we will—"

"Honored General," interrupts one of Scipio's most trusted tribunes, a one-eyed veteran of the Trasimene and Cannae battles, "some of us have been talking about this. If we could take another day or two to organize ourselves, we could essay a more traditional frontal attack."

Scipio takes a deep breath, exhales it loudly, and glares at him. "I cannot believe I am hearing this again! There is a time to be careful and a time to be opportunistic, Spurius. You know me—I am a careful man, accounting for every detail and planning for every eventuality. But today, our motto is *acta non verba* (deeds, not words). We attack now, while Hasdrubal is in disarray."

He turns and looks reprovingly at the dozen tribunes. "Understand, we are going to ambush Hasdrubal because it is the superior strategy, not because we need time to plan some silly formation march up the side of a mountain!" With a final glare at his wayward officers, he turns to Laelius, who has been polishing his sword with a scrap of linen, clearly ignoring the entire discussion. "Laelius, go see to your side. I am going to mine." He turns to the rest of his officers. "You doubt me, yet I have brought you nothing but victory. I tell you now, we will be at the top of that hill before the sun sets. If not, I will resign my command."

Without another word Scipio marches back to his horse and vaults upon it. As the officers rush out to prepare their men, Scipio rides over and looks down at Laelius. "Remember what that Carthaginian Hanno did when he fought in these mountains. Do not fight the land, Laelius:

make it your ally. Look for the most level terrain and follow it up. Switch back and forth."

Laelius nods, then a grim smile breaks across his face. "This will be a good test of our new swords, won't it? Bet you were hoping for a few more minor engagements before we used them like this!" Laughing, he spins about and rushes to his marines.

The battle horns sound. The velites and the Iberian light infantry stamp up the steep incline toward the ridge, with Marcus Silenus leading the Roman contingent. Several times, the hardened old warrior must pause for laggards to catch up to his relentless lead as the men scramble and trip over the rocky ground. The Balearics and Libyans rain javelins and stones down upon them, so thick that dozens of the well-shielded Romans and Ilergetes fall about the landscape. The legionnaires and tribesmen pull their most seriously wounded behind a protective tree or bush, but the rest bandage their wounds as best they can and continue, rabid to engage the men who wreaked havoc upon them.

Within half an hour, the velites and Iberians mount the front of the first ridge and push into the waiting enemy formations. The Balearics swarm down onto the Iberians on the Romans' center-right side. Armed with only a javelin, sword, and small wooden shield, the elusive islanders strike then retreat, only to swarm back to attack again. Mandonius' men chase after them, throwing their thick iron javelins at their backs. The determined Iberians' spread out and eventually encircle the Balearics, cutting off their escape. Mandonius' men rush into the islanders, hewing through their light armor with their cleaver-like falcatas, cutting off hands and limbs. After losing scores of men to the Iberians' frenzied onslaught, the Balearics retreat toward the top of the hill.

The staunch Libyans in the center and left have marched forward in phalanx formation, delving into the velites coming over the ridge. The Roman lines give way, but Marcus pushes to the front. He stabs down a Libyan captain and beheads his guard, exhorting his men to follow him.

Marcus' centurions and tribunes muster the young men to follow their leader. They gradually beat back the Libyans from the ridgeline, until the velites are fighting on level ground.

Mandonius' men shift their attack from the retreating Balearics, cutting into the side of the Libyan phalanx. The Ilergetes shove their large oblong shields into the Libyans to knock them off balance, followed by quick javelin thrusts to the Libyans' torsos. Furiously assailed from two sides, the Libyans desperately muster a counter charge into the more vulnerable velites, killing many of the young men with sword thrusts. The centurions drive the second and third lines forward over the bodies of their compatriots, and the velites hold long enough for the Ilergetes to penetrate the Libyans from the side, disorganizing their formation.

The Libyans regroup and gradually follow the Balearics in retreat up to the high plateau, back where the rest of Hasdrubal's army waits. Energized by their small victory, the Iberians and velites lunge after their retreating enemy, but Marcus Silenus wisely halts their charge, allowing time for Scipio's and Laelius' hillside legions to move up and around them. After a breather, Marcus' men march up the hill, killing stragglers and wounded as they go.

When Scipio sees the first of the Balearics retreating up toward the main camp, he signals for Laelius to begin his flanking attacks. Scipio loops his infantry around one side of the hill as Laelius does the same on the other, each searching for the most level and unobstructed paths upward. As per Scipio's orders, the legionnaires and marines divide into centuries of eighty men to better negotiate the terrain. With no opposition to slow them, the men quickly weave past to the edges of the first shelf to continue up to the plateau. Wearing their new hobnailed sandals, the Romans manage to scramble over small boulders and damp rocks with a minimum of slippage and injury, adding to their speed.

On the hill plateau, fresh Carthaginian forces wait to repel the velites and Iberians, and their retreating light infantry weaves through them to the back lines. Hasdrubal orders his finest Libyan and Iberian heavy infantry to concentrate in the middle, unaware of the legions that are closing in on him from the sides. The Carthaginian general keeps twenty elephants at the ready behind the center troops of Iberians, waiting to send the animals in for maximum shock when it is most required.

The velites and Iberians crest the plateau and move toward the heavy infantry. Hasdrubal rides over to confer with Yaroah about the frontal assault. As he does, he spies a glint of bronze on the side of the hill, away from the main force. Then the glint repeats a hundredfold, and he sees Laelius' marines and cavalry pouring over the hillcrest on his right. With dawning alarm, Hasdrubal looks to his left and sees Scipio's heavy infantry emerging on the other side, heading toward his infantry in the middle. Hasdrubal screams orders for the Numidians to attack, and they rush out toward Laelius' cavalry.

Yaroah leads thousands of his Libyan infantry over to repel Scipio's men, but Scipio's centuries are already breasting the ridge in force. Once upon the ridge, the legionnaires quickly fall into manipular formation, ready for the enemy's charge. Scipio rides ahead of his men, eyes agleam with the excitement of an impending victory. "Into them!" he screams over his shoulder, waving his Romanized falcata, the Gladius Hispanicus. "We have the day! Into them!"

The marines and legionnaires engage an infantry totally unprepared for their new swords and sword-fighting tactics. The Carthaginians are ready to defend against the standard Roman thrusts and stabs, only to find their enemy swings a heavier sword overhand that delves through shield, armor, and flesh. The Romans' looping blows crush scores of Carthaginian skulls before their enemy adapts and raises their shields. By then it is too late, however.

Scipio's and Laelius' men break the attackers' front lines, pressing them back into their fellows. On the hillside, the Roman cavalry occupy the Numidians by fighting them on foot and then leaping back onto their horses to chase them down, a tactic the Numidians have never seen. With the Numidians' mobility limited by the uneven terrain, the Romans can easily catch their nimble opponents, lancing them with their javelins or chopping into their exposed legs. Many of the equites fight on foot with their backs protected by a boulder or tree, forcing the Numidians to slow their charge. For the first time in history, the Roman cavalry outmaneuvers these fearsome Africans.

The Roman pincers slowly close in, throwing the Carthaginians' center into confusion. The enemy commanders ride bravely into the mêlée and fight to restore order, battling their mounted counterparts and shouting orders to their captains. Hasdrubal leads a phalanx of Libyan heavy infantry into the fray against Laelius' marines and sends another phalanx toward Scipio's men. The redoubtable Libyans refuse to be broken, and the Carthaginian resistance finally halts the pincer's closing.

Laelius grabs the stallion of a fallen legionnaire and rides to the front of his marines, goading them to break the Libyans. He gallops down to the side of the hill, where the Romans are cutting apart the Numidians. Summoning his cavalry commander, he pulls two alae of riders from the fray and leads them up the hill toward the Libyans.

As Laelius crests the hill, he is intercepted by a tall and regal young man who guides his black horse with his knees, his shield and lance at the ready. Masinissa, rebel prince of the Numidians, has seen Laelius' helmet crest and knows he is a commander. If Masinissa can kill or capture him, Carthage's support for his rebellion is almost guaranteed, as well as the hand of Gisgo's daughter, the wondrous Sophonisba. He plunges eagerly toward Laelius, his spear at the ready.

Laelius is occupied with a Carpetani chieftain who has run up and grabbed the reins of his horse, hoping to pull him down. Laelius jabs his pilum at the sturdy little man, but he dodges back and deflects the thrusts with his shield, slashing Laelius across his thigh. Laelius yells, more in frustration than pain, throws down his javelin and pulls out the falcata he has carried since his wars with Hannibal. He circles his horse about the foot soldier, chopping at his head, hewing chunks from his round wood shield until naught is left but a semicircle dangling from the chieftain's arm. Laelius chops into the shoulder of the man's shield arm, cutting it to the bone. The chieftain runs screaming back into his ranks, blood gouting from his shoulder.

Grinning derisively, Laelius hurls taunts at his retreating opponent in the limited Iberian scatology he has learned from Mandonius and Indibilis, not knowing the man cannot understand him. He pulls his horse about to head down the hill when Masinissa appears, galloping across the ridgeline at him. The Numidian levels his lance at Laelius as he nears. As Masinissa closes upon him, Laelius veers off and swings a vicious cut at him. Masinissa blocks the blow without stopping and wheels about to charge again, faster than Laelius thought possible. Closing upon Laelius, the Numidian shifts his lance at the last minute. The point eases past Laelius' shield to catch his armor's shoulder strap, leveraging him off his horse and crashing him onto the slippery, blood-soaked ground.

The Numidian thrusts his lance at Laelius' eyes as he rises to one knee. It is a death blow–for anyone who does not have Laelius' exceptional speed. Laelius flicks his head sideways, and the lance passes by him. With a vicious swing of his falcata, Laelius breaks the head off Masinissa's lance, leaving him with a splintered pole. Masinissa grins in admiration and vaults onto the ground. He draws out his Roman short sword, a blade he took from the last tribune he killed, and stalks toward Laelius.

Masinissa and Laelius circle each other. They slash and parry, falcata ringing against sword. Laelius cuts out several chunks of Masinissa's short round shield before the Numidian learns to angle off his blows. Laelius, in turn, is almost killed by the prince's feint and countercut, deflecting one slash just before it reaches his throat.

Laelius can feel himself growing weary; his bleeding thigh is taking its toll. He knows Masinissa can overcome him by simply staying on the defensive as Laelius bleeds out. Desperate, Laelius adopts a tactic he learned a decade ago, when he watched the Campanian gladiators practice at the Ostia docks.

Laelius charges headlong at Masinissa and raises his falcata high for a crushing head stroke. As Masinissa raises the tatters of his shield to block the swing, Laelius spins on one leg and kicks him viciously in the lower stomach, knocking him breathless to the ground. Quick as a striking snake, Laelius swings his falcata down to sever the African's head. Just as quickly, Masinissa rolls sideways and scrambles to his feet, bent double from the pain of the kick. The two gasping opponents face each other, deciding their next tactic.

The Numidian straightens up and braces himself to charge, when he hears the screams of warriors coming from behind him. He looks over his shoulder and sees Indibilis charging toward him with his Ilergete riders, chanting "kill, kill," as they plummet toward him. Masinissa runs for his horse and springs onto it in one motion, galloping away before he has settled on top of it. Laelius watches him disappear as Indibilis draws up.

"Who was that black demon?" asks Laelius as he retrieves a bandage from his belt purse and wraps it about his leg.

"Masinissa," grunts Indibilis. "Bad fighter—sneaky quick. You lucky you alive."

Laelius curls his lip at the Ilergete, a haughty gleam in his eye. "He's the one lucky to be alive!" He watches Masinissa join the rest of his cavalry and rush away from the approaching Ilergetes. "We'll meet again, I'm sure," says Laelius. His bandage knotted, he mounts his horse and sprints across the plateau, looking for Scipio.

Fighting on the other flank, Scipio has jumped off his horse to join his infantry in the front line, determined to restore their momentum. He fells a lumbering African with several cuts to the man's abdomen, then steps further into the fray. His alarmed tribunes rush men to protect him, and band wedges through the Libyan front lines. The Romans slowly cut their way through the last of the enemy's light infantry, and penetrate farther into the plateau.

The Libyan heavy infantry tread through the remains of their light infantry fellows and march headlong into Scipio's men. The veteran fighters thrust their spears out from the gaps between their large circular shields, their movements as structured as a Roman attack.

The Africans are led by a thick hulking Libyan who swings an enormous wood cudgel, bashing in his opponents' shields and armor as he breaks through the Roman lines. A brave centurion steps in to halt the hulk's advance, lunging in low for a thrust at his bowels. The Libyan deftly steps around the thrust and crushes the top of a centurion's helmet. Blood pours from the Roman's mouth and nose; he is dead before he hits the ground. As the grinning brute steps past the dead soldier he notices Scipio to his right. His grin widens when he recognizes the plumed crest of a commander. The hulk stalks toward the general, ramming aside anyone in his way.

Scipio sees the Libyan rampaging toward him. He cannot understand what the Libyan is shouting, but he recognizes the tone: he is challenging Scipio to battle. Scipio swallows, daunted at the prospect of the gigantic Libyan captain, but he turns to face him. One of Scipio's senior tribunes abruptly rushes between them to protect his general, deftly jabbing his gladius into the giant's midsection. The heavy blade deeply pierces the Libyan's side, and he roars with anger. The Libyan bashes the Roman's shield aside with his cudgel, and back swings to pulverize the side of his head, pounding a fist-sized hole in his skull. The tribune flies sideways to the earth, his brain crushed. The Libyan nods with satisfaction, grins predatorily, and closes in on Scipio.

Scipio rushes at the Libyan commander, hoping to surprise him. The man crouches low, his shield in front of him, holding his cudgel ready for a killing blow. Scipio feigns a strike to the midsection, and the African responds as he did with the tribune, swinging his shield to knock Scipio over. Scipio quickly steps back, and the Libyan's shield whooshes past him, leaving his other arm vulnerable. Scipio stabs into the African's sword arm, skewering the middle of his cabled forearm.

The Libyan cries out and drops his weapon as Scipio lunges in to pierce his throat. But the Libyan throws down his shield and jumps onto Scipio, moving inside his sword thrust. He crashes Scipio into the earth.

The massive Iberian holds Scipio's arms in an iron grip as Scipio convulses futilely beneath him. Scipio pitches harder, but he cannot break free. His mind races, and he remembers a legendary story about the Battle of Cannae, how an incapacitated Roman had chewed off a Carthaginian's nose and ears before he died.[xxvii]

Scipio lurches against the steely grasp of his enemy, throwing his shoulders from side to side. Cursing, the Iberian bends down to pin him more securely, shoving his head next to Scipio's. With a strength borne of desperation, Scipio lunges up and bites into the man's throat, spitting out chunks of flesh and gnawing into his windpipe. The African grasps his throat with both hands and tumbles off his prey, his blood gouting over Scipio as he rolls out from under the Iberian. Scipio jumps on top of the chieftain and grasps the Libyan's curly black hair in both hands, bashing his head on a boulder until he can see brains dangling from the back of the his skull. Even then, Scipio's terrified bloodlust prompts him to pound his enemy's head again and again, grunting with satisfaction each time the skull strikes stone. Trembling and sobbing, Scipio staggers from the corpse as several legionnaires arrive to succor him. They take one look at Scipio, and freeze in their tracks.

Laelius has ridden over to check on Scipio. When he sees Scipio's horse riding free, his stomach churns with dread. Laelius careens through the individual battles around him, warding off attackers, shouting Scipio's name. He spies Scipio standing behind the front infantry line. Laelius smiles and gallops over to have a word with his friend, but his relief becomes chagrin when he draws near. Scipio stands dazedly before him, wearing a mask of blood, with tatters of flesh hanging from his teeth, looking more like an beast than a patrician general. The legionnaires protecting him stare wonderingly at each other.

"General?" one of them ventures, but receives no reply.

Laelius pitches off his horse and hurries over, pulling a linen scarf from his belt purse. Without a word, he pours water on his cloth and wipes Scipio's face, gently tugging the gore from his mouth. "Scippy?" he says quietly. "Scippy?"

As if waking from a dream, Scipio's eyes focus on Laelius. He blinks his eyes and shudders. "My horse," Scipio mutters, "where's my horse?"

"Perhaps you should go back to the rear lines for a minute," says Laelius gently. "We've got the battle in hand, there are no worries!"

Scipio stares at his friend for a long minute, then he looks about for his mount. He turns to one of the legionnaires, points to the left of him, and bellows, his voice trembling but stern. "Get me my fucking horse! Now!" Scipio turns back to Laelius, and his face softens. "Thanks for your help, thanks truly," he says, squeezing Laelius' shoulder. Scipio glances back at the front lines. "Get some of your cavalry onto my right flank and attack those infantrymen. We're going to drive those bastards over the cliff."

Laelius stares silently at Scipio, then trots off to find his equites. Two alae of cavalry soon come crashing into the Libyan flanks, breaking their formation and tumbling them down the hill. As the Roman infantry press their newfound advantage, Laelius looks over his shoulder at Scipio. He can see him screaming orders at his tribunes, bloodlust reddening his face. *What has he become?* Laelius wonders.

As Scipio re-enters the battle, Hasdrubal is raging across his rear phalanxes, preparing an all out assault. He gallops over to the elephants and orders the mahouts to prepare them for a disruptive charge into the Roman center. He signals for Agon to come to his side. "When the elephants break into the middle, your Libyan cavalry should be right behind them," he shouts over the din. "We'll drive them back over the edge!" Agon nods, and rushes off to prepare his riders.

Marcus Silenus is leading the battle in the center, fighting with the Iberian and Roman light infantry. He sees the elephants lining up behind the enemy ranks, their mahouts climbing onto their saddles, and instantly grasps Hasdrubal's intentions. Relinquishing command to Mandonius, Marcus grabs several javelins from his velites and pushes through an opening in the battle lines, stabbing his way toward the elephants, knowing he must stop them before they initiate their implacable charge. He nears an elephant at the end of the row and hurls his javelin into the mahout on top of it. The pila plunges through the mahout's cheekbone and out the side of his head, and he tumbles off his beast. Marcus rushes up and stabs his knife into the elephant's trunk, it's most sensitive part. The beast bellows in pain and crashes into its neighbor, knocking off the mahout for Marcus to dispatch.

Marcus is dashing at the next elephant when a sarissa plunges through his right shoulder, and the javelins drop from his hand. Agon has caught up to him, and Hasdrubal's Master of Horse wheels about to lance the commander again. Marcus deflects the thrust with his shield arm, his right arm hanging useless. A grinning Agon turns and gallops back at him, his sarissa poised for a killing stab. The ambidextrous Marcus drops his shield and grabs one of his throwing knives from his belt, hurling it at Agon's head. The agile Master of Horse deflects the throw with a swipe of his shield. But Agon misses Marcus' following throw, his shield over his head from swiping off the first. The leaf-shaped blade disappears into Agon's eye socket, and the screaming officer careens into the back lines as his Sacred Band ride over to catch him. Marcus dashes to the elephants and stabs several more in the trunk, sending them into a colliding frenzy with their fellows.

The beasts rampage through their own lines, trampling and scattering Hasdrubal's heavy infantry before they stampede down the hill to safety. Seeing their opportunity, Indibilis and Mandonius lead their Iberians into the disorganized Libyans as Scipio's and Laelius' men pinch into them from the sides.

Hasdrubal sees that his army has been thrown into confusion and is being slowly encircled by the relentless Romans. Expecting to savor a quick Roman defeat, he sees thousands of his men being killed and captured, with half of his elephants rampaging off to the hills below. And he knows the day is lost.

With a muttered curse, Hasdrubal shouts for his trumpeters to sound the retreat, and the horns blow across the Carthaginian lines. Knowing the Romans will be occupied with the men they have encircled, Hasdrubal leads the remaining half of his army through their makeshift camp and out along the Tagus River road, heading to a more defensible position at higher ground, there to await the arrival of Gisgo and Mago.

The Romans have encircled thousands of Hasdrubal's Iberians, Libyans, and Balearics. Only the swift Numidians have escaped, disappearing into the surrounding hills. The Carthaginians and Libyans fight until they are bunched so tightly they cannot move, and then they surrender.

Several Iberian tribes fight on, however. Fearing that the dishonor of surrender will deny them a place in the afterlife, hundreds of Carpetani and Celtiberi tribesmen rush headlong into the oncoming Roman horde, seeking death in battle. Others swallow vials of the *ranunculus sardonia* plant, a poison buttercup that quickly kills them, leaving them with the horrifying rictus of a sardonic smile. When the victorious Romans see the dead warriors smiling at them, they scramble away in terror, believing the dead's spirits are mocking them. The Ilergetes are left to finish the tribesmen, laughing at their superstitious compatriots.

The late afternoon sun angles it light across Hades' new mown field of recruits, row upon row of the valiant dead. The Roman army moves from killing to capturing, stripping their prisoners and collecting their spoils. Grabbing a few tables and chairs, Scipio sets up an open-air command post in Hasdrubal's camp. His tribunes report that over six thousand of the enemy lie dead, and another ten thousand have been taken prisoner. Fewer than two thousand of Scipio's men have been lost, many of them the valiant Iberians and young velites that led the charge up the hill. Scipio gives Mandonius and Indibilis the pick of the first three hundred horses from the Carthaginian corrals,[xxviii] knowing that word of his extravagant honorific will quickly spread among the tribes.

Over half of Hasdrubal's army, the invincible army that felled the elder Scipios and wrested the country from Rome, has been lost to Scipio, who has shown the people of Iberia that the Three Generals can be beaten. More importantly, he has shown the same to the people of Rome.

Now, he need only send an emissary to Rome to report his victory, one who is respected by everyone. That can only be one person.

*　*　*　*　*

ROME, 208 BCE. "Marcus! Marcus Silenus! Is that you?" The sturdy older man thrusts his tree branch crutches forward, hobbling energetically to catch up to the man concealed beneath a gray hooded cloak. When Marcus turns about, a broad grin creases the elder's sun-browned face. "I knew it! My gods, it has been a long time, centurion!"

Marcus looks about to ensure no one is looking and pulls back his hood. He smiles broadly and hurries back to greet the one-legged man. "Cassius! It has been a god's life since last we met. I am blessed to see you!" Marcus slaps the man's back and squeezes his muscled shoulder. "You look well, better than most of my legionnaires, I do swear! Retirement must agree with you."

Cassius laughs. "Ah yes, retirement." He looks down at his remaining leg and looks up at Marcus, his blue eyes twinkling. "As if I had a choice, after old Hannibal took my leg at Cannae! Ah gods, what a monstrous affair that was. So many lay dead, I had to stand on top of the bodies when I fought, trying not to slip on the guts underneath my feet." He shakes his head, and his eyes grow distant. "We learned then we were not so fucking invincible, didn't we?" Cassius looks at Marcus and his grin returns. "But I hear things are better in Iberia, isn't that where you are? You took Cartago Nova, and Baecula. General Scipio must be doing something right, eh?"

"He is quite ingenious," says Marcus. "As clever as Hannibal himself, I would swear. But the crown hangs heavy on his head. He ages thrice with every battle."

Cassius bobs his head and grins knowingly. "Ah, Marcus, give him time. Experience lightens the weight of decision. His father Publius was one of our best. And the Scipios always thought of Rome first."

Marcus nods. "I think he is the same, at much cost to himself." Marcus points to a side street. "Will you walk with me? It is but a short distance."

Cassius laughs. "I would go with you to Pluto's latrine, my friend!" He waves one of his crutches under Marcus' nose. "Do not let this minor inconvenience fool you. I can still take you in wrestling, two falls out of three!"

"Looking at your arms, I would say that is indisputable!" Marcus adds with a grin. He pulls the cloak back over his head, and the two walk slowly through the narrow tenement streets on the south side of Rome, a mile and a world from the Forum.

The old veteran fingers Marcus' plain cloak. "What brings you down here? Why the cloak? You are beloved as one of us. No plebian would dare accost you." He laughs. "Other than a few ladies!"

"I but seek a quiet visit before I return to Iberia. To come home for a while, that I may remind myself of who I am." They turn into another side street and walk up to a narrow courtyard that is bounded by six insulae, five-story mud-and-stick apartment houses. Marcus walks to the front of the open courtyard and pauses there, looking carefully at the face of each tenement, at the hordes of people hanging from the open walkways that switch up to the higher stories. The bottom level is lined with small shops: butchers, potters, candle makers, and undertakers.

As the two old soldiers approach, they hear a furious argument coming from a corner of the courtyard. Marcus sees a patrician heatedly berating a carpenter about the selling price for four beautifully carved wooden chairs that stand before him. The stout man curses the stringy little carpenter and demands a lower price, but the carpenter shakes his bowed head. The patrician says a word to his two sturdy slaves, and they begin pushing the carpenter around as the patrician shouts his demands for a lower price.

Marcus turns to Cassius. "Apologies. Please wait for me."

Marcus stalks over toward the patrician's company. Without a word he reaches up and chops the first slave on the back of his neck, stunning him. Moving with battle speed, Marcus is on the second slave before he can react to the fall of his compatriot. Marcus' fist disappears into the large man's solar plexus, and he falls gasping to the ground.

Marcus turns to the patrician, who has covered his face with trembling hands. "Give this man fifty denarii for the abuse you have given him. Now." The patrician fumbles into his purse and gives the silver coins to the amazed carpenter. "Do you know who I am?" Marcus asks the patrician, who mutely nods. "Pray no misfortune befalls this man, for I shall hold you accountable. Now go."

Ignoring his two fallen slaves, the man hustles past Marcus and heads for the street. There is a flash of movement, and the patrician pitches face forward onto the muddied street. Amid the laughter and cheers about him, Marcus slowly returns his right foot to the ground, looking at his sandals. "These hobnailed caligae are good for something," he observes. With a nod to the carpenter, Marcus returns to Cassius.

"Would you do me a favor, old friend?" asks Marcus.

Cassius quits laughing long enough to reply. "For you, certainly. That scene was worth a year of my life!"

Marcus puts his hand on Cassius' shoulder. "Pomponia Scipio is in need of an able guard and assistant for her household. It would honor me if you would help her. She is a tough but fair woman. Her domus is a good place to work, and live." Cassius' eyes open with surprise, aghast at his good fortune. Marcus leans closer to him. "If you could go today, that would be best."

Cassius gulps and looks down at the rags he wears. "I ... I am not prepared to meet such a one, Marcus. Look at me!"

Marcus shakes his head. "This one sees beyond the guise. Just say that her old knife tutor has sent you. You will be most welcome."

"Gratitude, my friend," says Cassius, his head high as his eyes glaze with tears. "I will do you honorably."

Marcus nods. "Of that I am certain." For a moment, the legate's military demeanor returns, and his voice grows peremptory. "I will see Pomponia Scipio tonight, and I had best learn that you have been to see her, centurion. Or I will seek you out!" With a final pat on the shoulder, Marcus turns away from Cassius. "Excuse me now. I must travel this last part alone."

Marcus walks to the back of the courtyard, edging his way through the meandering pigs and chickens, dodging the dogs and children that swarm everywhere. He carefully steps between the chatting women that fill the stairsteps, and makes his way inside. Marcus plods up the rickety slat steps to the fifth floor, the level with the cheapest rooms. He walks down the narrow hall to knock on the wall next to a doorway covered with a worn horse blanket.

The blanket is pushed aside, and a dark-skinned young woman looks at him, cradling an infant in her arms. She looks at Marcus' stern face, and her eyes bulge with alarm. Marcus raises his hands to show they are empty. "Apologies for the intrusion, madam. I used to live here." He reaches into his belt purse and extracts a handful of denarii. "I wonder if I might step inside for a minute while you wait out here."

The woman's emotions—apprehension, greed, concern, and suspicion—race across her face as she looks at this severe man. "I wait below," she says in the heavy accents of North Italia. Her small hand snatches the coins from his palm, and she hurries down the stairway.

Marcus walks inside and stands in the middle of the tiny main room. He hears the pigeons cooing and scrabbling on the thin roof above his head, just as he did when he lay on this floor as a child, waiting for his father to return from the night fishing boats. The rich smells of the insulae—smoke, garlic, roasted meat, and excrement—bring back memories of times spent with his long-dead parents. Of the night the grim men came and told his mother that his father was lost overboard. How he lied about his age to enter the Roman army, determined to support his mother by fighting his way to a centurion's pay. Of the time he returned with a gold crown for his hand-to-hand combat championship, only to find his mother dead from the wasting diseases of squalor and hopelessness, his triumph empty.

The man-killer feels his eyes grow heavy and moist. He takes a deep breath, and another. Seeing a beaten old crib in the corner, he walks over and dumps the contents of his purse onto the tatty blanket that covers its stick frame, a small fortune of silver and gold. He pulls the blanket over the wealth, fingering the humble fabric. After a final look around him, he stiffens his back and marches out the door.

As he steps out from the insulae, he sees a throng of locals before him, filling the courtyard.

"Hail, Marcus Silenus," says a voice in the crowd.

"Salve, Bane of Carthage," shouts another.

Marcus sees the young woman standing on the side, and he bows his head to her before he pushes his way through the throng, walking swiftly back toward the Forum. A large group of boys follow him, skipping and shouting, but they soon tire of his unrelenting pace. And he walks alone.

VIII. WAR ON THREE FRONTS

SIERRA ALCARAZ, IBERIA, 208 BCE.. "Curse the gods, does it ever get warm up here? Throw more wood on that fire!" Mago stomps around the council chambers of the mountain redoubt of his Carpetani allies, rubbing his hands together. Gisgo and Hasdrubal watch him from their chairs at the oak plank meeting table.

"You always had thin blood," snipes Hasdrubal. "Me, I like this cold. You are the one who should be going to South Italia to help our brother, not me!"

"Forget about the fire," growls Gisgo. "What in Mot are we going to do next?" He looks accusingly at Hasdrubal. "You've lost almost half your army, and you haven't even got there yet!"

"You worry overmuch," retorts Hasdrubal. "I lost mostly Iberians, and I can recruit more. Besides, the Gauls are always eager to kill Romans. Once I get over those damned Alps, I will meet with the local chieftains. We will buy the Gaul's alliance." Hasdrubal laughs harshly. "I'll have plenty of time. North Italia has long winters."

"I don't think you should go until we've destroyed Scipio," interjects Mago. "We have almost seventy thousand men between the three of us, and he's only a few days' march from us. Let's squash this Roman bug now, before he recruits more of the natives." Mago spits on the ground. "The little bastard has already lured away Indibilis and Mandonius, those traitorous wretches!"

The ever-cautious Gisgo purses his lips. "Ah, it would not be an easy fight, Mago. Our scouts say Scipio has entrenched himself in Hasdrubal's old camp and shored up its defenses. He has felled every tree within sight to build his walls and prevent ambushes." He smirks. "The boy knows us too well."

"What do we care?" splutters Hasdrubal. "We still outnumber him. My best men, the Libyans and Sacred Band, they are ready for a fight. We should march there and challenge him to open battle on the plains of Baecula!"

"Your lust for revenge clouds your eye," says Gisgo. "This Scipio is too unpredictable. He is using new formations and weapons." Gisgo slowly shakes his head. "Of certitude, I would love to nail him to a cross, but we must wait until we can surprise him." He looks at Masinissa, standing stoically in the corner. "Or fight him on terrain where we can use our cavalry advantage."

Durro, Carthage's Council of Elders representative, has quietly observed this heated war council. He studies the Generals' faces as much as he listens to their words, looking for the meanings beyond their words. When they turn to discussing a concerted attack on Scipio, the wealthy old merchant finally intervenes, his aged voice resonant with authority. "May I remind you, General Hasdrubal, your prime directive is to succor Hannibal, that we may overthrow Rome and win the war in Italia." He takes a linen kerchief from his thick robes and dabs his runny nose. "Winter is coming, Hasdrubal, and you must cross the Pyrenees and Alps before it arrives."

"We will first rid ourselves of that little prick," spits Hasdrubal. "And then I will set out for the mountains."

The older politician studies the chambers' thick stone walls as he speaks, ignoring Hasdrubal. "As I have said before, the Council has decreed more men and money for Iberia. It will come when Hanno arrives. But he does not come until Hasdrubal goes. It is that simple."

Gisgo studies the stately Elder, who gazes calmly back at him, his hands tucked inside his flowing red-purple robe, a statue of calm decisiveness. Gisgo bites his lip. "It is best you go, Hasdrubal," he finally says. "Mago and I will return to our home base until Hanno arrives to help us expand our allied forces. Then the three of us will attack Scipio."

Mago nods. "I suggest we follow our earlier plan. I will set sail for the Balearic Islands and hire more of their mercenaries. They are cheap and fierce." Mago looks at Durro. "You said coin was coming for mercenaries?" When Durro nods, Mago continues. "Gisgo, you take my men back to Gades. You will be safe, Scipio would not dare attack such a concerted force."

Durro gives a dry chuckle, surprising the three commanders. "From what I have seen, it is best you do not anticipate what this young man will do. Unless you can predict the unpredictable."

*   *   *   *   *

BAECULA, IBERIA. Once again, as he did at Cartago Nova, Scipio is attending to his least favorite task: adjudicating the sea of requests and complaints that follow the conquest of a city.

The first topic is the most disputed: what to do about Hasdrubal's surviving army. Scipio's spy network has proven its worth; the speculatores informed him that Hasdrubal is leading his army toward the Alps, to cross into northern Italia. Marcus Silenus and the older tribunes argue for following Hasdrubal and destroying his force before it crosses into the mother country. Scipio fears the proximity of Gisgo's and Mago's armies and argues against it. If Hasdrubal were to turn and confront them, he reasons, the Romans could be trapped between armies in the front and rear, and summarily destroyed. After some heated discussion Scipio orders a cohort of light infantry to follow Hasdrubal, accompanied by four turmae of cavalry. They are to track the army's movements and attack its vulnerabilities. In essence, their mission is to run Hasdrubal out of Iberia so that he is no longer a threat to Scipio's army.

The rest of the council meeting is devoted to the fate of the captured soldiers: who will be enslaved, who will go free, and who will be ransomed. Scipio's tribunes have made the more obvious decisions, such as the enslavement of the Carthaginian and Libyan soldiers. But Scipio and his council must now set ransoms for the nobles and high-ranking officers and decide the fate of the captive Iberians. All this is done with an eye to expediency: caring for captives consumes costly manpower and food, as Felix the quaestor constantly reminds Scipio.

Deciding the fate of captives is a military tactic as important as winning a battle, and it is treated with great seriousness by Scipio and his officers. Scipio has a list of Iberian captives, grouped by their tribes. When he and his council deem a tribe sympathetic to their cause, they immediately free that tribe's warriors. Men, women, and children joyously begin their journey home, with hundreds of them staying to fight as allies.

For those tribes that have resisted the Romans, Scipio offers an arrangement that is the reverse of the Three Generals' approach: Roman and Iberian emissaries will travel to the tribes' strongholds. If the tribal chiefs swear friendship with Rome, their captives are released. If the tribes maintain allegiance to Carthage, their people are sold as slaves. It is a quick and profitable process for the Romans because the slave merchants have already crowded into Baecula; they readily appear after every major conflict, eager to buy humans from the winners.

When the emissaries contact the tribes, many swear allegiance to Rome. Scipio's diplomacy nets him thousands of Iberian allies and prevents the Carthaginians from gaining them. Those who resisted have replenished his war chest with an abundance of slaver money for weaponry and supplies.

As their last item of business, the council must determine the fate of a handful of captured Numidian warriors. The Africans are a staunch ally to Carthage, so their fate is readily apparent: sell them. Scipio is about to motion for enslavement when a tribune mentions there is a singular person of interest among the captives, a boy much too young to be a soldier, but who was nevertheless captured in battle when he fell from his horse.[xxix]

The tribune tells Scipio that the boy's dress, jewelry, and bearing indicate that he is from a powerful Numidian family. Intrigued, Scipio orders the youth to be brought before the council. They examine this willowy young man who looks at them with an equanimity beyond his years and station.

Scipio smiles at the young man. "You are barely beyond a boy," he says to him through his interpreter. "How did you come to be fighting us?"

The youth looks levelly at Scipio. "While my uncle was busy, I crept into the back lines with my horse, thence to fight your sluggish cavalry. But I'm not a boy," he scolds. "I can fight as good as any man!"

Scipio smiles. "I suppose you can, if you can stay on your horse." The laughter among the tribunes makes the boy stamp his foot angrily, as if they were impertinent slaves.

"What is your name? And who is your uncle?" Scipio casually inquires.

"I am Massiva, General Scipio. My uncle is Masinissa, rightful king of the Numidians, bane of the false king Syphax," replies the boy proudly.

At these words the council members' humorous mood disappears. "Masinissa!" exclaims more than one of them, anger coming to their faces.

Scipio's brother Lucius jumps from his seat, his normally placid face red with anger. "Masinissa helped kill my father and uncle," he blurts to his fellow officers. "They murdered hundreds of our men at Cannae! His Numidians have plagued us for years!"

An older tribune stands up from the council table. "Lucius speaks the truth. We should crucify this boy, as revenge for his uncle's depredations."

Massiva watches the faces of the officers as they debate his fate. He does not understand Latin, but he knows all too well the gist of what is being said: these men are not pleased with who he is. His boyish eyes begin to glaze with tears of fear, but he stands erect, maintaining his calm dignity, determined not to besmirch his family name.

Scipio studies the faces of his officers for a minute, and the room is silent. They notice his right hand twitching, a sign he is in the throes of a difficult decision. "Would you like to return to your uncle?" Scipio finally says.

The boy's shoulders slump with relief, but his face is proudly expressionless. "I ... I would desire that very much."

Ignoring the protests of his officers, Scipio turns to Quintus, his staff assistant, a powerfully built man who lost his shield arm at Baecula. "Release this boy. Give him a fine horse and an escort of a dozen of his countrymen. See that they leave camp safely." Scipio stands up. "This concludes our business."

Laelius starts to exit with the rest of the officers, but he abruptly walks over to Scipio and leans into his ear. "Word of your decision will get back to Rome, you know. The Latins will rejoice in slandering your 'weakness' about the Iberian captives, and this boy Massiva."

Scipio shrugs, and a look of weariness returns to his face, one that is never gone for long. "Ah, would their simple cruelty of killing captives worked to our advantage, it is the easier course. But this is as much a war of diplomacy as it is of strategy. I must win it on both fronts." Laelius looks away and says nothing. He heads for the door, and Scipio shouts at him good-naturedly. "You worry too much about Rome! Marcellus will triumph against Hannibal, and he will become dictator. Then the Latin dogs can bark all they want."

*   *   *   *   *

VENUSIA, 208 BCE. Marcellus is feeling the political pressure. He has just returned to his camp from Rome, where he spent a morning in the Senate defending himself against the Latin Party's latest accusation, that he refused battle with Hannibal. His defense is succinct and logical: his men needed recovery time after suffering heavy casualties in repelling Hannibal during the previous battle. Several veteran generals stepped forward to support him, but Flaccus demeaned Marcellus' strategy on the Senate floor, and demanded a vote of censure.

Marcellus left with the Senate still mulling a vote of censure. He knows he must best Hannibal soon, or he will be recalled when his consulship expires, leaving Hannibal to prey upon the weaker Roman generals. And so he has joined forces with his fellow consul Crispinus to challenge Hannibal to a final, decisive battle.

At the Carthaginian camp three miles away, the scouts give Hannibal the same report for the third day in a row: Marcellus' and Crispinus' two armies are arrayed on the open plain, challenging him to battle. Maharbal, Hannibal's second-in-command, is clearly frustrated by his commander's inaction. "I can prepare the men by tomorrow," he urges. "The Gauls and Libyans are rested. It is the perfect time for an assault! We can rid ourselves of that buffoon once and for all."

Hannibal frowns at his impetuous captain. "Old Marcellus is anything but a buffoon. He is the only general that has soundly defeated us. And now he has Crispinus' army with him. I have pondered our stratagem for this battle, and I have a way we can use the land to our advantage." Hannibal motions for Maharbal to follow him out of the tent, and he quickly marches to the edge of their camp, looking across a plain of scrub and meandering streams, a flat landscape broken only by a hill dotted with trees.

"A perfect landscape for a battle," Maharbal enthuses. "Our Numidians could sweep past the Italia cavalry while our infantry hold their legions at bay, and strike them in the rear."

"Perfect terrain, if you are a Roman," Hannibal says sarcastically. "They can employ their heavy infantry to full advantage." Hannibal is silent for several moments. "You are right about one thing: the Numidians will be the key. But we will use them for an ambush, not a battle. That served us well the other day, did it not? We came down that hill by Petelia and killed the two thousand Romans who were marching on the road to Locri—with very few casualties."

Maharbal looks skeptically at his general. "Where do you see us holding an ambush? On that hill? You want thousands of our men to all come swooping down from there? It's hardly large enough to hold a herd of cows!"

Hannibal shakes his head. "The hill is the bait. We do not need to put thousands on it. We will send a hundred Numidians to the hill late tonight, when the Romans have ceased their patrols." Hannibal points to the edges of the wide plain. "You see those forested lowlands on the sides there? That's where we plant five hundred of our swiftest Numidians. It looks like it is too far away to surprise any troops that are on the plain, but the Numidians can cross that space in the swish of a horse's tail."

"Very well, but Marcellus is not going to send out his army unless we march out for battle."

Hannibal looks irritated. "I don't want to fight their army out there; we have no terrain advantage. We will refuse battle but attack their scouts and foragers—and any skirmishers they send at us. That will keep them from marching at us for at least a moon. That gives me time to finish my recruiting from the nearby towns."

Maharbal shakes his head. "I am not sure the Romans will fall into another ambush. They would have learned from Trasimene and Cannae, would they not?"

Hannibal shrugs and grins. "You would think so, but these Romans are slow learners! Our camp spies tell us that Marcellus and Crispinus are extremely eager to fight us and gain the glory of a victory—just as Varro was at Cannae, when he thought he had the upper hand." The Bane of Roma looks across the plain, where he can see the smoke of distant fires. "When men are so eager for victory, they do strange things," he says reflectively.

Hannibal abruptly changes mood, happily slapping Maharbal on the back. "I want you to direct this ambush, my doubting friend! You can keep those impulsive Numidians in their place until it is time spring the trap."

Maharbal sighs. "As you say, Commander." He cocks an eyebrow at Hannibal. "Though I doubt this trap will catch anything other than a few rabbits!"

The next day, Marcellus and Crispinus are again standing in front of their legions, the army arrayed as a challenge to Hannibal. "Well, Marcellus, we have shown the men that Hannibal fears us," says Crispinus. "Now we are beginning to look a bit silly! Those plains are as empty as my son's head." He gestures toward the waiting cavalry lines on the flank, where his son stands in the forefront, chatting with his fellows. "I should have never brought him," Crispinus gripes.

Marcellus surveys the empty plain, staring at the barely visible hill in the distance. "We can take that hill and move our camp around it. That will give us a lookout position to study Hannibal's encampment."

Crispinus smiles ruefully. "Well, the action would at least silence our tribunes. Several of them have been clamoring to grab it before Hannibal does." Crispinus winks at Marcellus. "Taking it would be something to report to Rome, too."

Marcellus chuckles. "I take your point. Let's ride over there and investigate it."

Crispinus looks at Marcellus, surprised. "You and I? Not the scouts! Is the way clear?"

Marcellus points out to the plain. "You can see our scouts are already patrolling out there. They were all over that hill yesterday, and it was barren of everything but a few deer." Marcellus grins and stretches his arms. "By Jupiter, let's get out of this camp for a while, I'm bored!"

Crispinus bites his lip, uncertain. "Very well. But what about that augury of the goat you sacrificed this morning? The front lobe of its liver was missing. The priest was very disturbed by that." xxx

Marcellus waves his hand dismissively, an enthused gleam growing in his eye. "Yes, but the second goat's liver had a lobe that was abnormally large, so that balances the scales! We have Hannibal in front of us, Crispinus. We just have to go and get him before he sneaks off, as he is wont to do." He stares reprovingly at his younger consul. "We'll take plenty of men with us. You are not apprehensive, are you?"

Crispinus fidgets, then shrugs. "No, honored Marcellus, let us seize the day."

Marcellus grins. "Excellent. Aulius, come over here!" shouts Marcellus, calling to the allied commander. "I need fifty of your extraordinarii to accompany the three of us, and two hundred of the Etruscans—they will be offended if they aren't involved. We will go investigate that hill." The squat, bushy-haired Fregellian claps his hands to signal his acknowledgement and immediately shouts orders at his captains.

Marcellus and Crispinus soon ride out from the front infantry lines, cheered on by the many men who are also bored with the army's inaction. The two consuls lead the cavalry along the broad dirt road toward the hill, conversing about how to place the new camp around the hill, and how to attack Hannibal from there. Fresh scouts gallop past them and rush toward Hannibal's encampment, only to return and report that there are no Carthaginians on the plain. Marcellus receives the information in good humor and presses on. He sends an Etruscan rider back to the camp, ordering the officers to begin preparations to move the army toward the hill.

As the two consuls approach the hill, Maharbal stands atop his horse in the trees east of the plain. His Numidians are lined up under the squat oaks and pines that grow there, so well hidden that several Roman scouts ride past them, conversing. The immobile Numidians listen to them, their lances at the ready if they are discovered.

When Maharbal sees the Roman squadron drawing nigh to the hill, his eyes spark with interest. *Hannibal may be right*, he thinks. *We may trap a scouting party today.* Then Maharbal sees that the two lead riders are wearing the flowing scarlet cloaks of commanders, and his eyes gleam: he realizes that Marcellus and Crispinus are leading the party. *Oh Mother Tanit*, he prays desperately, *make those Numidians stay quiet up there.*

Breathless with excitement, Maharbal carefully guides his horse between the foliage until he comes to an opening that is flanked by trees, invisible from the plains. He takes out a small ladies' mirror and flashes it twice toward the hill, then repeats it. There is a winking flash from the top of the hill, and then another. Maharbal exhales in relief: they know they are to wait for him to attack.

The Roman reconnaissance squad comes up to the road leading up the hill, entering a wide and shallow depression that leads to its base. A faint thundering catches Marcellus' ear, and just as he turns to check it, his men shout the alarm: enemies are attacking! Marcellus gapes at the hundreds of Numidians who are storming across the plain toward them.

"It's an ambush! We're out here in the open!" Crispinus shouts.

Marcellus sees panic setting in on the faces of the mercurial Etruscans; he knows they are ready to bolt back to camp. "Head for that hill, Crispinus! We'll make a stand there!" The two consuls lead their men at full gallop through the shallow depression and head for the hill's welcoming trees.

A hundred Numidians explode from the hill's base and crash into the surprised Romans, spearing the front line Etruscans with their ten-foot lances. The doughty extraordinarii rush to the fore and clash with the lightly armored Numidians. The determined Fregellians hurl their pila into the riders, felling a score of them. Exhausting all their javelins, they draw their short swords and plunge into a swirling horse fight with their duck-and-dodge counterparts. Aulius, Marcellus, and Crispinus are in the van of the cavalry, leading their men toward the protection of the rocky hill.

The Roman unit's determined assault fells a dozen Numidians. As he stabs an attacker's thigh, Marcellus shouts for his men to make one final push through the Numidians, arcing his dripping sword forward. No sooner does he finish his command than Maharbal and the rest of the Numidians crash into their rear, fragmenting the Etruscan lines. Maharbal rides directly for Marcellus, determined to kill his army's most noisome enemy. He pulls a javelin from the scabbard on his back and casts it toward Marcellus' chest. The old general sees it coming and deftly blocks it with his scutum, the short spear sliding off its curved surface. Maharbal curses in frustration. He grabs a Numidian's long lance and spurs his horse toward Marcellus.

As Maharbal nears the Sword of Rome, a grim-faced Aulius collides with Maharbal's mount and knocks him to the ground. Maharbal springs up immediately and jerks up his small shield to block a killing head cut from Aulius. As the Fregellian rides past him, Maharbal thrusts his sword into Aulius' side. The commander yells in pain and reflexively yanks back on his horse's bridle, pulling his mount up short. In a flash, Maharbal rushes in and stabs Aulius' horse in the neck, and the beast collapses onto the ground with Aulius underneath.

Maharbal swoops over the dazed Aulius, repeatedly stabbing his short sword into the Fregellian's screaming face. Leaving his opponent to his death throes, Maharbal recovers his lance and runs toward Marcellus, who is engaged with two mounted Numidians. The Carthaginian dodges behind several riderless mounts to conceal himself, weaving his way toward Marcellus' unprotected back. When he sees the aged consul struggling to remove his sword from a fallen Numidian's chest, he rushes in and shoves the lance into the back of Marcellus' neck. The bloodied spearhead emerges from Marcellus' forehead. The consul has only a moment to clutch at it before nightfall descends on him.

Marcellus crashes to the bloodied earth. A horrified Crispinus rides over with a handful of brave Fregellians, slashing demonically at any Numidians that dare confront them. Maharbal sees the Romans coming with murder in their eyes. He quickly mounts his horse and races back to the protection of his Numidians in the rear.

The Etruscans see Marcellus fall and cry out in dismay. Without a backward glance, they gallop pell-mell toward the safety of the Roman camp. Maharbal sends a squadron of his Numidians in pursuit, and they lance many of the madly fleeing Etruscans in the back, dashing from one victim to the next.

Crispinus musters his score of surviving Fregellians. They retreat back along the road, maintaining a defensive formation. Most of the Numidians pursue the easier Etruscan prey, but many come at

Crispinus' retreating force, hurling the last of their javelins. One catches Crispinus in the shoulder, but he pulls it out and rides on, shouting for his men to stay together. Another javelin arcs in and pierces his upper back. The consul grunts heavily and slumps forward, clutching tightly to his reins as he starts to slide from his horse. Two of Crispinus' men rush in to prop him up and pull his mount toward camp.

Lusting to kill both consuls, Maharbal leads a squadron of Numidians at the wounded general. When the squadron nears Crispinus, the Fregellians surprise Maharbal's men by charging into them with sword and shield, beating back their charge. Then the camp gates fly open, and hundreds of Roman cavalry stampede out from camp, screaming their determination to kill the Carthaginians. Maharbal bellows for his men to retreat. They dash for the Carthaginian camp, collecting the rest of the Numidians on the way. The Romans pursue them but they are soon outstripped, so they surround the remainders of Crispinus' party and guide them safely back.

Inside the Roman camp, Crispinus is eased into a bed in his command tent. The camp healers attend to his wounds as best they can, but when asked about Crispinus' welfare, they can only bow their heads. Crispinus summons his remaining strength and directs the move of the camp farther north into the sheltering mountains, safe from Hannibal's depredations. The next day the army moves out. Four days later, consul Crispinus dies.

Maharbal throws Marcellus' body over the back of a horse and leads it back to camp, where he is received with great rejoicing. Hannibal receives news of the successful ambush with mixed feelings. He is aware he has cost Rome its greatest general, but he has also seen his most worthy opponent felled by a cowardly spear thrust from behind. *Would I had the chance to face him*, he thinks, looking at Marcellus' body. *We deserved for one of us to kill the other.*

Hannibal burns Marcellus' body and sends the ashes back to Rome, addressed to the consul's son. With Marcellus gone, Hannibal's thoughts once more return to Rome and to ultimate victory in next year's spring campaigns, to thoughts of having his brothers join him for Rome's final destruction.

*   *   *   *   *

ROME. With the death of its two consuls, Rome is thrown into a malaise of fear, confusion, and mourning. Not since the destruction at Cannae has the mighty city been more fearful for its survival. Once again, parents quiet their children with the admonishment *Hannibal ad portas* (Hannibal is at the gates), which had all but disappeared since Marcellus returned from Sicily to Rome. Despite the edicts against public mourning enacted after Cannae, the sounds of lamenting can be heard throughout Rome. From the gritty plebian apartments on the Aventine Hill to the patricians' plush domi near the Forum, the mothers sob at night for their children's welfare, and men make plans to flee the city with their families.

The Nine Days of Sorrow are conducted citywide for the two consuls, a mourning rite normally observed by members of the immediate family. The ceremonies and outcries are especially elaborate for Marcellus, the people's favorite. But not all Romans mourn Marcellus' death. Where all of Rome sees a tragedy, the Latin Party sees an opportunity. The upcoming consular elections have a dearth of able candidates, so Flaccus, Fabius, and Cato plot the election of two Latin candidates.

Amelia and Pomponia are devastated. Marcellus was more than the best hope for defeating Hannibal; he was the best opportunity for a future of public education and enculturation, for land reform and income redistribution. The two women discuss these matters as they return from the Forum's funeral orations for Marcellus, walking along with the hordes of mourners.

Amelia and Pomponia enter the Scipio domus, remove their black lace veils, and repair to the atrium, not bothering to change from their dark blue mourning dresses. As they stretch out on couches, a house slave brings them a plate of fruit and cheese. They moodily pop some bits into their mouths while they plan their next actions.

"You know what happens next," says Pomponia. "The Latins will push to have one of their own elected as consul. I have heard it will be Marcus Livius."

Amelia stares at her. "What? The man convicted of hoarding war booty for himself from his Illyrian victories? He confessed and exiled himself from Rome! I heard he became an unkempt old hermit."

"Well, he is back now, all clean and dressed up, thanks to the Latins. I daresay he would be more than willing to push through the Latin Party's 'agrarian reforms' for the rich."

Amelia pulls a plum from the tray, squeezes it for ripeness, and pops it into her mouth. "If that be the case, we need to start a propaganda campaign against him. My street artist friends are eager to decorate the town with new slogans."

Pomponia chews on her lower lip, thinking. "I think our time would be best spent in campaigning for a consul who will oppose whatever Livius proposes. A natural enemy, as it were. But he must be a capable general, or Hannibal will destroy him in a blink."

Pitching plums into the atrium pool, Amelia laughs. "Well, that certainly narrows the field to one, doesn't it? Gaius Nero, your son's old colleague in Iberia. The man who testified against Livius when they were censors." [xxxi]

Pomponia nods, her eyes bright. "Yes, I had thought the same. My son spoke well of him, as a man of honor and an able fighter. But his nomination would be opposed by many in the Senate."

"But it would be embraced by many on the streets," rejoins Amelia. "In that respect I can campaign ably for his election among the plebs. My workers are people of the streets. They will know who to talk to, and where to place our messages."

"I think I know someone special to talk to about the plebs' support," muses Pomponia. "I just have to find some shabbier clothes."

Several days later, a stooped figure hobbles through the clogged passageways of the Aventine Hill, using a cane to lurch past the stinking tanner's booths and bawdy street courtesans, working up the pebbled path into the canopy of the hill's stone pine trees. Pausing to sit upon a stone bench on a side trail, Pomponia straightens up and throws back the hood of her worn cloak. Although she is a lone patrician woman in a sea of slaves and workingmen she is unperturbed, trusting in the common man.

A man soon trudges under the trees to join her. He is a slight and bony man wearing a simple gray tunic several sizes too large for him, his face as broad and flat as a plate, seamed and leathered from years of working in the elements. The man salutes Pomponia with his three-fingered right hand, the missing digits a testament to his craft as a fisherman, men who often lose a finger or two in the nets.

This Corvinus Lucinius, the Tribune of the Plebs, is altogether an unimpressive man, until he looks at you. His green eyes transfix you with the unwavering gaze of his full concentration, as if he were reading your very soul. His thrust jaw and tight-lipped mouth evidence the determination he manifests in every undertaking. For forty years he has worked tirelessly for the betterment of the workingman, teaching himself reading and public oratory. In that time he has accomplished much for his station. Were he born into a higher family, the dauntless man would be leading Rome's legions today. Corvinus stands in front of Pomponia and slightly bows his head.

"Salve, noble Pomponia, friend to man," he says in a deep raspy voice. "The gods honor me with your presence."

Pomponia nods back with a welcoming smile. "Ave, Corvinus Lucinius. Gratitude for meeting me here."

Corvinus nods. "The gratitude is mine. You did venture alone where mishap is common for one of your station ... and gender."

Pomponia self-consciously brushes back a strand of her red hair, looking about. "Yes, well, I needed a place where patrician eyes would not be about. I wanted to talk to you about the consular elections."

Corvinus grunts with disappointment. "Marcus Livius is all but elected, I fear. Flaccus and Fabius have spoken out for him in the Senate. That young Cato has been delivering laudatory speeches in the public square, and he draws many to hear him."

Pomponia wrinkles her nose with disgust. "You know what Livius will advocate if elected, don't you?"

"I am afraid so," Corvinus sighs. "Under the guise of agrarian reform, they will import more slave labor to ease the cost of farming, replacing more freedmen. The most skilled slaves will be used in place of Roman craftsmen, and they too will be unemployed." He shakes his head. "So many capable men lie idle already, when they but seek a working wage!"

Pomponia pulls out a small scroll, its wax seal broken. "This is a record of the last Latin Party meeting. Do not ask me how I obtained it." She unrolls part of the scroll and shows it to Corvinus. Pomponia points to some writing at the top of the scroll. "Do you see here? Flaccus and some other Senators will propose laws to make it easy to foreclose on any farmland with more than two years of overdue taxes. That means our legionnaires could return to find their wives and children evicted by the government for which they fought, because a rich man purchased their land for back taxes."

Corvinus eyes' flame bright with anger. "That will not happen during my tenure, I swear it. I will veto any such measure from the Senate, if that was what you came here to know."

Pomponia's smile turns grim. "Ah, but therein lies the problem, Corvinus." She unrolls the rest of the scroll and points to a section near the bottom of it. "Flaccus and Fabius plan to nominate two people to replace Marcellus and Crispinus, candidates they no doubt control. When the candidates are elected as consuls, they will nominate Marcus Livius to be Dictator, ostensibly to be unencumbered by politics to war against Carthage. Of course, this will give Livius the imperium of absolute rule, as Fabius had when he was Dictator. Then you would be powerless to stop Livius from enacting these reforms." She puts her hand on his forearm. "*We* would be powerless to stop him."

The Tribune of the Plebs is visibly shaken, but he recovers and looks at Pomponia with a wry smile. *He does not daunt easily*, she thinks. "And true to your reputation, Domina, you have a solution to this?"

"Not a solution, but a proposal. You know Gaius Claudius Nero?"

Corvinus laughs. "I would not be a Roman if I did not! He fought nobly in Iberia. Only your son has done more for Rome."

Pomponia shrugs off the compliment. "Yes, well, my young Scipio may yet be a solution to this mess, but not for years to come." She leans forward and takes Corvinus' work-worn hands into her own, pulling him a step closer. "I want the plebs to throw their support behind Nero, to clamor for his election. The Century Assembly that votes for the consuls cannot ignore the will of the people. The Senate will be afraid to fight the Assembly on this. They are afraid the plebs will go on strike again, and bring this city to its knees!"

"It would not be too difficult to gain the Assembly's support," reflects Corvinus. "They already favor Nero, as they did Marcellus, that finest of men. But why choose Nero?"

Pomponia stares directly into his eyes, willing him to see the honesty in what she says. "Nero and Livius are enemies. The Latins know that as consul Nero would never nominate Livius for dictator, so they will abandon that plan and work to ensure Livius' election as consul, so they have someone to moderate Nero's plebian sympathies."

"So, Nero's election will not defeat the Party's aims, but it will mitigate their power." He grins ruefully. "A moderated success, at best."

"As so often happens in politics," Pomponia replies emotionlessly. "This is but a battle in the war for Rome's future, Corvinus, between the forces of empire and the forces of kingdom. Winning is not as important as not losing, because losing puts a dictator in power. And with your help, we will block that."

Corvinus looks at her for several long moments, reading her face. Then he nods. "For the sake of my people—not the Hellenic Party—I will build support for Nero."

Pomponia nods slightly. "Excellent. Can you start tomorrow, with a public oration? That mouthy Cato needs a counterforce."

Corvinus cannot help but laugh. "Yes, yes, I will. By Minerva's owl, you are a most puissant woman!" He looks at Pomponia with concern. "But you are a woman. nonetheless. I pray Flaccus and his ilk do not find what you are about. Even your boy's genius may not save you."

Pomponia smiles grimly and pats his hand as she stands to leave. "Gratitude for your concern about Flaccus, but that ship has sailed, although I know not where it will land." She pulls the cloak over her head, grabs her cane, and hobbles down the trail. Corvinus watches her, unmoving, until she fades from sight.

Two months later, as early winter eases into Rome, Gaius Nero and Marcus Livius stand next to each other in the Senate, looking uneasily at one another, as each is sworn in as consul. Nero is assigned to combat Hannibal in south Italia, while Livius is designated to intercept Hasdrubal in the north. Rome is caught between two Carthaginian armies that are moving to join together. Nero and Livius must prevent their joining, else Rome is lost.

*　　*　　*　　*　　*

TARRACO, 208 BCE. A distracted Scipio receives the news of Nero's and Livius' election with barely a nod, lost in plotting a way to defeat Mago's and Gisgo's armies. That night, when all the officers and city officials have finally left his town headquarters, Scipio goes to a battered trunk and retrieves two thick, yellowed papyrus scrolls. He opens the first book and revisits the history of Alexander the Great. Reading about the brilliant Macedonian general's battles, Scipio notices that Alexander defeated superior forces with unconventional infantry and cavalry placements, surprising his enemy. Impressed, Scipio inks several notes on the scroll, like a schoolboy preparing for a lesson.

When he is finished with Alexander's tome, Scipio turns to the story of Cyrus the Persian and the bold tactics he used to defeat the Babylonians, once diverting a protecting river so that his men could march across it. *I must make my enemy's expectations my ally,* Scipio muses*, by doing the opposite.* Then he thinks of the murderous genius of Hannibal, using the rivers and winds to defeat the Romans. *And the weather and terrain, I must recruit them, too.*

When Scipio is finished, he carefully stores the two scrolls and goes to the open map of Iberia, where there are two wooden phoenixes marking the location of Mago's and Gisgo's conjoined armies near Gades. *They would never expect our cavalry to be a threat*, he thinks. *Or us to fight in darkness.* Yawning, he places several Roman horse figurines in that part of the map and heads to bed.

*   *   *   *   *

VALENTIA, EASTERN IBERIAN COAST. Masinissa stands at the overlook of a long ridge in the Sierra Martes mountains, observing the Roman infantry as they tramp into the camp they are building in the river valley. He can see Laelius riding about with a squadron of his guard, directing the heavy cavalry to protect the marine legion that is bringing up the rear. The Numidian prince strokes his horse's neck as he weighs the risks and benefits of attacking the marines. *We can catch them before they have time to form ranks*, he reflects. *Kill a hundred before their cavalry comes out.*

Masinissa waves over Gala, his captain, and prepares to order the charge. Then two cavalry squadrons ride out from the camp, and he abandons his stratagem. *Wait until eventide*, he cautions himself. *That is always a good time to hunt.* The Numidian prince sends orders to his three thousand riders: rest until dusk, and then prepare to kill the foraging parties. Masinissa amuses himself by watching the Romans lay out their massive rectangular camp, quickly pitching officers' tents between the stick-drawn outlines for streets and corrals, digging out trenches and latrines in perfect lines. *They are like ants*, he muses wonderingly, *the greatest engineers of all.* Then he chuckles. *And the worst horsemen. Why do they jump off their horses to fight?*

At dusk Masinissa sees a few scouts ride out from camp, but there are not enough kills to warrant giving away his position. He summons Gala to his side to make new attack plans. Gala is a prince of Eastern Numidia. He and his men have joined Masinissa so that they can fight against King Syphax, the Numidian who decimated Gala's tribal nation. In return for Gala's service, Masinissa has promised to restore the lands that Syphax stole from his tribe. Gala is a short and blocky man, but like all Numidians he is graceful on a horse, capable of guiding his mount with his knees and throwing javelins with deadly accuracy at full gallop.

"Tonight, Gala, you will take two hundred men to those two farms we saw back down the road. The Romans will be foraging there tomorrow, I am certain. When they are fully engaged in gathering food, destroy them."

Gala puts his hand over his heart. "It will be so."

Following his directive from the Carthaginian generals, Masinissa has haunted Scipio's army since it departed Baecula, as Scipio leads his force toward winter camp at Tarraco. Mago has left for the Balearic Islands, hoping to recruit more slingers and infantry. Gisgo has taken their army to Gades. Only Masinissa remains to fight: his men have doggedly followed Scipio's victorious Romans as they went to Cartago Nova to cache their plunder, then moved up the coast. Now the army is nearing Tarraco, and Masinissa's time grows short to attack the Romans. He is not eager to engage Scipio's army with his limited force, but the ambush will demonstrate his commitment to Mago and Gisgo's mission. *I can use this trick only once*, he thinks. *Scipio will have a defense prepared if we try it again—or an ambush of his own.*

Masinissa and his men bed down on the ridge for the night, watching the Romans below. The next morning he sees four thirty-man squadrons riding out toward the farmlands, presumably to secure provisions to supplement the army's food. Slowly, in single file, he leads his men down the fifteen-hundred-foot plateau into the densely forested foothills near the plain. And there he waits, to see if Gala will accomplish his mission.

Hours later, Masinissa sees what he has been waiting for. The Roman cavalry is riding back toward camp, but this time the riders are dirty, bloodied, and exhausted. Masinissa holds his men until the bulk of the force is in the center of his line, and then he charges. Thousands of Numidians dash out across the plains at the returning cavalry. The Numidians whirl through the disorganized Romans, darting in between them from every angle and wielding their lances with deadly efficacy. Within minutes more than fifty Romans are dead on the ground while the rest hurtle for the safety of camp. The Numidians give chase, cutting down stragglers from behind with their javelins and short swords. As the life-and-death chase nears the camp, Allucius leads hundreds of Iberian cavalry out from the camp gates, screaming their tribal battle cries. Masinissa quickly calls for a retreat, and the Numidians rush back into the hills. They weave through the trees until they arrive at a prearranged spot, far back in the mountains.

Several hours later Gala leads his riders into the Numidian's hidden camp. Masinissa stands by a large campfire, cursing softly as he uses a vinegar-soaked rag to staunch a slash in his side. The prince sees Gala looking at his wound with concern. "The Roman bastard had a falcata, can you believe it? He cut right through my shield and got me in the side." Masinissa grins. "But that kept him occupied long enough for me to put a lance in his eye. How went the ambush?"

Gala lays down his sword and small round shield and pulls his javelin sling from off his back. He stretches his arms. "It went well," Gala concludes. "There were quite a few of them, but we stayed low in the grain fields, keeping the horses down. When they came in through the road between the fields, we sprang up on both sides of them." He chuckles heartily. "They must have thought the fields were sprouting Numidians!"

Masinissa nods. "Good, I take it you killed many of them."

Gala pulls off his tasseled silver helmet. "At least a score, but they did give us a surprise, and many escaped. Instead of jumping off their horses, they stayed on them and circled about to fight us, like they were Africans!"

Masinissa grimaces, confused at Gala's news. "They fight like us? This is Scipio's doing!" He looks over his shoulder. "Massiva!" he shouts. His young nephew appears from the surrounding shadows, a horse comb in his hand. "Fetch Gala some Rioja," the prince commands. The boy nods enthusiastically and dashes off.

"How is he?" asks Gala.

"He is well. Scipio returned him unharmed, but the boy had to promise him that he would not fight against Rome or its allies." Masinissa chuckles. "I think Scipio did it more to make Massiva feel like a man than to protect his troops. Now he tells everyone he had to promise mighty Scipio that he would not harm him!" At that they both laugh.

The willowy youth soon returns with two brimming wood cups. Gala drinks deeply, smacking his lips. Masinissa sips his, lost in reflection of the day's events. "You are right, Gala. The Romans fight differently now. I saw that same style earlier today, when we surrounded them. I'd wager that Scipio is training his men to fight like true horsemen, not infantry on a horse." He grins ruefully. "That is not good news for us!"

Gala frowns. "They are still unpracticed at it, though, and vulnerable. Would we had Mago's army here for a full assault, instead of all this raiding and running horseshit. We'd wipe them out and be off to Africa to take care of Syphax!"

Gala holds out his empty cup, and Massiva runs off to fill it. "Mago will be returning from the Balearics with new recruits," Masinissa says, "and Gisgo is still at Gades, waiting for Hanno to come over." He rubs his forehead and grimaces with disappointment. "The Three Generals have become a bit … cautious. I think they fear Scipio's guile. He surprised them at Baecula, chasing Hasdrubal out of his own camp. Now they want to grossly outnumber him before they fight. And while they recruit, Scipio builds his army." Massiva returns with a refilled cup; Gala takes it and waves him away.

After a deep drink, Gala hawks and spits into the fire. "Pfah! Winter is here now. Those two should snuff him out before we go to winter quarters!" Gala eyes his empty cup and drops it. "If there is nothing else, I am to bed." Masinissa waves him away and Gala totters away from the fire.

"Fear not!" Masinissa calls after him. "We shall crush him in the spring." When Gala has gone, Masinissa reflects on the truth of his words. *The Carthaginians are weakening. They scatter to the four winds to gather allies, but Scipio steals the Iberians from under their noses.* Masinissa looks at the men squatting beside their small campfires, men who followed him to this strange land because of his promise to liberate Numidia. *Perhaps we should throw our lot with the Romans, just ride down the mountain and surrender our services.* He looks over at his nephew, Massiva, combing his black Numidian pony. *Scipio might promise me support against Syphax, as the Three Generals did. At least I could believe him.*

Masinissa pulls out a braided silver chain from beneath his breastplate and opens the hinged silver capsule it supports. His long wiry fingers carefully pry open the capsule. Inside, on a bed of purple, lies a single lock of raven hair. He looks at it and then holds it to his nose, savoring the trace of jasmine that yet remains: Sophonisba is there with him. *If I join Scipio, Sophonisba would be lost to me. Gisgo would give her to Syphax.* The young prince gently closes the locket and tucks it back inside his tunic, where it hangs next to his beating heart. Hands on hips, he stares silently at the fire. "Shit!" he finally says, and stalks off to make his rest.

*   *   *   *   *

TARRACO, IBERIA, 207 BCE. Zargoza, Supreme Chieftain of the Belli people, is finding it difficult to bend his knee because pride cramps his legs. But bend it he does, finally, in homage to the mighty King Scipio, the man that has triumphed over his nation's oppressors.

The chieftain has kneeled to no man since he was a young warrior, a red-haired dreadnought who won his rule by right of combat. The middle-aged Celtiberian now wears a bulge on his stomach where there was once but a sheet of muscle, but his sinewy arms are still thick as a boy's thighs, his eyes still fiery with determination. Zargoza towers a full six feet from the ground, though his neck is bent with the blows of many battles. He is one of most influential leaders of northern Iberia, and his visit is a coup for Scipio.

Zaragoza has watched in silent fury as the Belli's neighboring tribes were brought under the rule of the Three Generals. Those who would not be hired as mercenaries were conscripted through torture, imprisonment, and bribery, their leaders crucified. Zargoza had fought off the advances of Hasdrubal and Mago, but he willingly genuflects before the young man who stands directly in front of him.

Scipio has risen from his commander's seat on the dais to walk down and meet Zargoza as an equal, aware of the respect it demonstrates to the tribal onlookers. The consul is dressed in full ceremonial armor, the purple-bordered red cape of an imperator flowing over his shoulders, the title his men gave him after his victory at Baecula. Scipio's aged interpreter has followed him down the steps and stands at his side as the young general takes Zaragoza's arm and pulls him up.

"Arise, noble Zaragoza. We are here to ensure that no Iberian has to kneel to a foreigner."

The chieftain raises his head and stands up slowly. His green eyes stare into Scipio's face for a long moment, and then he extends his arm and envelops Scipio's shoulder with his right hand. "King Scipio, I heard the stories of your punishments and mercy, given only to those who deserve them. Such a man is to be respected. I give you this." Zaragoza reaches into his belt pouch and extracts a thin gold coin with a wolf imprinted in it. The coin is divided into two halves, each with identical Celtiberian markings. The chieftain gives half to Scipio. "This is a sign of our mutual friendship, if you accept it."

Scipio bows his head slightly in acknowledgement, and he looks solemnly at Zaragoza. "Ruler of the Belli, I do accept your friendship. Know that you are now a friend to Rome." Following the Belli's contractual custom, the large barbarian embraces Scipio in a bear hug, his face solemn. Scipio's eyes widen with surprise, but he awkwardly returns the hug, his face buried in Zargoza's reeking wolfskin vest.

Allucius, Laelius, and Marcus Silenus are standing by Scipio's vacated seat. When they see the chief grab Scipio, they grasp their sword hilts and step down the dais. Before they can near him, however, Zargoza stands back and places both his hands on Scipio's shoulders. In a booming voice he chants thrice: "Your friend is my friend, your enemy my enemy, your triumphs my joy."

Looking at the seamed face of the mighty warrior in front of him, his simple words so sincere, it is all young Scipio can do to keep his eyes from moistening. "Your enemies are my enemies, Friend of Rome," he stammers.

Zargoza hears the interpreter's translation and nods. He takes his half of the coin and shows the back markings to Scipio. "Wherever you go in the Belli nation, if you show your half of the wolf, you will be safe and welcome. Death comes to any that spurn you—this is known to all."

Scipio fingers the coin. "I shall see you tonight, my friend. There is a great feasting for you and our new friends, the Ilergetes."

Zaragoza's eyes become slits. "Ilergetes," he sniffs. "Goat fuckers. I will be there." The chieftain stomps toward the doors. Two large red-haired youths join Zaragoza near the door; by all appearances they are his sons. They give their father his broad-bladed battle axe and follow him out the door.

Scipio watches the regal barbarian push his way out into the street bustle of Tarraco. *Two sons*, he thinks, *will I live to have children? Or was my dream a lie?*

Laelius, Marcus, and Allucius now join him on the meeting room floor, visibly relieved. "That was the last of them," Marcus says. "No more petitioners, merchants, or chieftains."

Scipio smiles gratefully as Laelius theatrically sniffs him. "Gods above," he expostulates, "I thought that monster was going to smother you. The stink alone could have killed you!"

Scipio stares at the door, his tired eyes melancholy. He bends and coughs violently for a minute, but pushes himself upright. "That man has more nobility than most men in the Senate. I wager I could walk naked through the Belli nation with this wolf token about my neck and return unharmed."

Marcus Silenus' mouth twitches. "General, for my sake do not attempt that. For a variety of reasons."

Allucius and Laelius stare at Marcus in amazement. "Do I hear aright?" exclaims Laelius. "Does the man-killer have a sense of humor? I knew I would be a good influence on you!"

Marcus turns his head slightly to look at Laelius, his face impassive. "You have always been a shining example to me—of what not to do or say."

Laelius feigns hurt as young Allucius addresses Scipio. "Zaragoza will bring thousands of Celtiberians to your side. This is a great victory, General."

Scipio rubs the back of his neck and smiles at the graceful young Iberian. "I learned much about battles from my tutors and scrolls. But only now am I learning how to fight. The real wars are fought in the interim between the battles, when recruits and resources are so at stake. Thank Juno the Carthaginians fight that war with imprisonment and torture, else we might not be here!"

Scipio rubs his hands together, summoning some eagerness. "But winning we are, and tonight we will celebrate with a large feast. We will have five new allied tribes attending. Finish your business by dusk because tonight Bacchus visits us." Allucius and Marcus nod and walk toward the exit. As they do, Scipio coughs again. Marcus glances over his shoulder, looking at Scipio with concern. Scipio waves him away, and Marcus marches out the door. When they are gone, Laelius and Scipio sprawl out on the floor, pushing and jostling each other, acting like children dressed in battle armor.

"You look very tired, Scippy," says Laelius. "Perhaps I should fetch you a masseuse. Or a young girl or three!"

Scipio shakes his head. "Neither will quell the dreams that Febris visits upon me. And the voices. I still hear them, Laelius, the innocents at Cartago Nova, screaming as I murdered them."

Looking at his beloved friend's face, Laelius bites his lip to keep from crying. He musters some bravado and slaps Scipio on the back. "Nonsense! That was the best thing you could have done, Imperator.

Old Marcus was right: mercy is only appreciated when you prove you are capable of the opposite. You saved hundreds of our men's lives. Maybe thousands!" He shakes Scipio's shoulder, as if trying to wake him from his melancholia. "Look, your work is done here for now. You have met with the tribes, and our men are practicing their new maneuvers. All is in order, and winter is upon us. Why in Hades don't you go back to Rome?"

Scipio's shrug registers his ambivalence. "There is still much to do here. And I do not relish facing a Latin-infused Senate, that is for certain." He manages a smile. "But I do miss my heart Amelia. Seeing her would make the abuse worthwhile."

"So what keeps you here? You do not think we are capable of surviving without your guidance?" Laelius chides. "Do you think Marcus and I cannot visit the rest of the neighboring tribes, or oversee our men's training? When did you become so arrogant?" He looks seriously at Scipio. "Rome will demand you return to report to them anyway, if for no other reason than to prove that they still have power over you. Would you rather it be two months from now, when the Generals may spring an early attack? You can take Lucius with you. It will be a family reunion!"

Scipio blows out his cheeks and sighs. "I have much to do. But I do see your point. And there is a … delivery I must soon make to my mother, regardless."

Laelius crooks an eyebrow at him. "Is this another 'mystery ship' that will go to some hidden dock at Ostia?"

Scipio looks away from him. "I do love you, Laelius. But as I have told Felix, the less you know the more you benefit." Seeing Laelius' disappointment, he shoves him playfully. "Very well! You have convinced me. To Rome I will go! I will send the letters of announcement tonight, via a bireme."

"Be it so," replies Laelius happily. After a final shove, Laelius kisses him on the cheek and stands up. "Good. I wanted to be rid of you anyway!" Still grinning, he strides out the door.

When he is gone, Scipio stands alone, lost in reflection. "Quintus!" he shouts, and his one-armed assistant appears. "Ready two triremes for passage. I sail to Rome on the full moon. Lucius will join me, and Felix." Quintus hurries off, and Scipio looks back toward the entry doors. *Perhaps the dreams will stay here. And the voices.*

*   *   *   *   *

LIGURIA REGION, SOUTHWESTERN ITALIA COAST, 207 BCE. Hasdrubal is pleased with himself. He has pushed his fifteen thousand men over the winter Pyrenees and escaped any pursuit from Scipio. Within days of descending from the mountains, he occupied the fortress of Genova without losing a single man, being welcomed as a liberator from Roman rule. Now he has settled in for the winter, making the town chief's mansion his headquarters, a sacrifice the chief gladly made after a bit of garroting. Hasdrubal waits comfortably for the impending spring, when he can move to join Hannibal. In the interim, he works hard to replace the allied forces he lost at Baecula. He has started with the Ligurians, a fierce but undisciplined mix of Gallic tribes.

Hasdrubal has summoned the region's most powerful chieftain and is entertaining him with a juggler and a fool while they sit at table. But the performers do not amuse Ambrix, the head of the Ligurians. He has come to Genova's lofty halls to join Hasdrubal in battle against Rome. His tribe joined Hannibal's army a decade ago, and they stormed down into Italia, killing many Romans and gathering much plunder. Now he wants to renew his alliance. But this haughty little Carthaginian has proven to be nothing like his graceful and dignified brother, who treated the Ligurians with respect. Were it not for the gift sacks of silver and the chance to plunder Rome, Ambrix would kill this impudent dwarf with his bare hands. He has done so to others more powerful, for less offense.

Ambrix fingers the inscribed solid gold torc he took from a tribal king he killed, playing with the thick neck rope as Hasdrubal drones on about his prowess in Iberia. Ambrix is not a fool; his spies have informed him about Hasdrubal's fate at Baecula, so he has already caught the Carthaginian general in a lie. But Ambrix reminds himself that the Carthaginians are the mortal enemies of Rome, as are the Ligurians and the rest of the Gauls. An enemy of his enemy should be his friend. Especially when that friend is connected to Hannibal.

The Gaul's reverie is interrupted when Hasdrubal poses a question to him, and he focuses back on the smallish general. "… and so I promise, Ambrix, that with the fall of Rome you will be granted the aforesaid provinces in North Italia, is that agreed?"

Ambrix stares down at Hasdrubal, then looks into the distance. "That is what Hannibal promised us years ago. And he is a man of his word."

Hasdrubal bristles. "Yes, well, my beloved brother is certainly a man who keeps his word. But you have to deal with me now, don't you?" Hasdrubal is almost a foot shorter than the towering chieftain, yet he grins insolently into the man's ice-blue eyes, knowing he has the upper hand. The Ligurians are desperate for money and victory. Most of all, they fear the loss of their fields to the land-grabbing Romans.

"Your wives and children will have their own place here, safely within the city. No harm shall come to them, as long as you keep to your part of the bargain." Hasdrubal holds up the sheepskin agreement that both had marked.

The Gallic chief fixes this little dark man with a look of stone. "You have my word and my mark," Ambrix growls. "There is no need for you to threaten my family."

"For certain, for certain," Hasdrubal says, bobbing his head in mock agreement. "Your honor is known to all. Oh, here is something you may like to see." Hasdrubal walks over to a corner of the room. His bronze bull lies there, its compartment door open, emanating a faint odor of roasted flesh. "This is my bull," he says nonchalantly. "It has been very valuable to me over the years. I have gained much valuable information from using it." Hasdrubal strokes the fire-discolored back of the bull, running his finger along its thick seams. "It has been my punishment of choice for transgressors, too," he adds, without looking at the Gaul. "The Iberians became quite loyal to me, after a time."

Now Ambrix's eyes are shining with repressed fury. He clenches and unclenches his massive right fist, grasping for his absent sword. "I will bring ten thousand men at winter's thaw. You will deliver two wagonloads of silver then. Agreed?"

Hasdrubal extends his arm. "It is agreed." The stern Gaul envelops Hasdrubal's forearm in a steely grip and Hasdrubal winces in pain but returns the gesture with all his strength. They hold their grasps briefly, then Ambrix turns about and exits the hall, the Sacred Band guards returning his weapons as he leaves.

Hasdrubal sneers at the chieftain's back, rubbing his forearm. "Fucking Gauls" he grouses. "They are so big they think they can have their way with anyone. But not me! He will learn that!" He gestures for wine and gulps a deep goblet of red, smacking his lips. He looks over at his Sacred Band guards. "I'll put them on the front line," he shouts to no one in particular. "Use them up to wear out the Romans." He hawks and spits. "Then they will be worth their money!"

Later that night, Hasdrubal clears the maps off his table and fetches a sheet of thrice-beaten papyrus from a small wooden chest. Dipping his stylus into a jar of purple Phoenician ink, he begins to write to his brother.

Hannibal:

I am well; I trust you are the same. My mission in Northern Italia has been successful. I have recruited thousands of your old friends the Ligurians. More will soon come to my side, I am certain.

You have voiced your concerns about this young Scipio, calling him a prodigy. I hope it comforts you to know that Mago and Gisgo await the coming of Hanno, and they will venture forth toward Scipio in spring. His destruction is imminent.

I am over the Pyrenees and will soon cross the Alps and head toward Umbria to join armies with you, as we had discussed. I can meet you near Trasimeno, the site of your great victory, at the full spring moon. I have brought much of my siege equipment. We will topple Rome's walls and batter in their gates. The Barcas will soon make history, brother. Carthage will rule the world.

Hasdrubal carefully rolls up the sheet and seals it with his wax seal. He summons a messenger squad of four Gauls and two Numidians. [xxxii] They take the message and depart immediately. Hasdrubal follows them out the door of his commandeered mansion and listens to their horses' fading hoofbeats, reflecting on the spring campaign. *Hannibal has not been able to overthrow Rome,* he thinks. *If it falls when I arrive, I will be the one idolized in Carthage. Then we will see who is the genius.*

*   *   *   *   *

ROME, 207 BCE. The legionnaires from Capua tramp through Rome's massive portal gates and flow past the shouting citizenry that surrounds them. With their gaze locked on the cobbled streets ahead of them, the soldiers are impassive to the plebs' screaming pleas for information about loved ones. The legion's legate rides in front on a roan stallion, directing his veterans to the Forum Square, heading for their welcoming celebration. All Rome rejoices: the legion brings a ray of hope to its inhabitants, after months of fearful turmoil.

After Marcellus' and Crispinus' deaths, a rumor flashed through Rome that Hannibal would be marching toward the city, as he did several years ago. Rome's citizens grew anxious and panicky; families flowed into Rome from the outlands to seek safety while patricians flowed out toward Capua and the other southern cities. Commerce slowed to a snail's pace, and the loss of profit prompted the Senate to recall one of Rome's last remaining legions of veterans. With the legion's arrival hope is restored, and the city rejoices.

That night, in the midst of Rome's uproar, Scipio's two ships approach the port at Ostia. Gliding in under the light of the full moon, he is coming in a day earlier than he had notified the Senate. The docks are almost empty at this late hour, the reason he timed his arrival then, and everything is going in accordance with his plan.

Lighting a torch, Scipio waves it at the captain of the ship behind him, and he returns the signal. The second trireme eases away from Scipio's ship, heading to a subsidiary portage that is far from any prying eyes on the dock. There, the captain will turn the ship's stores over to Pomponia's attendants, who will unload a series of sealed barrels and whisk them to the family domus.

Scipio's older brother Lucius is at the prow of the ship with him. As the second ship slides from sight, his normally placid face registers confusion. He turns to Scipio. "Where is that ship going?" he asks, his hands flapping nervously as they are wont to do when confronted with something he does not understand.

Scipio squeezes Lucius' forearm and smiles. "I told you before, it is a shipment of Iberian wines and foods. The merchants who are buying them own that old Greek dock to the north of us." Lucius is still bewildered, but he nods acceptance, having learned that his brother's mysterious ways have a way of working out.

Felix stands behind the two of them at the ship's rail. He alternates between watching the lights of Ostia and looking reprovingly at Scipio. "I should have inspected that cargo," Felix grouses, "and negotiated with the merchants myself!"

Scipio raises his eyes heavenward. "You have received an inventory list and a bill of sale with my signature, as you did at Cartago Nova. That should be sufficient to your duties."

Scipio turns away from the quaestor and shouts some orders to the ship's captain. The ship veers toward the large center dock as Felix steps closer to Scipio, determined to pursue the matter. "I know you were an adept bargainer when you served as aedile, General, but doing all the purchasing yourself is highly irregular." When Scipio says nothing, Felix stamps his foot. "I shall have to include this in my report," the older man huffs.

Scipio turns and fixes his quaestor with a cold look. "You are an honorable man, Felix. Perhaps too honorable for Rome's good. Include whatever you see as the truth, but do not discuss this with me again." He turns away. "I have a war to win."

The ship raises its three banks of oars and eases near the front of the center dock walkway. The deck hands toss ropes to the burly dock slaves who pull in the ropes and draw the ship close enough for the sailors to jump off and tie it down. Two cloaked figures walk out onto the walkway, watching the sailors tie down the ship. Aboard the ship, Lucius looks at the two figures and tugs on Scipio's tunic. "Is that Mother down there?" he asks, his face happily expectant.

"Hmm …," Scipio murmurs. "They look like two porters to me …."

Lucius looks confusedly at Scipio. "They are too small to be porters, aren't they?" he says.

Scipio smiles. "Why yes, you are right! We'd better go see who they are."

As the two brothers step onto the gangplank, the first figure throws back her cloak and her red hair cascades down her shoulders. Pomponia waves her hand furiously in greeting, tears streaming from the corners of her eyes. Lucius scrambles down the gangplank and disappears into her embrace, sobbing like a lost boy found. Pomponia pats him on the back, kissing his head, as she smiles up at Scipio. *My mother is Juno personified,* Scipio thinks, *a motherly queen.*

The second figure pulls back her hood and reveals herself as a fine-featured young woman with a crown of auburn ringlets and jade green eyes. It is Amelia, Scipio's fiancée, seeing her love for the first time in three years. When Scipio steps from the ship onto the gangplank, she shoves her way through the surprised marines and dashes up into his arms, almost knocking the both of them into the night-dark water, much to the amusement of the debarking seamen.

Scipio whirls her off her feet and carries her down to the dock, their faces locked in one long kiss. He stands her on the walkway and savors the sight of her. "Amelia, oh gods, you came to see me! You still care!" He looks down, boyishly embarrassed. "It was … I mean … it is so long since we have been together. I just wasn't sure if …."

She looks at him with mock anger and punches him in the shoulder.

"You were not sure of what?" she chides. "You are always so sure of yourself. You were not sure of me?"

Amelia extends her right forehand under his nose. In the torchlight he can see she wears a ring shaped as two hands clasped together, the one Scipio gave her for their engagement. "When you gave me this, I became one with you. When you left, half of me went to Iberia. I cannot be complete until you—only you—are with me again."

Scipio kisses her hands. "And I was but half a man until we met. Forgive my doubt. It was only borne of fear for my loss. I am yours."

The deck hands, marines, and oarsmen now fill the dock, hauling out their personal sacks of belongings, eagerly heading to their own reunions. But this bustling press of soldiers parts like water as Pomponia moves through them, men bowing their heads at the sight of her. Pomponia puts her hands on Scipio's shoulders and kisses him once, deeply, on his mouth, and smiles at him through her tears. "My son, I did so miss you. I am so proud of what you have done. Your father would be so happy if he could see you!"

Scipio embraces her as Lucius sidles over to stand next to Amelia, holding her hand as they did when they were playmates together. Pomponia hugs Scipio again and whispers in his ear. "Your letter said you had another 'shipment' for me? Is that right?"

Scipio stands back and looks seriously at her. "Yes, from Baecula's treasury," he says softly. "A present from Carthage. Not as much as Cartago Nova, but substantial nonetheless." He waves toward his docked trireme. "And the Senate has enough coin and treasure to sustain our legions for years to come, may the gods preserve us from that being necessary."

Pomponia squeezes Scipio's hand. "I will keep it for our people, as the need becomes evident." She turns to Amelia and Lucius, gaiety in her face and voice, an excited mother once more. "Time to celebrate our family reunion! We have a nice little evening celebration waiting for you two, with all your favorites. Let us away to home!"

Scipio and Lucius grin. "I am glad we are feasting now, Mother," laughs Scipio. "I will likely lose my appetite after I appear before the Senate!" Scipio gestures for their personal guard to follow them, and the happy foursome walk down the dock toward the town of Ostia, toward the carpentum (covered coach) that waits for them on the city street.

Hours later, as the family reclines on couches while they dine, Scipio details the Iberian campaign, from the conquest of Cartago Nova to the victory at Baecula. Lucius listens silently for the most part, filling in a detail now and then. Amelia and Lucius excuse themselves to visit the stone block restrooms in the back.

When they are gone, Pomponia rises from her couch to sit next to her now-famous son. She strokes his head soothingly, as one might a child. "I have a favor to ask, beloved, though I am sure you are tired of people asking for such."

Scipio pops a plum into his mouth and smiles. "If it is within my power, gladly will I do it!"

She fidgets with the hem of her robe, suddenly embarrassed. "I want you to give Lucius more power, more of a role in the war. Your success is hard on him, dear. Everyone attends to you and ignores him."

Scipio's face takes on the stern guise of a general. "I allot responsibilities to each man based on earned merit," he says flatly. "Lucius has received more than he has earned."

Pomponia closes her eyes and bites her lip, fighting her irritation. When she reopens her eyes, they have the look of a parent toward an impudent child. "I know Lucius is a bit … easygoing … but he carries the Scipio name." She looks penetratingly at him, hating herself for what she must say. "If death should befall you, he could become a general to Rome. And you would throw him into that role without command experience!"

Scipio glowers at his mother. He hears the happy chatter of Amelia and Lucius returning to the dinner. Pomponia's eyes never leave him, waiting. "I will give him a significant mission when I return to Iberia," he replies moodily.

Pomponia strokes his cheek. "Gratitude, my love. You have given me much."

After another hour of conversation, Amelia rises from the couch and stretches. "It is time for me to return to my home," she says languidly. "Let me walk you back. Those streets are dangerous," says Scipio, as Lucius and Pomponia smile knowingly at one another. "Yes, very dangerous," chirps Lucius, as Scipio makes a face at him.

"Don't forget to have your guard follow you," teases Pomponia. Scipio makes a face. "I can't get rid of them!" he says.

"Well, maybe you better get rid of them tonight," laughs Lucius, and his mother smiles, patting his arm.

Soon they enter the domus of Amelia's dead father, General Lucius Aemilius Paullus, who was killed at Cannae. Amelia dismisses the slaves. The two of them remove their sandals and pad through the quiet mansion until they arrive at Aemilia's bedroom, entering through the thick doorway curtains. No sooner are they inside than Amelia opens the side buttons of her long flowing stola and shrugs it off, leaving her in a brief wispy tunic of golden sea silk. Holding Scipio's eyes in her own, she eases the tunic over her head and stands before him, nude.

Scipio's breath catches in his throat. The young woman he left three years ago has become a mature woman now. Her breasts are fuller, her hips more rounded, her look more challenging. He can barely keep his hands from trembling as he removes his clothing and steps forward to clasp her against him, feeling her breasts press against his chest, and her pubic mound swell against him.

She leads him to her sleeping platform and eases him down onto his back. She strokes his chest and thighs lovingly as Scipio caresses her breasts and sides. Scipio's phallus rises and darkens, and he moans softly, awash in the pleasure and pain of unfulfilled desire.

Amelia reaches into a small pot of olive oil and rubs some into her hand. "Dearest heart, I would love you inside me, but we are not yet married. I would not anger the gods by giving my virginity before then, when you are still at war." She smiles as she caresses her hands together. "But we have other ways, don't we?" Slowly, lovingly, she runs her fingers over Scipio's stiff member, trailing her fingers along the underside of his phallus. He moans and thrusts himself upward, his body demanding more. "The courtesans showed me how to do this," she says and begins to expertly twirl her fingers around him, again and again. Scipio cries out, and begins to tremble. As he convulses, she dips her head. taking all of him in her mouth. He buries his hands in her beautiful auburn hair, stroking her head. All too soon, he cries out as he expends himself, and his moans slowly die.

They lay together, side by side, staring into each other's eyes. Scipio strokes her shoulder, then her back, running his hand down to cup her buttocks. He gently turns her on her back and lies on top of her, his chest on her pubic mound. He kisses her breasts and moves his lips down her smooth, firm stomach until his tongue penetrates her. Now it is her turn to cry with pleasure, to grasp his hair, to convulse in the final throes of climax.

They are quiet together, touching fingertips. Then Amelia rises on one elbow and looks at Scipio. Her finger pushes his sweaty hair from out of his eyes. "When will you return for good, carissima? When will Iberia end for us?"

Scipio sighs. "Sooner than I may have wished, I fear. I have heard the Latin Party presses for me to be recalled, as they tried to do with Marcellus. That cur Flaccus wants to send Fabius or another Latin there, with more legions. Then the Party would have the glory."

"Can we stop them?" Amelia asks. "Your mother and I could mount a support campaign for you, as we did with poor Marcellus."

Scipio shakes his head. "There is only one way. I must engage Mago and Gisgo as soon as possible. If I can defeat them, Iberia will be ours."

"Pray you are allowed to return to Iberia," Amelia says. "I am sure Cato will be in the square tomorrow, denouncing your campaign!"

Scipio nods. "He is dangerous because he speaks with an honest zeal. He believes in the austere values of Rome long ago, when it was little more than tribal farms." He kisses Amelia and rises to dress himself. "My eyes grow heavy, carissima. I must return to my home. It would not do for me to be seen coming out of here in the morning."

Two days later, Scipio is standing in front of the crowded Senate chamber in the Curia Hostilia, listening to Flaccus rail against him. "I have talked to Scipio's officers and men," says Flaccus, standing in the front row of Senators. "They say he employs tactics that are very un-Roman, very … foreign, if I may say so." Flaccus raises his voice and points toward Cato, who is sitting on the side in the commoners' section. "Let me give you an example that Cato has told me months ago—he can verify my words. When Scipio and Cato were training our new recruits, Scipio did train his men to use a foreigner's sword, an Iberian falcata. Then he schooled our equites to ride like a bunch of barbarian Numidians!"

Hearing some Senators grumble at the news, Flaccus takes his cue, and his voice takes a tinge of outrage. "And now he has his army fighting like these savages instead of fighting like Romans, we who are the most powerful warriors in the world!" He sweeps his arm across a large group of Hellenic Party Senators sitting on the left side of the semicircle, bored men who watch him as if he were a unentertaining comedian. "The Hellenics have done this," Flaccus declaims to the Senate. "To make us ashamed of our heritage, that they may make us into decadent Greeks!"

The Senate erupts into accusations and arguments, but Scipio calmly waits for the babbling furor to subside. At last he speaks. "You may quarrel with my strategy or tactics because many of you are veterans of our wars against Gaul, and Macedonia, and Illyria." He looks levelly across the entire row of Senators, ignoring Flaccus, seemingly staring each patrician in the eye. "But you cannot argue with the results, can you? Cartago Nova and Baecula have fallen. And the results fill your treasury." *If not your pockets*, he says to himself.

Portly old Numerius Tullius stands up and the room grows quiet. He is a veteran of four wars and is one of the richest men in Rome. Tullius is also a covert member of the Latin Party, posing as a disinterested third party to sway independents to the Latin cause. "I would argue with some of your results, General Scipio. From what I have heard, you had the chance to destroy Hasdrubal after your victory at Baecula, to chase him down and catch him on the march. But you let him escape across the mountains. And now he moves to join the Carthaginian in Bruttium. We have had to send Marcus Livius' army north to confront Hasdrubal, instead of joining Nero to battle Hannibal. And thus we have had to divide our forces and put our armies at risk on two fronts!"

Scipio raises his head high, defiant. "I not only allowed Hasdrubal to leave Iberia, I put a legion at his back so he couldn't return!"

A younger Senator jumps up. "He admits his folly!" he shouts with outrage, sparking a new wave of murmuring.

Scipio looks at the Senators as if they were naughty schoolchildren, no longer cowed by being in their presence. "Mago and Gisgo's armies were coming to join Hasdrubal's," he intones. "Had I ventured forth to fight him, I risked their hordes attacking me from the rear while I engaged him. I could have lost the entire army. It would be Cannae all over again."

He counts three fingers out to the Senate "One of them I can defeat. Two together and I still have a chance. But all three at once, each with a veteran army the size of my own? That was an impossibility!"

A number of Senators yell their approval of Scipio's words, but he remains stoic, waiting. He has always been adept at anticipating his enemy's next move, and he can guess what Flaccus will say next.

Flaccus stands atop his bench seat and spreads his arms wide, as if imploring his Senate mates to follow him. "You have heard General Scipio admit that he refused to engage Hasdrubal and prevent his assault on Rome." He points his finger at Scipio. The young general stares back at him, arms crossed, imperious and impervious. "I move we recall Publius Cornelius Scipio from Iberia, on grounds of military incompetence!"

The Senate chambers resonate with shouts of "Aye," "Nay," "Lies, Latin Lies!" and "Nero, Nero!"

Creesus, the aged leader of the Senate, has been quietly sitting in his tall overseer's chair to the right of Scipio, facing his peers. But now the dignified patrician rises, straight as a spear, and booms his bronze-bottomed staff onto the stone floor, calling the Senators to order. Amidst much grumbling and argument, the Senate quiets enough for Creesus to be heard. "Order!" he commands. "Let each speak in turn."

Senator Tullius stands. "I think we should give serious consideration to noble Flaccus' motion. We know he does not make such accusations lightly." A dozen Senators hoot at his comment, but Tullius continues. "We should conduct a vote on this."

Before anyone can respond to Tullius' words, Consul Gaius Claudius Nero walks out from the Senatorial ranks and stands next to Scipio, facing the Senators. "As many of you know," he says grimly, "I was not overjoyed to have my men given over to Scipio at Tarraco, and thence returned to Italia."

Flaccus chuckles loudly. "It was at best a capricious act by Consul Galba, noble Nero." He winks at his fellow Senators. "But knowing Galba to be a devout disciple of Priapus, it was probably because he was bribed with gold—golden-haired pussy, that is!"

After the scattered laughter subsides, an irritated Nero resumes. "Fellow patricians, I was angry that this untried young general was given my command at Tarraco. And I was disappointed that he engaged the Three Generals with his limited force, instead of assuming a defensive posture."

Nero paces across the floor in front of the Senate, his head bowed, seemingly weighing his next words. "You know me as an honest man, and I tell you now: not even Cincinnatus or Dentatus could have achieved so much, so quickly, with so few resources."

Four Senators rise and voice their "Nays."

Nero glares at them and his voices booms out. "Scipio's plan was sound. Were you to have given him the two extra legions he requested, or the coin to woo more Iberians to his side, I would disagree with letting Hasdrubal escape. But you, in your infinite fear of Hannibal, have chosen to put your efforts into killing the bear when you should starve it to death. That is Scipio's plan, and it is most praiseworthy. Be you not so stupid as to deny it."

The Senators are silent, save for some heated whispering between a knot of Latin cronies, debating the wisdom of challenging Nero. Creesus eyes the silent Senate, and his eyes twinkle. "Do I hear a motion for the recall of Publius Scipio Africanus?" Flaccus starts to rise, but Nero glowers at him, and he sits down, his mouth a line of frustration. Creesus waits for another awkward minute, and then he stamps his staff. "There is no motion. We shall proceed to the next order of business, horse allotments for Sicily. Thank you for your time, General."

Scipio's face is the essence of gravitas, but his eyes are bright with triumph. He bows stiffly to the Senate leader and nods at Nero before he marches for the Curia Hostilia's exit, where scores of citizens peer in from the open doors, gaping at the proceedings.

Nero catches up to Scipio and whispers into his ear. "The inn at the Via Castulo, at dusk." Scipio nods his agreement and strides out into the cool morning air. He pauses on the top steps of the Forum, looking down across the bustling city he so loves. He takes a deep breath and blows it out, then another.

His right hand begins to twitch uncontrollably. Scipio pulls his cape over his hand and glances around, fearful someone has seen his infirmity. He hustles down the steps to join his guard and head for home, to seek solace in his family until he meets with Nero.

As late afternoon melts into early evening, Scipio stands by a nondescript inn on the Via Castulo, in one of the city's oldest sections. It is a dirt-street area populated by bakers, builders, and craftsmen of all stripes: plebians who earn a meager but respectable living. Scipio wears a plain gray tunic without any ornamentation, save for a wide leather belt and a dagger. His personal guard is a quartet of speculatores from his intelligence unit. The spies are dressed in peasant clothes, their winter cloaks concealing their swords. Lounging in alleyways and side streets, they look at everyone but Scipio.

Nero soon joins Scipio out front of the inn. The veteran soldier is dressed as inconspicuously as Scipio, in a plain white tunic. Scipio and Nero clasp forearms. "Gratitude for coming," says Nero. "There are some things you should know, privately."

Scipio orders his men to remain as he follows Nero into the inn. Scipio peers into the open portal of the sprawling bar, looking at the crowd of workingmen who are talking, arguing, and playing dice games. "It is a bit noisy," grins Nero, "but that means no one will overhear us." He places his hands on his hips and savors the scene. "In truth, I prefer the honest stink of workingmen to those tepid patrician perfumes … and perfumed patricians! Here are men who speak with honest tongue, however crude." Scipio nods and follows Nero inside, where they find a rough-hewn oak table in a corner, teetering on its tree-branch legs.

Nero starts to head for the wine server when a scrawny gray-haired serving maid appears from the crowd, using an old wooden cavalry shield as her tray. "Wine?" she rasps.

Nero nods. "Yes. Give us some Caucinian. And some food." The woman nods and disappears.

"They have the wines from Falernum here?" Scipio asks in surprise.

Nero nods. "The owner is from the town of Campania over there. He has some of the best wines in the city, from his family's vineyards." He puts a finger to his lips. "Tell no one. This is my own little hideaway."

The serving woman returns with a tray of fresh-baked roundbread and a bowl of olives, accompanied by two large pottery cups of Caucinian, a heavily alcoholic white wine. "Here you are, Generals," she says.

Nero gapes at her. "You know who we are?"

The crone grins. "Oh, I attend the Forum ceremonies, honored sirs. I have heard both of you speak."

Nero nods. "I am impressed. I just didn't expect it."

She looks critically at Nero. "Just because I serve this ignorant lot doesn't make me one of them," she snips.

Nero stares at Scipio, a restrained smile on his face. "Apologies. I did not recognize you as a student of politics." Nero gives her denarii. "Keep an eye on us, and return soon."

As the old woman moves to the adjoining tables, the two men talk about soldierly issues: the cost of grain, digging latrines in rocky soil, the amount of armorers to take with you on the march. Scipio waits, knowing something is on Nero's mind. As they finish their second cup of wine, Nero looks sternly at Scipio. "I have harbored some resentment about Tarraco, as you know. I suspect your mother had something to do with my recall from Iberia, to give you the opportunity for victory. Regardless of all that, I admire your boldness in taking Cartago Nova, and surprising Hasdrubal at Baecula. It is a pity you could not finish him."

"You heard my reasons," Scipio retorts with equanimity, despite his buzzing head. "If I would have lost, Rome would be lost."

Nero tilts his head noncommittally. "Your logic was sound, though I might not have risked attacking Baecula. But that was why I called you here. I want to talk about Hasdrubal." Nero looks about him for eavesdroppers. "The magistrate in Tarentum intercepted a message from Hasdrubal, intended for Hannibal.[xxxiii] His messengers became lost and showed up at one of our allied towns, asking for directions. He says he will meet Hannibal near Trasimene, at the full spring moon."

"Livius' army is not too far from there," says Scipio, growing excited. "He can prepare to fight him."

Nero frowns. "Yes, *if* he will fight him. I fear he has too much of Fabius the Cunctuator in him, content to nip at Hasdrubal's heels while he marches to join his brother!" Nero waves his hand impatiently. "Another wine," he shouts. The attendant materializes behind him with

317

two full cups.

"I figured as much," she smirks, and disappears.

Nero takes a deep drink, and a deep breath. "I have decided. I am going after Hasdrubal myself, a week before the spring moon. When I return to my army in South Italia, I'll take seven thousand men north to join Marcus Livius' army. I'll get him to join me, or I will fight Hasdrubal myself."

Scipio looks doubtfully at the older man. "Your army is under Hannibal's very nose. He will notice your departure and follow you. And you will be in the same predicament I was."

Nero laughs. "I learned from your march to Cartago Nova, I must admit. My army will travel as light as yours, under cover of darkness, using your misdirection tactics." Nero takes a deep draft of his wine and belches heartily, pleased with his plan. "After we have gone west for some miles, we will turn north and march under cover of darkness all night. By dawn, no one will know where we are. Five more days, and we are up by the Metauro River. Hasdrubal will have to come past there to join his brother."

Scipio nods appreciatively. "What about food?"

Nero picks up a loaf of roundbread and turns it about in his hand. "I will send envoys ahead on our route. With luck, the farmers will provide for us as we come past. We will carry almost nothing, as you did."

Scipio looks suspiciously at Nero. "The Senate has approved this?"

The wiry older man drains his cup in one gulp. "Fuck them," he sneers. "Half of them want Marcus Livius to win without me, so the Latin Party can take the glory. The other half would piss about for months before they made any decision." Seeing Scipio's skeptical look, he glowers. "Look, who knew you were sneaking up on Cartago Nova? No one, and it was best no one knew! We are soldiers, Publius Cornelius Scipio. We do what we must, however we must."

Nero's eyes start to droop, and he raises himself from his chair, looking down at Scipio. "I still don't like the way I was treated at Tarraco, whoever is to blame. But I wanted to show you that not all Romans are so hidebound as old Fabius or Livius. I, too, will play some tricks on the Carthaginians. And some on the Senate, for that matter!"

Nero slaps Scipio on the shoulder as he stumbles out. Scipio grasps Nero's hand before he leaves. "Remember, Hasdrubal is Hannibal's brother. He will use the terrain or weather to gain advantage."

The consul nods solemnly and walks out the door. Scipio sits back thoughtfully, and then a small grin breaks across his face. He waves his hand at his gnarly server. "A cup of your best Faustian, the twenty-five-year-old stuff." He sees the woman's eyes widen. "I care not the price. I am celebrating. The student has become the teacher, after all these years."

*   *   *   *   *

LUCANIA, 207 BCE. Hannibal sits by a small campfire, cooking his evening meal over a spit. Maharbal, his gruff cavalry commander, squats uncomfortably next to him, looking wistfully at the comfortable confines of the Carthaginian command tent. "Do we have to eat out here all the time?" complains Maharbal. "Why don't we eat inside the tent, on that nice table?"

"Why? Our men have no tables, no big tents," Hannibal growls. "We need no special favors that make us soft. Have you forgotten what happened to us when we indulged ourselves at Capua? We became soft as patricians, and just as dull-witted!"

"Forgive me, Leader," comes a voice behind Hannibal and Maharbal. They look over their shoulders to see a Numidian rider standing behind them, a papyrus scroll in his hand. "A message from Hasdrubal," The messenger says, as he holds out the scroll. Hannibal sees it bears the goats-head seal of the house of Barca. Hannibal opens the scroll and studies it, squinting his eye to read the tiny script. He closes the scroll and smiles. "Hasdrubal is coming south to join us at Trasimene."

Maharbal's eyes widen. "Join us? Where is he? How many men does he have?"

"He is going to Placentia," says Hannibal, "with over thirty thousand men. He recruited ten thousand Gauls while he was wintering in the Po Valley. And he managed to drag his siege equipment over the mountains by following my old trail. That is amazing!" he says proudly.

"No more amazing than you crossing the Alps in winter," notes Maharbal. "It is already the stuff of legends."

Hannibal waves off the compliment. "We will have enough men and equipment to break Rome's walls. They will sue for peace or die! And we can finally win this damned war!" Hannibal hurries to his tent and scrawls a reply to his brother, sealing it with wax and stamping it with the goat's-head figure of Baal, the Barca seal. He gives the scroll to his chief messenger, who immediately rides north toward Hasdrubal's camp.

When he is some thirty miles north of Hannibal's emplacement, the rider heads down a dirt trail to an abandoned farm, where he enters a thick grove of olive trees. Nero is there, sprawled in the shade with his legion's legate and a squadron of his guard. An older Greek man sits on a blanket under a tree, carefully inspecting his satchel of candles, waxes, seals, and stylus writers.

The messenger hands the scroll to Nero, who hands it to the Greek. The old man studies the seal, fingering it carefully. He rummages into his bag and selects several seals that have Baal's face on them. Picking one, he shaves off some of the border, and etches some details onto the goat's-head figure. "I am ready," rasps the Greek.

The Roman general breaks the seal, reads it aloud to his legate, carefully rolls it back up, and gives it to the Greek. The older man meticulously scrapes off all traces of the seal wax, blowing away the shards. He lights a candle and melts a metal cup of the same color wax, which he pours onto the place where he removed the seal. The artisan stamps in his version of the Barca seal, and blows on the wax to harden it. Nero gives the messenger a purse of coins, and the messenger tucks the resealed scroll into his pouch and dashes out from the grove.

General Nero watches the rider fade into the distance, his eyes alight with excitement. He walks to his horse and jumps onto it, turning to his men. "We know where he'll be. Quickly now," he says. "We march at dawn. Gods help us arrive in time."

*　　*　　*　　*　　*

TEMPLE OF BELLONA, OUTSKIRTS OF ROME, 207 BCE. He is a plain-looking man of indeterminate age and average height and build, with sandy brown hair, brown eyes, and an unkempt beard. Were anyone to look at him, he would avert his gaze submissively. The man is altogether a forgettable figure. It is a look the man has cultivated since he retired from the Illyrian army, where he was one of its most deadly stealth warriors, infiltrating enemy camps to slay officers in their sleep, using his sixteen-inch dagger.

Now he works as a sicarus (dagger man), an assassin for hire in Rome and its provinces. None who hire him know his name or place, nor does he know theirs. One Illyrian butcher in Rome is his only point of contact, and even that man knows nothing of his background.

The assassin sits on the temple steps adjoining its sacred fig trees, which are budding out to celebrate winter's departure. He waits for his latest contract to arrive, tapping his foot on the steps. The sun is setting this chill day, and all worshippers have returned to the city long ago. Whoever comes here now will be his man.

As the last light of day fades, a solitary hooded figure—tall and gaunt—appears from the pine grove to the side of the temple. The sicarus gestures for him to seat himself, but the man shakes his head. "I have trouble sitting," he replies testily. "That is one of the reasons I am here."

The hooded figure reaches into his thick gray robe and pulls out a bulging rawhide bag of coins. He extends it to the assassin, who tucks the bag into his belt pouch. The hooded man then extends a hand with a scrap of bound papyrus in it. The Illyrian takes it, unties it, and reads the single name engraved therein:

Pomponia, mother of Publius Cornelius Scipio

The sicarus nods and pockets the scrap. The hooded figure starts to leave, when the assassin tugs at his robe. "A woman?" asks the Illyrian. "Why?"

"Because she overreaches her station," replies the cloaked figure. "Because she endangers Rome," he adds angrily and then snorts. "And because she is truly a pain in the ass."

IX. THREE VICTORIES

ABRUZZO REGION, SOUTHEAST ITALIA, 207 BCE. Moving with practiced efficiency, Nero's infantry paces quickly along the wide dirt road between the local farmers' fields, the round-shouldered Apennines rolling by on their left. His messengers have notified the area farmers of the army's incursion into their territory, and hundreds of men and women line the roads with food for their liberators—bulging sacks of corn, wheat, and barley; baskets of grapes; barrels of wine and oil; even live chickens and pigs. Leading the vanguard of his thousand cavalry, Nero waves enthusiastically at the generous locals. He will take this road on his way back, and he plants the seeds of future donations. His six thousand legionnaires hurry past the welcoming peasants, moving faster than any infantry has ever gone, save for Scipio's men.

As the last lines of the army pass, a line of horses and wagons pauses to collect the proffered foodstuffs from the locals. The wagons are attended by the hundreds of adventurous civilians who joined Nero's force as it went by their homes. There are young field hands barely in their teens and army veterans who received their land for meritorious service in the first Carthaginian war. The young carry pitchforks and scythes for weapons, ready to fight with anything at hand, as the farmers have done since Rome was a kingdom. The veterans are often dressed in tattered armor and rusty helmets, proudly wearing their badges of service from earlier wars. They come because this is their best chance to save their lands and families from the Carthaginian hordes who have plundered them in years past. Nero welcomes these valiant recruits, but he does not slow down for them: they must make his pace or be left behind.

Nero's army gradually grows to ten thousand men. Days later, as dusk looms, he rides back and forth along the line of march, exhorting his men to a faster pace, knowing The Metauro River is nigh. He is determined to arrive at Livius' camp by midnight, to sneak in under Hasdrubal's guard.

When the sun sets, Nero sends out two Gallic spies he has recruited for his army's trip to North Italia, aping Scipio's use of speculatores. The Gauls return with information that the Ligurians are acting as scouts for Hasdrubal. They relate Hasdrubal's coercive recruitment of the Ligurians, holding their families hostage and threatening them with torture. No stranger to the behavior of the proud northern tribes, Nero hatches a plan.

Nero sends out his senior Gallic scout with a signed offer for the Ligurian scouts. Nero offers them amnesty and a bag of gold for their scouting services, services they will provide Hasdrubal, not Nero. All they have to do is perform a bit of misdirection while scouting for Hasdrubal, when the time is right. Nero watches the Gaul gallop off. *Scipio was right*, he muses. *Win the fight before the battle starts.*

* * * * *

PORT OF GADES, SOUTHWESTERN IBERIA. Gisgo is enjoying himself immensely as he looks out to sea, but he is having a difficult time deciding which he enjoys more: Is it the sight of Hanno's Carthaginian fleet sprawling across the horizon, coming in to join him? Or is it the sight of the three burning Roman triremes that were caught between Gisgo and Hanno's patrols, with Laelius' men jumping into the chill spring seas? Hope and revenge are equally enjoyable, he decides, and he raises his wine cup in a salute to both.

Rhodo Gisgon, the NightBringer, stands next to his commander, watching the fleet navigate toward the port docks. The Sacred Band champion is pleased to see Hanno's force arrive. Now Gisgo may summon the courage to face Scipio again, and Rhodo can kill more Romans.

Since the fall of Cartago Nova, Rhodo has volunteered for every one of Gisgo's reconnaissance and raiding parties, that he may slay the men who sacked his city and humiliated him. Everywhere Rhodo has gone he has left a trail of Roman corpses, but the one victim he seeks has eluded him: the fierce little man who fought him to a standstill at Cartago Nova, the man General Scipio called "Marcus." Rhodo and he exchanged a look that was an unspoken agreement: neither would rest until the other was dead. Rhodo knows the man is a legion commander for Scipio, meaning his death would bring glory to him and seriously cripple Scipio's army. And so Rhodo sharpens his sword and dreams of their reunion, anticipating their next encounter with all the eagerness of an unrequited lover.

Hanno's ships land safely, easing in to the massive port docks. The Carthaginian general is soon at dockside. Hanno is a tall and severe older man with an immaculately groomed grey-black beard. The scion of a wealthy merchant family, he is a general with a modest military record, despite his years of service. Hanno is a longtime opponent of the war against Rome—and against Hannibal's intrusion into Italia, believing both are bad for commerce. For that reason, the Council of Elders has chosen him to join the Iberian generals, that he might temper the Barcas' imperialistic urges with their mercenary goals.

Gisgo eagerly welcomes Hanno and his fully paid mercenaries. He leads Hanno's ten thousand men through a celebratory parade into the Carthaginian stronghold. After Hanno has refreshed himself and changed into the silken robes he favors, Gisgo leads him to a reception with his army's commanders. To honor Carthage's Phoenician heritage, the officers dine on traditional Phoenician dishes of dates, cabbage, lentils, and sea-salted fish, all washed down with ample quantities of the region's lusty Palomino wine.

After dinner, Gisgo and Hanno interrupt the festivities to make several announcements. Gisgo announces that the North Iberian recruiting efforts have gone well, with thousands of Celtiberians adding to the Turdetani and Carpetani recruits. With Hanno's men now joining them, the Carthaginian army stands at sixty thousand men, the largest army Gisgo has ever had. This causes much rejoicing among the officers, who still feel the sting of Scipio's victories at Cartago Nova and

Baecula.

Then Hanno steps forward. Brandishing a scroll from Carthage's Council of Elders, he breaks the document's seal and unrolls it, theatrically reading its contents: the Council of Elders declares its support for Gisgo, Hanno, and Mago to pursue the defeat of Scipio, promising recurrent installments of money and men for that purpose. Gisgo stands next to Hanno, and they declare their intent to attack Scipio's army at Tarraco and then destroy Marcius' outpost on the Ebro River. They announce that Mago will return in a fortnight from the Balearic Islands, and the Three Generals will be reconstituted with Hanno in Hasdrubal's stead. Their sole mission will be to retake Iberia from Rome.

The announcements are received with great rejoicing, and the celebration continues late into the night. As the feast dissolves and men return to their quarters, the attending slaves clean up the leavings of food and wine, tucking away any edible remainders for their families. After all the officers are gone, a portly older slave ducks out from the meeting chambers and pads down a side street to an alleyway, entering a small tailor's shop. The slave has a hushed conversation with a young Iberian in charge there, and the youth closes up his business. Soon, a night rider departs out the back gates of Gades, galloping toward Tarraco.

$$* \quad * \quad * \quad * \quad *$$

METAURO RIVER, MARCHE REGION, ITALIA, 207 BCE. "Light another torch!" Marcus Livius orders as he rolls out his scouts' map of the Metauro River area. He places a red soldier carving next to Hasdrubal's emplacement, then two black ones for his and Porcius Linius' camps. "We are less than a mile away from him now, Porcius. We can attack at the next dawn."

Porcius Linius frowns dubiously. "Now? Claudius Nero will be here in two or three days. Why not wait for him? The scouts say Hasdrubal has over 30,000 men and a dozen elephants, and he is protected by the river on one flank. It will be a costly fight."

"And what is the cost if we let him slip away and join Hannibal?" comes a voice from the tent entrance. A roadworn Nero walks into the tent, his grin glowing white in his sunburned face. The consul and praetor stare at each other, amazed at Nero's early arrival. Livius musters some enthusiasm for seeing his old political enemy and walks over to shake his arm.

"Nero! How in Jupiter did you get here already?"

Nero removes his dusty helmet and sits on a stool, still smiling. "I stole a march from Scipio's march!" he says with a grin. "We travelled light, no food or tools. And moved like the wind." He throws open his hands and laughs. "We don't even have any tents!"

"Where are your men? Did they come in the rear gate?" asks Linius, looking out through the tent flaps.

Nero gestures toward the east. "They are camped in that last line of trees before the plain starts. They will come in late tonight. I have about nine or ten thousand men. It is hard to estimate—more kept joining as we went!"

"Well, we are overjoyed to have you, consul," says Livius tonelessly. "We will wait two days for your men to catch their rest and then go at Hasdrubal."

At those words, Nero jumps up. "Nay, no such thing. We did not march day and night to sit on our arses while Hasdrubal sneaks away! Let us to battle as soon as we can organize our men!"

The praetor and the consul look at one another, and a silent decision is made. "Very well," says Livius, putting a third Roman figurine on the map. "Let us talk about the day after tomorrow ...."

That night, as Hasdrubal lays in his tent, his scouts tell him of a bugle call sounding in the Roman camp, signaling an arrival. He rises from his sleeping cushions and walks outside, looking toward Livius' emplacement. *It is the middle of the night*, Hasdrubal wonders. *Why was a welcome horn sounding?*

The next day, a suspicious Hasdrubal sends all his scouts out to closely monitor the Roman camp. They return with news that a number of emaciated horses are now in the Roman corral, and a number of men at the river were sunburned, signs of them being engaged in a severe march.[xxxiv] Still, his scouts say there are no new tents in camp, casting doubt that any sizable force would have arrived last night. But Hasdrubal is a Barca, wise in the ways of war and deception, and he is not convinced. He remembers last night's Roman bugle call, the series of notes that is given when a notable presence has entered the camp. He calls a quick meeting of his commanders, and they make plans to evacuate the camp during the night.

Slowly, silently, the entire Carthaginian army eases out of camp that moonless eve, leaving only enough men to tend to the campfires they leave as a ruse. Hasdrubal's two Ligurian guides lead the army north along the river, ostensibly to find a place to cross over into the protecting lands of Gaul.

Hasdrubal rides in the front with Agon, his Master of Horse. They call out to the Ligurian scouts in front of them but receives no answer. He sends his Carthaginian scouts into the darkness to find them, but no one is there. After an hour of futile searching, he realizes that they have abandoned him. He directs his men to search the river for a crossing point, but the river is far below the bluffs on which they march, and the search is futile.

In the meantime, the two Ligurians show up at the Roman gates, demanding an audience with Nero, who enthusiastically welcomes them. They impart the direction and location of Hasdrubal's army. "Well done," says Nero, "you have fulfilled our contract." The consul gives each a bag of silver and sends them out to join his scouts. Then Nero summons Livius and Linius.

The dawning sun rises on two entirely different armies. The Carthaginian scouts meander slowly along the banks of the Metauro, searching for a crossing, while tens of thousands of soldiers lie scattered about the landscape, sleeping. The Roman infantry files out in organized lines of march, and thousands of cavalry ride ahead, focused on catching Hasdrubal's army to slow its progress until their legions arrive.

The Roman cavalry soon closes in on Hasdrubal's army, but they are discovered by his scouts. The Libyan and Numidian cavalry sally forth to engage the equites in an extended skirmish, halting the Carthaginian army. Hasdrubal knows that the infantry cannot be far behind, so he reluctantly orders his commanders to prepare for battle. By early afternoon, Nero, Livius, and Linius arrive with their men and quickly draw up into battle formation.

Hasdrubal can see he is outnumbered, but he is undaunted. He knows he must use the terrain as his ally, as his brother Hannibal would do. He moves his men back to a place where the riverbank protects his right flank from a full-scale attack, and the hilly left side defends the left flank from the penetration. He sends his Gauls into the left-side hills, knowing its disjointed ground suits their disorganized methods of attack and defense, and they can hold the Romans at bay there. To the right he places his Iberian and Libyan infantry and his cavalry. True to his word, Hasdrubal places Ambrix and his Ligurians in the center behind his dozen elephants. He plans for the Ligurians to forestall the Roman heavy infantry while his best men forge in from the right. With a quick prayer to Baal for victory, Hasdrubal rides out to the front of his men and awaits the Roman attack.

Nero watches the Carthaginian army's deployment. He remembers Scipio's warning about the Barcas using the landscape and unconventional tactics as weapons. Believing he can improvise better than his Livius and Linius, he volunteers to take the Gauls and fight in the trees. The three decide that Nero will take the forested hill while Marcus Livius engages Hasdrubal and his Iberians, with the praetor Porcius Linius deploying his two legions against the Ligurian center. The army quickly draws into its formations. The Roman cornu sound the attack, and the cavalry hurtle toward Hasdrubal's lines as the legionnaires tramp steadily forward.

The Roman cavalry swarm into the mounted Numidians and Iberians. The Carthaginian cavalrymen fight fearlessly, but they are greatly outnumbered and many soon fall before the Romans. Many of the equites soon leave the slaughter to aid their legions against the staunch

Iberian and Libyan infantry.

The Carthaginian elephants charge into Linius' center, breaking through his legion's ranks and trampling scores of unfortunate legionnaires. The Ligurians seize the opportunity and rush recklessly into the Roman hastati, buckling their lines. The battlefront is now a constellation of individual battles, many of which the unyielding Ligurians win by circling about until they can slash into a legionnaire's unprotected lower back, penetrating their livers and kidneys.

Cato fights in the midst of Linius' center, and the young tribune shouts for his centurions to order a change of lines. The centurions blow their whistles, and the weakening hastati step back between the advancing principes. With Cato walking in front of them, the veteran warriors stamp forward as a solid wall, jabbing and thrusting in between their protective shields. Many a Ligurian charges the wall of Roman shields, only to receive a thrust in his chest or bowels. The principes step over hundreds of wounded Ligurians, and the following hastati methodically dispatch them.

The Ligurians step back apace and catch their breath as the principes prepare for them, deflecting the stones and spears the Gauls rain upon them. Fresh tribesmen from the Ligurian rear jostle their way to the front, eager to repulse these stubborn little Romans. Ambrix screams out a battle cry, and the Ligurians riot out into the waiting principes. Cato waves a signal, the whistles blow, and the principes march forward, step by step, cutting their way deep into the barbarian lines.

Behind the Roman center, the rampaging elephants have trampled their way to the rear, where the veteran triarii spear their mahouts and jab the undirected pachyderms along like unwary cattle, goading them until the elephants rumble past the battle and out onto the plains, out of the fight.

Nero's men assault the hillside Gauls time and again, fighting them individually among the trees. Drinking, cursing, and shouting, the immense Gauls jump out between trees and swing down with their two handed broadswords, beating back the Romans. The determined Romans kill many of them but they cannot gain a victory: their movements are blocked by the trees, hampering their cut and thrust tactics. The disjointed battle is a standoff, and Nero grows frustrated.

Then he remembers Scipio's words about improvising against the Carthaginians' tricks. He recalls his men and evaluates the situation as the Gauls jeer at them from the forest. It occurs to Nero that the outnumbered Gauls are as unable to leave the hillside as his men are to penetrate it. Nero assigns four cohorts of veterans to keep the Gauls engaged via skirmishes, and he rides out with his remaining seven thousand men marching behind him. His infantry march at the triple-time speed they have practiced and are soon skirting behind Livius' legions.

Nero directs his men to form four abreast columns and hustle through the narrow gap between the Carthaginian lines and the river, ignoring the Carthaginian forces until they are completely behind them. Once they are in the Carthaginian rear, Nero orders his men back into formation, and they charge into the back of the Iberians and Libyans, throwing them into confusion.

By now the Roman cavalry have disposed of the last of the outnumbered enemy cavalry. The Roman Master of Horse follows Nero's flanking maneuver, and thousands of riders circle behind Marcus Livius' battling infantry to chop into the Carthaginians' unprotected flanks near the river. After exhausting their pila, most of the riders dismount and charge into the enemy, breaking their ranks.

In the center, the front line maniples are refreshed by the ones behind them. But Ambrix rallies his men to charge back into the Romans, and the Ligurians push the legionnaires back. Then Ambrix falls down, pierced through the neck by a javelin, and several legionnaires stab him to death. Cato and the other tribunes scream for their men to go forward, decimating the demoralized Ligurians, and the Carthaginian center bows inward.

Hasdrubal and his men are being hit from the front, back, and side. The Libyans, Iberians, and Ligurians are gradually pushed together and encircled. Agon fights his way to Hasdrubal, his left arm dangling useless from a bone-deep gash in his elbow. He points to an opening in the rear lines, behind the last of the Ligurians. "Hasdrubal, the battle is lost. This way!"

Hasdrubal wheels his horse to flee, but he pauses for a moment to survey the carnage that was his army. In a flash of insight, Hasdrubal grasps the fate of the battle, the fate of Hannibal, and the fate of Carthage.

"Fuck it," he spits, his eyes moist with sorrow. Screaming his coarse insults, he waves his sword over his head and charges head-on into the Roman cavalry as Agon rushes to join him.

* * * * *

ROME. With a weary smile on her face, Pomponia weaves her way through the crowded streets, following the throngs to the Temple of Jupiter for the final celebration in this, the third day of citywide thanksgiving for Nero and Livius' victory.

When Rome discovered that Nero left to join Marcus Livius' army, the populace became very anxious. From the lowest slave to the most senior Senator, all realized that a subsequent victory by Hasdrubal would open the Barca brothers path to Rome, with few left to impede them. Thousands of Romans inundated the temples to pray for salvation, and just as many filled the popinas and tabernas to drown their anxieties. The city held its collective breath, waiting for its fate.

Rumors trickled in from Umbria and Toscana: that Hasdrubal suffered a grievous defeat, that ten thousand Carthaginians were killed and just as many captured. But only the most foolhardy dared believe in them, having experienced encouraging reports about the Roman disasters at Trebia, Trasimene, and Cannae. Plebs and patricians collected by the gates interrogating everyone who came through them.

Then Nero's and Livius' four envoys trotted through the city gates one afternoon, waving and hooting like schoolboys on a holiday. Once inside, they confirmed the victory rumors and sent the city into a paroxysm of rejoicing. Romans of all stripes crowded around the messengers, constantly touching their horses and bodies, as if to confirm that they were real. The Senate dispensed with its partisan bickering and unanimously declared a three-day holiday, replete with ceremonies, sacrifices, and gladiatorial contests.

Pomponia and her friend Cornelia Furius have joined the city's revelers. Both are dressed in their best jewels and robes, as are the rest of the citizenry. Cornelia is the widow of an equite who was killed while fighting under Publius Scipio in Iberia, and the two women share a special bond of grief. Pomponia misses having her future daughter-in-law with her, but she knows Amelia is out spreading banners that celebrate Nero's victory, using the celebration as an opportunity to increase his political popularity. *My god,* Pomponia thinks, *the girl never takes a holiday. She will exhaust my poor son*!

When the day's ceremonies are finally over, Pomponia and Cornelia weave their way through the main streets toward the Scipio domus, to conclude the day with a celebratory feast. They chat happily as they walk along, not noticing the bent, hooded figure that follows them through the crowds.

The two women take a shortcut through a side street, and the cloaked figure darts into a street parallel to theirs, hurrying to reach an alleyway that connects to their street. He rushes down the alley until he reaches its juncture with the women's street. He pulls out a long knife, waiting for them to pass by. As their laughter becomes louder, he crouches and prepares to spring, using the maneuver that is part of his livelihood: two slashes and the women are dead, throats cut to prevent an outcry.

The man stiffens, eyes bulging from his head. He scrabbles at the keen, thin blade that has appeared from the center of his spurting chest. A muscular forearm throttles his windpipe as the man bucks his life out, and the thief collapses without a sound.

A plain-looking, brown-haired man pulls the dead thief into a door alcove and props him up like a sleeping drunkard, covering his wound. He sprawls next to the corpse and puts his arm around him as Pomponia and Cornelia walk past, arm in arm. They glance at the two men but pay them little attention; the city is filled with sprawled celebrants today. Once the women are gone, the man casually walks back down the alley, satisfied with his work. It is a point of honor that the hired assassin will kill Pomponia himself. Her death is his, and no one will interfere.

*　　*　　*　　*　　*

LUCANIA, SOUTH ITALIA. Hannibal stands on the walkway that borders his permanent camp's thick timber walls. He gazes across the valley floor at hundreds of Roman campfires twinkling in the moonless night, so numerous it seems as if the night sky itself had fallen to earth. Nero's camp is sprawled out there in front of him, as it has been since the new moon. *He has not challenged us for battle,* Hannibal wonders. *What is he waiting for?* Hannibal's camp spies have been useless: they only know Nero's command tent has been quiescent for days and the overheard conversations of centurions and tribunes do not reveal any new plans or actions. *It is as if the entire army is waiting for something,* Hannibal thinks as he listens to the Roman's watch horns. *But waiting for what?*

To amuse himself, Hannibal again draws out a mental plan to attack the camp, using the trees and hills for an initial ambush and the river to protect his rear lines. It is all for play, however, because he will not attack until he hears from Hasdrubal. If Hasdrubal is near Lucania, Hannibal will wait until he can join forces with him before he attacks. Their combined might would easily destroy Nero's army, and they could then march unopposed to Rome. If his brother is farther north, Hannibal plans to leave under cover of darkness, join forces with Hasdrubal, and make Nero chase after them while they march to Rome, giving them the strategic advantage. Either way, Hannibal can see the stratagems and tactics he would employ to destroy the consular legions, and the peace demands he would levy upon Rome. The thought occasionally crosses his mind: *burn Rome to the ground, as that bastard Cato keeps demanding they do to Carthage.* But he recalls the carnage of Cannae, and Trebia, and Trasimene; of the towns he has burned and innocents put to the sword. He cannot fathom another mass murder. *You won't have to do that. They will have to sue for peace,* he tells himself.

The rapid pounding of hooves distracts him, drawing nigh to where he stands. Hannibal stares into the blackness below him but he cannot discern the rider's whereabouts. The pounding grows louder, then it is followed by a soft thunk below him, inside the camp, and the hoofbeats fade into the night. He can hear a mumbled, urgent discussion between two guards below.

"General?" says one of the guards. "I beg you, come look at this." Hannibal climbs down a ladder into the courtyard. In the torchlight, he can see two Carthaginian soldiers standing at attention in front of him, looking very apprehensive. One of them holds a red linen sack with a spread eagle crest upon it, obviously of Roman origin. Hannibal walks over to them, his interest piqued by the bag the one guard clenches in both his hands. Hannibal stands next to them, and the guard wordlessly extends the bag to The Carthaginian, his eyes large with concern.

Hannibal takes the sack, noticing it is discolored on the bottom, and looks inside. There, lying on a bed of finest red silk, is the head of his brother Hasdrubal.[xxxv] One eye socket is carefully stitched together, masking the gouge of a missing eyeball. The cheek cuts and neck stub have similar closures. *He was cut in many places*, Hannibal thinks dully. *He did not go easily.*

Hannibal cradles the sack in his arms and stumbles back to his command tent. He waves out his attendants and collapses onto a broad wooden stool, staring into the sack at his brother's face. Soon tears dribble from his eye, and his body convulses with repressed sobs.

"What are you doing in there, Hannibal? We are to talk!" barks a voice from outside the tent. There is an argument outside, then brash Maharbal barges through the tent flaps. "I thought I'd have to kill the guards to get in here," he says irritably. Then he stops, noticing Hannibal's expression and the sack he dumbly holds. Without another word, Maharbal walks over and looks into the sack. He heaves a deep sigh, and looks at Hannibal. "Now what?" is all he says. Hannibal does not respond. He stares out with an infinite look in his eye, as if studying a far-off shore. Maharbal shifts about uneasily. "General?" he inquires.

Hannibal turns his head toward Maharbal and blinks rapidly, as if rousing himself from sleep, or a dream. "I see clearly the destiny of

335

Carthage," ^{xxxvi} he says heavily. "There will be no attack on Rome. We will gather our Lucanian allies and move south to Bruttium. There, we have friends and allies. Rome cannot touch us there." He sighs. "In Bruttium, we have something resembling a family."

*　　*　　*　　*　　*

BAECULA, IBERIA, 207 BCE. "... And there are thousands of them, King Scipio, many, many Celtiberians, I swear. Down in the southern valley, not far from here." The Olcade sheepherder twists his rag cap nervously, looking at his feet. He has rode fourscore miles to advise Scipio of the enemy's presence, knowing Scipio is a sworn friend of the Olcade—hoping to receive a reward.

Scipio is perched on a large throne-like wooden chair, with Laelius, Lucius, and Marcus Silenus standing about him. A bag of coins rests on one of the chair's planked arms, and a broad-bladed cutting knife is on the other. The herdsman shifts about nervously. He has heard stories of Scipio's treatment of informers: speak the truth, and you will be well rewarded; sell a lie, and you lose your tongue.

The herder is shown a map of the region, and he points to the Baetis River valley south of Baecula, near the coastal foothills. Scipio turns to Lucius. "Send out two scouts. If they see any Carthaginian forces, they are to take a census and return immediately." Scipio watches him hurry off, enthused about his task. *I am keeping him involved, Mother. I pray it does not cost us.*

Scipio smiles gently at the trembling herdsman. "Thank you for this information. Please be our guest here until the scouts return." Scipio looks over his shoulder at the captain of his personal guard. "Put our friend in the grain house for the night. See that he has wine and food." The captain leads the frightened tribesman toward the door, but the peasant stops and looks entreatingly at Scipio. "It will just be for the night," Scipio soothes as the herdsman is tugged out the door.

The general immediately turns to his officers, his voice urgent. "I need you to prepare a reconnaissance force. If our scouts confirm this man's story, you must act at once. Mago and Hanno are recruiting allies from every region of Iberia. They may be out by the valley, under our very noses, talking to Hasdrubal's old allies."

The scouts return the next day, bearing puzzling information. They could not find any large bodies of soldiers, but several large Numidian scout squadrons were patrolling the lowlands by the mountains. Scipio scratches his head at the news, and he orders Marcus Silenus to investigate. "Take two legions with you, Marcus, just to be safe. Our spies in Gades say that Mago, Gisgo, and Hanno have built their army to sixty thousand men, so there might be a larger force than a mere patrol."

Marcus salutes in acknowledgement. "No tents, no baggage," Marcus says curtly. "Twenty-five miles a day." Scipio nods his agreement, and Marcus strides from the room, already focused on his purpose.

Laelius leans in toward Scipio. "You think they have sixty thousand? After what you did to them at Baecula?"

Scipio nods. "Many of the Celtiberians in the north have not heard of us, and they are in the Carthaginians' hire, though only the gods know how they find money to pay them, now that we have their mines."

The next day, Marcus leads his army down the Baetis Valley road that undulates over the area's rocky scrubland. The Roman scouts roam to the sidelands off the road, looking for enemy presence, but each day they return with nothing, other than an occasional sighting of a rider in the distance. On the third morning, as the army finishes another cold breakfast, one scout returns early, galloping to the command tent. The scout finds Marcus Silenus out in front, garbed in nothing but a loincloth, lifting and throwing a small boulder for exercise. "Two camps," the scout blurts excitedly. "Two camps less than a mile apart from each other! Iberians and Carthaginians, I saw them there!" He points to the southeast.

Marcus tosses the boulder aside and looks at him, unperturbed. "How many? Cavalry or infantry?"

The scout shrugs. "There were too many scouts about, so I rode back here immediately. But there are many men in each place. Thousands."

Marcus pulls the surprised scout off his saddle as easily as one might lift a child and holds him in front of his face. "Go back and find out. Do not return until you do. Take Coriolanus with you." The scout departs, and Marcus summons his tribunes for an emergency meeting. Within two hours the legions are weaving through the concealing lowland scrub, heading toward the enemy camps. The two scouts return with alarming news: the two camps are only three miles away from the Romans, in a clearing near the foothills. One is an unprotected sprawl of some ten thousand Celtiberians, who appear to be recruits. The other is a fortified camp of four thousand Libyan and Iberian infantry, backed by Numidian cavalry. Marcus calls a conference to plan their attack.

Tribune Spurius, a veteran of Cannae and Trasimene, hears the news with a measure of disappointment. "We are outnumbered by half, if their reports are correct. We should hold our place until we have reinforcements."

Acteon, Marcus' brash and haughty Master of Horse, laughs at Spurius. "Pfuff! I have a thousand cavalry. We can ride them down ourselves!" Marcus glances at Acteon, knowing he has little experience with the whirlwind Numidians and that he is eager to make his place among his famous ancestors. A man whose men are means to an end.

Marcus looks over the broken terrain about them. "If the Celtiberians merge with the Carthaginian camp, General Scipio will have to lead our entire army down here to wedge them out. We strike now." He walks over to one of the many outcroppings that seem to grow from the soil here and places his hand on it as if it were a favorite horse. "I have learned from Scipio's tactics, and Hannibal's. We make the terrain our ally. Here is how we gain advantage ...."

The sturdy ex-centurion grabs Acteon by the shoulder and drags him to a man-sized outcropping. Marcus mimics fighting with his back to the rock. "Acteon, the Numidians are very slippery. They will try to strike you from behind. Tell your men to use these rocks as protection, keeping their backs to them." He stares balefully at the impulsive young commander. "No formation attacks. Your mission is to hold the

Numidians at bay from our infantry, not destroy them. If you try, they will slip by you. Say you understand."

The haughty patrician tries to hold Marcus' demanding stare, but his gaze breaks. "As you command," Acteon replies.

Spurius has been watching this scenario with a smile on his face, but it quickly fades when Marcus pivots to him. "Spurius, we cannot hold shield-to-shield formation on this ground. Our gaps would be uneven. We will use line of sight to maintain discipline. The centurions will ensure no man advances past his fellows. Staggered rows to fill the gaps between the front lines."

Spurius unhappily looks at the furrowed ground. "The principes will have trouble stepping forward as a unit to replace the hastati."

Marcus nods. "Forget that There will be enemy penetration on broken ground, regardless. The principes are to engage any enemies who move beyond that first line, wherever it is. And the triarii take any beyond the second. We will not have Celtiberians ravaging through our cohorts. Now we go."

The Romans weave over and around the scrubby bushes, stunted trees, and ubiquitous boulders. They draw within a mile of the Celtiberian camp, and then two Numidian scouts detect the glint of Roman iron, and rush to report the assault. One gallops toward the Celtiberians, and the other plunges toward the Carthaginian camp.

Marcus knows it will not be long before the Libyans and Iberians will be upon them, so he must destroy the Celtiberians before they arrive. He double-times the legions toward the milling Celtiberians, who are hastily organizing themselves into a semblance of battle lines. As the Romans draw within a half mile of the barbarian recruits, a plumed and purpled Carthaginian commander dashes past the front of the legions and into the Celtiberian camp, coming from the direction of the Carthaginians.

By the time the Romans have crossed another quarter mile, the recruits are flowing out to engage them. There are four thousand

Celtiberian heavy infantry, followed in the rear by five thousand light infantry. Leading this mob of thousands is the Carthaginian commander and his Sacred Band. As the enemy draws near him, Marcus can see the commander looks like Hannibal himself, and he knows it is Mago, Hannibal's brother, who directs the attack.

The Romans pause at a javelin's throw from the onrushing horde. The legionnaires pull their shields next to their bodies and draw their swords, waiting.

Screaming battle cries, the barbarians dash forward and crash into the waiting Roman lines, slavering for their first Roman kills. The legionnaires methodically block and stab, then step forward around the rocks and bushes, monitoring their comrades' position so that they can maintain a line. The northern Celtiberians fight by dashing about from foe to foe, chopping at them with their two-handed greatswords, but they soon find that the broken ground makes them easy prey for the methodical Romans. Even when the knots of the inexperienced Celtiberians fight through the front infantry lines, the veteran principes are there to cut them down. After an hour of battle, the Romans have decimated the heavy infantry and are delving into the lighter ones. Mago rides about fearlessly, shouting encouragement and threats, but to no avail. The Celtiberians flee for hills and home, done with fighting the Roman machine.

The Romans barely have time to pause and reorganize before a new threat presents itself. Hanno appears, leading two thousand Libyan and Iberian infantry from the far camp, with hundreds of Numidian cavalry. Marcus orders his legions to turn and face the oncoming threat. As the cohorts wheel about, Acteon's five hundred cavalry gallop out to engage the Numidians before they clash into the infantry. Young Acteon himself leads the charge, waving his sword and shouting, eager for glory.

A milling, swirling cavalry fight ensues over the uneven landscape. The Romans use the dismount-remount tactic they learned while wintering at Tarraco, under the direction of Scipio. The riders jump off their horses when they are next to a protective rock or tree, using it to protect their backs while they slash down any Numidian that attacks them. When their foe is felled, they remount to chase down another. The lightly armored Numidians fight gamely, but the terrain hampers their deadly mobility. Many a proud African rider is left crawling in the dirt, mortally wounded.

The Romans lose scores of men as the Africans refuse to yield the field. Proud Acteon is cut down by Mago himself, lanced through the forehead as he tries to extricate his sword from a Numidian's skull. A decurion sees Acteon slide off his horse and charges his squadron of thirty equites at Mago and the Sacred Band, determined to rescue Acteon's body. The frenzied riders cut down half the Band before Mago and the rest flee to rejoin the Numidians.

Mago's two thousand foot soldiers march into the legionnaires, their center manned by phalanxes of Libyan heavy infantry. For this engagement, Marcus orders the principes to replace the hastati, and the battle takes on a new color. The veteran Libyans are as methodical and refuse to give ground. The Iberians on the flanks wield their falcatas with deadly efficiency while fending off Roman thrusts with their oblong shields. Many of the natives grab a field boulder and hurl it into the sides of their opponent helmets, stunning them for an easy killing blow. More legionnaires fall to the terrain-wise Iberians than to any foe.

The fight is a standoff for several hours, but the Carthaginian force is greatly outnumbered, and they eventually weaken. While the Roman center holds the Libyans in position, the rear cohorts deploy their newly learned mobility to split from the main legion and outflank the Iberians, sealing them in from the sides and then the rear. Soon, the Libyans and Iberians are an island in a sea of Romans, their men too densely packed to fight with any alacrity. Step by step, the methodical legionnaires cut down the circumference, stepping over the twitching corpses of their opponents to cut into the next one.

When only a few hundred Libyans and Iberians remain, a horn sounds thrice from the middle of the enemy force, and the infantrymen throw down their arms. The hastati and principes cease their attack and begin binding their opponents. The triarii oversee the capture, their long spears at the ready. Marcus Silenus pushes through the cluster of unarmed enemy, heading for their center. He comes to a frightened man in a purple tunic and silver helmet.

"Who are you?" Marcus demands.

"Hanno," he replies, "Supreme General of the armies of Carthage. Please, do not kill me!"

Marcus takes Hanno's plumed helmet from him, a souvenir of his first victory as absolute commander. "Kill you? Do not fear, 'Supreme Leader.' Your ransom will feed Rome's coffers." Marcus sniffs at the cowering man. "You have the same rank as Hannibal? Carthage is indeed doomed!"

Mago is lancing a Roman rider off his horse when he hears Hanno's horns sounding his surrender, and Mago knows the battle is lost. He shouts a retreat order to his men, and the Numidians pound away for the Carthaginian camp, relieved to cease fighting on such a awkward landscape. As the sun sets on his disastrous day, Mago leads his remaining infantry and cavalry southwest toward Gades, hoping to join Gisgo's army.

Evenfall settles over the bloody field while the victorious Romans carefully gather their fallen comrades and burn them in a mass cremation. Acteon's equites wrap his body for transport back to camp, but Marcus commands that he be burned with the rest. "He was a brave soldier, but no more so than his men, whom he put at risk," Marcus says to his surprised tribunes. "Think you his wealth made him deserving of a finer burial?"

The prisoners are put to work stripping the belongings from their perished comrades and mounding their bodies for cremation. For several Carthaginians, the anguish of tending to a friend or brother is too great; they grab a found weapon and rush at their captors, to kill them or escape—anything but become a slave. These men are summarily killed, their bodies left to the crows and dogs.

That night, the camp of Marcus Silenus is filled with the laughter of men who rejoice at cheating death another day. Marcus has dismissed his guard so he can walk alone among his soldiers. In especial, Marcus spends time with the centurions, the brothers of his soul. He grins at their rude jokes, shares their bread and wine, and laughs at their praise disguised as insults. He is at home.

It is past midnight when Marcus Silenus returns to his command tent. The commander divests himself of his battle-stained armor and lies naked upon a thinly padded pallet in the corner. As he pulls his wool cape about him, he recalls his recent visit to the spare tenement of his childhood, of the unfortunates who live there and the unfortunate he had been.

Marcus looks into the corner of his tent and sees Hanno's crested helmet gleaming in the torchlight, the flickers rippling over its dents and furrows. A wracking sob comes to him, then another, as he looks heavenward and smiles through his tears. The warrior swallows hard, pulls the cape more tightly about him, and disappears into sleep.

*   *   *   *   *

CORDOBA PROVINCE, SOUTHWEST IBERIA. Mago only has to follow the smoke to find his destination. He has led his surviving troops back toward Gades along their original line of march, knowing Gisgo will be leading his sixty thousand men that way toward the Baetis Valley. As soon as Mago sees plumes of black smoke rising in the distance, he sends his scouts to confirm his suspicions. They return with news that Gisgo's army is there, bivouacked in front of the crumbled walls of a town of Roman allies that they have just sacked and burned.

After Hasdrubal's defeat at Baecula, the town welcomed a diplomatic visit from Scipio and allied itself to his cause. Gisgo was aware that other allied towns were considering the same arrangement, so he decided to use this town as a representative lesson to any others who would betray the Carthaginian cause. And he has made his point very vividly. The main road to the town is bordered with crucifixes, each one holding a beheaded torso of one of the town's citizenry: man, woman, and child. Each victim's head lies at the foot of the cross, with a blood-scrawled Iberian sign over it reading "Where was Scipio?"

Once the town gates were rammed open, Gisgo loosed hordes of his Balearic recruits upon the town to show them the benefits of fighting for the Carthaginians. After murdering the male citizenry, the Balearics ignored troves of gold and jewels for the one treasure they desired: women. The cries lasted all through the night, and the crucifixions began in the morning.

Mago's bedraggled force joins Gisgo's men on the plains, where they are feasting on the plundered stores of the unfortunate town. Gisgo is taken aback at the news of Hanno's capture, but he is pleased that this political emissary from the Council of Elders will no longer hamper his and Mago's plans. Two days later, Gisgo and Mago march northeast toward Marcus Silenus' army, intent on wiping it out and moving to eliminate Scipio.

But the burning town's smoke has attracted more than Mago's army: the exploratores from Scipio's intelligence unit has found them out. The quartet spends the morning in the hillside trees, taking a census of the Carthaginian numbers and equipment. By afternoon they are riding back to Baecula.

Scipio receives the census with dismay, then determination: this is his chance to remove the rest of the Three Generals, and their numbers will not dismay him. He musters his thirty five thousand men and marches south to join Marcus Silenus' force. Once there, he leads the army onto a plateau above the upper Baetis, giving him a strategic advantage over any who approach. Scipio appoints Laelius as acting Master of Horse in place of Acteon, and the two soon find an ambush point among the hills in the valley entrance. Scipio sends his exploratores out to follow Gisgo and Mago's progress, and then he waits.

But Mago is the brother of Hannibal Barca, the master of ambush and entrapment, and he is not so easily fooled. When his scouts report the position of Scipio's army, Mago rides out on a reconnaissance mission and sees that Scipio's army has a height and terrain advantage, and controls the passage into the valley. This grievously disappoints him. Like Hannibal, Mago will not fight unless he has the terrain advantage, which Scipio possesses.

Mago confers with Gisgo, and the two generals decide to retreat to Gades for the remainder of the campaign season, there to add more recruits to their army. On the way, crafty Gisgo spreads tens of thousands of his men into the walled towns that are allied with Carthage. To defeat the Carthaginian army, Scipio would have to lay siege to each one, an impossible task during these waning months of the campaign season.[xxxvii]

When Scipio learns that the Carthaginians have left, he organizes an extended pursuit of them and moves his army to hunt them down. When his army encounters the first heavily garrisoned town on his way, the Carthaginian plan is revealed to him: Gisgo and Mago will not fight this year. Scipio reluctantly leads his army back toward Baecula, to prepare for winter quarters. But before he departs the area, he decides that the Carthaginians and their allies must be given their own lesson. And Lucius will be the teacher.

*   *   *   *   *

ORONGIS, SOUTH-CENTRAL IBERIA. Lucius Scipio is confused. He has tried to be diplomatic with these Iberians, riding to their town gates to request a parley. His brother has wooed many tribes to his side by simply negotiating with them. But these Bastetani, they hurl rocks at him from the walls, eagerly joining the town's Carthaginian soldiers. Lucius desperately wants to show his brother that he can be a capable commander; he cannot return to Baecula without a victory. But he does not know how to achieve it.

Lucius is there to take over Iberia's largest city of Carthaginian supporters. Orongis is a wealthy mining town that has tall stone walls, a fortress so redoubtable that the Three Generals have used it for their southern base of operations. With winter coming, Scipio does not have time to overthrow all the towns that Mago and Gisgo fortified with soldiers on their retreat to Gades. But overthrowing their most powerful one could make the region's towns more amenable to a Roman alliance. Lucius has been given the honor of securing the victory, with Laelius and Marcus Silenus there to advise him. But so far, all he has found is confusion and frustration.

That night Lucius convenes with Laelius and Marcus, pacing about as he rants his frustration. "They won't even talk to us," he complains.

"Perhaps if we offer a golden bowl as a gift. Or a white horse?" Laelius looks at Marcus, sharing a knowing look. "There are two thousand Carthaginian soldiers in that city. What would you expect, roses from the ramparts?"

"*Acta non verba* (deeds, not words)," states Marcus. "We must conquer the city, not waste our time on idle talk."

Lucius throws his hands up. "Yes, easily said! But those stone walls are thick and high, and it would take months to lay siege to the city. We would be in mid-winter!"

"Brrr, I do not welcome sitting on this frozen ground," says Laelius, hugging himself. "Eating cold porridge while the Carthaginians sit in the warmth of their city homes, coming out every now and then to hurl stones and spears at us."

"Nor do I, Laelius," scowls Lucius. "Perhaps we should focus on attacking their side gates and ramming through them. The mains are too thick, and we certainly can't ram through stone walls." The three commanders are silent as they consider these words.

"Stone?" muses Laelius. "I think you have the answer there, Lucius. Remember the old proverb our tutor Asclepius taught us? *Gutta cavat lapidem non vi, sed saepe cadendo* (A drop hollows out the stone not by force, but falling many times)?"

Lucius frowns at him. "Yes. So?"

Marcus nods. "I see the point. We do not have to break their walls. We have to break their will."

Lucius looks at Marcus, a pupil eager to please his teacher. "So they give up? Via a siege?"

Marcus shakes his head, his eyes shining with recognition. "No, not by siege, by constant attack. We will wear them out, make them think resistance is futile."

"Yes. But without wearing ourselves out," adds Laelius. "And perhaps that may be done." He fingers his brocaded cape. "Hmm … we have ten thousand infantry, and a thousand cavalry. I can see how we will 'dribble our drops' …."

Two mornings later, Lucius leads ten cohorts of three hundred men out toward the city, carrying scores of attack ladders. Behind them a century of men tow a dozen ballistae: massive, horizontal bow-like instruments that hurl large projectiles at deadly speeds. The cohorts grab the ladders and swarm at the city walls, throwing them up along the front perimeter.

Inside Orongis, the soldiers and citizens swarm to the ladders, hurling stones at those ascending and throwing out grappling hooks to pull up ladders and their legionnaires.

While the escaladers attack the walls, the ballistari crank back the thick horsehair bowstrings on their ballistae. They load boulders into the projectile channel and release the tightly drawn ropes, sending hundred-pound river stones whirring toward the walls, to pulverize ramparts and defenders.

Dozens of relentless legionnaires fight their way up the ladders to the walkway. They join handfuls of their fellows and rush into the defenders. Small battles break out all along the walls; some men fall to the sword, and others are hurled screaming over the walls. The Carthaginian veterans are not easily daunted, and eventually they beat back their attackers with their sheer numbers. They reorganize the wall defenders and throw off the assault ladders, ignoring the deadly stones that hurtle about them.

The assault continues until late afternoon. Then the Roman cornu sound a retreat, and the weary legionnaires march back to camp, leaving their ladders and ballistae. The Orongis defenders cheer mightily and hurl insults at the Romans, celebrating their defense.

Then the battle horns sound again, and the Orongis defenders watch in dismay as Marcus Silenus marches out with a fresh set of 3,600 Romans, tramping directly toward the walls. The attack resumes for another four hours, until nightfall, when the second wave of attackers retreats. The town defenders cheer again, but the cheers are more muted.

There is a short, quiet respite. Then the horns blow, and Laelius rides out with a third wave, these carrying torches. These attackers use the ballistae to hurl flaming timbers into the city. They attack the walls from the rear as well as the front, spreading out the defenders. The assault continues through the night as the soldiers and townspeople muster their dregs of energy to repel the invaders and put out the fires.

Early dawn comes silently; the night wave has finally withdrawn, and no new attackers emerge from camp. The city defenders sleep at their posts, exhausted from their continuing action—and from fear. Below them, the women and children gather bring the defenders food, but most are too tired to eat. All is blessedly quiet, for an hour.

The cornu sound, and Lucius leads out the day's first wave of attackers. They return to the battle site, pick up the ladders stacked in the rear of the field, and begin loading rocks into the ballistae.

Word spreads through the city: the Romans are attacking again. The citizenry is thrown into a panic; they heard about the massacre of resisting civilians at Cartago Nova, and of General Scipio's mercy to those who surrender peacefully. The town inhabitants gather in the square, and arguments erupt about surrendering versus resisting. Finally, a Bastetani chief stands on the temple steps and shouts that people of his tribe should follow him out of Orongis, to leave the Carthaginians and Romans to fight it out. Several Carthaginian soldiers rush to quiet him, but they are stabbed to the earth by the chieftain's tribesmen. He shouts for his people to grab a shield to protect their head and to leave their weapons behind. Hundreds rush the gates and quickly overpower the sentries. They throw open the gates and dash out into the plain, carrying children and possessions with their one free arm, the shields held over their heads.

Lucius sees hundreds of shield-bearing people running down the road toward his emplacement.[xxxviii] Then he sees the open gates behind them. "Attack!" he shouts to his Master of Horse. "Get the cavalry through those gates!" His commander leaves to follow Lucius' orders, and Lucius calls for his velites to follow him as he rides toward the oncoming Iberians. When he is within spear cast of them, he pulls up and waves his sword forward. Four hundred light infantry rush in and hurl their javelins into the crowd, throwing low to go beneath the townspeople's shields. Then they rain another round of javelins upon them, and another. Lucius stares in horror at the fallen Iberians: now he can see they have no weapons, now he can see women lying dead, now he can see the children.

He turns to shout a halt, but his cavalry thunder by him, drowning out his desperately screamed orders, trampling through those Iberians who are still standing. The Romans crash through the closing gates and pour into the town square, using their falcata-like swords to hew down any who try to stop them. The triarii infantry rush in behind the cavalry, their twelve-foot spears transfixing scores of Carthaginians.

The escaladers and legionnaires at the base of the walls see their men enter the main gates, and victory looms before their eyes. They grab picks and axes and frenziedly attack the side gates, chopping and ramming until they give way. Marcus and Laelius rush their cohorts into the town, and the city is filled with the Roman army. The last defenders on the wall throw down their arms, and the victory is complete.

Marcus and Laelius ride out to notify Lucius of his triumph. They find him squatting among the dead townspeople on the main road. Staring down at a dead child. Weeping.

When Lucius' army returns to Baecula, Scipio receives his brother with great glory, remembering to fulfill his promise to his mother. The news about Hasdrubal's death in Italia has also arrived, and he seizes upon the opportunity to build morale by his favorite means, a lavish celebration.

Scipio gives a masterful speech about his brother's valor and cleverness. Laelius and Marcus Silenus stand quietly behind their general, content to let gentle Lucius have the glory for once in his life. Scipio places a golden crown on his brother's head as the Romans and their allies cheer. But Scipio cannot help but notice the haunted look in Lucius' eyes, an inner pain that says the lovable child is gone forever, leaving a morose man in its wake.

Days later, the early winter rains begin to fall. Scipio leads his army toward Tarraco for winter quarters. He sends Marcius with a legion to the Ebro River garrison, to guard against any Carthaginian incursions to Italia. Lucius is sent back to Rome with the prisoner Hanno, that he may have the glory of leading him before the Senate and purchase some surcease from war's horrors.

For Scipio, the winter will be preparation for battle. Local tribesmen must be recruited, equipped, and trained to Roman discipline. Scipio knows that a final battle for Iberia looms in the spring, and he will once again be outnumbered. Somehow, in this quiescent season, he must figure out how to reduce that advantage, by men, weapon, terrain, or stratagem.

X. ILIPA

ROME, 206 BCE. Pomponia dances about the sunny atrium, so happy with her life. Lucius has returned safely from Iberia, bringing the Carthaginian Hanno in chains. When he appeared before the Senate with his prisoner Hanno, her son was received with great approbation—especially when he reported the millions of denarrii gained from the Baecula triumph.

And her youngest boy, once so quiet and studious, he has somehow managed to defeat the dread Carthaginians again, giving Rome some hope for the future. Pomponia was proud to see Lucius praised before the Senate, but she knows him too well to believe that Hanno's capture was not somehow his brother's doing. *My son has kept his promise. He has given Lucius a chance.*

Even Roman politics are turning in favor of Pomponia's beloved Hellenic party. Nero has proved to be the people's hero, his march to the Metauro River already a legend. At Rome's celebration of their victory, Marcus Livius' own men celebrated Nero more than their own general They made many jibes and jests about Nero, a sure sign of their regard.[xxxix] Pomponia expects Nero to be nominated for dictator by the plebs and patricians, and she has already met with him about his election.

In their covert meeting at the Temple of Bellona, Nero assured Pomponia that he will appoint Lucius Veturius, his army's Master of Horse, as his proconsul. Lucius is an equite from one of Rome's wealthiest families, but he is also a staunch supporter of the plebians' welfare and education. With Veturius' appointment, the funds Nero has surreptitiously given her will go to the commoners' causes. And the Hellenic party will rise to prominence.

As Pomponia skips around, a cloak-shrouded beggar shuffles across the street from the Scipio domus. He sees the door is propped open while a house slave sweeps off the front stoop. The beggar pauses, watching the slave sweep her way down the street walk. He looks about the street to ascertain it is empty and sidles toward the opening. His right hand is hidden inside his rags, clutching something.

Pomponia swishes by the doorway corridor, and the beggar rushes forward. As he pads up the steps, two tall Egyptian slaves materialize to block the doorway, their arms crossed. "Off with you," one of them commands, in impeccable Latin. "Now, or I take a stick to you." The beggar pauses and calmly studies the two slaves, as if he is making a decision about them. His right hand fingers something in his cloak as they take a step closer to him.

Cursing under his breath, he turns about and shuffles down the street, past the sidewalk sweeper. As he passes her, the girl puts down her twig broom and gives him a small coin. "Blessings!" she says gaily. He looks at the coin in his palm and glares at her. Then he barks a laugh.

"Gratitude," he growls, and slides past her. She stares at him for a moment, dumbfounded at his rudeness. Then she resumes her task, singing all the louder.

*   *   *   *   *

GADES, SOUTHWESTERN IBERIA, 206 BCE. "We can either attack him now before he gains strength or wait for him to attack us. There will be no other choice," states Mago.

A Turdetani chieftain jumps up from his seat at the meeting table, a large gray-haired man with a bronze caplet covering his wrist stub. "Attack now! My men grow restless for plunder," he blurts. "If we do not fight, I take them back to Corduba. The Turduli steal our livestock and women! I go kill!"

Gisgo glowers at the angry barbarian. "You think you will just pack up your eight thousand men and leave? You go nowhere without our approval, lest we send your wife and children to fight in your stead!"

He nods toward Mago on his right. "But I see the wisdom of moving now. The Scipio boy gathers allies in the north. The Celtiberian tribes are joining him."

Gisgo rises, walks to a large papyrus wall map of Iberia, and puts his finger on Baecula. "He is still in the valley, meeting with the Carpetani and Edetani. If we move on him now, we can pick the place of battle." Gisgo slowly pulls his finger southwest from Baecula to a fortress symbol in the Guadalquivir River Valley near Gades. "Here, by our garrison at Ilipa, several days north of us. We take our army there, establish position, and wait him out. What say you?"

There is little dissent to Gisgo's proposal. With spring approaching, the Carthaginians and their allies are restless to end Scipio's threat and spend the rest of campaign season purging the Roman outposts from Iberia, restoring their mines and allies. The only arguments are about the division of spoils, which is always a disputed point among the mercenaries. That issue is soon settled, and Mago and Gisgo dismiss the meeting. The Iberian leaders file out immediately, their eyes filled with excitement for battle. Masinissa, however, remains behind. He motions for Gisgo and Mago to talk with him. With a suspicious glance at each other, they sit and face the Numidian prince.

Masinissa clenches his right fist. "Syphax grows ever more powerful," he says testily. "He incurs on my tribe's boundaries. My father is too ill to fight—I have told you that." He pounds his fist on the table. "Send the Libyans with me to Numidia. Let the Romans wait until summer. I promise I will return with thrice my Numidians. We will storm over the Roman cavalry as if they were riding goats."

Mago looks at Gisgo, each waiting for the other to speak. "We did promise to help you, and that we will do," says Mago calmly. "But we cannot allow Scipio to gather strength. We squash him first, then you will have two phalanxes of our best men to aid you." Mago jabs his finger into his own chest. "I will go with you myself, by Baal's balls!"

Masinissa shakes his head vigorously. "Too long to wait. My father cannot last."

Gisgo grins at him. ""Have you forgotten our other part of the bargain?"" he says unctuously. ""Perhaps you should visit Sophonisba to refresh your memory. She is out in the back." He sees the resentment on Masinissa's face and adds, "She has inquired about you every day, you know."

In spite of himself, Masinissa's eyes gleam. "She is of some interest to me," he says offhandedly. "And it would be rude not to inquire of her welfare."

With a knowing look to each other, Gisgo and Mago stand up and leave for the door. "She is out there with her favorites," Gisgo says over his shoulder as he and Mago laugh.

The regal young prince frowns, angry with himself for being so easily manipulated. He rubs his long-fingered hands together, deciding what to do. With a deep sigh he rises and walks out the back of the meeting room, into the back lots near the stables. He sees Sophonisba there, a willowy, black-haired beauty wearing only a soggy wool tunica. She is using a sponge on a pole to scrub the sides of the gigantic Boodes, her favorite war elephant. Since arriving with her father in Iberia, Sophonisba has grown from darling child to sultry woman, so stunning she is known even among the Gauls and Celtiberians of the distant north. Masinissa's breath catches at the sight of her. *Gods help me; she is the most beautiful woman I have seen.*

He swallows and nonchalantly approaches her. "I do believe you missed a spot on the top of his head," he says.

Sophonisba's almond eyes open wide with surprise and delight. She blesses him with a broad smile. "Ah, Prince Masinissa! Perhaps you would do me the favor of reaching up there and washing it for me!"

Masinissa cranes his neck to look at the top of the elephant's head and laughs. "Perhaps I shall. Do you have a siege ladder handy?"

She laughs, takes his long-fingered hand in hers, and kisses it. "You are a welcome sight, noble prince."

"I am blessed to see you," Masinissa says, folding his long hand over hers. He feels his phallus stir against the thin linen of his robe and wills it not to rise any farther. "You know I would see you every day if I could. As my wife."

Sophonisba looks shyly at her feet. "That is ... not an unwelcome idea. But it is not mine to say." She looks solemnly into his eyes. "I must follow my father's wishes ... whatever I feel." Her face brightens. "But your alliance with us is a boon in your favor. Father speaks often of your loyalty. And he says he couldn't win the war without you and your wonderful cavalry!"

Masinissa's eyes take on a distant, troubled look. "Loyalty to him and loyalty to my people. I pray I can serve them both."

Sophonisba is about to reply when Gisgo walks in from the side of the field. "Masinissa! Mago and I would have a word with you about Ilipa. We need to discuss strategy."

Masinissa gives Sophonisba's hand a final squeeze and walks across the lot toward Gisgo. *He wants a strategy against Scipio? Expect the unexpected.* He looks over his shoulder and sees Sophonisba still watching him. She waves, and his heart constricts. *Whatever I must do, I cannot lose her.*

* * * * *

TEMPLE OF CYBELE, PALATINE HILL, ROME. Gaius Claudius Nero stands alone at the top of the temple steps, listening to the birds greet the morning. He has sent his guards out of hearing range, not knowing the topic of his meeting with Cato. Nero is still groggy from last night's victory celebrations, and he leans his head against a tall column next to the statue of Cybele, carved as a regal matron leading a chariot drawn by four lions. The general wears a simple white toga today, hoping to remain inconspicuous from passersby, even though it is still too early for any temple visitors.

Cato walks out from the interior of the rectangular little temple, clad in his customary unadorned gray tunic. He nods at the consul. "We are alone," he says to Nero, by way of greeting.

Nero looks about him. "It is a pleasure to see you again, Tribune. But why did you want to meet out here at a temple? You are certainly welcome in my house."

"I would be assured that we are not overheard," Cato replies as he studies the graceful carvings on the temple facade. "It is a beautiful building, is it not? Just built this last year, when you were out fighting in south Italia." He stares up at The Cybele. "The priests brought this statue of the Great Mother from Greece so that she could help save us from Carthage." Cato smirks. "Cybele and I have that in common: I am dedicated to saving Rome—from Hellenic corruption. So I thought it ironic that we meet here, given your Hellenic sympathies."

"You asked me out here just to point out our political differences?" says Nero irritably. "You belie your reputation for efficiency, my friend."

"Oh, there were other reasons, consul," adds Cato sarcastically. "For example, I know you have a fondness for meetings at temples. You went to the Temple of Bellona to consort with Pomponia about the hundred thousand sesterces you gave to her."

Nero stares silently at Cato. "You know of that?" he finally says.

Cato eyes him resentfully. "Hellenics are not the only ones with plebian friends. An attendant observed you. And overheard."

Nero snorts. "There was nothing to overhear. We were friends rejoicing in the victory at Metauro. If you Latins say anything else, it will be a lie."

Cato shakes his head. "Consul, you have stolen war plunder that was due the Senate and given it to Pomponia Scipio. I know this by testament of two of your own centurions, who facilitated the transfer." Cato looks away from Nero. "This is not welcome news to me," Cato says. "You may have saved Rome when you decimated Hasdrubal's force. But if I have to, I will speak about your theft in the Forum—and bring witnesses against you."

"Do your worst, boy," snarls Nero. "I am not ashamed of anything I have done. I fear not the wagging tongues of you or your cronies."

Cato shakes his head. "Fabius and Flaccus do not know of my visit. Were Flaccus to know of this, he would pack the truth with lies, I know." Cato bites his lower lip. "I feel complicit in your crime by not telling him, but you have saved Rome. You do not deserve the calumny of politicians."

Nero leans against the temple column, suddenly spent. He sighs. "Gratitude for that, anyway. So, is that all you came to tell me?"

Cato stares up at the taller man, and sighs regretfully. "You must withdraw yourself from consideration as dictator and name your fellow general, Marcus Livius, as dictator. Then I will consider this matter closed."

Nero's face flushes. "Marcus Livius! That salt merchant? I will not! He will name his patrician friends as consuls, soft-handed politicians who have no idea how to lead an army!"

Cato waits for Nero's emotion to dissolve from the air. "You know me as a man of truth. I can assure you that Lucius Veturius, your Master of Horse, will be one of the consuls named. And Livius' own Master of Horse will be the other. A Hellenic and a Latin, both honest soldiers. The two most suited to rule. When they become consuls, Livius will resign his dictatorship."

"You cannot promise such things," spurts Nero. "Livius listens to no one, much less a tribune such as yourself."

"Livius has promised me he will do all of this if I secure the honor of the dictatorship for him, though he will not know the reason you declined it." Cato raises his right hand. "I pledge this as a sacramentum militare (sacred military oath) to you, consul. May the gods take me if I lie."

The proud consul rubs the back of his bowed head, pacing about in a circle. Cato's eyes sadden at seeing the great man in such a plight, but they become stern when Nero looks back at him. "I ... I must think on this," Nero mutters.

Cato vigorously shakes his head, his lips tightly compressed. "No time for that. The elections are at the end of this week. I will speak of this matter in the Forum tomorrow, if you do not withdraw at tomorrow's Senate meeting."

Nero looks at the ground. All is silent for moments, save for the birds' chirping. "It will be so," he says then looks at Cato. "I did this only for the people of Rome. Not a coin went to me."

"You may think you serve a greater purpose," Cato says. "But theft is theft. I leave you to your conscience." He starts to walk away, then turns to look at the forlorn general. "You will be forever known as the hero of the Battle of the Metauro, a savior of Rome. That much you deserve."

Cato quickly walks down the hill and into the teeming side streets of the Forum. He walks hurriedly down a side alley until he comes to a secluded place. He leans against the wall and vomits, his arms shaking as he braces his head against the cool limestone wall.

*   *   *   *   *

ILIPA, SOUTHERN IBERIA, 206 BCE. Scipio, Marcus Silenus, Lucius Marcius, and Laelius have their first tactical meeting at their Ilipa Valley camp. The Roman army marched into Ilipa yesterday evening from Baecula, arraying themselves across a low ridge that fronts the broad valley floor. Three miles away, the Carthaginian army is dug in on a similar ridge at the exit to the valley, waiting for battle.

"What is the census?" asks Scipio gloomily, fearing he already knows the news. "Quintus! What is the camp count?"

The grizzled old centurion holds up the clay tablet in his one remaining hand, squinting at the figures in the low dusk light inside the tent. "Four Roman legions for twenty thousand men. Two allied extraordinarii for eight thousand infantry. Counting in the Celtiberians, we have ten thousand Iberian foot soldiers. And three thousand Roman and allied cavalry."

"In toto, forty-one thousand," Marcus says. "Hmph. How many do

Mago and Hasdrubal have?"

Quintus stares at some marks on the bottom of the tablet. "The scouts could not get close enough to their camp to tell. Our speculatores at Gades told us the two generals left there with sixty thousand infantry, four thousand horse, and thirty-two elephants. They were going to collect more men as they passed by those towns they garrisoned on their flight from Baecula." He shakes his head, frowning. "Likely seventy thousand in total."

"And many of those will be their Libyans and Carthaginians, the rest Iberians with a lot of seasoned Oretani and Turdetani," says Scipio. He looks at Marcus Silenus and Laelius with a grim smile. "It appears they have a slight numerical advantage."

Laelius rolls his eyes heavenward. "Yes, you could say that. And Vesuvius is a slightly tall hill. That's a lot of men over there." He looks at Scipio meaningfully. "It will require some ingenuity to defeat that horde."

"The valley floor is flat and featureless, at least," adds Marcius. "That suits our infantry. But it also pleases their Numidian cavalry."

"True, Marcius, we will have to find a way to negate that," Scipio says to the old tribune. Scipio has called in Marcius and his men from the northern Ebro garrison, knowing his former trainer at Tarraco is an expert in the new mobility tactics of the cohort formation. Scipio will have to use every man he can muster, even his treacherous Celtiberians, the men who fought against his father and uncle.

The young general paces about furiously, hands behind his back. He halts and faces his officers. "This is how I see it. If we battle the Carthaginians on the plains, neither side will have a terrain advantage, nor any element of surprise. Their Libyans and Carthaginians are experienced fighters, so they will not easily be routed. They have more elephants than we have ever seen, and almost twice our men. So as commander in chief I must ask you, do you think should we engage them? We have not established camp yet, there is still time to depart."

It is quiet for a moment, and then Marcus speaks. "What is the alternative, General?" he says. "To sneak away in the night like Carthaginians do? To go hide behind our walls?"

"Gisgo and Mago are losing money and allies to us," notes Lucius Marcius. They have to defeat you. The moment we leave, they will stalk us wherever we go."

"You have won over most of the local Iberian tribes," says Laelius. "If we were to retreat now, they would find out and leave us." He smirks. "Besides, I have some ideas on how to take care of those elephants. Remember what Flavus did to them?"

Scipio looks into each of his leaders' faces, but sees naught but resolve. And trust. He looks away for a moment, hand twitching, contemplating the enormity of what he will say.

"I agree with all those reasons, but I wanted to hear them from you. And for you to hear them from each other." He takes a deep breath. "It will be done. One final battle for all of Iberia." Marcus, Marcius, and Laelius merely nod, but their eyes betray their eagerness.

Scipio feels the chills and shaking of his returning fever: Febris will no doubt visit him, and soon. He summons himself. "Tomorrow we meet in late morning to discuss tactics, after camp construction is underway." His commanders don their helmets and swords and march out to finish their evening tasks. Scipio catches Laelius' arm as he passes by. "Do you have time for a bit of relaxation, a bit of play before everything becomes too serious? I fear I shall need that tonight."

Laelius frowns in mock anger. "What? I was planning to have my death mask made tonight! I wanted to have it done while I'm still pretty, not all hacked up by Iberian swords!" He laughs reproachfully when he sees Scipio's face. "Yes, I do jest. I swear to Jupiter, you are becoming so gravid you cannot tell a joke or a joker anymore."

After pouring out two cups of Rioja, the two take out an eight-by-eight board of squares. They cross their legs and sit on the ground to begin playing a game of latrunculi, their favorite pastime. The object of the game is to jump your stones around to pin your opponent's piece on each side so that it cannot move, in which case the stone is removed. Laelius has played the game since he was an urchin on the docks of Ostia, winning food money from the dock hands.

They play several games, and Laelius repeatedly takes Scipio's stones by flanking them so that they cannot move to the side, and then putting one of his own in front so that Scipio cannot advance. After winning another game, Laelius lifts his head from the board with a triumphant smile. It quickly fades when he sees Scipio's flushed face. "It's the fever, isn't it?"

Scipio nods, manages a tired smile. "I think I have had enough beatings for one night. I am to bed. It will be a long night ahead."

Laelius pushes himself up from the ground. Arms over each other's shoulders, they walk to the tent exit. "Do not worry, Scippy. You will think of something. … *We* will think of something. We always do!" Laelius kisses Scipio deeply and slaps his back. "Now go to bed. You don't have to be a genius until tomorrow!" Scipio laughs feebly and shuffles over to quench several candles. He topples onto his sleeping cushions. Soon he sleeps, and soon come the visions.

Scipio is back on the battlefield of Cannae, a mere boy again. He is leading his cavalry turma into their fight with the Numidian riders, who swirl about and block his men from entering into the main fray. He again sees Hannibal's trap unfold, how the Carthaginian centerlines bend inward under the Roman heavy infantry attack, and how the foolhardy Romans follow the center retreat until they are surrounded on each side. He sees Hannibal standing on a rise overlooking a sea of Roman dead, joking with his Sacred Band about the Romans' predictability.

His father Publius appears to him in his battle armor, bearing the chest and face wounds of his death during the Battle of the Upper Baetis. Publius Scipio's face is worried. "Beware the treachery of the Celtiberians," his father urges, blood trickling from his wounds. "They did flee me when I needed them most."

The camp horns sound the changing of the morning watch, and Scipio wakes groggily from his sweat-soaked bed pallet, his fever broken. He props himself upright with his arms, reflecting on his vivid dream. Febris has sent him clues for victory, but what are they? He cannot copy Hannibal's Cannae strategy; Hannibal's brother Mago would easily sniff it out. But his father was right: he must worry about the Iberians fleeing if the tide of battle turns, lead by the unstable Celtic Iberians.

Still half-asleep, the images of his night with Laelius come to mind, of laughter and roughhousing while they played their board game. He sees the pieces on the board, the different formations of the stones, of how Laelius would entrap him. And he remembers Hannibal joking with his men about the Romans. *Our predictability can be my ally*, he realizes. *The Carthaginians have used it against us. Now we will use it against them, and play our own board game.*

Scipio vaults from bed and shouts for his guards. "Summon my commanders!" he bellows. "Have them here within the hour!" Laelius, Marcus, and Marcius are soon in his tent, their faces puzzled. He dismisses everyone else from his presence and sends his guards out of earshot with orders he is not to be disturbed.

Bending over the large table map of the valley, Scipio moves the Roman and Iberian figures into position against the Carthaginian ones. "Our strategy is simple: we will put our worst against their best," says Scipio, "in ways they will not expect." Scipio explains his plan, adjusts it to their criticisms, and finally sees their faces light with enthusiasm. The morning is spent arguing over tactics, with voices alternately rising in anger and excitement, punctuated with occasional laughter.

In late afternoon Scipio's officers finally exit the command tent, hurrying to fulfill their assignments. There are new plans and orders for their tribunes, ones that will bear much explanation. No Roman has fought as they will fight.

*   *   *   *   *

ROME. Pomponia is devastated when she hears the news of Nero's refusal to become dictator and horrified when he names Livius in his stead. She storms over to his domus but he refuses to see her, and she eventually returns to her manse and sulks. With a Latin sympathizer as one of the consuls, Pomponia knows there is little hope that consul Lucius Veturius can push forward any city taxation reforms before he leaves to pursue Hannibal. There is only one avenue for political change now: the plebians. She sends a house slave out to request a meeting with her friend Corvinus, the leader of the ten Tribunes of the Plebians.

Two days later Pomponia eases out from her domus in her commoner's disguise, pushing through the vendors' shops on the Forum's main street and turns left for the Aventine Hill. She does not notice another commonly garbed figure following her at a distance, dressed in beggar's rags.

Pomponia weaves through the bustling Aventine and takes the winding temple trail up through the trees, passing by several small groups of descending worshippers. Finally she comes to the Aventine Triad temple dedicated to Ceres, Liber, and Libera, the patron gods of plebians. Corvinus Lucinius is there waiting for her, standing inside the marble columns of the small, circular temple. The old fisherman is still garbed in the odiferous and stained tunic he wore in his morning's work at the docks, but he carries himself with a Senator's dignity as he walks down to greet Pomponia, kissing her lightly on the cheek.

As they embrace, a shabby figure materializes from the column behind them. Flaccus' hired assassin dashes at them, casting off his beggar's garb. The sicarius clutches his sixteen-inch dagger, prepared for a fatal plunging stroke. He raises it over his head, and he closes on Pomponia, aiming for her heart. Corvinus hurtles himself between Pomponia and the man, grasping the assassin's sword arm with his left hand and clasping the man's right with the stubbed fingers of his other. With a strength born of his years pulling heavy fishing lines, the old fisherman stands the assassin up and bends him backwards. The sicarius eventually goes to one knee, but there is a sudden shrug of movement from him, and Corvinus falls sideways, pierced through the heart.

Pomponia has clambered to her feet, but the killer is on her, knocking her onto her back and crawling onto her. She reaches inside her robe for one of her throwing knives, but the Illyrian grasps her wrist and twists it out of her grasp. "I was told of your little knifey tricks, bitch," he exults. He pins her struggling arms with his knees. "This is from Flaccus," he says as he and eases his razored blade into her throat.

The sicarius yells and grasps at the back of his neck, and looks at his blood-filled hand. An aspen-shaped throwing knife clatters to the marble steps. He screams as another knife point thunks into his shoulder and wobbles out as he grabs it. Her hands free, Pomponia reaches quickly into her sleeve and yanks out a double-bladed knife. She thrusts it into his bowels, pulling it sideways with all her strength to cut across his lower stomach. The Illyrian screams in agony and falls off her, clutching at the intestines that protrude from his cut, his feet kicking futilely.

Pomponia scrambles up and sees Amelia facing her, hands pressed to her mouth. Her eyes are glassy with terror as she watches the sicarius writhe on the ground. "I just wanted to follow you, to see what you were doing," Amelia babbles. "I didn't mean to spy, but I thought maybe you were in danger, sneaking about without anyone to follow you. I did like you taught me, threw them hard. But they didn't stick. I didn't throw them very hard. I should have put one through his skull, the bastard. ... I'm sorry."

Pomponia dabs some of the blood from the front of her robe and walks over to kick the moaning Illyrian. She raises a trembling hand to smooth her hair and pulls her old clothes over her raiment. Composed, she kisses Amelia on the cheek. "I knew not your courage. I am proud to call you daughter." She grasps Amelia's hand and quickly pulls her down a side trail. They have not gone far when they hear the screams of someone discovering the assassin. "We must go," Pomponia says, her arm around Amelia's shoulder, gently guiding her forward. She touches the spot where the knife was on her neck, shuddering. "This was Flaccus' doing," she growls. "I swear to Bellona, sister of Mars, this will be a debt thrice paid."

*   *   *   *   *

ILIPA, SOUTHERN IBERIA, 206 BCE. The Romans are cooking their morning porridge when they hear the camp trumpets sound the alarm: the Carthaginians are coming. The legionnaires rush to put out their cooking fires, but the centurions pass through them and tell them to take their time and finish their food. They know this will be their men's only meal of the day, and it is crucial to sustaining energy during their battle. The Romans return to their simple repasts, but many walk to the front of the camp walls and look out anxiously at the thin dark line stretching out across the plain. The Carthaginians are there, massing in battle formation, challenging the Romans to come forth.

Gisgo is in the center of his army, surrounded by his staunch Libyans, the battle lines stretching out of sight on either side. Rhodo Gisgon is at his side, exuberant with anticipation. The center Libyans are flanked on each side by thousands of Iberian infantry, impatiently pounding their shields for battle. To the far left of Gisgo stands Mago and his thousands of Libyan and Sacred Band cavalry, waiting to charge. On the right Masinissa commands his proud Numidians; they dash about in circles and chase each other across the warm dusty plain, restless for engagement.

Gisgo barks an order, and the elephants come forward, filling a column on each side of the Libyans. Gisgo intends to send the elephants first, to wreak shock and awe on the Roman front lines, destroying their disciplined formations.

For hours, the Carthaginians wait for the Romans to appear. As the afternoon sun creeps toward the horizon, Gisgo orders the men back to camp. Slowly, the vast force turns about. When they start to march back to camp, the Roman army appears in the distance, tramping steadily toward them. The Carthaginian horns recall battle formations, and the army hastily resumes its position as the Romans close in. Mago and Gisgo can see Scipio in the center, riding on a white horse, his red cape flowing. Marcus Silenus and Marcius march behind him, directing their Roman and allied legions. They see Laelius riding a black stallion on the flank, blindingly resplendent in his burnished bronze armor and gold embroidered tunic, waving on his Roman cavalry.

Scipio halts the army within a half mile of the Carthaginians. Gisgo glares across the distance at Scipio, willing him to attack. *Why are they coming out here so late?* he wonders. He shakes his head and commands his men to sustain their formations. For two hours, as the shadows lengthen over the vast forest of spears and helmets, the mighty armies remain poised and motionless, the tension palpable. The only sounds are the scattered challenges and insults hurled from both sides, punctuated with nervous laughter at a particularly telling comment.

The sun begins to set, and Mago signals for a return to camp. The Carthaginians file back in, looking over their shoulders at the motionless Romans, puzzled at their un-Roman behavior. Many tell themselves the Romans are afraid of them, but in their hearts they know better.

The scenario repeats itself three days in a row. The Carthaginians march out early and challenge the Romans to battle. The Romans march out toward the end of the afternoon and pause within a quarter-mile of their enemy. Both sides wait for hours in the withering heat, and then the Carthaginians leave at dusk's onset.

After the Romans return on the third day, Scipio calls his officers to him. "I think Mago and Gisgo are at the end of their patience. They will attack tomorrow or the next day, regardless of what time we come out. It is time to spring the trap."

Marcus Silenus steps to Scipio's side and faces the officers. "You know what you are to do," he says sternly. "Get your men to sleep early. Tomorrow is the day of our lives." There are scattered questions, and then the officers stride out, conversing animatedly.

Scipio watches them leave, his right hand twitching. When everyone is gone, he goes to a corner of his tent and stands at his portable lararium (altar), bowing before the pottery figurines of his family and ancestors. He pours some wine on the ground as a sacrifice and prays: *Fortuna, come to us tomorrow. Help the Carthaginians sleep long and soundly.*

An hour before dawn, the legionnaires wake to the sounds of soft clinking: the cavalry are quietly bridling their horses for a dawn raid.

As instructed, the men crawl out from their eight-man tents and consume a heavy breakfast of bread, fruit, olive oil, and cold porridge. They fill themselves with water and run to the latrine trenches. Time is short; they must be on the march by daybreak.

The rising sun dapples the thickly clouded sky as Laelius trots out from camp, riding at the head of the Roman and allied cavalry. Allucius, prince of the Oretani, rides at his right. The prince captains his remaining thousand riders, men eager to avenge their fellows' death. Thousands of velites ride on the backs of the horses, their sling bags filled with large pebbles, their packs carrying a brace of javelins.

The cavalry dust has hardly settled on the ground before it is again disturbed by the trampings of thirty-eight thousand infantry Every able-bodied man is leaving camp as Scipio seeks to maximize the striking force of his outnumbered army. Zaragoza stomps along in front of his thousands of hoary Belli warriors, swinging his battle axe as if it were a toy, laughing with his two axe-wielding sons. Zargoza casts a disdaining eye at the Ilergetes marching next to him.

Mandonius, their leader, returns the stare. "You watch how we kill," he shouts at Zaragoza. "You learn something."

The Ilergetes laugh, and Zaragoza spits on the ground. "We see who has the most heads come sundown!" he shouts. His stout young sons wave their fearsome weapons and scream, anxious for glory and plunder.

Colchis' northern Celtiberian tribesmen tramp along on the other side of the Ilergetes, tall and heavily muscled men hefting double-edged greatswords. Scipio visited Colchis two months ago during his winter quarters, at which time the rangy old chieftain pledged his men to Scipio for the promise of self-rule. The Celtiberians ignore the Iberians, their cold eyes fixed on the horizon, looking for the first signs of an enemy to fight.

As Scipio's army closes in on the Carthaginian camp, the enemy soldiers scramble madly out of their tents, shocked awake by a frantic chorus of battle horns. Mago stands outside his command tent, wearing only a linen sleeping tunic, shouting for his officers. The Carthaginian forces hastily don whatever armor and weapons they can grab as their commanders scream for them get to their formations. Without taking food or water, the soldiers scramble to the alignments they have mustered for the last three days to counter the Roman formations.

As Mago and Gisgo's men rush to the front of the camp, the Iberian, Libyan, and Numidian cavalry thunder past around them, rushing to the fight. They do not have far to go: Laelius is rampaging the Roman cavalry about the earthworks in front of the camp, joined by Iberians led by Indibilis and his young cousin Allucius. The Roman horsemen hurl their javelins into approaching riders, saving their last ones to duel with their mounted opponents. Their Iberian allies aim their long lances with both hands, their shields over their backs. They spear many an unwary Carthaginian rider, crashing them to the earth. The velites jog in toward the battle, having dismounted earlier to give the cavalry the element of surprise.

The cavalry battle seesaws for a short while. The Romans break through into the front of the camp, but the Carthaginians regroup and drive them out onto the plain. Then the velites tramp in to bolster the cavalry, and the tide turns. The light infantry wield their slings to great effect on the lightly armored Numidians, striking them in the head as they dart about, their elusiveness no escape from a speeding missile.

The cavalry and velites push the enemy back into their camp, back into their own men rushing into formation. Then the deadly Balearics arrive and sling their volleys into the Roman forces, felling scores of them, and the battle moves out again into the plains.

By now, Mago and Gisgo have finished organizing their infantry and elephants. They ride out in front of the army to assure the troops are arranged as they were the previous days: Libyan infantry in the center, Iberians on each side of the Libyans, and Numidian and Iberian cavalry at the end of each side. They ready their men to help their cavalry when they hear the sound of Roman cornu in the distance.

The Roman cavalry and light infantry suddenly fly back toward their camp, and Mago and Gisgo begin to wonder if the attack was no more than a raid. Then, as the cavalry dust settles, the two commanders can see a constellation of weapons and armor glinting in the distance, and they know this no mere skirmish. Soon, the Romans' legionary and cohort standards come into view, tall gilt poles with the emblems of an eagle, ox, boar, and wolf for each of the four legions, with a sea of bobbing poles with cloth squares and numbers for the cohorts. Scipio's army is coming again.

Mago is puzzled at the sight because the standards are displayed on the right and left flanks of the half-mile wide army line, not in the center. He turns to Gisgo and points out toward the approaching lines. "Their legions aren't in the center! What do we do?"

"What the fuck can we do?" Gisgo shouts angrily, his face red with frustration. "We can't change formations—we'd expose our flanks! Gods be cursed!"

As Scipio's army closes upon the Carthaginian front lines, the generals realize their fears are true. The Belli, Ilergetes, and Celtiberian infantry are arrayed in loose squares in the center, where the Romans had been the past three days. Now, two Roman legions and an allied legion are on each side of the tribesmen. Contrary to military tradition, the Romans have put their legionnaires, the heart of the army, on the flanks.

Mago frowns at the surprise arrangement, but Gisgo pushes his shoulder. "It is not to worry. We outnumber them." He waves for one of his Sacred Band commanders to come to him. "Bring up the elephants!" he shouts. The elephants trundle out four abreast, flanking the Libyan infantry in the center. The elephants' mahouts ride astraddle their beasts' necks, ready to stampede them into the enemy.

Scipio trots along in front of the two legions on the right, with Marcus Silenus fronting the two on the left. The Romans flank their Celtiberian and Iberian allies in the center, leaving them little room to escape or retreat, other than running into the Romans behind them. Scipio has made a move worthy of a win at latrunculi, moving pieces to give him the personnel mismatches he desires. His next move will be to pin the Carthaginians, and he knows it will be much trickier.

When his army is just out of enemy sling range, Scipio raises his right arm, and the cornu sound a halt. The army stands there, waiting, as the hot spring sun rises higher in the sky. Scipio's Iberians and Celtiberians stir about restlessly, cursing and shouting at the thousands of Libyans across from them. The legionnaires and Italia allies stand silent and calm, knowing the purpose to their inaction, conserving their energy.

The two armies stalemate each other for several hours as the cloudy, humid day grows ever longer and warmer. The Carthaginians' deprivation of food and water begins to tell. Some soldiers waver in line; others crouch or sit, prompting their commanders to curse them upright. In particular, the cold-weather northern tribes wilt in the heat.

After some hours, Scipio decides the deprivation and temperature have had their desired effect; he knows the time is ripe. There is still enough daylight left for a complete victory—for one side or the other.

Scipio reaches into his side pouch and takes out a small bronze icon of a woman with eagle's wings spreading out from her back. He remembers Amelia's words when she gave it to him as he left Rome to return to Iberia. *This is Nike, the Grecian goddess of victory. She blesses those with strength, speed, or guile. You, my love, have all three. Use them and she will surely bless you.*

Scipio grasps the Nike figure tightly in his fist, opens his hand for one last look, kisses it, and restores it to his pouch. He scans the enemy lines stretching out of sight to his left, at the two columns of elephants tramping for release, and at Mago and Gisgo atop their chargers in the center. He pulls out his falcata, takes a deep breath, and waves it into the air. The battle horns sound the charge.

Scipio's Iberian and Celtiberian center slowly marches forward, a step at a time, directly toward the redoubtable Libyans. The legions on the flanks, however, march briskly forward, moving ahead of their center, heading straight for the enemy Iberians that flank the Libyans. Gisgo rides over to Mago, waving his arm at the approaching Romans. "They're attacking the Iberians! Get our Libyans after them!"

Mago shakes his head. "We can't! We'd expose our backs. They have to hold the center."

Gisgo curses in frustration. "Then I'm sending the elephants!"

Gisgo shouts orders to two of his Sacred Band officers, and they gallop over to the elephant columns. The elephants trundle forward toward the Romans, intent on crashing their lines to make them easy prey. The Romans continue their march forward, distancing themselves from the slow-moving Iberians in the center. As the elephants near the legions, hundreds of triarii dash out from behind the principes and hastati. Running forward with their twelve-foot spears, the old veterans head straight for the elephants. Scipio has heard about Flavus' brave charge into the elephants at the Battle of Canusium, and he has incorporated the tactic. Having studied the elephants' positioning for three days, he knows exactly what to do.

Operating in units designated for each elephant, the senior infantry spear down the mahouts, then goad the elephants toward the Carthaginian cavalry on the flanks. Bellowing their anger, the pachyderms stampede toward the Numidians and Iberians. The elephants crash into Mago and Gisgo's cavalry, throwing them into milling disorder. As the elephants stampede about, the legionnaires move in to clash with the confused Iberian infantry, methodically cutting through their disorganized lines.

With his infantry occupying the Iberians on the flanks, Scipio signals for his cavalry to attack again. The cavalry bursts out from behind the legions, with Laelius leading the Roman cavalry on a looping turn around the left edge of the Carthaginian army, as another cavalry officer does the same on the right. The Roman cavalry hurtles past their distracted Numidian and Iberian opponents and turn to envelop the Iberian infantry from the rear, delving into their disordered ranks. The velites follow their cavalry and strike into the rear lines, pushing the remaining Iberians toward the center.

By this time the Libyan and Sacred Band infantry in the center are engaged with the fierce Celtiberians and Iberians, and can offer little help to their allies. Slowly, the Carthaginian army is pushed together and pushed backwards, leaving a trail of bodies with each step of retreat.

Mago gallops off to muster the cavalry for a counterattack. Gisgo fearlessly rides to the front lines of his Africans and exhorts them to retreat in order, maintaining their phalanx formation. Fighting with each step they take, the Libyan and Carthaginian infantry fell many of the Iberians who face them, even as the Iberians at their sides begin to retreat past them toward camp.

Rhodo is in the center of the staunch Africans, fighting like a demon possessed, intent on driving the Iberians back. He spies Zaragoza at the forefront of his troops, splitting the brains of a Sacred Band officer. Rhodo shoves his way through the fighters and rushes at the Belli chieftain.

As he levers his axe from the Carthaginian's head, Zaragoza sees the sinewy warrior rushing at him, the purple phoenix imprinted on his snow white cuirass. Zaragoza knows this man must be a champion. With a roar of enthusiasm he rushes at Rhodo, swinging his axe over his head. Quick as a striking snake, Rhodo dives under Zaragoza's charge and stabs him in the side as he passes. Zaragoza roars in pain but quickly spins about, grinning at his grim-faced opponent. He steps forward more deliberately and aims a low swing at Rhodo's head. Rhodo blocks the blow with his shield, but the force of the blow knocks him sideways. He stabs his sword at Zaragoza's chest, but the Belli knocks the blade aside, drops his axes, and grabs Rhodo's sword arm. The mighty Zaragoza slowly twists Rhodo's arm back until his sword falls, pushing him to his knees.

The NightBringer grimaces in pain as a grinning Zaragoza pushes farther, intent on breaking his arm. So intent is he on his kill, Zaragoza does not notice the gleaming steel edge on Rhodo's round shield. As the chieftain leans over farther, Rhodo thrusts his shield edge up into Zaragoza's neck, its razored edge slicing into his jugular. Zaragoza's eyes widen with alarm as he grasps at his burbling throat. Rhodo springs up and saws his shield deeper into the chieftain's neck, using it like a knife. Zaragoza's head falls back between his shoulders, dangling from a single scrap of skin, and he is dead before he hits the ground.

The Belli's two sons cry out and rush at the Carthaginian, tears of rage on their face. Rhodo coolly hurls his javelin through the face of the nearest youth and dispatches the second with a thrust to his throat. He leaves the three dead men to return to the cheering Africans on the front line and stands in front of them, challenging any enemy to confront him. One after the other, Rhodo cuts down any Iberians who dare venture out, refusing to retreat. The Libyans and Carthaginians rally behind him and attack with renewed vigor, stalling the Romans' victory momentum. The fighting pauses as both infantries exchange front-line fighters.

During the respite, a solitary Roman figure comes from the left flank of the line, striding purposefully through the twenty-foot space between the armies, heading toward Rhodo. The Carthaginian champion is leaning on his shield when he sees the Roman approaching.

"You at last!" Rhodo shouts. "Our time has come." He turns to the Africans. "This one is mine."

Marcus Silenus closes in on Rhodo, and the Carthaginian steps to the middle of the opening between the armies. Marcus had been leading the attack on the Carthaginian flanks when he saw the center's retreat slow, and then stop. He saw the phoenix-crested figure at the head of the African lines and knew it could be only one man, the one he fought to a standstill at Cartago Nova—whom he knew he would face again.

Marcus leaves the infantry charge to his captains and rides behind the Iberians' front lines until he is opposite Rhodo, where he dismounts and enters the opening between the two armies. As he draws within six feet of Rhodo, he raises his scutum high and draws his falcata. "To the death!" he shouts. Rhodo nods, understanding the gist of Silenus' message.

Rhodo jogs forward and immediately rams his round shield into Marcus' rectangular one. The two infantries watch raptly, cheering on their champion, their conflict forgotten. The combatants dance about each other, blocking thrusts with their shields and lunging with quick counterthrusts. Both know there will be no easy openings for a kill stroke; this will be a fight of attrition.

In a short space of time, Marcus is bleeding from a dozen nicks and cuts. Rhodo dances from his thrusts and counters with lightning speed, levying quick slashes into Marcus' unprotected legs and arms. *This is like fighting a serpent,* Marcus thinks, unperturbed. He grimly stalks the elusive Rhodo, who seems to be content with playing a waiting game, looking for just the right opening while his opponent bleeds out his energy. Marcus knows that eventually the trickles of blood will weaken him quickly in this hot sun, and he must soon act. As Rhodo essays a quick charge, Marcus leaps forward and rains sword blows upon his shield, the field ringing with the force of his blows. Rhodo retreats under the barrage, keeping his shield in front of his face, moving sideways to make Marcus follow him. When Marcus Silenus hews out a section of Rhodo's steel-edged shield, Rhodo swipes his sword broadside onto Marcus' fist, and the blade crunches his knuckles. The falcata falls from his bleeding hand.

A predatory smile crosses Rhodo's face. He steps over the sword and rushes at Marcus Silenus, his blade a flick of lightning as it gashes Marcus' chest and shoulder. Marcus retreats behind his shield, twisting it rapidly to block the quick strikes, stepping carefully so that he does not slip in his own blood. He can feel his strength ebbing. He must use his own element of surprise, something the Carthaginian would not expect from a Roman.

As Rhodo aims a telling thrust at his face, Marcus raises his shield to block it. Shielded from Rhodo's view, he darts his hand behind his back and pulls a small throwing knife from his belt as he retreats, concealing it in his palm. Marcus lowers his shield just enough to see over it. As Rhodo shoves his shield into Marcus' scutum, the Carthaginian's shield drops beneath his face for an instant, and an instant is all the old warrior needs. With a snap of his wrist, he flings the leaf-shaped blade into Rhodo's eye socket, and it disappears into his head up to the handle. Rhodo has only time enough to touch the blade before Marcus is at him with his second knife, gashing his throat open. The NightBringer slumps to the earth, choking out his life.

Gasping for breath, Marcus retrieves his sword and looks at the Africans, who stare dazedly at their fallen champion. Marcus turns toward his Iberians and waves the sword over his head. "Advance!" he screams, and the chieftains echo his call. The Iberians charge forward and buckle the lines of the dispirited infantry, and the Libyans and Carthaginians begin a desperate flight toward camp.

On the right wing, Scipio has seen the Carthaginian lines retreat and then stiffen, unaware of Rhodo's presence. When the enemy center ceases their retreat, he rides about through his cavalry lines, urging them into the crumbling flanks of the enemy Iberians about the center. Then, Scipio sees the enemy center again retreat, and he becomes a man possessed, sensing victory. He charges headlong into the Iberian infantry, forcing his cavalry to follow him.

The Roman cavalry stampede through the foot soldiers, skewering hundreds with their javelins, cutting down others with their swords. The onslaught is too much for the Iberians. They collapse toward the fleeing Africans, and a mob retreat ensues. Scipio rides over to the thousands of velites who attacked the Carthaginian rear and urges them into pursuit. The lightly armed young soldiers chase after the unprotected backs of their retreating enemy, and hundreds fall to the young men's javelins. The enraged Belli seek to avenge the death of Zaragoza, and they swarm murderously into the retreating Africans, followed by the Ilergetes and Celtiberians.

Gisgo screams for order, riding from Iberians to Africans, but fear has taken command. The enemy forces scramble for the low hills that lead into their camp, leaving the road paved with tens of thousands of their dead. Mago's Turdetani allies break through the Romans on the right flank and flee toward the forested hills, heading back to their tribal lands. The Romans allow them to flee unharmed, following Scipio's dictum to spare future allies. Carthage's other Iberian allies see them flee unmolested and follow suit.

Scipio finds Laelius on the far flank, exhorting his cavalry to pursue the escaping Numidian and Iberian riders. "We have them," Laelius exults, his bloodied face radiant. "This is their ending!"

Scipio looks back at him with a commander's face, grim and unyielding. "Storm the camp. Do not stop until all are dead or in chains."

Laelius nods, a bittersweet smile on his face. "Okay, Scippy—General Scipio. Death and destruction, it shall be."

Fighting in the midst of a maelstrom of Laelius' cavalry, Masinissa watches the retreat of the main Carthaginian force. He grasps the fate of the battle, and he has a quick decision to make: stay and fight, risking his men, or desert the defeated Carthaginians, losing his chance for Sophonisba's hand. He charges back into the fight, lancing down several of the Roman cavalry that swarm about his men.

Then Masinissa watches a knot of his riders cut down by cavalry encirclement. He sees the Romans' Iberians riding into the fray, beginning to enclose his cavalry and limit their mobility. He sees the loss of his men, and himself, and Numidia, should he stay and fight. Masinissa grabs his saddle horn and blasts three short notes, sounding the retreat. His hornsmen echo the command, and he dashes toward the hills, waving his men to follow him, tears streaming down his face.

The Carthaginian army is in full-scale retreat, men dropping arms and armor to run faster. Scipio watches his legionnaires and allies stream by him, eager for revenge upon a weakened foe. Satisfied, Scipio calls Laelius and Marcus to his side. "Now is our time," the general exults. "Maintain an orderly attack, but do not stop until we are out through the other side of their camp!"

Several raindrops splash on the three commanders, then the drizzle becomes a stream, and finally a torrent. A thunderstorm pours over the field of battle, blinding the pursued and the pursuers. Horses and men struggle through the thick mud, walking on bodies to keep their footing. Laelius shakes his head. "This does not look like it will go away."

Scipio stares up into the sky, eyes blinded by the downpour. "The gods have sent us a sign. There has been enough killing today."

Marcus looks sideways at him. "*Enough* is when there are no more to kill," he says.

Scipio issues the retreat command via his field tribunes, and the horns sound the recall. The drenched and weary Romans cease their slaughter and slowly turn about, marching in formation back to camp.

As dusk settles, Scipio arrives at his command tent and removes his weapons. He washes the blood from his limbs and walks to the front of the tent to await his officers. Laelius is the first to arrive, running headlong into Scipio's tent to bathe, stripping off his wet clothes and wriggling into a tunic. Marcus Silenus approaches the tent on foot, seemingly oblivious to the rain. He steps inside and removes his battered helmet. Then he pulls out a large scrap of cloth from his belt and carefully places it on the map table. It is a white linen square with a red-purple phoenix on it. Scipio and Laelius nod in salute, knowing its source.

A horse's whinny brings Scipio to the tent entrance. He sticks his head out and sees a bandaged Oretani chieftain slumped in his saddle, holding the reins of a horse with a body tied face down across it. Scipio walks out, lifts up the head of the corpse, and looks into Allucius' sightless eyes.

Scipio stands there for a minute, stroking his young friend's hair as if he were putting him to sleep. He gently releases his head and returns to his comrades in the tent. "Allucius is dead," he intones and pours a cup of wine. Laelius and Marcus Silenus bow their heads and follow suit. They spill a bit onto the ground for the gods and drink a tribute to their fallen comrade, draining their cups. All is quiet for a minute, then Scipio looks up at his two commanders, his face baleful. "Tomorrow, we end this thing." They raise their cups in acknowledgement as the rain tattoos the weathered tent roof.

The next day, as the Roman army organizes for a final assault on the Carthaginian camp, the day scouts return with alarming news: Mago and Gisgo escaped under cover of night, moving their army through the Baetis River Valley for Gades. Scipio is buckling on his breastplate when Laelius gives him the news. He immediately summons the senior legionary tribunes and tribal chieftains. "The Carthaginians have fled their camp. Laelius will lead our cavalry after them, and the velites will follow." He summons Laelius to face him, that the officers may witness his orders to Laelius. "You are to catch the Carthaginians and engage them on the march, harassing them until our army can catch up to you."

Scipio gestures for Marcus Silenus. "We will strip the army down to a basic pack, as we did on the march to Cartago Nova. Five days of cold provisions—no more. If we do not catch them by then, we will starve until we do!" After receiving some final mustering orders, the officers dash to reorganize their men. Two hours later, the cavalry ride out from the camp, followed by the velites. By early afternoon Scipio leads the heavy infantry out on a double-time march, determined to catch the Carthaginians.

The pursuit plan works perfectly. Laelius' Roman cavalry soon catch up to the Carthaginians and instigate a series of attacks and skirmishes that slow Mago and Gisgo's march. The velites catch up to the cavalry, and the skirmishes develop into small battles as Mago and Gisgo have to put their men into battle formation to defend themselves, slowing them further.

The next morning, Scipio's infantry catches the Carthaginians as they attempt to find a fording point across the broad Baetis River. With a superior force against a disorganized enemy, there is no need for subtle strategy, only killing determination. Scipio leads the charge toward the Carthaginians' disordered ranks as his cavalry rushes to keep up with him.

The Roman and allied riders penetrate the flanks of the remaining Iberians, cutting them down from behind. The infantry clashes with the Libyans and Carthaginian soldiers, but they fight tenaciously, reluctant to besmirch their honor by fleeing again. After an hour the Africans give ground to overwhelming numbers, and their phalanxes begin to break apart. Sensing defeat, the remaining Iberians flee from the conflict. The Roman cavalry charges into the Carthaginian infantry, and the slaughter begins, the fight devolving into little more than the butchering of cattle.[xl]

Mago takes his remaining Sacred Band soldiers and flees by boat, determined to reach Gades. As his staunch Libyans fight to buy him time, Gisgo leads the last 6,000 men up a steep ridge for a final stand,

where they built a makeshift defense upon the highest of the hills.[xli]
The Roman army essays the steep hill several times but is repulsed. As
night draws close, Scipio calls a halt to the futility. He calls Marcus
Silenus to his side.

"You are to stay here until you take that hill, and all upon it," Scipio
orders. "I leave you with two legions and a thousand cavalry." Marcus
nods his agreement. Scipio starts to walk away, then suddenly whirls
about, his face a stone. "Accept no requests for 'peace talks' or
surrender! They used that trick on Nero."

Marcus looks at him wonderingly, studying the stern man who has
replaced the boy. "But what if they throw down their arms?" Marcus
can see Scipio's right hand shake as he struggles with his decision.

Reflexively, Scipio reaches into his belt pouch and fingers the Nike
figurine from Amelia. "Very well," he finally says, with no small
measure of regret. "Imprison them. But kill any who try to escape."

Marcus spins on his heel and marches off, and Laelius walks up
behind Scipio. "I heard you talking to him," Laelius says, his voice
heavy with concern. "I thought you would have wearied of such a
slaughter, with all your nightmares about Cartago Nova."

Scipio stares straight ahead, eyes unblinking. "I kill to kill the killing.
We will not allow this to turn into Italia's fourteen-year war." He
shrugs his shoulders and forces a wan grin. "The nightmares will
continue anyway, my friend. At least they will have different
characters."

* * * * *

Three days after Ilipa, Scipio is leading his victorious army on a long
march back to Tarraco, stopping to commandeer the Carthaginian
garrisons that surrendered to him, replacing Carthage's network of
allies with his own. There are still some holdouts to the north and west,
but he will deal with them in time.

Scipio's army is approaching the Ebro River when his scouts return
with news that thousands of Numidians are arrayed on the plains,

waiting for the Romans' approach. Laelius is at Scipio's side, and he becomes excited. "The Numidians are back! I can send out our cavalry with the velites on their backs," he exclaims. "It worked well at Ilipa."

Scipio shakes his head. "Numidians standing quietly on a plain? That is not their style. Perhaps they are inviting a parley. Let us see if Masinissa leads them."

"It could be a trap, you know," adds Laelius.

Scipio shakes his head. "Were it a Carthaginian force, I would be more worried," he replies. "But this is not Masinissa's war. He fights only for aid to defend his tribe."

Laelius puts his hand on Scipio's shoulder. "I've been fighting against that raiding bastard for two full moons! He attacked your father's army at Castulo—for all we know, he killed Publius himself! How can you trust him?"

"Masinissa may switch loyalties, but he is not treacherous. He keeps his word until he gives it again." Scipio sighs. "Besides, I cannot afford the luxury of revenge."

Scipio's army halts their march when the Numidians come into view, hordes of the world's best horsemen lined up before them. A solitary rider approaches the Roman lines.

Scipio squints to see who it is. When he sees it is Masinissa, riding alone, Scipio summons one of his interpreters and trots out between the front lines. "Hold!" he shouts to his guard. As Masinissa draws near, Scipio sees that he is unarmed, and Scipio raises his right hand in greeting.

"Hail, Masinissa, Prince of Numidia," says Scipio gravely. The tall, lithe prince awkwardly raises his hand in greeting, as if the act was unfamiliar to him.

"Hail, King Scipio," he says, and the two awkwardly clasp forearms. When he hears the word "king," Scipio knows the purposes of Masinissa's arrival: capitulation and alliance.

"I come in peace. I no longer fight for Carthage," says Masinissa.

"And of what import is that to me?" says Scipio, knowing its import.

"You are a man of honor. You did free my nephew Massiva, without ransom or punishment. That I have not forgotten." He sweeps his arm to take in his thousands of riders. "My men and I would join forces with you, against the Carthaginians."

A brief smile flits across Scipio's face. "Against Hanno and Mago? It may be a bit too late for that now, noble prince."

A knowing smile crosses Masinissa's face. "Iberia is yours, but you are not stopping there, are you?"

Scipio looks away, ignoring the question. "Of certitude, I would welcome your cavalry. What seek you in return?"

"My father is dead," Masinissa says bluntly. "Syphax's tribe is taking our land. I would have you support our tribe to overthrow him and make me king of a unified Numidia." Masinissa holds a spread hand in Scipio's face. "I will bring you five thousand more Masslyles to join me. We will be an army unto ourselves."

"I cannot pledge to overthrow Syphax," Scipio states. "But I pledge to give you my support to unite Numidia. And I promise you will gain much from our alliance."

Masinissa bows his head forlornly. "I believe you, Publius Cornelius Scipio. But I fear I will have already lost that which is most precious to me, just by joining you."

Scipio looks inquiringly at Masinissa. When he adds nothing, Scipio continues. "Well then, take your men off horse while I address my men about your ... conversion. Then follow us to Tarraco. We will make our plans there."

With the Numidians in tow, Scipio's army continues its victory march on to Tarraco. Marcus Silenus soon joins Scipio there, entering the costal fortress with several thousand captives, although Gisgo had escaped him. For Marcus' defeat of Rhodo, Scipio awards him the coveted corona aurea, a gold crown given to a legionnaire who defeats a powerful enemy in single combat. But Marcus is abashed that Gisgo escaped down the Baetis River during their battle. He tries to return the crown, much to Laelius' awed amusement. Scipio adamantly refuses to take it. Soon, he sends Marcus and Lucius back to Rome with the captives, to gain the honor of the victory.

Summer shades into a peaceful fall as Scipio sows the seeds of a Roman empire. He reinforces Marcius' garrison on the Ebro, making it a potent and permanent presence in northern Iberia. And he begins seeking a location for the first Roman colony outside Italia, a homestead for Roman and allied veterans.

Scipio's fledgling intelligence unit again proves its worth. His Iberian spies report that Gisgo has sailed back to Carthage, and Mago barely holds on to Gades, vainly trying to bribe the local tribes to reinforce his skeleton army. With Iberia free from Carthaginian control, Scipio freely travels to the numerous Iberian tribes. Each visit is decisive as he reaps their allegiance—or their destruction.

Carthage's control of Iberia is broken, but the war is far from over, and so Scipio turns his thoughts to Hannibal. And to Africa. And to Carthage itself.

I. VICTORY'S PRICE

NORTH AFRICAN COAST, 206 BCE. "I wish I had an ox to sacrifice," grouses Scipio. "That might get us going." The winter winds have deserted the fleet, leaving the oarsmen to slowly stroke the ship along toward Africa. Scipio paces nervously on the deck of his quinquereme, anxious to attain Siga before nightfall. "These pissy wind gods abandon you just when you need them most," he complains.

"Perhaps you should pray to Zephyrus, the Greek god of wind," snipes Admiral Laelius, irritated as Scipio's land-lover ways. "I would wager our Roman gods know you are a Hellenic sympathizer. They are likely to be Latin Party members, being wealthy and powerful, so they will surely not support you. Seek the Greeks!"

"Your humor is sometimes out of place, Admiral," grouses Scipio, which only prompts Laelius to laugh at him.

"You are certainly of a mood, Scippy," he chuckles. "You should not have come, I think. Sailing is best left to sailors!"

Scipio snorts. "What choice did I have? Syphax would not sign the treaty you brought him unless I signed it with him." He looks out toward Africa, watching for signs of wind. "It may be a trap, but I will take the risk to get more allies. I just don't want to bob along out here in the middle of the sea, easy prey for the Carthaginians."

"Then we should increase the oarsmen's pace." Laelius retorts. "If we get the wind, they can ease off." Scipio nods, and Laelius barks the order. The ship's 180 oars quicken their smooth dipping into the deep blue waters, and the massive ship slowly speeds up. Scipio calms down, although Laelius notices he looks anxiously about the empty seas, searching for Carthaginian patrol ships.

After several uneventful hours, Laelius spies the rocky bluffs of Rachgoun Harbor, the gateway to Syphax's inland citadel at Siga. Standing at the ship's curved prow, Laelius admires the immaculate stone harbor, at the myriad little fishing boats that speckle its turquoise waters. Looking for a place to dock, he notices six large ships that are tied to the front pillars. His mouth falls open.

"Scipio!" he shouts. "Over here! When Scipio draws close, Laelius points at the vessels. "I swear, those look like Carthaginian triremes!" The words no sooner leave his mouth than the faint sounds of battle horns drift across the sea. The two friends watch dozens of ant-sized men swarming busily on all six triremes, hurrying to set sail. "Ram speed!" yells Scipio. "We have to get to the harbor before they come out!"

The quinquereme's oars thresh into the water, and the large ship gains speed, but the triremes are already being tied off from the dock. Scipio grits his teeth, knowing they will not reach the protection of Syphax's harbor in time. He turns to Laelius. "Arm the oarsmen. We'll have a fight to the death on our hands." Scipio pounds his fist onto the mast. "Damn, we were so close!"

Laelius is strapping on his greaves when he feels his hair stir, then whirl into his face. He looks behind him and a grin splits his face. "The wind!" he cries, "the wind is back!" Scipio raises his hand to feel it, and smiles. "Hoist all the sails!" he shouts. "Hoist them now!" The quinquereme's sails billow out and the ship surges ahead. It soon noses into the front waters of the enormous bay, putting it under the protection of Syphax's realm, just as the triremes sail out to meet them. Scipio can see the Carthaginian commanders at the prows of their ships, glaring angrily at him as their ships turn about. *So close to losing all*, Scipio thinks. *After all these years, a capricious wind decides my fate.*

The quinquereme eases into an empty dock, as far from the triremes as possible. As Scipio and Laelius descend the gangplank, a lean, hawk-faced man walks out to greet them, surrounded by a retinue of Numidian guards. The man wears a golden brown robe edged in silver, a thin gold diadem across his crag-like brow. Scipio knows he must be Syphax, lord of the Masaeslyi tribe of western Numidia. "Hail, King Syphax," Scipio says, with the slightest of bows. The Numidian raises his right hand in acknowledgement, and waves for Scipio and Laelius to approach.

Scipio's eyes widen at the sight of the sturdy little man standing next to Syphax. The Carthaginian general Gisgo glares at Scipio, his face showing his disappointment at not catching Scipio at sea. *Now this is an odd turn of affairs* is all Scipio can think, an awkward smile upon his face.

"The esteemed General Gisgo did favor us with his presence on his way to Carthage," Syphax purrs. "Most unexpected. But most welcome, of course."

Gisgo nods briefly at Scipio and looks at Syphax. "I thought I should pay a visit to our old ally, noble king. To celebrate your lifelong friendship with us."

"Ah yes, friendship," muses Scipio out loud. "If I remember my military history aright, Syphax, you were our ally in the first Carthaginian war. We even sent a praefectus castrorum to train your troops."

Syphax shifts about awkwardly. "Well, yes, you are both correct. Changing times beget changing alliances, you know... But let us be off to my palace, honored guests, that you may refresh yourself before we dine. There is much to talk about, with the both of you."

Gisgo eyes Scipio resentfully. Scipio steps forward and extends his arm. "At least tonight, let us be comrades in arms. We can talk about our common enemy--the politicians back home!"

At that comment both Gisgo and Syphax laugh, Syphax loudest of all.. Gisgo touches his hand to his forehead, by way of a salute, and smiles tightly. "Your point is well met, General Scipio. Tonight we are but fellow soldiers, sharing bread and wine."

A relieved smile splits Syphax's face, and he strokes his close-cropped beard. "Nobly spoken, General Scipio! And nobly accepted General Gisgo. Now, to my palace. I have prepared a feast that will be the stuff of songs!" The Numidian king turns and heads down the dock, as Scipio and Gisgo walk on each side of him, glancing speculatively at one another.

True to their word, Scipio and Gisgo spend the night amiably feasting, drinking wine, and sharing stories. They tactfully avoid talking about their battles at Baecula and Iberia, and endure Syphax' rants against his rival Masinissa, rebel prince of eastern Numidia. Syphax presses them both about making troop commitments to his war against Masinissa. Mago refuses, and Scipio will only promise to help end the war between the Numidian tribes, To his relief, Syphax has not learned that Masinissa has secretly joined Scipio.

Ever cordial and entertaining, Laelius regales the party with stories of his roughshod childhood on the docks of Ostia and the back streets of Rome. After several cups of wine, Scipio and Gisgo commiserate about a general's common complaint: having military decisions made by businessmen and officials who have never laid hand to sword.

Scipio dutifully listens to Gisgo declaim the sheltered merchants who dominate Carthage's Council of Elders, and he almost feels sorry for him. *Cato was wrong*, he realizes. *We do not have to destroy Carthage to win the war. We just have to make peace more profitable than resistance.*

The next morning there is a final meeting between the three leaders. Gisgo and Scipio agree to leave at the same time, so one will not gain a diplomatic advantage with Syphax. When Scipio boards his ship, he carries with him a signed treaty between himself and Syphax, a declaration that there will be no war between Rome and western Numidia. Scipio now has an alliance of the second most powerful kingdom in Africa; a man who can supply considerable troops and food for an African campaign.

Gisgo carries no such treaty. As graciously as he could, Syphax informed him that Carthage, Numidia's rival for control of Africa, will lose the war. And Syphax will be waiting when they do.

The Roman quinquereme pushes off from the dock and opens its sails to the welcoming wind. Scipio calls Laelius to his side and they have a brief, muted, discussion. Laelius gapes at Scipio's words, then nods his agreement. "Set sail for Cartago Nova," Laelius yells to his captain. The quinquereme slowly heels to the west. "Weren't you going to sail to Rome after we landed at Tarraco?" Laelius asks. "Amelia grievously misses you, I know. And your mother."

Scipio only stares out at the glistening whitecaps, his face impassive. "We must eliminate the last traces of rebellion in Iberia. Rome and home will have to wait. "He looks at Laelius, his eyes filled with a distant stare. "And Africa awaits us."

When Gisgo boards his trireme he finds Altos, his fleet captain, waiting for him. "What news from the meet, Syphax?" the grizzled old captain inquires. "Did you learn more about the Roman's weaknesses, how to drive the Scipio boy from Iberia?"

Gisgo laughs derisively, and shakes his head. "Now that I have seen Scipio in the flesh, I have greater admiration for him than I had for his many military victories." He shakes his head forlornly. "I do not doubt that Syphax and his kingdom will soon be in the power of Rome. Now let me be." Gisgo repairs to the prow of the ship, watching Scipio's quinquereme ease out from the harbor. *No, Altos, the question is not how we lost Iberia,* Gisgo thinks. *It is how we can hold on to Africa.*

The Carthaginian general wracks his brain to think of something he can offer Syphax, something that will sway his loyalty. After rejecting money and territory as options, he grudgingly admits that he must offer his most prized possession, the one treasure that all men desire.

Sophonisba.

ABOUT THE AUTHOR

Martin Tessmer is a retired University of Colorado professor and administrator. His previous ten books have ranged from online training to hiking guides to ancient Roman History. He lives in Denver, Colorado.

ⁱ Priapus. Wikipedia. http://en.wikipedia.org/wiki/Priapus/

ⁱⁱ http://en.wikipedia.org/wiki/Maharbal

ⁱⁱⁱ http://en.wikipedia.org/wiki/Battle_of_the_Silarus

^{iv} Cato, *De Agri Cultura*, trans. Andrew Dalby (Devon: Prospect Books), Chapter 2.

^v Livy, *Hannibal's War: Books 21–30,* 27, 1, 378.

^{vi} Priapus. Wikipedia. http://en.wikipedia.org/wiki/Priapus/

^{vii} http://en.wikipedia.org/wiki/Ancient_Roman_bathing

^{viii} http://www.famousquotesonline.info/quote.php?category=anger

^{ix} Richard Gabriel, *Scipio Africanus: Rome's Greatest General* (Washington, DC: Potomac Books, 2008), 94.

^x http://www.livius.org/ap-ark/appian/appian_spain_17.html

^{xi} http://en.wikiquote.org/wiki/Cato_the_Elder

^{xii} Gabriel, *Scipio Africanus*, 97.

^{xiii} Plutarch, *Roman Lives*, trans. Robin Waterfield (Oxford: The University Press, 1999), 17.

^{xiv} Plutarch, *Roman Lives*, 16.

^{xv} Livy, 26, 50, p. 375.

^{xvi} Gabriel, *Scipio Africanus*, 99.

^{xvii} Livy, 26, 48, 373.

^{xviii} Gabriel, *Scipio Africanus*, 100.

xix Livy, 27, 13, p. 396.

xx Plutarch, *Roman Lives, Vol. I, Marcellus*. trans. John Dryden, revised by A.H. Clough (Boston: Little, Brown, and Company, 1885).

xxi Wikipedia. http://en.wikipedia.org/wiki/Cato_the_Elder

xxii Livy, 26, 51, 376.

xxiii Appian, *Appian's History of Rome: The Spanish Wars*, trans. Horace White (Loeb Classical Library, 1912), 18, 85.

xxiv Livy, 26, 50, p. 376.

xxv Livy, 26, 50, 376.

xxvi Gabriel, 122.

xxvii Livy, 22, 51, 121.

xxviii Livy, 27, 19, 407.

xxix Livy, 27, 19, 407.

xxx Livy, 27, 26, 416.

xxxi Livy, 29, 37, 361.

xxxii Livy, 27, 43, 436.

xxxiii Livy, 27, 43, 437.

xxxiv Livy, 27, 47, 441.

xxxv Gabriel, 117.

xxxvi Livy, 27, 51, 447.

xxxvii Livy, 28, 2, 450.

xxxviii Livy, 28, 3, 451.

---

xxxix Livy, 28, 16, 469.

xl Gabriel, 122.

xli Livy, 28, 16, 469.

53549969R00223

Made in the USA
Lexington, KY
09 July 2016